"The serial killer thriller takes to the high seas in *Steel Fear* as an elusive murderer stalks his prey through the steel corridors of a U.S. Navy Nimitz-class aircraft carrier. Lovers of both serial-killer thrillers and military novels will be turning pages late into the night, as former Navy SEAL Brandon Webb and award-winning author John David Mann draw us deeper and deeper into this unique, suspenseful, and authentically detailed game of cat and mouse."

—MICHAEL LEDWIDGE, co-author of
fourteen bestselling James Patterson novels

"[A] highly original update on a classical mystery trope . . . The authors effectively integrate former Navy SEAL Webb's military experience into the plot, making every detail ring true."

—*Publishers Weekly* (starred review)

"Former SEAL Webb and coauthor Mann . . . hit all the right notes in their fiction debut, which blends the high-tech trappings of a military thriller with the crushing claustrophobia of a locked-room mystery (if that locked room was home to more than 5,000 people, along with 90 aircraft and a handful of nuclear reactors). Like Lee Child in his Jack Reacher novels, the authors can do more than power a pulse-racing narrative. . . . For readers who can't resist a bureaucracy-battling action hero, there's a new kid on the block (or boat)."

—*Booklist* (starred review)

### By Brandon Webb & John David Mann

NONFICTION

*The Red Circle*
*The Making of a Navy SEAL*
*Among Heroes*
*The Killing School*
*Total Focus*
*Mastering Fear*

FICTION

*Steel Fear*
*Cold Fear*

# STEEL FEAR

 Bantam Books | New York

# STEEL FEAR

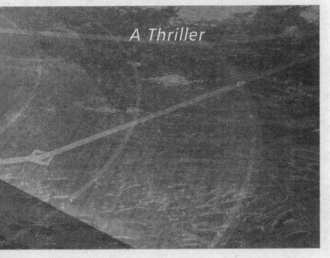

*A Thriller*

Brandon Webb & John David Mann

2022 Bantam Books Mass Market Edition

Copyright © 2021 by Brandon Webb and John David Mann
Excerpt from *Cold Fear* by Brandon Webb and John David Mann
copyright © 2022 by Brandon Webb and John David Mann

Published in the United States by Bantam Books,
an imprint of Random House, a division of
Penguin Random House LLC, New York.

BANTAM BOOKS is a registered trademark and the B colophon
is a trademark of Penguin Random House LLC.

Originally published in hardcover in the United States
by Bantam Books, an imprint of Random House, a division of
Penguin Random House LLC, in 2021.

This book contains an excerpt from the forthcoming book
*Cold Fear* by Brandon Webb and John David Mann.
This excerpt has been set for this edition only and may not
reflect the final content of the forthcoming edition.

ISBN 978-0-593-35630-2
Ebook ISBN 978-0-593-35629-6

Cover art direction: Carlos Beltrán
Cover design: Faceout Studio/Jeff Miller

Printed in the United States of America

randomhousebooks.com

2 4 6 8 9 7 5 3 1

Bantam Books Mass Market Edition: May 2022

# Contents

Diagram of USS *Abraham Lincoln*    xiii

I. The Seam of the Weld    1

II. Bolter    99

III. Crossing the Line    155

IV. Monster    225

V. The Other Shoe    295

VI. Rubik's Cube    369

VII. The Storm    441

Epilogue    501

Note from the Authors    513

# USS *Abraham Lincoln* (CVN72)

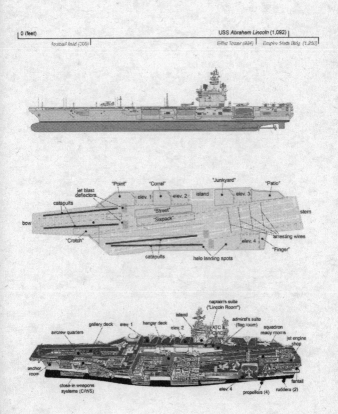

0 (feet)

football field (300)

USS *Abraham Lincoln* (1,092)

Eiffel Tower (984) | Empire State Bldg. (1,250)

"Point"  "Corral"  "Junkyard"  "Patio"

jet blast deflectors

catapults

bow

"Street"

"Sixpack"

elev. 1  elev. 2  island  elev. 3

stern

"Crotch"

catapults

helo landing spots

elev. 4

arresting wires

"Finger"

captain's suite ("Lincoln Room")

island

admiral's suite (flag room)

gallery deck  elev. 1  hangar deck  elev. 2

ATC (CVIC)

squadron ready rooms

aircrew quarters

jet engine shop

anchor room

close-in weapons systems (CIWS)

elev. 4  propellers (4)  rudders (2)

fantail

# I

# The Seam of the Weld

# 1

Shivers rippled over Monica Halsey's naked skin as she peered into the steel mirror and splashed water on her face. Monica needed to be on her game tonight. She was close to earning her helicopter aircraft commander qualification, and tonight's hop was a critical step in that process.

Because Papa Doc was flying with her.

She shivered again. Lord, why did they keep the AC up so high in this place? She pulled on a red-and-black undershirt—squadron colors—then fished out a tan flight suit, stepped into the legs, pulled up the suit, and slipped her arms into the sleeves.

His name wasn't really Papa Doc, of course, it was Nikos Papadakis, and he was a control freak and a bully. Which was unfortunate, because he was also her commanding officer.

Papa Doc didn't like her. She didn't know why. Some security issue, probably; his daddy hit him or the big kids teased him or Lord knew what, but whatever the reason, it was a problem, because he held the keys to the kingdom—the kingdom in this case being Monica's HAC qual.

Which Papa Doc had the power to quash.

She zipped her flight suit up the front to mid-sternum, rolled up the sleeves to mid-forearm.

Focused on her HAC, and on what lay beyond that.

A tour at the Pentagon, some high-profile posting, maybe an admiral's aide? Tough job to get, and well worth it. If she did an excellent job there (and she would) she'd have people in high places looking out for her. Proceed to O-5, commander, and then O-6: the promised land. As a captain all sorts of posts would open up to her. Command of a ship. A cruiser. Even a carrier. Why not? And after captain came admiral. There'd been plenty of female admirals in the navy by now, even one full-ranked female four-star. The admiral of their own strike group was a woman. Not impossible at all.

*Eyes on the prize.*

The most important event shaping Monica's life occurred ten years before she was born. In 1983 a thirty-two-year-old astronaut named Sally Ride flew the space shuttle *Challenger* and became the first American woman in space. On a third-grade school trip to the Houston Space Center Monica learned all about Sally Ride, learned that girls could actually become astronauts, and at the age of eight she fell in love. From that day on she wanted to fly more than anything in the world.

She bent down, slipped on her brown oxfords, and began lacing them tight.

In junior high she learned about Kara Hultgreen, the first female navy combat aviator, and her ambition shifted from astronaut to fighter pilot. She also learned that the USS *Abraham Lincoln* became the first Pacific Fleet carrier to integrate female aviators into its crew in 1993, the year Monica was born. It was on the *Lin-*

*coln*'s flight deck that Hultgreen flew her F-14 Tomcat.

Monica looked again at her reflection in the polished steel. "And here we are," she whispered.

The USS *Abraham* freaking *Lincoln*.

She glanced around the dimly lit stateroom. Anne, one of her roommates, lay back on her rack, headphones on, murmuring incomprehensible phrases. Anne was sucking another foreign language (Mandarin, this time) into her voracious brain. Kris was on flight duty, gunning her F/A-18 somewhere up there through the Mesopotamian murk. The fourth rack, the one above Anne's, was empty now. Monica forced herself not to look at it. The sight still put a knot in her stomach.

She reached for her toothbrush and squeezed on a pearl of toothpaste.

She'd learned a few more things in junior high, too. She learned about something called the "Tailhook scandal": eighty-three navy women assaulted or sexually harassed. (That one happened two years before she was born.) That in 1994 Kara Hultgreen also became the first navy female aviator to die, right off the *Lincoln*'s flight deck—and that the crash that killed her was blamed on "improprieties" in qualifying her for flight status, "given her gender."

For Flying While Female, in other words.

And Sally Ride? In a press conference just before that historic first flight in '83, reporters asked her if space flight would "affect her reproductive organs" and whether she cried when things went wrong on the job.

"Shit fire and save the matches," was Gram's comment when Monica told her about it.

Monica was fifteen when she read about that humiliating press conference, and that was the day she formulated the guiding philosophy she'd held to ever since.

*Never back down.*

She looked in the mirror, gave her hair a few quick brushstrokes, and snapped everything into place with a hair tie.

Ready for battle.

# 2

She opened the stateroom door, ducked her head, and began threading her way through the labyrinth. The nighttime safety lights provided her just enough illumination to see her way, their faint red glow giving the painted steel passageways an even more claustrophobic feel than usual. A lattice of wires, exposed pipes, and conduit brushed by overhead, like strands of web in a giant spider's lair.

Eerie how quiet it got in here at night.

If you put all the ship's passageways end to end, Monica'd heard, they would stretch out more than twenty miles. She'd asked her crew chief once just how big a carrier was. He told her about two brothers he knew who'd deployed at the same time on the same ship. From the day they left port to the day they returned seven months later the two never once bumped into each other. "That's how big," he said.

More than three thousand ship's crew, plus nearly three thousand more with the air wing on board: some six thousand souls packed into this steel honeycomb. Like a small city folded in on itself. She'd heard of crew members getting lost even after weeks on board.

Monica never lost her way, not once.

Though she did crack her head a lot those first few weeks.

As she ducked through another doorway Monica thought again—for the thousandth time—of the inconvenience her height saddled her with here on the *Lincoln*. It was like living in a hobbit shire, only this particular hobbit shire was interlaced with a thousand narrow, nearly vertical steel staircases—"ladders," in Navyspeak, never "stairs"—and punctuated by compact, capsule-shaped doorways with openings raised a few inches off the deck, so you had to remember to high-step through. Look down to make sure you cleared the edge and *SLAM!* Another whack to the head.

She ducked again, then on through a few more doors, down two steep, narrow ladders, and into her squadron's ready room for a cup of hot Black Falcon coffee. Best coffee on the ship.

Quick op brief, then into the riggers' loft, where she and the other crew donned their inflatable vests—"float coats"—and white flight helmets.

Moments later she was out in the labyrinth again with Papa Doc and two other crew members. Up another steep ladder and through a heavy hatch to the outside—where they all paused, momentarily immobilized by the blast of saturated heat.

Even at night the Persian Gulf was sweltering.

The four stood for a moment on the steel catwalk, eyes adjusting to the darkness as their bodies adapted to the heat. Looking down between her feet into the darkness, Monica could hear the ocean rushing by five stories below. Sailors who jumped from here with suicide on their minds might hope to drown, but only those few sorry souls who survived the fall got their wish.

She followed the others up the five steel steps and out

onto the *Lincoln*'s massive flight deck, where every day was the Fourth of July.

*WHAM!* She was expecting it, but still the sound made her jump. A hundred yards from where Monica stood one of the flight deck's steam catapults slammed against its stock, sending a fighter jet screaming off the bow end of the deck and into the air with a *whoosh* and disappearing into the dark.

*CRASH!* A second jet pounded into the deck's stern to her right, its tailhook snagging one of the four arresting wires strung across the deck like booby traps. The cable shrieked as it stretched out into an elongated V, slowing the jet from 150 mph to zero in a two-count to stop it from careening off the deck's angled landing strip.

Goggled and green-jerseyed handlers rushed forward to chock and chain the beast. Monica knew them all by their gait and gestures, had each one's physical signature memorized. Her crew's lives depended on these guys.

*WHAM!* Another cat shot, and *whoosh!* another jet disappeared into the dark.

*CRASH!* Another 25-ton beast pounded into the deck.

Insanity.

Her big brother had told her that the contrast between below decks and above was like night and day. That didn't even come close. Life below was like living in a steel ant colony. Up here, everything was a mass of exploding chaos—yellow-jerseyed "shooters" signaling jet launches with their elaborate ballet; white-shirted "paddles" feeding the incoming pilots chunks of complex data with a wave of their glowing light sticks; green-jerseyed Martians swarming everywhere, checking and double-checking every facet of the machinery before takeoff. The roar of jet blast as the next pilot rammed the throttle forward, sending a blaze of blistering exhaust back into concrete-and-steel blast deflectors raised on their servo motors just in time to catch the inferno. The air boss up in the tower, all-seeing, his amplified voice booming above the din, directing everything like a benevolent Eye of Sauron.

And that smell! That heady mix of diesel fumes, jet fuel, and salt air. Every time Monica stepped off the catwalk and out onto the deck it hit her again, like echoes of a first high school kiss. She couldn't get enough of it. Wished she could bottle it.

Launching and landing these jets was the most dangerous job in the world—and it was up to Monica to provide the safety net. The *Lincoln* carried forty-eight fighter jets and just six helicopters, but the helos were always, *always,* the first to lift off and last to land in any launch cycle, circling the ship's starboard side in three-hour shifts so there would always be at least one helo in the air with a rescue swimmer on board, suited up and ready to plunge into the drink in the event a plane went down.

Every helo squadron had its own motto. "One Team, One Scream." "Train to Fight, Fight to Win." "Our Sting Is Death." All of which sounded to Monica more like they belonged to jet fighters. Not the Black Falcons, though. The day she'd been assigned to the Falcons and learned what their motto was, she'd felt immediately at home.

*"That Others May Live."*

Their helo was coming in now, winding up its final loop, another already in the air to take its place. As it settled onto the port edge of the deck in front of them, Monica thought again how much the Knighthawk resembled a praying mantis with its big cockpit-window eyes.

In the seconds before takeoff, she always said a silent prayer herself.

She'd be damned if anyone else on this deployment lost their lives. Not on her watch.

# 3

A pair of fuel handlers in their purple jerseys—"grapes"—rushed in dragging their long lines to gas up the bird as the two crews made a hot swap, Monica and the others buckling themselves into their seats, testing their comms, checking the digital readouts.

One of the grapes ran up to the pilot's window and held up a small glass jar. Fresh fuel sample for visual inspection. Papa Doc nodded: no visible contamination.

Tonight they were making an unscheduled ferry run to pick up a passenger in Bahrain. Pilot and co-pilot would trade off, one taking the stick while the other rode shotgun and worked the radio.

"Halsey. I'll fly her out. You take the stick on the leg back."

"Yessir." Normally the formal "Yessirs" and "No-sirs" were relaxed while flying, unless the pilot was a prick. Papa Doc was a prick.

Monica wondered once again what it was about her that Papa Doc so resented. Maybe it was her height; at six one she towered over his five nine.

Or maybe he just wasn't comfortable with her Flying While Female.

"*Hotel Sierra two zero six, Log Cabin, you are cleared for takeoff, spot one.*"

"Roger, Log Cabin," Monica replied. "Hotel Sierra two zero six, cleared for takeoff."

From here on the dialogue was pure mime: hand signals and glowsticks from the brown-jerseyed plane captain on the deck in front of them. Nothing like the elaborate takeoff dance for a jet—no yellow-jerseyed shooters, no slamming catapult, no blasting off the deck like a rocket. Their plane captain pointed directly at them—*Ready*—as two green shirts pulled out the forward wheel chocks and scurried off with them to the side. He spread both arms out to his sides in a T, then brought them straight up over his head, repeating the sequence several times in a series of overhead claps. *Lift off.*

Papa Doc pulled up on the "collective" (thrust lever) and Monica felt them lift with a whisper, tilting away to the port and leveling into their southbound flight path, where for the next hour they would chop away at the wet chunks of night air between them and their destination.

Monica stared out into the black nothing. Checked all her instrumentation. Out into the nothing again.

Flying in the Knighthawk was like being in a cave: the close confinement, condensation dripping from overhead pipes, everything draped in shadows from the glow of instrument lights, the steady soporific *whump-whump-whump* of rotors that could just about lull you to sleep.

Not a word from Stickman, their lanky rescue swimmer, in back. Nor from Harris, their crew chief.

This was the hardest part of flying, the part you never saw in movies: the monotony. The long stretches of empty time, having to stay sharp and alert even when nothing was happening. Mostly they would eat up the time with idle conversation, though with everyone on comms it was like having a conversation with the voices in your head. On some runs they'd ramble on for hours, pausing only when necessary to confirm a procedure or communicate with ATC. But Papa Doc frowned on too much chatter. On his watch, flights tended to be less like sitting around a campfire and more like going to church. Sit silent in your seat, join in from the hymnal when the time came, then sit back down. *Yessir*.

Monica steered her thoughts away from Papa Doc and onto the reason for their flight: their passenger, a Navy SEAL from Black Squadron, was coming on board solo, for what reason none of them knew.

Nor cared, as far as Monica was concerned.

SEALs: Sea Air and Land. Cream of the crop, elite of the elite, blah blah blah.

Monica had met quite a few SEALs and had taken an instant dislike to each and every one. As far as she could see, they were all arrogant, profane, and self-absorbed. The ultimate macho-supreme assholes.

Worse than Papa Doc?

Call it a tie.

She inadvertently glanced over in her CO's direction, then quickly looked away again. *Lord, I hope he can't hear my thoughts.*

The hour bled out in silence.

"*Hotel Sierra two zero six, Muharraq Airfield Control. We have you on visual, continue on course and maintain current altitude until advised.*"

"Two zero six, roger that," replied Monica.

Through the Knighthawk's windshield Monica could make out their destination, a small landing strip where they were to rendezvous with their SEAL guest and his officer escort.

The Bahrain tower spoke up again. "*Hotel Sierra two zero six, you are cleared to land.*"

As the bird lowered to the tarmac Monica spotted

the two men walking toward them, illuminated by runway lights.

Even from a hundred feet off she had zero trouble identifying the SEAL. He was tall, muscular, powerful, carried his fully loaded backpack as if it weighed no more than a paper boarding pass. He didn't stride so much as he loped, moving with a dangerous grace that made her think of the mountain lions she'd seen back home.

Perfect specimen.

*Asshole.*

As they drew closer she could make out the officer lagging behind the SEAL in his desert cammies, lugging the other man's kit bag and gun case. This little guy was totally eclipsed by the SEAL, not just a head shorter but almost a different species: thin wiry limbs, knobby joints, oversize eyes. *He looks like a marsupial,* she thought.

In the navy, rank was everything—who outflew, outperformed, outlasted whom—and SEALs were a breed apart. The short, awkward-looking officer might technically outrank the big guy, but the big guy outclassed him in every other way. The contrast was almost comical.

Marsupial, meet mountain lion.

Stickman leaned out the door and shouted over the din of the rotors. "We're here for Chief Finn."

The marsupial took the backpack from the mountain lion, stepped forward without a word, and boarded the helo.

# 4

Finn silently assessed the four other people in the bird, starting with the pilot. He could sense him regarding his passenger there in the back with disdain. An angry man. Finn never trusted angry men. This one was cursed with a chiseled face, classic Greek nose, olive complexion. A movie-star face. Nobody should be born that handsome. Good looks like that made it tougher to keep yourself in perspective.

Finn understood the type: his talents, his limitations. The pilot would never advance much further than where he was right now. He might be career navy but his trajectory was a dead-end street. Not that his ego was too big. It was too small. Too fragile.

Finn dropped the pilot from the sonar of his mind and moved on to the co-pilot.

Something about Finn had startled her when he first climbed on. She'd tried to hide it, but she wasn't skilled at concealment. She was on the stick now and focused on her task. She said something to Movie Star and Finn caught the echoes of a Texas accent, light on the twang. West Texas, his guess. Strong, possibly headstrong. Someone on a mission. No dead-end street here.

Tall, good features. Must have taken a ton of shit on her way to flying a navy bird. The naval aviation officer track was brutal. Just gaining admittance was an intense selection process, let alone getting all the way through it. Not easy to make it this far. Even harder to do so and not turn mean. Finn read the co-pilot as tough on the surface but still green. He sensed a sadness just underneath, too, like she was grieving someone or something recent.

The crew chief in the seat next to him interrupted his thoughts. "Welcome aboard, Chief." Finn looked at him but said nothing.

The junior guy, the crew's avionics operator and designated SAR swimmer, grinned at him. Black dude, introduced to Finn as "Stickman." Still had that new-guy sparkle. This was a kid who had not yet seen death up close.

Finn nodded.

They all had their jobs to do. He saw no reason to interfere or interrupt.

He didn't speak a word the rest of the flight.


The helo threaded its way through the invisible corridors, slipping in on the carrier's port side as fighter jets exploded off the deck's bow and came screaming in aft to catch the big arrestor wires. Finn watched through the Knighthawk's side window, absorbed in the skill of it all.

According to Kennedy, a carrier flight deck was one gigantic bolt-action sniper rifle, three and a half football fields long, only instead of firing steel-tipped 10-gram rounds it shot 25-ton fighter jets, firing and reloading at the rate of one every twenty-five seconds. Finn thought about the jet pilots strapped into their multimillion-dollar machines, being shot off the deck into the dark like bullets.

The idea of being encased in a supersonic steel tube like that made his balls clench.

The tall co-pilot put their bird down on the deck like a mother's kiss on a baby's cranium. She was good. He noticed her glancing in the pilot's direction, trying not to look like she was doing it. Checking for signs of his approval. Professionally, though, not emotionally. Finn suspected she didn't give a shit about his approval emotionally. Good thing, because she was never going to get it, not from him. No one was.

The young SAR swimmer slid open the cabin door. Finn followed him out and down onto the flight deck's hot surface. The crew chief, Harris, walked him over to the edge, where they clambered down a short metal ladder onto the catwalk. Harris stepped through a hatch into the ship's interior.

Finn hesitated.

So here he was. Boarding an aircraft carrier, being carted back to the States.

Leaving his team behind.

Harris turned and saw him looking back to the south, toward Bahrain. "Chief Finn?" When the SEAL didn't respond he said, "Everything okay, Chief?"

Finn looked over at the other man. Nodded and followed him in.

Nothing was okay.

# 5

The Air Transfer Office was located on the gallery deck, the level directly below the flight deck. Several rows of vinyl-cushioned steel benches for outgoing passengers to sit and wait. Shelves and files lining the bulkheads, where they weren't cluttered with flight coats and helmets on hooks. Two desks, jammed into the two far corners. The place was crammed. Everything on an aircraft carrier was crammed. The only spaces Finn had ever seen more tightly packed were submarines and New York City apartments. Not that he'd had much experience in either.

There were two staff members, one officer and one enlisted. Neither had noticed him yet. His lightweight combat boots made no sound when he walked. Despite Finn's awkward appearance, when he moved he was the opposite of awkward. There were people who took up a lot of space when they entered a room. Finn seemed to take up no space at all.

Now the officer looked up and noticed him. Stood, leaned forward, and shook Finn's hand. "Welcome aboard, Chief Finn. Lieutenant Sam Schofield. Honored to have you as our guest aboard the Abe."

"Just a passenger, Lieutenant."

The officer paused. Hadn't expected that response. "Campion will handle your processing."

The young airman at the other desk flashed a quick grin and got down to business. Had Finn sign a log sheet. Gave him a slip of paper with a few key locations, including his berthing space and muster location. Explained how to read the "bull's-eye" location codes posted everywhere around the ship, in case Finn didn't already know.

The airman paused, then nodded apologetically toward Finn's gun case.

"We'll need to hold on to that while you're here."

Finn handed over the gun case, then set his kit bag down and dug out his sidearm. He ejected the magazine, racked the slide, and surrendered that as well.

"They'll be stored in the armory, locked and under guard," the kid added. "Safer for you, safer for the guns."

Finn looked over at the officer, Schofield.

"There's no lock on the door to the compartment where you'll be berthing," Schofield explained. He pointed at Finn's cellphone, which Finn had set on the desk while unearthing his sidearm. "Won't have much use for that, I'm afraid."

Finn glanced at the phone, then back at Schofield. "I should be getting a package. From command. How does that work?"

"We'll put a note on your door."

Finn nodded. "Okay." Then added, "Sir."

Finn's satphone was busted. It had happened the previous night while Finn slept. How exactly he still didn't know. When he woke up that morning, the thing was cracked in two. Best guess, someone had slammed a boot or rifle butt down on it in the dark. Probably stone drunk. Nobody owned up to it.

For all he knew, he'd done it himself.

His memory of the night before was blank.

Finn had put in for a replacement right away. Within hours he'd learned he was shipping out. They'd said they would send the replacement satphone out to him. He expected that could take at least a few days, more likely weeks. Military efficiency: hurry up and wait.

Finn had had the sense that he should travel light. He wasn't sure why but trusted the instinct. So he'd left his other gun case with his bolt-action .308 behind in Bahrain with Kennedy, along with his night vision goggles and a bunch of other tools. And the pieces of his shattered satphone.

The ATO officer ushered Finn through a maze of passageways to his compartment, a tiny space tucked in a portside corner just below the flight deck. Not too much smaller than a broom closet. Across the way, a few meters from the door, was a tiny head with a single toilet. No sink.

"It's not much," said the officer, "but you're probably the only enlisted man on board with a private suite."

Finn nodded. Officer humor.

Schofield was an interesting one, a mix of soft and wary. Big guy, strength to him, but the hands and musculature of an office worker. Had never done hard physical work. Not exactly street-smart; didn't have the kind of 360° awareness that came with life on the hustle—but Finn caught his eyes darting to the corners a few times. Habitual defensive posture. He'd been a target, not just once but often enough to grow reflexes for it. Yet he was no weakling. And the man projected something genuine. Not surprising he was an officer. Probably a good one, too; strong enough to lead by example, but he'd been a victim often enough to empathize with the ranks.

Finn had encountered two types of leaders in the military. There were those who grew to fill the high positions they were given. Who became bigger versions of themselves and used their elevated standing to protect the weak. And there were those who used the position to arrogate power to themselves. Who became smaller versions of themselves. Small men in high places.

He thought Schofield was probably the first kind of leader.

The lieutenant was wrapping up his summary brief. "We'll have a man here for you at 0600, if that works for you."

"A man?"

"Chief Donnelly, senior guy from the ops department. He's been assigned to show you around for a few days, point out spaces of interest, Chief's Mess, that kind of thing. Think of him as your personal tour guide."

"No need," said Finn. "Sir."

"You sure? It's no trouble. The Abe is a hell of a labyrinth."

"I'll find my way."

The lieutenant didn't push it, as a purebred bureaucrat would have. Good for him.

"Spent much time on a carrier, Chief?"

"Been a while. First time on a nuke."

Schofield nodded and looked around, as if weighing how to convey the enormity of the ship. "Chief's Mess is five levels below, on deck three, aft. Best chow on the boat. And XO says you've got an open invitation to the officers' wardroom on deck two."

"I'll find my way."

Schofield nodded and paused. Then said: "So, special assignment, we're told."

Finn looked at him. "Yes," he said. "Sir."

Schofield smiled with his eyes and gave a single nod.

"Well, it's an honor to have you on board, Chief," he repeated.

"Just a passenger," said Finn.

He closed the steel door between them and stood, alone.

*Special assignment.*

An antiseptic term, crafted to cover a lot of sins. Could be as simple as briefing a high-level committee. Or as complex as extracting sensitive intelligence from deep inside hostile territory. Sometimes a special assignment concluded when two men walked into a dark alley and only Finn walked out.

Finn set his backpack and kit bag down and glanced around the tiny space.

It felt like he'd been shuffled into a desk drawer.

He pulled the thin regulation wool blanket off the rack, rolled it up, and tucked it under his arm. Opened the door and looked out into the empty passageway. Stepped out and shut the door behind him.

*Special assignment.* The mother of all military euphemisms.

His best guess?

He was being shipped home in disgrace.

# 6

At 0600 the next morning a speaker outside Finn's compartment crackled to life, emitting a long, sharp whistle followed by a monotone voice: *"Reveille, reveille, all hands heave out and trice up."*

Which was lost on Finn, who'd been out most of the night anyway, walking the length of the gallery deck back and forth a dozen times, taking a different route with each circuit. It was what he always did in any new environment. Recon.

The gallery deck was trisected lengthwise by two long central corridors, port and starboard, like the twin avenues of a modern city. A similar pair ran the length of the mess deck, four levels below. From there, as on the rest of the ship, the tangle of passageways splintered off in all directions with no discernible logic, like the back alleyways of a medieval town. Given the sheer number of forks and turns, Finn guessed he could repeat his stern-to-bow-to-stern lap four or five dozen times and never walk the same path twice.

Reveille was also the breakfast bell, so he headed below to the mess deck. He'd already swapped his cam-

mies for a plain desert-tan flight suit to better blend in—
no patches, no platoon logo, just name tag and trident.

As he made his way aft he passed a line forming outside Jittery Abe's, the ship's coffee shop, serving a full
line of caffeinated libations hot and cold. Uncle Sam,
meet Captain Starbucks. The place didn't open till 0630,
but a swarm of some three dozen sailors had already
flocked to the scent like sharks to blood.

"Sssst!" he heard a sailor at the end of the line, a
corpsman, hiss under his breath to his neighbor. "Yo,
Billy." Nodding with his chin. "You in?" The corpsman
shot a quick glance down at his hand, then back at the
other guy. Finn caught a glimpse of a small handmade
white paper envelope and heard Billy decline softly:
"Not my thing, man."

Stealing and dealing: a court-martial offense.

Not his problem.

Finn kept walking.

For his first morning on board Finn opted for general
mess, right behind Jittery Abe's, where the rank and file
ate. He believed Lieutenant Schofield's claim that Chief's
Mess had the best food on the ship, but Finn didn't care
about the quality of the food.

He cared about the quality of information.

On a ship, meals were ritual, food was social fabric;
mess was the seat of morale. And sitting for a few minutes with his bowl of plain oatmeal, surrounded by
trays bearing reconstituted egg product, greasy bacon,
and mugs of corrosive coffee, listening to the scraps of
conversation and watching the body language, Finn
could already see: morale on the *Lincoln* was not good.
It had been a long deployment, and from all appear-
ances, not a happy one.

Everyone was itching to get out of the Gulf and head
home.

Leaving mess behind, Finn headed above to resume his recon.

Despite its unique function as the air wing's launch and landing strip, the flight deck was not the ship's central reference point. The "main deck," or deck 1, largely consisted of three gigantic bays that housed the planes, thus it was also called the "hangar deck." Additional decks were numbered downward from there: deck 2, deck 3, deck 4, and so on, while decks above the hangar deck were technically called "levels": 01 level; 02 level, with its aircrew quarters and squadron ready rooms; 03 level, aka "gallery deck," and finally the flight deck and its imposing control tower, called the "island," which itself encompassed minilevels numbering all the way up to level 10, where the radar dishes turned.

Since Finn's first priority was to locate areas of possible solitude that were open to the exterior, today he'd stay above the waterline, which meant deck 2 (mess deck) and above. On each deck he made at least a dozen laps, noting entries, exits, and choke points; offices and compartments, their functions and personnel; side passageways and hatches and where each led.

As he walked he observed people hurrying to their various stations and duties, from engineers and intel wonks, navigators and scheduling clerks, communication hacks and store workers, to the mechanics and medics and barbers and galley cooks and all the other worker bees.

With no room to pass in the narrow passageways, every encounter between two people was an exercise in deference and therefore a reminder of rank. Enlisted deferred to officer, junior officer to senior officer, black shoe (boat navy) to brown shoe (aviation community). Yet everyone without exception, when they got close enough to see that golden trident on Finn's chest, stepped aside.

In the grand poker of navy ranking, nothing trumped a SEAL.

A few times people stopped and asked, "Do you need directions, Chief?"

He didn't.

Years earlier, before BUD/S, Finn had done a tour as a sonar operator and rescue swimmer on the USS *Kitty Hawk,* the navy's last non-nuclear carrier. The *Abraham Lincoln* was a whole different ball game. Everything was newer, sharper, more modern. The dimensions felt larger here. There'd been no Starbucks on the *Kitty Hawk,* that was for sure.

The essentials never changed; you could walk off a World War II–era carrier and onto the flight deck of a modern vessel like the *Lincoln* and it would all feel familiar. Still, the devil was in the details.

And you never knew when the devil would show up.

Finn needed to know what had changed and what hadn't, where everything was, how everything worked. So he walked and observed and cataloged.

Something was bugging him. He couldn't put his finger on it. Not something wrong, exactly.

Something missing.

# 7

At 0900 the 1MC—the ship's PA system—coughed out a single long tone from the bosun's pipe, followed by that same bored voice: *"All available hands to the flight deck for FOD walk."*

Finn was already there, watching as ship's personnel formed a ragged line, edge to edge, across the bow.

The FOD walk—Foreign Object Debris walkdown, pronounced "fahd-walk"—was typically the first order of every day that included flight operations. All available hands were called topside to participate, officers included. If you were caught loitering below you were in for a quick ass-chewing and mandatory summons.

The FOD walk was serious business. It took tens of millions of dollars to put a fighter jet in the air; a seventy-five-cent bolt could ruin it. Any foreign object—the tiniest screw or scrap of metal wire, a misplaced shoestring or boot eyelet, a dropped pen—could be sucked into a jet engine and cause catastrophic damage to the aircraft. Not to mention the humans flying it.

To execute the walkdown, the crew would line up shoulder to shoulder in several rows, then carefully pace along the flight deck, starting at the bow. The vanguard line slowly moved aft, each person focused on the deck directly in front of them; every so often a sailor would bend down, pick up some found object, and continue on, additional rows following behind in ten-foot intervals to scour for anything the first row might have missed. When the whole phalanx reached the stern they'd about-face and perform the same operation over again, moving in reverse.

All found items were collected in FOD bags, then analyzed to trace them to their source. If you were the one who dropped that tiny screwdriver, well, you were fucked, because they could track that tool back to the specific tool kit it came from, and records would show who last took it out. You could run but you couldn't hide. Not from a FOD walk.

Finn watched as crew members shuffled into place, lining the deck.

Not loving what he saw.

A few clusters of pasty faces here and there, underdwellers from the ship's company. Bored pilots sauntering into the line with casual arrogance. Mostly the mob was composed of flight deck crew with their strange goggle-tan lines and colored jerseys. They all looked exhausted. And today's flight ops hadn't even started yet.

This was nothing like the FOD walks he remembered from the deck of the Battle Cat fifteen years earlier.

The USS *Kitty Hawk* had been one of the most beloved warships of the twentieth century. Also one of the most hated. Plagued with mechanical breakdowns and maintenance problems. All of which earned her a second nickname: "Shitty Kitty." But the damn thing stayed afloat for nearly fifty years. Finn had loved it there on the Shitty Kitty, for one reason, and one reason only.

Captain Tomaszeski.

Captain Tom's leadership sent ripples of pride and quality flowing throughout the ship. He created an esprit de corps that expressed itself on the flight deck, at mess, in the polish and gleam of every passageway. That turned even something as routine and burdensome as their daily FOD walkdown into something to look forward to.

Finn's very first experience of a FOD walk on the Shitty Kitty had erupted with an amplified bass drum's *thump, thump, thump* booming from the air boss's PA system, joined by a deep blast of electric guitar—a single struck note, its long reverberation bending away at maximum fuzz and maximum volume. Then another long downward-bending note.

And then: Ozzy Osbourne, screeching out the opening lines of "Iron Man."

And then another voice—*"AHHHHHHH"*—the air boss, known on the flight deck as the Voice of God, blasting out of the hyper-amplified flight deck PA system—*"AHRIGHT, KITTY HAHK, welcome to this mahnin's edition of yah FAHHHD WAHHHK!"*

Yes, Shitty Kitty's VOG happened to hail out of Boston. God spoke Southie.

*"AHHHHHH, little Black Sabbath comin atchahh-hhh . . ."*

Command on the Shitty Kitty definitely knew how to hold your attention. You couldn't call it "fun," exactly, it was a FOD walk and serious as a coronary. But there was a spring in people's step, a sense of shared purpose, a feeling Finn identified as a *spirit of camaraderie*.

Finn did not experience this himself. The whole concept of camaraderie was something of a mystery to him. But he knew it when he saw it. For example, among the men in his own platoon.

He knew its absence when he saw it, too.

It was staring him in the face right now.

No music there on the deck of the *Lincoln,* just the

sounds of the wind and shuffling feet. Like prisoners of war lining up in the frigid yard.

Now the ragged line was in motion, oozing along the flight deck. Finn noticed body language, posture, and facial tells. The deck-status LSO (landing signal officer) passing a young photographer, the two studiously avoiding each other's eyes, unwittingly telegraphing an illicit relationship. Two guys who'd obviously been drinking the night before (although alcohol was strictly forbidden on board) and a third who'd been hitting it already this morning. He saw the guy who'd offered Billy the little white envelope in the coffee line, could see his dilated pupils.

*Christ on stilts,* Kennedy would say if he were seeing this.

And they were finding way too many items. Yes, the whole point of the walkdown was to find misplaced objects—but there shouldn't have been *this* many objects there to start with.

This place was FOD, all right: Fucked On Delivery. The operation was a mess. Which meant there was a mess somewhere in the leadership.

Small men in high places.

As if on cue, Finn felt the faint heat of someone's gaze fixed on him from above. He swiveled his neck to look up. A thin angular face looking down on him from sixty feet above, standing out on the little balcony they called "Vulture's Row." Steel-gray captain's eyes, flanking an eagle's claw of a nose, radiating mistrust.

Which Finn radiated right back.

*Duly noted.*

# 8

Ship's library, waiting his turn till the next common-use PC came free.

Schofield the ATO officer was right: Finn's cellphone was useless here. There was no wireless service out on the open ocean, and no Wi-Fi on board. No point. The place was one gigantic steel honeycomb. No way to make a Wi-Fi signal penetrate all that steel.

Until his replacement satphone came, the library's PCs would have to do.

Though even then, email and web access would be limited. There was no such thing here as private email—it all went through DOD email that was tightly monitored—and the meager bandwidth made browsing the Internet tediously slow, social media sites all but impossible.

CNN blatted away on the big screen in the corner, nobody listening. At some point someone would switch it off and start the day's cycle of films. No doubt *Top Gun* would at some point make an appearance. Or maybe *Hot Shots,* depending on the irony level of whoever controlled the TV.

Finn read the ship's "Rules to Live By" posted on the bulkhead:

> Any display of affection between shipmates while on board the ship is strictly prohibited. Out of the way places on the ship are off-limits for any male-female meetings. Close proximity viewing of movies on computer or DVD player, hanging out, or leaning on or against another person is forbidden. (Must maintain 1 foot distance between individuals.)

Good luck with that. Finn noted one pair "studying" in back, nearly down each other's pants.

He finally got his PC, checked his two Gmail accounts.

No email yet from Kennedy.

Which shouldn't have surprised him. "Give me twenty-four," Kennedy had said when Finn told him he was leaving. Which Finn had understood to mean, "Give me twenty-four hours to talk with command, and I'll contact you and explain exactly what the hell is going on." That was yesterday afternoon. Technically speaking, not quite twenty-four hours yet.

So no, it shouldn't have surprised him. But it did. Kennedy was a guy who underpromised and overdelivered.

Finn sent short emails to a few of his platoon mates. Then sat for a full minute, thinking about doing some Web searches.

Decided against.

Clicked on NEW MESSAGE and entered into the TO box:

squidink28@gmail.com

Finn had a girl. Up in Washington, near the Canadian border. Carol.

Finn and Carol lost their virginity to each other some two decades earlier when they were both fifteen. To date, she was the only girl he'd slept with. The other Team guys ribbed him about this, of course. Ragged on him for not hitting on other women the way the rest of them did. But Finn didn't see the point. "Don't you like sex?" they'd say. Of course he did. When he and Carol had sex Finn felt like he was diving into the deepest, clearest water. *Becoming* the water. When he climaxed, he became the entire ocean. So yes, he loved sex. Would it be better with someone other than Carol? He didn't understand the question.

One of the guys asked him about it one night while they were waiting to take down an enemy compound in some backwater in Helmand Province.

He and Carol, Finn explained to the guy, had similar backgrounds. Not the same, but parallel.

In Carol's case it was a stepfather with a predilection for staying home and raping the girls while mom was out hustling spare change. One gray day Carol's older sister up and shot them both, then turned the little .22 on herself. Carol rode the foster home bus till she hit the age of majority, then took an actual bus west across the country to start over.

In Finn's case it was . . . whatever it was.

Childhoods best left forgotten. Not identical, but similar.

"So she's like, your soul mate?" the teammate said. Finn said "Okay" and let it go at that. He didn't really know what bound them together. Maybe it was just that they seemed to be traveling in roughly the same direction.

"'Scuse me, Chief. You finished?" A sailor waiting his turn.

"Not quite," said Finn. He typed in his message to squidink28:

> I'm on the water. If you hear anything, don't believe
> it. I'm good.

After clicking SEND he checked his IN box again. Still nothing.

*If you hear anything, don't believe it.* Why had he written that? He didn't know. Whatever prompted it was at the far edge of his thoughts, like a blur in his peripheral vision, something he couldn't quite see but had learned to trust.

Something pinged.

An unopened email, sitting there.

A reply from squidink28.

He clicked.

Just one line. No sig block, no name, nothing else, just three words.

> Give em hell.

He smiled and hit DELETE. Cleared the cache, closed out the browser, and stood, relinquishing his spot to the next sailor in line.

He spent the next few hours walking the upper decks again, focusing on the outermost passageways and mentally cataloging the dozens of locations that opened onto the exterior, where sailors might slip out to sneak in a tan or attempt some hurried surreptitious sex. Depending on the state of security on board. Which Finn suspected was less than gulag-level.

Down on the hangar deck Finn noticed a partially open hatch just ahead that led to the outside. A master-at-arms, his head stuck out the door, was in the process of chasing away some slacker who'd been sitting out there reading. Finn stepped back into the concealment of a narrow alcove and observed.

"I catch you farting around out here again, sailor, and I'm gonna paddle your fanny, just like your momma used to do." The MA's voice was high-pitched and gravelly.

The man waited while the kid climbed back inside, then shut the hatch behind him and followed him down the passageway and out of sight.

Finn opened the hatch and stepped out. He was standing on a small platform, stuck onto the ship's hull like a steel barnacle, that housed a gigantic six-barrel Gatling gun, one of the *Lincoln*'s two close-in weapons systems, or CIWS, pronounced *sea-whiz*. Finn figured no one came out there for any official purpose beyond the occasional maintenance.

He looked around and nodded. He liked this spot.

Much better than his broom closet.

Back inside, Finn made his way toward the rear of the ship, past the huge hangar bays and the jet engine mechanics shops, and poked his head out onto the rounded deck off the ship's stern, called the "fantail."

He walked the length of the empty fantail a few times, back and forth. This was where they dumped the biodegradable trash and it stank of rotting garbage.

A ship's fantail was also a favorite spot for suicides—one reason it was normally under tight security patrol.

Out of curiosity, Finn sat down on a capstan the size of a throne and gazed out at the ocean for another fifteen minutes.

Not a soul appeared.

# 9

Less than a hundred feet away, sequestered in her office deep inside hangar bay 3, Monica sat hunched over her desk, focused on a big three-ring binder, frowning in concentration. Toward the back of her desk sat a silver-plated Rubik's cube, an award she won in a junior high math competition for conceptual modeling in calculus. In place of the usual six colors, each of the nine subsections making up each of the cube's six sides was set with a configuration of one to six small onyx dots, like dice, so that when you solved the puzzle, one face was all ones, another all twos, and so on.

As maintenance officer, Monica was responsible for all their shop's work. In theory, her maintenance chief ran the show and she was there mostly to give him support from up top when he needed it. But Monica took a very hands-on approach to her shop. To a lot of the guys, maintenance officer was considered a gritty job for a woman to manage, a viewpoint that would have royally pissed her off if she let herself think about it. The fact that she was an O-3 in a post normally reserved for an O-4 had made earning the shop's respect an even higher bar. She'd cleared it.

Monica had already been through her usual morning rounds, climbing over and around and under the birds under review, checking their mechanicals, ticking boxes off her lists. She wasn't on flight duty till later, which meant she could sneak in a quiet hour or two with the binder.

As she reread the page her left hand reached reflexively for the silver cube and began manipulating it, turning its faces one way and another while she parsed each line of text.

> STOCKDALE ATC: Hotel Sierra two zero four, you are cleared to land.
> PILOT: Roger, Control—hang on.
> [Brief pause.]
> PILOT: Control, we have a problem. We, hang on—
> [Brief pause.]
> STOCKDALE ATC: Two zero four, say again please?

That was the moment, right there. *Roger, Control—hang on.*

Twenty seconds later the entire craft was sinking to the Gulf floor and her four friends were dead or dying.

Monica thought about the possibilities hidden in that pivotal moment. *Control, we have a problem.* What problem, exactly? Low fuel? Maybe suddenly, dangerously low, maybe a leak sprung somewhere? But Diego or Micaela would've seen that immediately and said something. Unless . . . maybe the fuel gauge was malfunctioning? But no, it was working perfectly on their last maintenance check just hours earlier. She flipped forward a few dozen pages. A perfect report. There was her signature. Right there on the page. Just like the last ten times she looked.

*Algebra, Mon. Quantify the knowns, then solve for X.*

She turned back the pages, starting again from the

beginning, trying to understand where flight two zero four had gone so badly wrong.

> **STOCKDALE ATC:** Hotel Sierra two zero four, you are cleared to land.
> **PILOT:** Roger, Control—hang on.
> [Brief pause.]
> **PILOT:** Control, we have a problem. We, hang on—
> [Brief pause.]
> **STOCKDALE ATC:** Two zero four, say again please?
> **CO-PILOT:** [inaudible] altitude!
> **CREW:** Hey, what [inaudible]—
> **PILOT:** Brace for ditching—
> **CO-PILOT:** Altitude! Alti—
> [Silence for 4 seconds.]
> **STOCKDALE:** Two zero four, come back?
> **STOCKDALE:** [Inaudible curse.]

Monica closed her eyes and felt the seawater clutching at her ankles, climbing her legs and torso like poisonous vines—

She reached out, flipped the binder shut. Let her breathing slow back to normal.

The helo had been on approach to the guided missile destroyer DGG *Stockdale,* planning to refuel before heading back to the *Lincoln,* when the event occurred. Black Falcon 204 inexplicably stalled out a few hundred yards above the surface, then arced like a lawn dart into the black Gulf waters.

The *Stockdale* immediately launched a small boat with their standby SAR swimmer on board. They were at the crash scene within seconds, but by that time the Knighthawk had sunk out of sight. No crew were recovered.

Best guess was that all four crew members had been knocked out on impact, but there was always the possibility that one or more came to in time to realize that they were upside down, submerged too deep to use their emergency breathing devices, being dragged down to their deaths in the dark.

What were they each thinking, those last few seconds before impact? And the seconds that came after, as the bird broke into pieces and flooded with brine?

There had, of course, been investigations. Flight ops were suspended for a week. Endless questions, microscopic scrutiny. There was even talk of grounding every Knighthawk in the fleet while they combed for possible design flaws that might have contributed to the event. But the determination was reached within days: no design flaws, maintenance had been impeccable, procedure sound as a dollar. Once they ruled out mechanical failure and fuel issues, that left one thing.

Pilot error, pure and simple.

Most likely scenario: Diego, the pilot, had suffered a vertigo attack and didn't realize how low he'd flown, and by the time his co-pilot saw what was happening it was too late to pull out.

*It should have been me.*

Monica pushed back and stretched, arms over her head, then looked up at the framed quotation over her desk, a passage from Harry Reasoner, the ABC News reporter, written during the Vietnam War days:

Helicopters are different from planes. An airplane by its nature wants to fly and, if not interfered with too strongly by unusual events or by a deliberately incompetent pilot, it will fly. A helicopter does not want to fly. It is maintained in the air by a variety of forces and controls working in opposition to one another, and if there is any disturbance in the delicate balance, the helicopter stops flying, immediately and disastrously. There is no such thing as a gliding helicopter.

This is why a helicopter pilot is so different a being from an airplane pilot, and why in general, airplane pilots are open, clear-eyed, buoyant extroverts, and helicopter pilots are brooders, introspective anticipators of trouble. They know if something bad has not happened, it is about to.

That quote used to live in the Black Falcons' ready room. When they took it down, after the crash, Monica quietly commandeered it, brought it down to the hangar deck, and hung it directly over her desk.

"You can't punish yourself." That's what their flight surgeon told her. "You have to let it go." But she couldn't. Monica grew up outside a town called "Muleshoe," somewhere between Lubbock and Amarillo, a fact her teammates never failed to kid her about. If helo pilots had call signs the way jet pilots did, hers would be "Muleshoe." As in, *stubborn as a mule's shoe.*

She looked at the heavy silver cube in her hand. As a kid she'd learned that you could follow certain sequences, called "algorithms," to arrive at given conditions. There were a huge number of different possible solutions, but she'd mastered them all. She didn't even have to think about it: her fingers knew the sequences.

Like she knew the sequences of how to pull out a stalled Knighthawk.

What if she had been piloting that night? What if Papa Doc hadn't been such a flaming jerk and let poor Diego have the rest he so badly needed? He'd been pushing the kid, pushing him way too hard. He was always pushing everyone too hard.

If it had been Monica in that pilot's seat, and not Diego, would that have changed anything?

Would it have changed *everything*?

A service was held on board for all four crew members; families were notified, personal effects packed up and flown off the boat. Life went on. And still Monica couldn't accept it.

She pulled her chair forward again, reopened the binder, and slowly leafed through the pages, her left hand absently working the silver cube, twisting and turning its many faces, feeling for the *click*.

# 10

The ship's mess facilities were all available 24/7, but the most popular meal by far was the late-night galley raid they called "midrats," short for "midnight rations." Which was why, at 2400 hours, Finn was seated at a table to the rear of the officers' wardroom, drinking spring water from a tall glass, observing a roomful of navy officers hobnobbing.

He heard a lot of boasts being tossed around—how many flight hours logged, how many traps (completed landings) and greens (landings with top marks). A lot of mine-is-bigger-than-yours. The interplay of rank, seniority, and track record reminded him of a bumper car course, the buggies all riding on egos inflated till they strained at the seams like tires pumped way over their spec maximums. A few of these people would levitate above the herd to become admirals and commodores, military icons and political heavyweights. But not most. Most would hit retirement young and spend the rest of their lives telling anyone who would still listen that there was nothing, *nothing* that compared to the rush of being shot off an aircraft carrier flight deck by a nuclear-powered slingshot.

It occurred to Finn that if the USS *Abraham Lincoln* was powered by the steady depletion of radioactive uranium, its air wing was held aloft by the steady depletion of unfulfilled ambitions.

He surveyed the space. The noisiest sector here seemed to be focused on a petite, black-haired ball of energy whom Finn remembered seeing in the Jittery Abe line, one the others called "Biker."

The last jet pilot to land that night, Biker had evidently made quite the entrance at recovery. "You see how she dropped that bird?" said one of her squadron mates. "No approach, just splotted it down on the deck. Blam! Like a mutt taking a dump on the street."

"Thank you, Gopher, that's very poetic," said the tiny pilot, as she stabbed a huge forkful of whatever it was she'd mounded up on her plate.

"Jesus, Biker, how the hell do you pack all that in?" said another brother pilot.

"High metabolism," she said between chomps. "I could eat you under the table."

"You know what, I think I'd like that."

"Fuck you, Ratso."

"My stateroom, oh two hundred."

"In your dreams, Ratso, not in mine."

Kidding around with the guys. A navy fighter-pilot squadron was like a college fraternity, except with no alcohol and twice the testosterone. This one, though, she was holding her own. No, more than holding. She *owned* the place.

Finn also noted the helo pilot, the angry handsome olive-skinned one, sitting off by himself and drinking a can of Monster. Projecting that distinctive aura of self-righteous self-sufficiency that suggested Movie Star was used to sitting alone, that possibly it had hurt his feelings at some distant point in time, the way others avoided his company, but that he'd long ago taught himself to believe it was his decision in the first place.

Despite Movie Star's careful efforts to hide it, Finn noticed him sneaking lingering looks every so often in the tiny black-haired jet pilot's direction.

So, Movie Star had a crush.

Far off in a corner Finn spotted the ATO officer, Schofield, sitting quietly with another pilot. The two were obviously in a relationship and thought they were doing a good job of hiding it, but Finn could read it from clear across the wardroom.

If there was one thing that telegraphed the existence of a covert couple on a navy vessel, it was the irritation factor. Not affection: everyone knew how to hide that. No, there was a kind of friction, as unconscious as static electricity, that was specific to romantically involved couples, specifically couples that had been together for some length of time.

These two were having a spat.

He watched the conversation go off the rails, the other guy getting upset, Schofield staying calm. Finally the other guy got up and left. After a few moments Schofield stood, too, and began making his way back toward the buffet-style row of steam tables. As he passed Finn's table he stopped. "Chief Finn."

Finn hoisted his glass.

"I meant to ask you about that package," said the officer. "Roughly what size are we looking for?"

"Small," said Finn. "A satphone."

Schofield nodded. "If you need an inside line meanwhile, anything beyond the ship's phone or common-use PCs, just holler. I'm sure we can set you up in CVIC with secure comms." CVIC: the ship's intelligence center.

Finn thanked him, said that probably wouldn't be necessary.

Schofield took two steps away, then stopped again and looked back at Finn. "You said you served on another carrier? An oil burner?"

Finn nodded. "*Kitty Hawk*. Oh-three to oh-four."

Schofield's face broke out in a grin. "The Battle Cat. If you don't mind my asking, who was your CO?"

"Tomaszeski."

Schofield closed his eyes, drew in a long breath, and let it out, dropping his normal tenor to a deep baritone: "*Good morning, shipmates!*"

Finn set his glass down and regarded the other man. "You knew him?"

"My first tour, a year after you. And every single day of that tour opened with the bosun's whistle and reveille call, followed by Captain Tomaszeski's daily address, which always started the same way—"

Finn joined in, the two men now speaking in unison:

"GOOD MORNING, SHIPMATES—IT'S ANOTHER MAGNIFICENT DAY AT SEA!"

Schofield gave a nostalgic smile. "And lo and behold, it was. It *always* was."

The two were silent for a moment. Then Schofield nodded at Finn's glass. "Refill?"

Finn didn't need more water, but he nodded and said, "Thanks."

While Schofield took the empty glass over to the beverage counter, Finn thought about Captain Tom.

Schofield had nailed it. *And lo and behold, it was.* Not that every day was specifically *magnificent*. The skipper would vary his adjectives. Sometimes the day was "stupendous," "excellent," or "phenomenal." An aspirational "perfect." A purely aesthetic "beautiful." But it was always some version of "amazing." Because Captain Tom wasn't just blowing smoke up their asses. To him that particular day at sea *was* magnificent. And no matter what bullshit was happening that morning,

no matter what plugged toilets or crappy food or aggra-
vating bunkmates threatened to plague your day, when
you heard Captain Tom pronounce the day "magnificent," you couldn't help but feel the same way.

Not that he stopped there. The skipper would then
walk them through the current plan for the day, where
they were headed and why, and then address whatever
complaints had been brought to his attention by his network of chiefs—not that they would always be fixed immediately, but they would at least be *addressed*, and that
was enough to make the intolerable bearable. Then he
would single out one division for that day's praise, and
close with a few words of inspiration that in anyone
else's mouth might have sounded corny but from Captain Tom were as real as blood and bones.

Schofield returned with two fresh glasses and took a
seat across from Finn, then raised his glass as Finn had
done earlier. "To Captain Tom. As the saying goes, I
would follow that guy through the gates of Hell and
back."

Finn tilted his glass and tapped it against Schofield's.

And all at once it clicked.

*That's* what had been missing since he set foot on this
ship.

No morning address.

No address at all.

He thought back to that pair of steel-gray eyes he'd
seen that morning, up on Vulture's Row. He'd been on
board the USS *Abraham Lincoln* for twenty-four hours
now, and he hadn't yet heard the sound of that man's
voice.

"Tell me something," he said. "When was the last
time you heard your captain here on the *Lincoln* give an
announcement or address?"

Schofield thought about that. "I guess that'd be
maybe four, five months ago. Just before we reached the

Gulf. Some joker tossed a chem light overboard one night. After we went through the whole man-overboard alert and muster call, the skipper got on the 1MC."

"And said what?"

Schofield pursed his lips and frowned. "Gave us all a tongue-lashing worthy of William Bligh."

Finn took that in. "When else?"

Schofield thought some more. Shook his head. "Honestly, that's the only time I can remember."

They both fell silent again as they drank.

So the guy had never talked to his people, not but once in eight months to bawl them out over some trivial screwup?

This was not Finn's idea of a captain.

Not by a long shot.

# 11

August 2, 0600. The whistle, the bored voice. *"Reveille, reveille, all hands heave out and trice up."* No "Good morning, shipmates!" No captain's address.

And no Finn. The broom closet was empty, its narrow steel rack swung up and latched to the bulkhead ("triced"). Its assigned resident had spent the past few hours exploring the lower decks of the ship where the under-dwellers worked, pacing out their days in the recycled air and sunless passageways below the waterline. If the pilots and officers were the *Lincoln*'s Eloi, down here was where the Morlocks toiled and slept.

Now, as reveille sounded and the ship's nighttime red lights switched over to daytime white lighting, Finn turned and headed back above to intersect with the breakfast crowd.

On deck 4, as he passed the gym they called the "Jungle," something brought him to a halt. The hormonal ozone of gathering human thunderheads. He slipped inside the gym to look for its source.

There, by the weight bench. The tall helo pilot who flew him in two nights ago, talking to a brick bunker of a guy who stood rooted there flanked by his two rat-faced buddies. Finn recognized the trio from mess the day before: an enormous redneck mechanic with his entourage of two. Brothers, he guessed. Same litter.

"Hey," he heard the pilot say. "You planning on re-racking those weights?"

Under the gym lights Finn could see her more clearly than from the back of her darkened helo. Her eyes were pale blue, the bleached color of prairie sky, her hair not Hollywood blond but long-years-of-work-under-the-sun blond. West Texas. Ranch country.

It wasn't hard to see what was going down here. Bunker Guy had just finished his lifting routine and left the weights lying in disarray—intentionally, Finn suspected, as a diss—and West Texas wasn't happy about it.

Finn suspected that West Texas wasn't happy about a lot more that had nothing to do with Bunker Guy, and that she hit the gym hard and often to work out whatever it was—that dark undercurrent of grief and anger he'd sensed two nights earlier on the helo, which he guessed she tried to keep hidden. But anger was like magma; it would always find its way to the surface.

Bunker Guy stood to his full height. West Texas was tall but this guy was enormous, tall enough to look down at her as he talked.

"Yeah, sorry about that, ma'am. Want me to spot you?"

Challenging her. Clearly had a death wish, talking to an officer like that.

West Texas looked up at him without blinking. "No, Tucker, I want you to rerack your weights. I'll wait."

He opened his mouth, then closed it again.

He had not gone about this strategically. Fully expecting her to be intimidated and back right the fuck down, he hadn't calculated an exit strategy in the event that she didn't. His only options now were to escalate, never a smart idea with an officer, or back right the fuck down himself and rerack the goddamn weights.

He reracked the goddamn weights.

Without a word the pilot lay down on the bench and began her routine.

Tucker turned and noticed Finn. His face curled into a snarl. "What. You here to rescue the lady?" Still trying to pick a fight. Maybe he couldn't take out his aggression on an officer, but he looked like he'd sure as hell be okay with decking this SEAL sonofabitch who thought his shit didn't stink.

Yup. Death wish.

Finn noticed Tucker's rat squad inching in toward their guy's flank. Backing him up. Like a street gang challenge.

Finn didn't move. "Fighting's not really my thing," he said.

Tucker rocked back on his heels and made a face of mock surprise.

"A *pacifist*," he said to his rat boys. "A fuckin' Navy SEAL pacifist." He *ark-ark-ark*'d a few times: his impression of a seal barking. Ratface 1 and Ratface 2 laughed in chorus. Tucker turned to Ratface 1. "You know what that is?"

The rodent reflexively obliged. "No, what?"

Tucker grinned. "That's what you call an 'oxymoron.'" Turning back to face Finn. "Are you an oxy*moron,* pacifist?"

"Let me think," said Finn. He tilted his head two degrees, then righted it again. "No. Just don't see the point." He gave a nod in the pilot's direction. "Besides, she didn't look like she was the one needed rescuing."

Ratface 2 blurted out a *haw-haw-haw!* before realizing he was running with the ball in the wrong direction, then abruptly shut up.

Finn turned back to the door. As he exited, he glanced over just in time to see West Texas shoot him an undisguisedly hostile look.

*Good morning, shipmates!* he thought. *It's another antagonizing day at sea!*

# 12

Finn arrived at Jittery Abe's just in time to stand at the end of the line next to a short, muscular kid in a red jersey. The kid nodded deferentially and took a step back, inviting Finn to get in line ahead of him.

"Oh, hey," said Finn, waving the kid back into place and taking the spot behind him.

The kid shrugged and nodded his thanks.

Finn nodded at the kid's jersey and lifted one eyebrow. "I-why ay-oh, why ay-ess, right?"

IYAOYAS: the ordie's creed. *If You Ain't Ordnance, You Ain't Shit*.

The kid broke into a grin. "Copy that, Chief!"

"Just Finn," said Finn.

"Finn." The kid's grin grew wider. "Like Huck Finn?"

"Something like that. What's your name, airman?"

"Tom, Chief."

Finn nodded. "Good to meet you, Tom Sawyer."

And just like that, the two were best buds.

*That's one*, he thought.

Finn had clocked this kid the day before, on the flight deck during FOD walk. Round face, stub of a nose, narrow thick eyebrows that lent him a thoughtful look. He was young, and not just in years, but he had solid character and it was clear that the guys he worked with trusted him. No doubt because he had a trusting nature himself. Finn would have bet money that this kid had a girl back home, and that by the time he got back his heart would be broken. But he'd get through it. Those who were gifted with a trusting nature, Finn had observed, had a certain naïve resilience.

A few minutes of small talk later Tom had his order and it was Finn's turn. He ordered a small coffee, black. Gave Tom Sawyer a two-finger salute and headed the other direction. Took the coffee with him down a passageway, hooked a left, tossed the coffee in the trash, untouched. Leaned against the bulkhead and checked his watch.

His first day on board Finn had drawn curious stares as he made his way around the decks. Today, as he walked the passageways in his desert tan flight suit, hardly anyone noticed. He'd become part of the fabric. It was always this way. Strange as his physical appearance was, he could blend in, then disappear. He was, after all, a sniper; he knew how to stalk.

After waiting three minutes he circled back around and got in line at Jittery Abe's again, this time stepping in right behind the master-at-arms he'd seen the day before at the portside CIWS mount, the one with the high gravelly voice.

The MA turned his head, noticed the SEAL insignia on his chest. Nodded.

Finn nodded back. Smiled.

Emboldened by the smile, the MA said, "Hey, can I ask you a question?"

Finn said, "You mean, a second question?"

The man's face went blank for a moment, then relaxed in a chuckle. "Ha. You got a point there. Yeah, a second question."

Now at the front of the line, the MA placed his order and turned back to Finn after paying with his Navy Cash card. Everything on board a navy ship ran on Navy Cash. That and cans of Monster, which were hoarded and traded like prison-yard cigarette packs.

"What exactly is a SEAL doing here? I mean, no platoon, no squad, just one SEAL?"

Finn opened his mouth, paused a second, then said softly, "That's classified." He leaned an inch closer and dropped his voice even further. "If I told you, I'd have to . . ." He glanced left, then right, then back at the MA. "Well, you know. Coffee, black," that last said to the barista.

The man chuckled again. "Copy that." He stuck out his hand and got a brief shake from Finn. "Mason. Frank Mason." He jerked a thumb at the MA standing next to him. "This here's Dewitt."

"Let me guess," said Finn, then tipped his head toward Frank's silent partner. "First name Ernest?"

Frank did the blank face again for a full three seconds, then barked a laugh. "Ha! Frank and Ernest. You're funny!"

Finn shrugged, then nodded in Dewitt's direction. "Hey. *He's* Dewitt."

Frank paused—then laughed out loud again, a high wheezy laugh. "Ha! That's good. That's really good."

Finn glanced at his watch. "Uh-oh. Gotta bounce. Later, gents." He stepped out of the line and started walking away.

"Hey," Frank called over. "What about your coffee?"

"You guys have it. I'll get one later."

*That's two.*

*Three, with Schofield.*

Tom the ordie, Frank in security, Schofield the ATO

officer. They were the first three nodes in his fledgling onboard HUMINT network. Human intelligence. His own personal grapevine and early warning system. Finn did this everywhere he went, and it worked every time. He'd done it in urban Iraq and backwater villages in Afghanistan. It had worked in Libya, Syria, Somalia, Yemen—

Yemen, mostly. Though in Mukalla, not so much.

No, it hadn't worked too well there, had it.

A whole settlement wiped out. Three dozen Yemeni locals slaughtered. On their watch. His and Kennedy's.

Hence the disgrace.

And no one could tell him how it happened.

# 13

Finn sat out on the little strip of catwalk by the CIWS mount, watching the fierce Arabian sunlight playing over the water. The *Lincoln*'s strike group was spread too far apart to see any of the other ships from here, but they were far from alone. The Gulf's surface was littered with little fishing boats, the ones the locals called "dhows." Flocks of black-and-white terns swooped in and out, following the larger dhows' wakes, diving for leftovers. To the north, he could just make out the Iranian coastline. They were currently on an east-southeast heading, beelining toward the Strait of Hormuz. About to leave the Gulf and start the homeward trek.

He reached down and picked up the large blank sketch pad at his feet, one of a dozen he'd bought at the ship's store, and a fresh charcoal pencil. The pencils he'd brought on board with him. Never went anywhere without them.

He began sharpening, his little finger looped through the steel ring forged at the end of the knife's haft.

The very first lesson he learned in close quarters combat training consisted of three words: "primary," "secondary," "tertiary." In plain English: always have a backup. And a backup to your backup.

His primary, a Remington .300 Win Mag, was now locked up in the ship's armory. His secondary, a Heckler & Koch .45 semiautomatic pistol, was keeping the Win Mag company. His primary and secondary were both gone.

This four-inch piece of steel was his tertiary.

Which suited Finn just fine. In an all-steel environment like this, bullets didn't make much sense anyway; ricochets would travel at near original velocity and be unacceptably risky. Besides, unlike most of his sniper school classmates, Finn was not a lover of guns. Before joining the military he had never even handled a rifle, and despite the fluency he acquired through SEAL selection and sniper school, it was still not his native language.

Finn set the knife down at his side and began to sketch.

A memory floated up. Final training exercise—FTX—at sniper school.

Their instructor was a holdover from the early days, when sniper school instructors thought they were glorified BUD/S instructors whose sole purpose in life was to break these guys.

And he hated Finn. Had spent the entire course trying to figure out how to flush him and his partner, Boyd. But Finn was just too good. "Little motherfucker stalks like a fucking patch of mist," Finn had overheard him complain to a colleague. "Melts into the goddamn scenery and pops up like a bad dream a thousand fucking yards away."

Boyd had sucked at stalking, but Finn coached him through.

When the FTX arrived the instructor set up an extra pair of watchers fifty yards in front of where he sat, determined to stop Finn from reaching the target no matter what it took. Finn stalked himself and Boyd right up to the instructor's perimeter, then set his rifle down, circled around to within thirty yards of the man's backside, and tossed a pebble at him. Popped him square between the shoulder blades. Which was the signal for Boyd to take *his* shot.

Finn passed.

Boyd passed.

The instructor was rotated back to some bullshit admin post.

Sometimes a rock was as good as a gun.

Just then Finn felt a shift in the catwalk beneath him.

He looked up. The ship was veering due south again. Reverting to that familiar box pattern, the carrier strike group's equivalent of treading water.

Finn understood what was happening. Ozone. Thunderheads. There was some diplomatic dustup with Iran and an order had come down. They couldn't transit the Strait yet, as much as the crew was aching to go. For the moment they were trapped here in the Gulf, awaiting word from Washington as diplomats and back-channel proxies arm-wrestled and the talking heads on CNN batted around their little balls of yarn while waiting for more catnip.

And still not a word from the captain. *Christ on stilts.*

"Hey!"

Finn looked over his shoulder and saw Frank, the master-at-arms, standing at the hatchway.

"Ha," Frank said, his glare softening to a smile when he saw who it was.

"Yo," said Finn, nodding with his chin. The knife was gone, salted away in a pocket the instant he'd heard Frank's approach.

Frank glanced out at the ocean and took a full breath

of the salt air. He looked to Finn like he might like to sneak out there himself and spend some time reading a book, too. The MA looked at the big Gatling gun, then back at Finn. "Whatever you're doing here," he said, "it looks . . . sketchy." He grinned, pleased with himself. Frank, the wit.

He came closer and looked at what Finn had drawn. "Whoa," he said.

Now Finn looked at it, too.

It was a nighttime scene, in meticulous detail, sparse shrubby vegetation surrounding a walled-in little cluster of houses. In the center, a large wooden doorframe set into a wall built of mud-brick and rubble. Though the scene was dark, gashes of heat lightning sliced open the sky, its pale glare sufficient to see that the door had been shattered to pieces.

Finn felt a shudder of revulsion.

"Hey, that's pretty good," said Frank. "Really lifelike. Where the heck *is* that?"

"Someplace scary," said Finn.

Frank chuckled. "Copy that." He stood up straight again. "All right, then. But see that you're in by ten thirty, young man, or I'll dock your allowance." He chuckled again and withdrew, leaving Finn alone out there.

As Finn had figured he would.

Make someone laugh and they trusted you. Finn didn't get it. But he knew it worked.

"*Whoa,*" he said in Frank's voice. And gave a soft chuckle, perfectly replicating the MA's high-pitched gravel.

The Team guys used to say Finn was a hell of a manipulator. He didn't see it that way. As far as he was concerned, he was just following the Golden Rule.

Interact with others the way they want to be interacted with.

He looked down at what he'd drawn. Carefully tore the page from the pad, crumpled it into a ball, and tossed it overboard. Then picked up his charcoal pencil and began again.

*Really lifelike.*

That it was.

And Finn had absolutely no memory of ever seeing it before.

# 14

Up in the library the TV was tuned once more to CNN, the talking heads going round and round about something out of Iran.

Hormonal ozone. Human thunderheads.

Finally a PC station freed up. Finn hit both Gmail boxes.

Nothing.

Not from his teammates. Not from Kennedy. Not from anyone.

It was now two full days since he'd had that telegraphic conversation with Kennedy. *Give me twenty-four.* Twenty-four meant twenty-four. His lieutenant would have been in contact by now if it was at all physically possible.

Which meant it wasn't at all physically possible.

Which would be the case, for example, if the whole platoon were back out in the field somewhere on some op or other, on comms lockdown. But that seemed unlikely. They'd been back from Mukalla for only a few days and were expected to be there at the base in Bahrain for at least another week, probably more.

Or which would also be the case if . . .

If what?

Finn couldn't come up with a plausible second scenario, and he didn't like that. Kennedy was the platoon's
OIC. Officer in charge. As platoon chief, Finn was their
top enlisted man, second in charge. He was not a natural born leader, not like Kennedy, and he knew that. But
these were his guys. His responsibility. They were counting on him.

Why wasn't he hearing from them?

He set up three brand-new email boxes, none identifying him in any way. Gmail wasn't like sending a letter
sealed in an envelope. More like sending a postcard. You
might as well spray paint your message on the subway
wall. Would his emails be read by someone on board?
Forwarded to some functionary up the chain of command? No doubt.

From each of the new accounts he sent a series of three
messages, covering a total of nine teammates. Each email
was the same: no subject line, just a two-word message:

I'm here.

He closed the PC's browser window. Glanced around.
Same couple in the back again, warming up to perpetu-
ate the species. He looked back at the blank screen.

Finn didn't care for the Web. He didn't like putting
himself out into cyberspace where his thoughts and
movements could be tracked and stored. But he needed
to know what was out there.

He opened a fresh window in the PC's browser, put
the cursor in the search window, and typed:

mukalla incident

Hit the NEWS tab, waited for the PC's snail's-pace
bandwidth to respond. Then scrolled through the search

results. Nothing pertinent. To focus the search he inserted the relevant date:

mukalla July 29 incident

Wait. Scroll. Nothing. He backspaced over "incident" and typed in a new phrase:

mukalla July 29 terror attack

No results, none that meant anything.

Finn glanced around the space. He was sitting in a corner of a crowded compartment—but it felt like he was alone out on a ridgeline, standing silhouetted against the open sky, the easiest target in the world. He didn't like being this exposed.

He deleted "terror attack," hesitated for a moment, then added one last word to the search string:

mukalla July 29 massacre

Looked at the blinking cursor for a moment. Hit RETURN. Waited.

And got nothing.

He cleared his search history, deleted the browser's cookies. Restarted the computer. He would swing by every few days to check for replies. Like walking the woods to check a string of traps.

His expectations were not high, though he could not have explained why.

# 15

Ship's pay phone. Another wait. Once he reached the front of the line and inserted his Navy Cash card, he was surprised how accessible it was. AT&T Direct Ocean Service. Another change since his tour on the Shitty Kitty.

He placed a call to Naval Support Activity Bahrain, the air base where he'd been stationed. Asked to be put through to his unit. A long pause. "They're back out in the field," he was told.

Unexpected.

He tried to press for more information, was unsurprised when he got none. Asked to be put through to supply, checking on a package that was supposed to be on its way to him. They put him on hold for two expensive minutes, then came back on. "We'll have to check on that. Try back later."

Which he wouldn't. He knew this military dialect and what it meant. Stonewalling. Nothing unusual there. Standard operating procedure. No reason to be concerned.

Still. In his experience, by the time you worked out a reason to be concerned it was already too late.

He looked at the phone.

It was thirteen hours later in Dam Neck, Virginia. Not ideal but still on the far edge of prime time. They'd all be up.

He tried calling the wives of four platoon mates, one after the other. Every one went to voicemail. He left no messages. On the fifth try he finally got through. A woman's voice said, "Hello?"

"It's me. Finn."

Silence.

"Jean? You there?"

The voice said quietly, "Don't call back." And broke the connection.

He spent the rest of the day walking the passageways, mostly circling the centers of power clustered at the foot of the island on the gallery deck: captain's suite, admiral's suite, air traffic control, intel offices, battle command, and so on. Didn't bother with lunch. Or dinner.

*Don't call back.*

When the light started to change he went down to the hangar deck and climbed out onto the big Gatling gun mount again, where he spent the next few hours with his charcoal pencils capturing frame after frame of darkening shades of gray.

The scene with the shattered door did not put in an appearance.

That night he crept up onto the flight deck catwalk, slipped on a pair of ear protectors, and poked his head a few inches above the deck to watch the flight crew in operation. Impressive, yet he sensed a kind of brittle fatigue. After nearly eight months at sea, the six thousand–odd people on board the ship were nearly worn out. Even the jets looked worn out, their paint fading, stenciled pilot call signs missing pieces of letters.

He reached out and felt the flight deck's surface. It

was losing its gritty edge and would soon need a resurfacing. Hell of a metaphor.

A Hornet shot off the prow and screamed into the night.

*Don't call back.*

The Dam Neck wives had never liked him, never trusted him, no matter how much the guys protested. It never bothered him. But the voice on the other end of that phone had been outright hostile.

*If you hear anything, don't believe it.*

What had they heard?

# 16

Papa Doc was flying with Monica again tonight, and he was driving her nuts. There was nothing to do on plane guard but keep the bird in the air and fly in endless D-loops, yet he was on her constantly, fussing and micromanaging as if this were her first time in a cockpit. By the end of the three hours, Monica's nerves were shot.

As they set down on the ship's port side, toward the stern, Monica noticed the SEAL on the catwalk. It was disquieting how he popped up everywhere, silently watching, observing everything.

No, not just observing. Like he was *memorizing* everything.

Marsupials. She'd looked it up. Born underdeveloped, with features that never quite caught up. The marsupial family included koalas, possums, and Tasmanian devils. Which, she wondered, was he?

When she stepped out of the Knighthawk and looked over toward the edge of the deck, he was gone.

Ten minutes later she was in her stateroom, undressed and lying back in her rack, talking quietly back and forth with Kris, her best friend, in the bunk below. It was past midnight and their roommate, Anne, lay fast asleep on the other bottom bunk a few yards away. The empty fourth rack, above Anne's, had belonged to Micaela, the co-pilot on the helo that went down. It was the loudest thing in the cabin.

"So how was Papa Doc?" Kris's hushed voice drifted up from below. It was Kris who'd coined the nickname, and she was the only soul on board who dared voice it out loud.

Monica replied with a groan.

"That good, huh?"

"Gracious as ever."

"Turd."

"Why does he so push my buttons?" Monica wondered aloud, not for the first time.

"Um, I don't know," replied Kristine, "maybe because he's your classic male chauvinist, a fucking racist, and unreconstructed homophobe asshole?"

"Jesus, Kris! Keep your voice down!" Slanderous words spoken against a superior officer could be held as insubordination and earn grave punishment. Court-martial, even.

"I tell you I caught him staring at me a few nights ago at midrats?" Kris commented.

"Ugh. You're kidding."

"And not in an arrogant-CO way, either, more like a pervy-peeper way. Like when a guy's trying to look down your blouse without looking like he's doing it?"

"Eww. What did you do?"

"Walked over and asked him if he needed help finding anything. Like his dignity. Or his dick."

"*Kris!*"

"Okay, not really. I did what any Tennessee girl would, stared back at him and batted my eyelashes till he turned red and looked away."

"Seriously? Jesus, Kris, why would you *do* that!"

"Because fuck him, that's why."

Kris was a natural target for men's attention, but she typically had no problem handling herself. Last few days, though, she'd been distracted. Jumpy. She'd even skipped breakfast that morning, which for her was practically unheard of.

She hid it well. The rest of the squadron saw only the top-gun swagger and Tennessee ballsiness, and they loved her for it. (A girl so gutsy she went by the call sign "Biker"!) Only Monica understood how fragile she was. She'd tried to bring it up a few times, but even as close as the two were, Kris held her feelings awfully close to her vest.

In the silence Monica felt the presence of Micaela's empty rack. Remembering how harshly Papa Doc had treated her, how she and Kris had found her weeping in her rack on more than one occasion after an especially brutal tongue-lashing.

"Quite a show you gave out there tonight," she said to change the subject.

Kris had made one of her signature night landings, smacking the deck like a meteor strike. Monica had flown more than a hundred missions and there'd been a few tense moments—but nothing in the Knighthawk came close to the experience of flying solo in an F/A-18, let alone *landing* the freaking thing. "Like setting a bucking bronco down on a postage stamp floating in a shark-infested pool . . . at night" was how her brother had described it.

"How you can pull that off is beyond me. I'd be terrified of crashing the damn thing."

"It's not the idea of crashing," said Kris. "I mean, what the hell, we're all gonna crash and burn at some point, right? But ejecting and ending up in the *water*? Ugh. I don't know if I'd make it."

This was something the two shared: an unmitigated aversion to the open water. Monica grew up around horses and ranches, Kris around motorcycles and urban blight. Naturally, as part of their pilot training, they'd both learned to swim at an expert level. But only Monica knew how terrified her friend was of ending up alone in the ocean.

"'Course you'd make it," said Monica. "You'd just float and let your strobe flash. We'd be on you in minutes." But she knew what Kris meant.

They went quiet again, both thinking about the downed helo crew. Ever since flight 204 went down their stateroom had felt haunted.

Hell, the whole ship had felt haunted.

It was Kris who broke the silence. "Do you feel . . . safe here?"

"What do you mean?" said Monica. "In the Gulf? Totally. And anyway, we're done here. We'll be heading home any day now."

"No, I mean here. On the ship."

"Shit, Kris—are you okay? Is anyone hassling you?"

"No, no, it's— Forget it."

She seemed almost . . . paranoid. Monica had caught her glancing over her shoulder a few times, as if there were someone following her.

"Hey," she whispered. "Have you noticed that creepy SEAL skulking the passageways?" She leaned over to look down at Kris—but her friend had already dropped off. Kris fell asleep the way she landed her jet. *Like a mutt taking a dump on the street.*

Monica gave a quiet laugh and settled back on her pillow. Let Kris sleep; she'd earned it. Her best friend was a fierce worker, not only in the grueling business of flying her Hornet but also in her "day job" as assistant ordnance officer for her squadron. Always made Monica smile to think about that. As Maintenance O, her own job was to make sure things didn't fall apart. Kris's was to make sure things blew up.

Staring at the overhead, she listened to the sounds of the last cycle of flight ops playing out just yards above, nothing separating them but a few inches of steel deck plating. Their stateroom was located directly under the 3 wire, the one all the pilots aimed to catch. The massive machinery that controlled it was housed right next door, and each time another jet crashed onto the deck it made an ear-shattering whine as the cable played out, followed by a shriek as it scraped back across the deck to rewind for the next trap. Earplugs helped a little, but nothing could block out that unearthly din.

Monica closed her eyes. Another long day starting just hours from now, but she was too stirred up to sleep.

She said a prayer, for Kris, for her squadron. For Diego and Micaela and the rest of the drowned helo crew. Nothing quieted her mind.

*Do you feel . . . safe here?*

She slipped off her rack, padded to the door, and cracked it open. Looked up and down the red-lit passageway.

Empty as a ghost town.

Back to bed. Curled on her side, eyes closed, searching for sleep.

She went through her "boldface," the emergency procedures you had to be ready to follow instantly and automatically, without stopping to check a list or search your memory banks, in the event of an emergency. Boldface if the steering quit. If a rotor blade snapped. If comms went out.

*Helicopter pilots are brooders, introspective antici-*

*pators of trouble. They know if something bad has not happened, it is about to.*

She finally drifted off into strange dreams of pushing her commanding officer out of their craft and watching him drown in the black water below.

# 17

Half-past midnight. Finn poked his head in the door at general mess. Not much was happening at midrats tonight. People were eating, staring at the TV, hardly talking. Everyone seemed to be in when-the-fuck-do-we-get-out-of-here mode. By now a good number of ship's company had figured out what Finn knew that afternoon: they were in a holding pattern. For how long? Who knew.

He headed above to walk the upper decks again. Through the ladders and passageways, noticing and cataloging the different ranks and ratings and body types and personalities. Unrated E-1s and E-2s, swabbing and polishing in their endless cleaning missions. Air traffic and intel crew clomping down to their berths after a long day on the island or in the cluster of offices at the island's foot. Flight deck crew and mechanics heading above to the flight deck or below to the hangar deck to service their various aircraft.

All at once, Finn felt a hot prickling up the back of his neck.

He stopped. Closed his eyes.

*Mukalla outskirts, dead of night. Their platoon had
silently surrounded the tiny compound. It was a classic
SEAL op, the thing they did best: breach charge, flash
bangs, zip ties, hoods over heads, and they'd be out of
there, prisoners in tow. In and out. The moment their
breacher blasted the door they would flow through that
compound like high tide through a sandcastle. If everything went according to plan. Though of course most
plans went to hell the moment the first shot was fired.*

Finn opened his eyes.

Remembering those last moments in the dark, waiting for the signal in his ear.

You never knew what you were running into in the
seconds after that breach charge went off. A wall of
steel-jacketed AK gunfire. The boiling hot flash of an
IED. Crazy-eyed men wielding razor-sharp daggers,
screaming women coming at you with their fingernails
and teeth. Or just a crowd of disoriented, terrified people jarred from sleep. You never knew.

It all depended on the quality of the intel.

In Mukalla they'd had bad intel.

Finn continued walking, clocking the various species
of nighttime personnel. A pair of yellow shirts laughing
quietly over some private joke, making their way below
to wash up and hit the rack. There went Schofield striding purposefully past in the direction of the fantail. Another handler in his green jersey and goggles, heading
the same general direction. Dozens of faceless individuals all going their separate ways yet all swimming to the
same rhythm, the endless pulse of the ship's vast metabolism: operating it, feeding it, cleaning it, maintaining it, servicing it.

He stopped again.

Now he remembered what it was that had stirred
that particular memory.

Those last few moments, waiting for the signal to breach that compound in Mukalla, he'd felt something.

A hot prickling up the back of his neck.

So why was he feeling it again now?

# 18

Sam Schofield had had enough. It was time to end this thing.

The navy's "Rules to Live By" notwithstanding, there was a good deal of latitude and tolerance on board the *Lincoln,* but if you pushed the boundaries too far they would eventually push back, and when they did they'd push back hard. You could find your whole career flushed down the toilet. Bennett just didn't seem to grasp this simple truth.

Schofield strode purposefully past a pair of chuckling yellow shirts and on toward the fantail.

Life in the ATO shack was good, his best assignment yet. But this relationship with Lieutenant Bennett, this had gotten out of hand. Bennett was needy, persistent, and increasingly demanding, and Schofield was tired of it.

He still had the note in his pocket, ripped from the envelope sitting on the pillow on his rack. Typed, on plain white paper. (*Typed,* for heaven's sake!)

> Sammy, we need to talk. Can you come meet me?
> Sponson G, by the fantail, at 0100.

*We need to talk*—seriously? Where did he think they were, in junior high?

Schofield was a reasonable guy, some might even say overly so. But the petulance, the possessiveness, the petty arguments over nothing! Sam wasn't used to this kind of drama, and God knew an aircraft carrier on deployment was the last place on earth for it.

Enough.

He arrived at the hatch to the exterior, grasped the handle—and stopped.

Was he overreacting?

Maybe he should blow off this rendezvous altogether, turn himself around and go back to his cabin. Confront Bennett quietly tomorrow in the light of day, when cooler heads prevailed.

Tempting.

He took a long breath in, then let it out again and slowly shook his head. It would be easy to let the anger dissipate, just let it go—but right now he needed to stay a little angry.

Right now, it was time to end this thing.

He pushed open the big steel hatch, bracing himself against the onrush of muggy heat. Ducking his head so he wouldn't slam it on the steel frame overhead, he walked out into the darkness and stepped to the rail.

He heard the hatch thud shut, felt the presence behind him, but he didn't turn around, just stood with his hands on the rail breathing in the hot soup of Gulf air. There was the distant *schuss* of the ship's prow slicing through the black water, the groans and creaks of great cords up on the flight deck holding their cargo fast. On the distant shoreline, oil derricks poked pinpricks of flame in the thickening dark; the moon's pale scimitar hung overhead, silently watching.

"I don't want to make this any more difficult than it

needs to be." Schofield kept his tone calm and even. "But all this *drama*. It has to stop."

The presence behind him said nothing at all. Which did not entirely surprise him, because really, what was there to say?

"I don't mean to be unkind," he added, then shook his head. For Pete's sake, why was *he* apologizing? "Honestly, your note took me by surprise. In fact, I didn't even think you were on board tonight." He began to turn and face the other man. "Didn't you have to fly a run over to Doha—"

A thousand needles stabbed him in the face, his eyes scalded shut by a savage yellow blast of pure pain. *Oleoresin capsicum.*

Pepper spray.

He staggered back against the rail, clawing at the air, fighting for breath, then felt a single needle stab him in the neck.

Not a metaphor.

An actual needle.

He managed to rake in one ragged breath, then another. Like forcing a cheese grater down his throat.

*What the hell, Bennett?*

He found himself seated on the catwalk flooring, back to the rail, legs splayed out, zip ties on his wrists, still blinded and fighting to breathe.

Something was happening to him, something taking control of his legs, his arms, his fingers.

Whatever he'd been jabbed with.

It was freezing his body into stone.

Before full paralysis could take effect, he pried open one burning eyelid. Looked in the face of his attacker.

Not the face he expected. But a face he knew.

*YOU? Why are you doing this!* he wanted to say.

But he couldn't speak.

Couldn't breathe.

Couldn't move.

The face leaned close. Hands held up two objects before his one open eye, so he could see them clearly.

A can of pepper spray.

And a box cutter.

*"We don't have much time,"* the voice whispered.

# 19

"GOOD MORNING, SHIPMATES—IT'S ANOTHER MAG-
NIFICENT DAY AT SEA! TODAY WE'LL BE REVIEWING THE
DRILL PROCEDURES FOR FULL MUSTER, BECAUSE, HEAR YE
HEAR YE, LADIES AND GENTLEMEN: ELVIS HAS LEFT THE
BUILDING AND THE SHIT HAS HIT THE FAN!"

His third morning aboard the *Lincoln*, Finn was sitting astride the big Gatling gun, gazing out at the ocean,
sketch pad in hand, when Captain Tom's voice went off
in his head.

He abruptly tossed his sketch pad onto the catwalk
and slipped down off the big gun, grabbed up pad and
blanket roll, and headed inside, making his way to deckhouse 3 on the hangar deck, his assigned station. He
was halfway there when the ship's 1MC erupted in five
long whistle blasts.

*Here we go.* Finn picked up his pace. The voice in his
head was right—of course, Captain Tom was always
right. The shit had very much hit the fan.

The fifth whistle blast was followed immediately by
an announcement:

"*Man overboard. Man overboard. All hands to mus-*

*ter, get your shipmates out of the rack. All hands safely and immediately to muster."*

The passageways were jammed with sailors rushing every which way, scattering like a disturbed anthill. Six thousand souls scrambling to get to their muster posts, all at the same time. It was a wonder there were no serious collisions.

Reaching the deckhouse, Finn gave his name to the petty officer with the clipboard, then took up position just inside the door, where he could watch the whole process go down.

The voice came over the 1MC again: *"Man overboard, man overboard. All hands to muster. Time plus one."*

The place was filling with staff. Everything was hushed voices and rustling pieces of paper. The XO had come down from the bridge to run the show.

*"Time plus two."*

Taking full muster was a complex operation—nearly six thousand individuals to be accounted for—and the crew at each muster station would be sweating right now.

Finn noticed a machine-gun turret of a guy planted a few feet behind the XO, watching everything. His lapel device made him a master chief—no, that was an extra star there: *command* master chief. CMC. Top dog on the enlisted side, second in stature only to the ship's captain.

As if hearing Finn's thoughts, the CMC's eyes fixed on him with a *Who the fuck are you and what are you doing on my ship?* look.

Good question.

*"Time plus three."*

The seconds ticked by. Around the rustling papers and whispered comparing of notes a silence, pregnant with irritation, swelled like smoke to fill the space.

*"Time plus four."*

The XO spoke into his phone handset, his voice simultaneously blasting throughout the ship over the 1MC:

*"The following personnel report to deckhouse 3 with their ID cards. LT James Bennett, Air. ET3 Jason Quarry, Combat Systems. ET2 Donna Moore, Supply. AD3 Jed Smalley, Supply. ADAN Kanisha Williams, Air. OSSN Kenny Frye, Operations. LS3 Warren Vincent, Operations. Ensign Melissa Gosling, Safety. LT Sam Schofield, Admin. LT Frank Hatch, Communications."*

Schofield. The ATO officer. Finn didn't recognize any of the other names.

Another twenty seconds ticked by.

*"Man overboard, time plus five."*

A guy showed up at the door, shamefaced and dripping with weak excuses, the defeated look of a sailor knowing he was in for one serious ass-chewing and probably worse than that. Gave his name to the orderly and was ushered to the back of the compartment. Two women filed in, gave their names, and joined him over at the wall of shame.

The XO held out the latest sheet handed to him and spoke into his handset again:

*"The following personnel report to deckhouse 3 with their ID cards: LT James Bennett, Air. ET2 Donna Moore, Supply. AD3 Jed Smalley, Supply. ADAN Kanisha Williams, Air. LS3 Warren Vincent, Operations. LT Sam Schofield, Admin. LT Frank Hatch, Communications."*

Seven names now. Once they had every name accounted for they would secure the drill. End of exercise. If not, they would start launching the helicopters and lifeboats.

More rustling papers, more hushed conversations.

A few more showed up, quietly giving their names

and lining up with the others to await execution. With the next repetition the list shrank to four. At *"Time plus seven"* there were just two names left: James Bennett and Sam Schofield.

"Bennett and Schofield," said the XO. "Great. Just great." He turned to the petty officer with the clipboard. "Randy?"

"Aye, sir?"

"Randy, where the fuck is Lieutenant Bennett?" he said mildly.

"I'm just checking now, sir." The petty officer spoke into a phone, low and urgent.

"What the hell," said the XO to no one in particular. "I can get here from anywhere on this ship inside of two minutes."

Thirty seconds went by, no one else saying a word.

*Bennett and Schofield. Great. Just great.* Given the XO's comment it wasn't hard to work out the math. Bennett would be the pilot Finn had seen with Schofield at midrats his first night on board. Schofield and Bennett were an item. And they were both missing.

An ensign rushed in the door and huddled with the petty officer, who then turned to the XO. "Sir, Lieutenant Bennett flew a run over to Doha yesterday afternoon, return flight down for later today. He's still there. We just talked to him."

The XO passed a hand over his face. "Well why in God's name didn't we already know that? Never mind. What's the story with Schofield?"

"He's still missing, sir. No one's seen him since he left the ATO shack last night at," he checked his clipboard, "twenty-three hundred hours, sir."

"Great," muttered the XO.

Now Finn spoke up.

"I saw him."

Everyone turned toward the door to see who'd

spoken—except the CMC, Finn noted, who kept his eyes trained on the XO, watching to see how he handled whatever the newcomer had to say.

"This morning," Finn continued. "About oh forty-five. Heading in the direction of the fantail." There was a pause in the room, and Finn added, "Sir."

Now all heads swiveled over to the XO—except for the CMC, who turned his attention to Finn. The two held each other's gaze for a three-count before the CMC broke off to listen to the XO's conversation.

Finn felt the shift in the soles of his feet.

The ship was pulling around.

# 20

By the time the ship had completed its turn their Knight-hawk was already in the air, Monica talking with ATC and a squadmate on the stick. Any nearby ships from the strike group were probably on their way to assist, and RHIB teams with their inflatable boats would be on standby as a backup measure—but in a search-and-rescue op like this the Knighthawks were the ship's first line of defense.

"Defense" in this case against the twin enemies of time and exposure.

The clock was ticking.

So far no one had any idea when the man went over, which made the operation immensely more difficult. The bridge would be working right now with the Combat Information Center to plot their search parameters. There was a tremendous amount of math involved, and Monica understood and appreciated all of it. Wind speed and current. Available manpower, helos and boats, both on the *Lincoln* and other nearby vessels from the strike group, plus each vessel's distance and rendezvous ETA. Time window of when the officer most likely went over, which in this case would be quite a large window indeed. Number of daylight hours available for the search. All that and more went into plotting the search grid. Then they would skew the resulting grid into a diamond pattern to account for drift. Which could be considerable.

All of which, given the uncertainties in this case, meant they would be combing an extremely large quadrant. If they didn't locate him quickly, they would keep searching. It could take days, but they'd find him. They had to.

Monica's thoughts turned to Schofield himself, his situation and his odds, bobbing out there in the water.

The fall itself was not trivial—as much as a sixty-foot drop, and the water's surface didn't compress like a foam mattress or air bag—but it was survivable. The threat magnified once you were in the water. You could easily be pulled under by ocean currents, or worse, pulled under by the ship itself as it passed. Overboards had been known to get sucked into the propeller vortex. No one survived an encounter with four pickup-truck-sized brass propellers in full spin.

On the other hand, Schofield was experienced. If he had fallen in, his body would have flooded with adrenaline. He would have focused instantly on putting some distance between himself and the ship to avoid getting dragged under, then waited for rescue. There was no significant sea state this morning, which would work in his favor. The water was far from freezing, though not as warm as it would be later in the day; probably a surface temperature of 75°F or so. Not frigid. Still, enough to induce mild hypothermia.

Time would be the big factor here.

Each flight suit came equipped with strobe light and whistle. If he were wearing a float coat it would inflate and his strobe would start flashing immediately upon contact with salt water. He would have blown the whistle, if he were able.

Unless of course he had gone over the rail intentionally.

In which case float coats and strobe lights would pretty well defeat the purpose, wouldn't they.

Which meant all four crew in that Knighthawk were thinking the same question, though none would voice it out loud.

Did he fall, or did he jump?

*He's out there right now,* Monica told herself. *He's out there floating, waiting for us. We'll find him.*


They'd been circling for nearly three hours when they got word: someone had found a note in his stateroom. Schofield jumped.

# 21

Captain William James Eagleberg didn't like making hasty decisions, nor did he respect those who did. Cautious by nature and made more so by training, he had not arrived at his station in life by acting on impulse. Right now, however, he was exhausted, his patience worn thin as a sheet of goddamn onionskin stationery.

Eagleberg had been up all night getting updates on the Iran situation. Then this morning, just as he had retired to his sea cabin in hopes of a stolen hour of shut-eye, they woke him to tell him some chucklehead had gone missing. Probably tucked away somewhere in a corner asleep. It was the last thing he'd wanted to hear, and the last thing he wanted to do, but he had no choice. After securing the go-ahead from the admiral he issued the orders to mount a search-and-rescue operation.

Then, not three hours later, they informed him a note had been found in the man's quarters.

A *note*.

"Balls," he muttered.

The man was an officer, head of ATO, a position of

not inconsiderable responsibility. Also gay, as Eagleberg had been informed. The pressures of his life and
station (and lifestyle, no doubt) had evidently got to
the man, and he came to the moronic conclusion that
he could resolve his issues by going over the rail and
gulping down a few quarts of Gulf water. And he'd
had neither the respect nor the consideration to hold
off on that decision till they'd gotten through the choke
point at Hormuz and out into the open sea. No, he just
had to execute his drama right then and there, as they
all sat at the Gulf's mouth twiddling their goddamn
thumbs.

No impulse control. An *officer*.

So here they were, holding up the progress of an entire strike group and investing the resources of the US
Navy into the futility of a search-and-recover mission
for the body of a man who in all probability would just
as soon stay unrecovered and unsearched-for.

Captain Eagleberg glanced at his watch for the ump-
teenth time.

Twelve hundred hours. High noon. Lieutenant Schofield was now occupying the efforts and attentions of
William Eagleberg's 5,750 total crew—make that
5,749—at the zenith of the day.

Twelve oh one hours.

The timing could not be worse. Shortly after learn-
ing about Schofield's note he'd heard from the admiral
again. The international diplomats had apparently
worked out solutions to Iran's hissy fit to everyone's satisfaction (though for how long was anybody's guess)
and they'd finally gotten the all-clear to transit the
Strait.

Except that now they couldn't.

Commanding officer of one of the most fearsome
warships on the seven seas, and he was powerless to

move it a foot, for Christ's sweet sake, because there was still a chance they'd find that belly-flopping officer floating somewhere out here.

Twelve oh two.

Well, to hell with it.

"Artie?"

Commander Arthur Gaines, his executive officer, crossed over from the other side of the bridge to stand by the captain's side. "Captain?"

"Give it another five hours. Then bring everyone in."

Gaines's face was total bafflement. "Sir?"

"I'll clear it with Selena. She'll sign off." Technically speaking, it was the admiral's decision, but she had her hands full with larger issues and would rubber-stamp Eagleberg's decisions. "I want my crew fed and rested and ready. We thread the needle tonight."

Hearing himself say the words, Eagleberg felt his shoulders relax. He took the first full breath he'd drawn in hours.

"We're getting out of here, Artie."

"Sir? *Tonight,* sir?" Gaines seemed unsure he'd heard the captain correctly. Another five hours would take no more than a modest bite out of the full search grid. Were they really going to call off a search without an urgent mission imperative compelling them to?

Eagleberg turned a cold look on his XO. "The man killed himself, Artie. I neither condone nor understand his decision, but he had his choice to make. I have mine. Five hours. Then call it off. Tonight we go on high alert, get those jets in the air, flight ops in full swing. Hormuz is no slow dance."

Arthur stared at the captain for a moment before remembering himself. He nodded vaguely. "Aye aye, Skipper."

Captain Eagleberg felt no need to explain himself to

his XO. He knew it might seem capricious, even cruel. It wasn't.

It was *necessary*.

This deployment had been one problem after another. And then that helo squadron disaster—he'd caught six kinds of hell from Selena for that fiasco, and no surprise. A $43 million Knighthawk and crew of four at the bottom of the Persian Gulf was no kind of blemish to have on your record. Someone's head needed to roll for it. If he'd had his way, that preening idiot Papadakis, the squadron's CO, would've been drawn and quartered, but the man had managed to come out of that investigation clean as a virgin's dipstick.

All Eagleberg wanted at this point was to finish out this deployment, get his admiral's star, and go ride a desk somewhere on the Beltway. God knew he'd earned it. But right now his promotion was hanging by a hair. Eagleberg may have become three-quarters politician and two-thirds administrator (and yes, that added up to a hell of a lot more than 100 percent) but he was still a sailor in his bones, and no fool. He could still feel the currents and read the winds. Sailor's instinct told him to get out of there *now*. The longer he stayed, the worse it would get. And the Iranians were so goddamn skittish; if some mullah farted in Tehran and the winds in Arlington shifted again, who knew if the Strait might shut right down—for real this time, leaving them stuck in there for days or even weeks? Or, God Almighty, for *months*?

Captain Eagleberg stood on the bridge of the USS *Abraham Lincoln* peering into the northeast at the distant coastline of Iran, and silently prayed the prayer of Job.

*Dear God, there is no one who compares to You. I come before You and humbly entreat You, in Your al-*

*mighty wisdom, to spare us from any more tests or torments, deliver us out of this Christforsaken bunghole, and bring us safely back to terra fucking firma.*

He bowed his head.

*In Jesus's name. Amen.*

# 22

That night Finn sat out on the portside Gatling gun cat-walk, watching the ocean, sketching in the faint illumi-nation of a waning crescent moon as jets blasted off the flight deck above. Incredible, that no one had spotted him out here and dragged his ass inside.

Incredible, that they were leaving the Gulf without completing their search.

This ship was a mess, all right. But not his mess. How had he put it to Schofield, that first night? *Just a passenger*.

Besides, he had his own concerns to worry about.

He took out his ring knife and sharpened the char-coal pencil to a fresh point.

The sea looked like hammered silver tonight, the moon's arc fracturing into a million slivers of glass on its surface. Finn knew exactly what that looked like gaz-ing up from underneath, dozens of meters down, diving under the hulls of great ships like this.

As part of their SEAL workup, Finn and Boyd had gone through a dive exercise, planting explosives on the hull of a destroyer in the San Diego Harbor. Visibility was close to nil and because their Dräger rebreathers emitted no bubbles, they couldn't orient themselves by the usual upward bubble trail from their exhale. The boom of the ship's generators was incredibly loud, and sound didn't work in water the way it did in the air—it pinged and echoed so that it seemed as if sounds were coming at them from every direction at once.

"It's easy to lose all spatial orientation," he'd explained when he told Carol about what happened. "The way to beat the panic is to find the seam of the weld on the ship's hull and follow it with your fingers. You have to ignore everything else, because the moment you go chasing after up and down you lose connection with the seam of the weld."

"And that was Boyd's mistake," said Carol.

And that was Boyd's mistake. When he lost orientation he fought to get it back. He let go of the seam, unclipped his buddy line, and went chasing after up and down. The more it eluded him the more frantic he got.

Finn couldn't reach him in time.

Those ballast pumps sucked in seawater with tremendous force. The ship was supposed to have shut down their pumps for the exercise, but some dipshit in admin forgot to pass along an order to someone else. Boyd got sucked into the ballast tank.

The next moment Finn's sniper partner was nothing but a cloud of red mist.

It was ruled an accident, of course. A tragic training mishap. No one was charged. The circle-jerk of military politics.

A few weeks later Finn was at the funeral, seated next to Boyd's stone-faced sister. Halfway through the service she leaned sideways toward him and whispered, "You're Finn?"

Finn nodded, smelling the coffee and stale funeral-home cookies on her breath.

"He told me, if it hadn't been for you, he'd never have

got through that sniper course. That he would've washed out and gone home."

Finn said nothing. It was true. Boyd was a phenomenal shot, but couldn't stalk worth shit. Finn had practically carried him through the course.

After a long pause the sister leaned closer, her hand on his arm now, and whispered directly in his ear.

*"I hope you burn in hell."*

Finn didn't blame her. Boyd shouldn't have died.

"Know what I think?" Carol had said after hearing the story. "In a court of law they'd probably find you insane."

Because?

"Because the courts define insanity as not knowing the difference between right and wrong—and as far as you're concerned that definition completely misses the point of reality."

How so?

"Right and wrong? Might as well chase after up and down. And in the dark there is no up and down. There's only the seam of the weld."

Finn had no response to that.

"So here's my question," she said. "For you, what *is* the seam of the weld?"

Finn didn't have an answer.

After a minute Carol said, "Know what I think?" She leaned over and whispered in his ear.

*"I think it's loyalty."*

Finn watched the coast of Iran recede, its oil derricks lighting the sky.

Was that true? Was that what kept him connected to Carol? To Kennedy?

Loyalty?

He didn't know. All he knew was, he was sitting here saying goodbye to a man he hardly knew.

They were leaving Schofield behind.

Finn had never been big on the leave-no-man-behind ethic, noble as it was. He didn't disagree with the sentiment; it was a good code and he'd fought for it himself, more than once. But he didn't believe in it. Some men got left behind. That was just how it was. It wasn't karma, it wasn't fate. They didn't deserve it or not deserve it. There was no reason for it.

No up, no down.

But Schofield should not have died.

He turned to a fresh page and went on sketching the glassy slivers of moon.

He thought again of Schofield the night before, striding purposefully past in the direction of the fantail. The hot prickling up the back of his neck.

The next moment, he'd been sitting out on the CIWS mount astride the great Gatling gun at dawn, hearing Captain Tom's voice in his head.

Two scenes, side by side in his mind, seamless, like a smash cut in a horror flick or a skip in an old vinyl LP.

And of the sequence of steps between those two moments? He had no memory.

No memory at all.

# II

# Bolter

# 23

Command Master Chief Robbie Jackson glanced down at his cooling coffee. Master Chief Jackson was not a patron of Jittery Abe's. He liked his coffee the traditional navy way: from the mess, black and nasty. A description that he himself had answered to on more than one occasion. Though he was not in fact a nasty man; an even mix of drill sergeant and Creole den mother, Master Chief Jackson was revered among his crew, even loved. Also feared.

No one aboard the USS *Abraham Lincoln* had ever seen him smile.

When he roamed the Abe's passageways Jackson moved like an Abrams tank that had taken a few semesters of ballet. This morning, though, he was planted behind his desk watching his coffee cool to the point of bitterness.

He took a sip. The brew tasted like scorched chicory cut with mud. Perfect, to his way of thinking. He set the mug down, its ceramic base making almost no sound as it touched the desk's steel surface, and thought about the man who had just left his office.

It hadn't been an easy interview. Lieutenant Bennett

had been having an illicit relationship with another officer, now missing and presumed dead. All of which meant this guy was torn up emotionally, which was understandable, and at the same time terrified that his career was about to slide into the ship's trash incinerator. Also understandable. Jackson had probed gently, asking the kinds of short, open-ended questions that lead to very long answers. Mostly he listened.

By the time he released Lieutenant Bennett from his office, he was satisfied on three questions, and greatly mystified on a fourth.

Jackson picked up his mug, swirled the bitter grounds, then set it down again.

He withdrew a sheet of plain white paper from his top desk drawer, placed it on the desk in front of him, and read the typed text one more time.

Tired tonight, really tired. Long day, long year. Just another clod, washed away, no piece of any continent. Perhaps some men really are islands after all. Another day, another dolor. Oh God, I'm so very tired of all of this. Weary to the bone.

*Just another clod, washed away.* John Donne, "No man is an island," and so on, but all mixed up. *Another day, another dolor.* Colum McCann? Jackson shook his head. Apparently the man liked poetry. He slipped the note into the desk drawer, pushed his chair back a foot.

So.

His first three questions seemed to have pretty solid answers. Had Lieutenant Schofield been especially depressed lately? Were there significant conflicts at work? Problems in his personal life?

No, no, and no.

That note notwithstanding, by all accounts Sam Schofield was not a moody guy. The opposite, if anything; steady, solid, looked up to by his peers. Yes, being a gay man in the military was no picnic. Still, from what Jackson could tell, there was no particular climate of intolerance, no overt hostility or pattern of discrimination. According to his staff, everything at the ATO shack was normal as eggs and grits that day. Nor was there any real crisis in his personal life, assuming Bennett was telling the truth, which Jackson was inclined to believe that he was. They'd had a minor spat the day before, but it was all patched up. No big deal.

So what possessed the man to type up this weird suicide note, then walk out to the fantail in the middle of the night and throw himself off?

# 24

First morning out of the Gulf. After a breakfast of plain oatmeal and smoked herring from a can, Finn headed above to the ATO shack. Campion, the young airman who'd processed him in that first night, was stationed at Schofield's desk, staring at some paperwork. Two others moved around the cramped space, going through the motions of office work as if they were all inhabiting the same bad dream.

The young airman looked up. Stood and shook Finn's hand, like he didn't know what else to do. "Morning, Chief Finn."

"Hey," said Finn. "I was sorry to hear about Lieutenant Schofield."

This was true. The world would be better off if Schofield were still here.

"I can't believe he's just, just . . ." Campion couldn't bring himself to say the words "dead" or "gone." "I mean, I wasn't like him, you know?" Finn nodded. Wasn't gay, he meant. "But man, I *loved* that guy. I mean, everyone did. You know?" Campion fought to keep his composure but couldn't stop his eyes from welling up.

Finn put his hand on Campion's shoulder. "I know, man. I know how you feel. I get it."

This was a lie.

Finn didn't have the slightest idea how Campion felt. Whatever muscle or tendon or connective tissue it took to make genuine empathy happen, it was missing from Finn's physiology. Or atrophied. Or maybe surgically removed when he was a kid. Whatever the deficiency was, Finn had no clear experience of compassion or emotional resonance. However he did have a great capacity for appreciation. If he couldn't quite feel what Campion was feeling, he could witness it, down to the finest nuance. So while it may have been a total fabrication when he said, "I know how you feel," he was fabricating from accurate observation.

It was a lie with a basis.

Campion looked up at him through damp eyes. "Thanks." He wiped his nose on his sleeve. "I don't know, man," he said. "I just don't get it."

Finn cocked his head slightly, doing puzzled concern. "Don't get what?"

Campion sniffled once and sat up straighter. "The whole, you know, suicide thing. I mean," he leaned forward and spoke in a whisper, "when that kid crashed their helo, we all felt terrible. That was awful." He took a big shaky breath. "But . . . Lieutenant *Schofield*?"

"Really," Finn agreed.

*When that kid crashed their helo?*

"I mean, what do I know," said Campion. "What does anyone really know, right?"

Finn nodded. What did anyone really know. He could go along with that one.

"But, man," the boy said. "I did *not* see that coming."

———

After determining that, no, his satphone replacement had still not arrived, Finn headed over to the library, where he waited for a PC. Checked all his email boxes. Nothing. Not from Kennedy, not from anyone.

*Give me twenty-four.*

People were, by and large, a mystery to Finn. He could read their intentions like a meteorologist tracked weather patterns, see inside them like an X-ray tech. But he didn't really understand what went on in there. Which made him wary. Human beings could always still surprise him. It was therefore a rare thing for Finn to put his trust in another person.

Lieutenant Michael Joseph Kennedy was one of those exceptions.

They'd been on the battlefield together. Charged into potential death traps together based on nothing but each other's read on the situation. Borne teammates' dying bodies on their backs while running through rubble and gunfire following no map but each other's instincts. People said that kind of shared experience created a uniquely strong bond. Finn didn't know about that. The whole idea of a "bond" was as mysterious to him as the inner working of quarks.

But what he had with Kennedy was special.

Part of it, Finn guessed, was that they were so different from each other. Finn built intel networks. Kennedy made *friends*. He had an ability to relate to anyone and everyone that Finn both admired and found baffling. Most people passed through life making friends along the way, but as far as Finn could see those friendships came and went. Not with Kennedy. He never let go of a friendship, ever. Even now, in his late thirties, he was still running around with the guys he'd known when he was three. He had a gift for it. Everybody's best friend.

And his sayings. "Scrotal disaster." (Said of especially fucked-up individuals or situations.) "Moses blows us." (Meaning: *Uh-oh, we're in trouble.*) And that grand catchall phrase, the ultimate expression of exasperation: "Christ on stilts." Which made zero sense to Finn (Why would Christ be on stilts? What did that even mean?), but he still found himself repeating the line. There was little about Kennedy that made sense to him.

But he trusted him.

Four days now and still no word.

Where was his platoon?

He needed to talk to someone up the food chain, someone in Coronado. Which was not a call he could make through AT&T Direct Ocean Service.

He headed below to the Public Affairs office, where he spoke with an ensign named Olivia, a writer for the ship's newsletter whom he knew from the Jittery Abe's line.

"I was wondering if you could help me out. I don't have my satphone, and I need to get a secure line with WARCOM at Coronado for a few minutes, check in with my command."

"Totally no problem," she said, practically gushing. "Let me just tell my boss and we'll hook you up." She trotted off into a suite of back offices.

Finn waited for a minute, then another. Not wanting to be conspicuous, he took a seat. He noticed the young photographer he'd seen blushing on the flight deck his first morning there when she'd looked at the deck-status LSO. A full ten minutes later Olivia came back, looking embarrassed.

"She says," Olivia straightened her spine and cleared her throat to make it clear that she was now quoting her boss, " 'I'm very sorry, I don't have the authority to grant that access.' "

"Oh, hey," he said. "Forget about it. No big deal."

Finn left the PAO and went to change into his service khakis with his SEAL trident and three highest ribbons—

Silver Star, Bronze Star, and Combat Action Ribbon—then walked over to the Combat Intelligence Center at the foot of the island. After gaining entrance and introducing himself, he explained his mission.

"I need to get a SITREP on my unit back on the beach." He jerked his thumb back in the general direction of the Arabian Peninsula. "I've been given clearance to inside-channel comms to Coronado, on authority from McDill." Which wasn't strictly speaking true but sounded true. He doubted they would bother calling SOCOM headquarters at McDill Air Force Base in Tampa to check.

In a most apologetic tone the ensign on the desk told him to wait there one moment while they set up a private space for him.

And came back more than ten minutes later, even more apologetic.

"I'm so sorry, Chief Finn. I'm being told we don't have the authority to grant that access."

Finn nodded. "I understand," he said. "Who do I see to put in for special permission?"

"Uh, just one more minute." Finn half expected him to back out of the compartment kowtowing.

A moment later a commander stepped out. "Commander Jacobsen," he said, gripping Finn's hand in an iron handshake. "How can I help?" Commander Jacobsen said this last in a tone that clearly conveyed the opposite meaning.

"Sir," said Finn. "I need to get a SITREP on my unit back on the peninsula. How do I get a secure line to Coronado?"

"You'd have to talk to the captain."

"How do I do that?" He knew the normal answer: fill out a form and wade through a week of red tape. He was hoping for something a little more streamlined.

The commander pressed his lips together and

frowned, then spoke slowly, as if in careful thought. "I don't know, he's a busy man."

Uh-huh. Message received.

He thanked the commander, adding a "Sir," and headed back to his broom closet to get back into his flight suit.

Schofield had said he'd make sure Finn would get access to inside-track communication if he needed it. Turned out he needed it. But Schofield wasn't there to help. As much as he wanted to give the man a wide berth, it looked like he'd need to talk to the captain himself. The question was, how to manage that? He couldn't exactly wait around for an engraved invitation.

He stepped inside his quarters and noticed an envelope placed neatly on the pillow on his rack, dead center. The hand-printed writing said "Chief Finn."

Inside was a printed, personalized card.

FROM THE DESK OF
CAPTAIN WILLIAM JAMES EAGLEBERG
COMMANDER, USS ABRAHAM LINCOLN
(CVN-72)

The printed message read:

> You are cordially invited to be the guest
> of the Commanding Officer at his mess.
> On August 4 at 1700 hrs in wardroom
> 2-200-0-L. Dress whites.

And in the bottom third of the card, there was the captain's signature in a sweeping calligraphic scrawl.

An invitation.

Practically engraved.

# 25

At 1645 Finn was decked out in his dress whites and being ushered into the captain's wardroom, where he was seated opposite the captain, who had arrived at the same moment. The captain's XO was seated to Eagleberg's right, the day-shift junior officer of the deck at his left. With its white linens and china and elaborate codes of etiquette, to Finn the setting had more the appearance of a state dinner in DC than a meal on a working warship.

Finn was introduced one by one to each person at the table. As they all took their seats Finn caught the junior OOD's eye and winked; he'd made friends with her at midrats. She gave back a quick grin.

"So: Finn," said the captain. "Is that, Finn . . . ?" When Finn didn't jump in with a response he prompted further. "First name? Last name?"

"Just Finn." After a moment he added, "Sir."

The captain glanced around with slight irritation at the clatter of soup tureens being placed on plates around the table. "I'm sorry, it's a little noisy. Justin? I don't think I got your full name."

"Just Finn," Finn repeated, no louder than the first

time. He was curious: Would the captain ask for further explanation, exhibit further irritation? Or let it go, and keep his powder dry?

The captain paused, no doubt waiting for another "sir" or "captain" to conclude the sentence. When he didn't get one he said simply, "Ah," took his soup spoon and fell to.

Finn did likewise, as did the rest of the table. The clatter of dishes was replaced by a soft chorus of sips and slurps. Finn was mildly impressed that the captain hadn't taken the bait.

"I trust you're finding your way around all right, making yourself at home on our little bark," the captain commented after a full minute of leek potato soup had elapsed. "Finding everything you need?"

"About that," Finn replied. "There's something I'd like to get set up, if possible. A few minutes with a secure line to Coronado, check in with brass there. Sir."

The captain nodded as he took another spoonful. "You should talk to the people at CVIC."

"I did. They said they didn't have the authority to grant access."

The captain looked up, his eyebrows lifting in surprise. Real or feigned, hard to say. "Is that right?" He looked over at his executive officer. "Artie? That doesn't seem right." He looked back at Finn. "We need to do something about that."

Then took a long thoughtful spoonful. And another.

"So, special assignment, we're told," the captain said. "May I ask the nature of that assignment?"

The captain hadn't actually directed his XO to do anything about the CVIC issue, Finn noted. Just changed the subject.

"I really can't say, sir," Finn replied.

True, strictly speaking—he couldn't have said even if he'd wanted to, because he didn't really know himself.

He knew why command *said* he was going home: to deliver a special debrief on their efforts in Yemen. But he didn't believe that. If it was true, it wasn't the whole truth. Which was what he hoped to learn from Kennedy.

The captain broke into a smile. He sat back in his chair as the mess stewards began removing the empty tureens.

"Naval Special Warfare. Underwater, under wraps, under the radar. Right, Artie? I expect ninety-five percent of Chief Finn's life is too classified to classify!" He chuckled. A murmur of chuckles circumnavigated the table.

That didn't seem to call for comment, and Finn offered none.

He noticed that the XO winced every time the captain called him "Artie." A microexpression, so fleeting that no one else saw it. Probably didn't even realize he was doing it. Finn sensed that the XO hated that nickname but would never let on, not to his captain. Finn had seen him in operation during that muster call, and he'd carried himself quite differently then. Not a right-hand man, but a man in charge. Not overbearing, not an asshole, but wearing his authority well. Bit of a shapeshifter, though. Sucking up to the captain the way he did now was entirely understandable. Once the captain got kicked upstairs, the XO stood a decent chance of taking his place on the bridge. The promotion path was not automatic. But possible. Which meant that until then he would stay close to his captain, close and protective.

Not necessarily the same thing as loyal.

"I have tremendous respect for everything you boys are doing back there," the captain was saying. He gave a vague wave of his butter knife in the direction of the stern and, implicitly, all of Asia, Africa, and the Middle East. "And I know you've made a lot of sacrifices, no doubt including many of your own friends." Pointing now at Finn with the butter knife. "Not easy, losing men you trained with, fought with, bled with."

To Finn it sounded like the captain was rehearsing the voiceover for a movie trailer, but here he decided to contribute a reply. "Tougher for you, I'd think."

"For us?" The captain frowned.

"Noncombat losses are even harder. You've lost an ATO officer and an entire helo crew, and not one of them in combat. Sir."

The captain stiffened. "Every loss is a hard thing."

There was an icy silence as the stewards began placing platters of Caesar salad. The Parmesan had been baked into the shape of a plane's tail assembly and placed jutting up on one side of the plate, with three flash-fried whole white anchovies laid out flat upon the bed of romaine. An aircraft carrier salad. Galley guys plying their trade skills. Good for them.

Finn took a bite of romaine.

"That has to be tough on morale, sir," he added. "You know sailors and their superstitions."

The XO, Gaines, broke his silence. "You think we should be worried about morale, Chief?" he said mildly.

"No. I mean, I wouldn't, sir. Maybe if you lost a few more."

Finn noticed the junior OOD's eyes grow wide. No one said a word.

Now the captain chuckled and took a bite of salad. "Some people," he said, then took another bite, chewing thoroughly before continuing. "Some people see you fellas in Special Operations as renegades. Outlaws. Troublemakers. As if you're not really part of the navy at all." He shook his head. "I don't see it that way. No. My view is this: you may be outliers, but you're outliers belonging to the same great organization as every other soul on this boat." He looked around the table, as if admonishing all assembled company. "From now until we dock in San Diego, Chief Finn, you are not a US Navy SEAL. You are a guest on our ship. As such, you're part of my crew, and I, for one, look forward to the men and women of my crew having the benefit of your example as a sailor of great achievement, discipline, and respect."

In plain English: *behave yourself*.

"You know what the man says," the captain continued. "The victorious warrior wins first, then goes to war; the defeated warrior goes to war first, then seeks to win." He stabbed another bite of salad, then paused, fork in midair. "However," he added. He placed the bite in his mouth and chewed thoughtfully while everyone else at the table waited for him to finish the sentence. Classic power move. Finally he gave a nod, speared a second bite, then paused yet again, fork held aloft.

"*However,* the wise warrior avoids the battle altogether."

Finn took another bite himself, chewed, swallowed. Then said: "Ruling a country is like cooking a small fish."

There was another awkward silence, this time broken by the captain bursting into laughter and holding up a fried anchovy on his fork. "Well these, in my estimation, are perfect!" He turned to a nearby server. "Compliments, Luis, please!"

The server nodded and with a murmured "Of course, Captain" withdrew to convey the captain's compliments to the chef.

# 26

**The captain was not happy.**

For five full minutes Arthur had sat silent, waiting. Part of his job description. When the skipper finally spoke up it was so abrupt he nearly flinched.

"Did you note the first thing that happened when our guest sat down tonight?"

Arthur frowned in thought. "You . . . asked him about his name."

The captain gave a sour smile. "That came next. Before that." When his XO had no reply the captain continued. "He *winked* at my junior OOD. And she smiled back."

Arthur raised his eyebrows. He had not noticed that.

Eagleberg nodded. "Oh, yes. I observe, Artie. I observe. Chief Finn has been making friends." He paused to swirl his Baccarat crystal brandy snifter and take a taste of the premium cognac. Against regulations, but this was his ship. "You know what they called me at the Academy, behind my back? Captain Know-It-All."

In fact, they'd called him "Captain Eaglebeak," but Arthur was not about to offer the correction.

"And they were right. I did know it all. That's how I

got to be commander of this ship. By knowing everything—*before* it matters. By having the answer before anyone else has even thought to ask the question. And you know what I know about this Lone Ranger knuckle-dragger we've got on board?"

"No, sir, what's that?"

The captain looked up from his crystal glass and peered at his XO for a moment before replying.

"Nothing. Not a goddamned thing." He took his final sip and placed the glass down. "I don't know why he's nosing around CVIC, or Public Affairs, or why he's grilling my crew members about misfortunes past. I don't know why he's patrolling this ship every day like a Bengal in a cage. I don't know why, if SOCOM has such a hard-on for him that they had to yank him from the field and pull him back to the States for some *special assignment,* they didn't just put the man on a C-130 to Frankfurt and points west.

"I don't know why the man is on my boat, Artie. And I don't like not knowing."

Arthur had always admired his boss's piercing intellect, but he found the man's paranoid streak worrisome. It was Eagleberg's job to manage the ship. It was Arthur's job to manage Eagleberg.

"And that comment," said the captain. "What the hell was that about? Ruling a country is like cooking a fish?"

"A small fish, sir," Arthur said. "You quoted Sun Tzu, *The Art of War.* He quoted Lao Tzu. *Tao Te Ching.*"

"I know that," snapped the captain. (He didn't, was Arthur's guess.) "But what the hell did he mean by it?"

Arthur shrugged. "Hard to say, sir."

*He meant you, sir,* he thought. *He meant, be careful how you treat the small fish.*

# 27

August 5. A warm breeze; rumbles of distant morning thunder.

Sailors called this the "time of no horizon," this brief stretch of transition from night to dawn, when light had begun to infiltrate everywhere without quite showing itself. Neuroscientists said it was in the moments between sleep and wake that the boundaries roping off conscious from subconscious were at their most permeable, imagination and intuition at their peak.

The time of no horizon was the ocean's intuition time.

This morning Finn sat out on the ship's fantail, perched on that big capstan, sketch pad on his knees, gazing out at the total absence of distinction. No sounds but the scratch of the pencil, the steady churn of the big brass screws below, and the wash of the sea.

Was this where Schofield had gone over the edge?

"Ashes to ashes, dust to dust," that's how they always put it in the funeral services, but it wasn't really like that: ashes and dust weren't where we came from, no, we came from the water, and the water was always there, waiting to claim us back.

Finn tried to picture the man, a few yards away, putting one leg up over the rail.

Not his mess.

*Just a passenger.*

Ignoring the lingering stench of garbage, he went on sketching the shifting shades of charcoal gray, pewter gray, battleship gray, ash gray.

Gradually, almost imperceptibly, the time of no horizon receded and distinct masses of color began to resolve. The sky grew lighter, the ocean darker. Up and down reasserted their presence.

Now, in their second day since threading the Strait, the air was already changing. It was strange to feel less humidity when you were completely surrounded by water, but on the open sea the atmosphere was drying out, leaving the cloying feeling of the Gulf behind them.

The ocean, too, was different here. In the Gulf it was always calm, as if it were going along with a pretense of domestication. Out here the sea didn't hide the fact that it was wild.

"Still here, Ray," whispered Finn. "Still here."

A low wind whipped around from the starboard and carried his words away.

*Sssss. Sssss. Sssssstillhhhhheeeeeerrrrrre . . .*

"You hate ships." That was Carol explaining Finn to himself, a task at which she was considerably skilled.

"Not true," Finn had objected. "I love ships."

"You love *water*. Everything about it. You love being in the water, under the water, out on the water. You love small boats, where you can smell and feel the water. Big ships, where you're shut in? Those you hate."

Finn didn't relate to the word "hate." But otherwise she had him nailed, dead to rights. As usual.

Carol said she felt safe with Finn because he was "such a fucked-up mass of contradictions."

Not true, Finn had said, knowing she would then demonstrate that it was.

"You love hunting, especially underwater," she said. This was true. He was lethal with a speargun. "But you've got this weird thing about guns."

Also true. So?

"So, you're an elite sniper who doesn't like guns. You despise authority figures but worship your lieutenant. You love water, hate ships. You're a fucked-up mass of contradictions."

So how did that make her feel safe?

"Your shit is out front, where I can see it," she explained. "It's the assholes who keep their contradictions hidden you have to worry about."

Finn smiled as he sketched.

*Sssssssstillhhhhheeeeeerrrrrre* said the wind.

He thought about Schofield. Thought about that hot prickling he'd felt up the back of his neck. He still didn't know what it was telling him, but he recognized the language.

Death had come to call.

"Death and I are old friends," he'd heard teammates boast, but he knew that was a lie. Death didn't have friends, only acquaintances. Death was still a mystery, even to Finn.

The prospect of dying did not especially disturb him, though. He'd spent his life knocking at death's back door. For as long as he could remember, Finn had always pictured death as a creature with a massive head and no arms or legs. Like a great wriggling invertebrate shark. Why, he had no idea. Maybe one day he'd find out.

Maybe soon.

Because death had come to call, and wasn't leaving yet. Finn could feel it stalking the ship.

For all he knew, it had already brushed right by him.

*"Reveille, reveille, all hands heave out and trice up."*

Oh six hundred. Finn closed the sketch pad and stood. Time for breakfast.

He needed to ask someone for a favor.

# 28

Stopping by his broom closet to drop off his drawing tools, Finn opened the door and froze.

Intruder.

A slender, narrow-shouldered sailor over by Finn's dresser, shuffling a mop around and humming to himself. He swayed slightly on his feet, almost as if he might fall. Drunk? Stoned? It took Finn a moment to understand.

He was dancing with his mop.

As the sailor began swiveling around toward Finn his tune reached its chorus and he went from humming to singing. "Ayy, ayy, ay, ayyyyy, canta y no llorr—"

He stopped, seeing Finn in the doorway, and stood stock-still, looking guilty as a tipsy husband caught on a 3:00 a.m. staircase.

A few seconds ticked by. Then Finn tilted his head a degree and raised his eyebrows in silent interrogation.

"I'm supposed, I'm supposed to clean the officers' staterooms," the sailor stammered.

Couldn't have been over nineteen. Looked about twelve. The lack of stripes on his sleeve said he was an undesignated E-1, no assigned rating. Bottom of the food chain. Got all the crap jobs.

Finn pointed to himself. "Not an officer."

"And guests. Officers and guests, I mean." The boy's face went crimson.

He had to be the worst liar Finn had ever seen.

"I'm not an officer, this is not a stateroom, and you don't clean it. I clean it. Me. Nobody else."

The boy looked stricken. As Finn held open the door, he collected his cleaning supplies and started toward the door.

"Hey," said Finn. "Can you keep a secret?"

The boy froze again, seeming unsure whether to reply.

Finn did the head-tilt, eyebrow-raise thing again.

"A secret. Yeah, sure." The boy spoke quickly and quietly now.

"You're probably wondering who I am, why I'm here. What my mission is, who sent me. That sort of thing."

The boy shook his head in vague denial.

"It's okay," Finn said. He nodded slowly.

The boy stopped shaking his head and began slowly nodding, too. He hadn't been wondering any of those things, of course, but he nodded along with Finn just the same. Interrogation 101.

"Well, I'm a SEAL, here on a secret mission. *Super* secret. International stuff. No one knows. Just you now." None of it true, of course. But exciting. "Don't tell anyone, right?"

The boy's face relaxed into a sly grin.

"Right?" repeated Finn.

The boy nodded, hard. "Right! No one."

Finn took a step back and gave a brisk nod toward the door.

The E-1 suddenly remembered where he was standing: in a cabin this SEAL didn't want him to clean.

"Right! Right." He pushed his mop and bucket out the door. Turned back and gave Finn a confidential look. Put his thumb and index finger to his lips and turned them like a key. "Not a word," he whispered, and he gave a conspiratorial nod.

"What's your name, sailor?"

"Luca. Luca Santiago."

"Finn," said Finn.

"Finn," repeated Luca softly, like an incantation. "*Vaya con Dios,* Finn."

Finn nodded and closed the door.

Another friend.

Luca Santiago. Dances With Mops. The last romantic. Clearly the guy lived in his own world. Didn't we all.

Finn got to work. Eleven minutes later he'd inventoried and examined all his possessions. Three of his brand-new charcoal pencils were missing. Nothing else.

He sat on his rack and considered the implications.

Who would have sent an E-1 to go through his stuff? And why take a few pencils?

# 29

General mess. The prevailing mood was a strange brew today, as it had been since they transited the Strait. Relief at having finally left the Gulf, curdled by a sense of gloom brought on by the failed search for Schofield. Finn had seen this kind of confused, depressed morale before. He knew it could sink an entire operation.

He also knew it wasn't that hard to change. All it took was a little leadership.

GOOD MORNING, SHIPMATES, THIS IS YOUR CAPTAIN SPEAKING! YOU ACQUITTED YOURSELVES WITH EXCELLENCE IN THE GULF, MADE ME PROUD. BUT DON'T LET THAT CREATE COMPLACENCY! WE STILL HAVE A LONG TRANSIT AHEAD OF US, A MISSION TO RUN, JOBS TO DO. STAY FOCUSED! STAY CLEAR! KEEP MAKING ME PROUD!

That would have done it. That would have cut through the fog and moved the emotional rudder. But they weren't getting that here.

And it was in leadership vacuums like this one, he knew, too, that incompetents and bad actors so often stepped in to fill the void.

"Hey, mornin', Chief! Mind if I . . . ?"

Stickman, the lanky rescue swimmer from Finn's helo ride.

"Morning, Mister Stickman," said Finn, nodding a *be my guest* at the seat across from him. "How you gettin' on?"

Stickman set his tray of pancakes, sausages, and re-constituted eggs down with a loud *clank*. "All good, Chief, all good." Reaching into an inside pocket he pulled out a thin red bottle, set it down on the table, unscrewed the tiny hexagonal top, and began shaking out drops over his eggs. He grinned at Finn. "Best piece of advice I got from my recruiter. '*When you go to sea, Stickman, bring your own Tabasco.*' "

Finn nodded. "Good to have friends who know." He slipped a small flat can from one pocket, pulled the pop-top lid, and forked half a dozen smelts onto his plate next to his mango slices.

This was why he'd chosen this particular seat, at this hour, in general mess. Stickman's table. People were creatures of habit. Completely predictable.

This was something that never ceased to amaze Finn: people who followed precisely the same routine every day. He couldn't think of anything more foolish. That was how burglars cleared your house. How pirates took down a ship. How Russia hijacked American elections. All they had to do was observe your routine. Once they knew that, they owned you. As if people were trained rats. Which, in Finn's observation, they mostly were.

"Hey," said Finn. "I wonder if I could ask a favor."

"You serious? Shoot."

Finn explained what he was after. To pass the time in the days ahead, he thought he might amuse himself by building a little shortwave radio receiver set. Given that Stickman knew his way around the avionics shop, could he lay his hands on a few components Finn needed?

The rescue swimmer once again told him to "shoot."

Finn shot. Laid out his short wish list and specs.

Stickman frowned, shook his head. "I don't know, that won't give you much range."

Finn said that was okay, he wasn't looking for range. Just looking to pick up the local stuff when they got close enough to whatever land mass. Did Stickman think there'd be any problem with the list?

Stickman laughed. "Seriously? No problem at all, Chief." Stickman was casual about it, but the gleam in his eyes said he was thrilled at the chance to do their esteemed guest a *quid pro bro*. "Might take a week or so."

"No rush," said Finn. "Got no place else to be."

"Ain't that the truth."

Finn heard footsteps coming toward him from behind, someone with a heavy tread. Heard a voice bark like a seal. *Ark-ark-ark.* Finn didn't look around.

Tucker walked past them with his tray, chuckling. Heading back to the food line.

Stickman watched him go, incredulous. "You know that guy?"

Finn nodded without looking up. "Tucker. Works down in the nukes. We're buddies."

Stickman leaned in. "Was he . . . *mocking* you?"

"Private joke."

They chowed down in silence again for a minute.

Then Finn spoke up again, quieter this time.

"Heard about that helo that went down."

Stickman stopped chewing. Paused, then swallowed. "Yeah," he said, his voice gone husky. "That was bad. You know it was way out, right, just off one of our destroyers?"

Finn nodded. Completely out of their control, in other words: no way Stickman or anyone else from the squadron could have participated in the rescue effort.

"They got a good crew down in the water, what I

heard, and fast. Still . . ." Stickman shook his head. "I was pretty tight with Diego. And his co-pilot, Micaela Katz? She was bunked out in the same stateroom as Lieutenant Halsey. The one on the stick the night we came to pick you up?"

Finn nodded again.

"*Roommates*. Tore her up pretty bad. She didn't show it, though, just kept on keeping on."

Finn set his fork down and spoke even more quietly.

"So, what happened? I mean, did they figure out what went wrong? Anyone in command go on the block?"

"Not really. Nothing mechanical, far as they could see. They called it 'pilot error.'" Stickman shook his head. "Whatever." He stood up with his empty tray. Finn did likewise.

"You know," Stickman said, then he leaned close and confidential. "It was supposed to be *her* flying. Lieutenant Halsey. CO yanked her at the last minute and put in Diego."

Finn whistled and said, "Ouch."

Stickman nodded, solemn. "Got that right, Chief. Ouch, big-time."

# 30

Jackson eased back into his chair and frowned. He'd just gotten an earful from Jimmy Suzuki, the ship's chief engineer, who'd stopped in to say his goodbyes. Suzuki was much beloved among the troops and had den-mother instincts second only to Jackson's. He'd met with the captain that morning to give him "some honest feedback." Shared his views on the decision to call off the search for Schofield and its impact on morale.

"You're a braver man than me, Jimmy," he muttered.

Within the hour, Suzuki was reassigned to one of the other ships in the strike group.

Jackson sat back and looked around his office.

The place was surprisingly chaotic for a man so fiercely dedicated to order. His desk was covered with crude clay ashtrays, tie tacks, and paperweights, his bulkheads papered with crayon drawings, grade-school achievement awards, diplomas, and half a dozen God's eyes of various sizes. He especially loved the God's eyes, more for the little hands that had made them than for the supernatural protection they were alleged to impart.

Kids.

As the highest-ranking enlisted man on the ship,

Jackson was responsible for the health, welfare, and morale of five thousand–plus men and women. The majority of these sailors were still kids, barely out of high school. Regular contact with family was next to impossible. Life on the carrier could feel impossibly busy, a blur of action and hustle. It could also be the loneliest place on earth. Sometimes people cracked.

Suicide was a major issue in the navy, growing worse each year. Active duty military were nearly 50 percent more likely to commit suicide than the national average.

How had they gotten to the point where they were losing more sailors each year to suicide than to combat?

He gazed over at the God's eyes.

*Decisions like canceling that SAR sure don't help,* they seemed to whisper back.

In the nineteenth century, so Jackson learned during his Master's studies, some bright social theorists came up with this concept, the Great Man theory of history. Heroes emerged from time to time, so they said, individuals of exceptional virtue who singlehandedly shaped the course of human events. Others argued that this idea was naïve, simplistic. Great men, the critics said—and it was always *men* in these theories—were simply the products of their time, not the other way around.

Call it the "Great Societies theory."

Jackson was a pragmatist. In his experience, the normal fabric of events would always give rise to thugs and petty tyrants. Influential, charismatic men—and yes, almost always *men*—of outsized ego and destructive impulse. Who, left to their own devices, would wreak unmitigated havoc.

Call it the "Terrible Man theory."

Jackson did not believe in the Great Man theory because he did not believe in Great Men. He did not expect nor want his sailors to become Great. He wanted them to become decent, effective human beings. Lymphocytes of the body politic.

Like Jimmy.

"Miss you already, Suzuki," Jackson murmured.

The chief engineer had also told him there was a rumor making the rounds, that a large shark had followed them out of the Gulf. That there was talk of the ship being under some kind of curse.

"*Mère Marie,*" Jackson murmured. This was exactly the kind of superstitious crap that messed with the societal immune system.

That made people do crazy things.

# 31

Finn had been sitting out on the CIWS catwalk for close to ninety minutes, watching the ocean and sketching, when he became aware of someone trying to observe him without his knowledge.

"You might as well come sit down," he called out as he continued sketching.

His stalker stepped out from around the corner, sat down a few meters off, and followed his gaze out at the ocean.

West Texas, the helo pilot.

After a while she spoke. "What's that, some kind of meditation?" Nodding at his sketch pad.

Finn made no reply.

"I didn't know SEALs meditated. Guess it takes all kinds."

Finn wondered where this was going.

"You have some kind of special mantra or something?"

"No, ma'am." He hesitated, then added, "No mantra."

They were silent. The wind rose and fell, moaning faintly as it slipped across the flight deck above.

The pilot spoke up again. "If you did have a mantra, what would it be?"

Finn thought, *She's good.* She'd picked up on the brief hesitation.

"I don't have a mantra," he said.

She looked over at him. "I see you everywhere. Are you stalking us?" Her voice suddenly sharp as the edge of a flint knife.

"Us?"

"Me. My roommate. Are you?"

Finn turned to a fresh page and continued sketching. "No ma'am. I'm not stalking anyone."

"You're talking to my guy. Stickman."

Finn nodded. "Good kid. Solid operator."

"He's my guy," she said. "On my crew, which you have zero business going anywhere near. As of now you're going to quit talking to him, quit distracting him. He doesn't need it."

In his mind, Finn smiled. "If I don't?"

"Then I kick your skinny ass and throw you off the boat."

Finn nodded. He could see her doing that. Kicking some guy's ass and throwing him off the boat. Tucker, maybe.

"I was sorry to hear about your roommate and her crew," he said.

A lie with a basis.

"Yeah," she said after a minute. Her voice had gone quiet and lost the hard edge. "Sucks."

After a few minutes of silence, she got up and slipped back inside without another word.

Finn continued sketching.

*If you did have a mantra, what would it be?*

"Still here, Ray," he murmured into the wind.

*Sssssssstillhhhheeeeeerrrrrre* the wind replied.

# 32

The guy in the yellow windbreaker ran the length of the rooftop six stories up as he chased the helicopter. When he reached the edge of the roof he jumped right off, grabbing onto the rope ladder as the helo bore him up and over the Kuala Lumpur skyline . . .

Twenty-five sailors sent up a lusty cheer.

Finn was back in the library again. Time to check the traps. As usual there was a line for the next free PC, so he was waiting, sitting at one of the long tables, viewing the big screen along with everyone else.

No talking heads today. Today it was *Supercop*, the nineties Jackie Chan comedy-action-crime flick. Cheesy, but a classic—and the last half hour was set in Malaysia.

Malaysia! Their next port of call. Still a week away, but the crew was practically counting the hours. Three sweet days of tropical freedom!

*Supercop* had just reached the climactic sequence over the city, where the helo flew its rope-ladder hitchhiker straight into a stone tower atop one of Malaysia's tallest buildings. Jackie slammed into the tower with a resounding *whack*, but refused to let go.

Twenty-five sailors laughed and groaned.

Jackie crashed through a huge billboard advertising Stuyvesant cigarettes but hung on to that rope ladder as the helo flew him higher and higher over the city.

Twenty-five sailors hooted and hollered.

The kid on the PC pushed away from the table, stood up, and walked away. Finn stepped over to the machine and turned it, repositioning the screen so that it faced the bulkhead. Then pulled the chair over and sat, his back to the bulkhead. Restarted the PC, reopened the browser.

Nothing in his regular Gmail accounts.

Opened one of his three new anonymous accounts. Nothing.

Closed that account, opened the next. Nothing.

Closed that account, opened the third.

Something.

A message, from stanl3099@gmail.com. No subject line. In the email's single brief paragraph, Stan L. had this to say:

> Hey man, good to hear from you. Smitty sends his
> regards, says when you hit port in Hawaii have a
> Molokai Mike on him!

Finn read it twice.

Then deleted it, emptied the email account's trash, deleted the account, quit the browser. And sat still.

*Hey man, good to hear from you.*

Stan L. had not heard from him. Stan L. was not among the nine teammates he'd emailed. Stan L. wasn't a teammate.

He didn't know anyone named Stan.

He didn't know anyone named Smitty.

And he didn't drink.

Not Molokai Mikes or anything else.

The message, though. The message was definitely for him.

"Holy shit!" exclaimed the guy behind him. Now Jackie was fighting it out with the bad guys on top of a speeding train—and here came Michelle Yeoh out of nowhere, racing alongside on a motorcycle, pacing with the train! "Yeoh's doing her own stunts, man!" the seaman said to his neighbor as the actress took her Steve McQueen moment and jumped, her bike roaring into the air and slamming down *right on top of the freaking train!*

Twenty-five sailors whooped and clapped.

Finn had tuned it all out.

Still staring at the blank screen.

The email was in code.

"Stan" was a Teams guy he knew from way back. Big Spider-Man fan. (Hence the pseudonym.) Got out a few years ago and now worked in the private sector, big defense firm. Stan had his ear to the floor. All kinds of floors. Quite a few walls and ceilings, too. Evidently Stan knew that Finn was in transit somewhere out on the Pacific, bound for Hawaii. What else did he know?

Smitty sends his regards

Smitty, i.e. Smith, i.e. someone anonymous. Someone not simply unknown but intentionally unknown. "Stan" was relaying a message from one of Finn's platoon mates. Who couldn't communicate directly himself.

Which meant something highly fucked was going on.

This was about the mess in Mukalla. Had to be.

Finn's platoon had been tracking reports of a cell operating in the area, terrorizing locals, assassinating civic leaders. Stealing what wealth there was to steal. Very bad actors. Also fiendishly elusive. Impossible to find. Then they tortured and killed an American journalist. That was a bridge too far.

Someone came up with the critical intel: the cell was holed up in a small compound, northern outskirts of the city. It was a simple mission, a classic SEAL op. Three squads, in and out, kill or capture. Finn's squad led the breach, Kennedy's came in from the rear, and the third squad hung back to cover their flanks and roll up any escapees. Door charge. Flash bangs. Zip ties and hoods, out and ready and—

And nothing.

No one there.

Empty compound.

Bad intel.

And while Finn and his team stood there holding nothing but the wind, five klicks to the east the bad guys were slaughtering a whole settlement of farm families. Three dozen civilians. Toddlers to great-grandparents.

Finn and the others didn't even hear about it until the next morning. Later that same day they were shipped back to Bahrain. And the day after that Finn was on a chopper out to the *Lincoln*, bound for home.

Officially, the platoon wasn't being blamed. But Finn could add 2+2 as well as anyone. Someone had to go explain their epic fail to the top brass. As platoon chief, Finn was elected.

At least that's what he'd assumed.

But not according to "Smitty."

According to "Smitty," 2+2 didn't equal 4.

Finn looked up. *Supercop* was over, CNN back on the screen. The place had just about emptied out.

He stood, left the library to go circuit the decks, thinking about Stan's email. The last six words. Which were the whole point of the message.

have a Molokai Mike on him!

Finn didn't drink. Not a drop. Not caffeine, not alcohol. Everyone who knew him knew that. "Stan L." knew that. "Smitty" knew that.

have a Molokai Mike
Molokai

Molokai. Known for its pineapples, sea cliffs (the highest in the world), and stunning tropical ecology. Also its lepers. Among the many gifts brought to the island by nineteenth-century European traders were smallpox, cholera, and leprosy. Soon the native Hawaiian lepers were exiled to the northern side of the island and declared legally dead.

Kalaupapa: most famous leper colony in history.

"Smitty" was saying: Finn was now inhabiting a leper colony.

He was saying: Finn *was* a leper colony. Cut off. Legally dead.

A leper colony of one.

Finn had thought he was going home to defend his platoon.

But they weren't blaming his platoon.

They were blaming him.

# 33

A few more days south of the Arabian Peninsula the oppressive shroud of wet air finally dispersed, gracing the inhabitants of the *Lincoln* with a dry breeze that made the flight deck crew just about weep with relief.

The drier air was a welcome change for the pilots, too, but the open ocean also brought more heat differentials, which meant more weather. As dusk approached, the sea state grew steadily rougher, and by midnight, with flight ops moving into the final launch cycle for the night, the ship was heaving and surging in twenty-five-foot swells.

Lieutenant Kristine "Biker" Shiflin's F/A-18 was the last jet to launch, which meant that ninety minutes later it was also the last to join that cycle's marshal stack, the tight-knit pattern planes formed in 1,000-foot layers as they queued for recovery. By the time it was Kris's turn to go, the sea swells were pitching at thirty feet and more.

"Alrighty, then," she murmured. "Bring it on." Cruising at 660 mph, adjusting for tailwind, headwind, and crosswinds while listening to the voice in her headset, she stared into the nothing and waited for the word to go.

There was no moon out tonight. Pitch-black skies, pitch-black water. Her "night in the barrel," as the pilots called it: a nighttime landing in the worst possible conditions.

"One zero five, marshal. Your push time is one-five," said the voice in her ear. Now there was a hell of a phrase. *Push time.* Like you were about to give birth.

It felt like no time at all had elapsed when the voice spoke again.

"One zero five, dirty up."

"One zero five," she replied.

She extended her landing gear and wing flaps ("dirtied up"), activated the whirring servo motor that lowered her tailhook. Shook her head and gave a low laugh. It still amazed her that this was how they did it: that their high-tech solution to the challenge of putting 25 tons' worth of incredibly sophisticated twenty-first-century machinery down on a moving ship's surface in the middle of the rocking ocean was to catch on to a little wire with a little hook.

Basically, the same technology she used to hang cheap art on her studio apartment wall back home in Tennessee.

Down below, in the Golden Kestrels' ready room, a dozen guys from Kris's squadron were sitting around munching popcorn, watching her approach on the CCTV, taking bets on which wire she'd snag or whether she'd miss altogether and have to do a bolter.

She missed.

The ready room filled with groans and cheers, depending on which bets each had placed, followed by more popcorn, more bets, eyes glued back to the screen.

Up in the empty blackness 1,200 feet over their heads, Kris came around to port, describing a gigantic U-turn in the sky, then circled the boat and began her reapproach.

The boat heaved, bobbing up and down in forty-foot swells now, the enormous brass propellers visible for a few seconds at a time, the monster baring its teeth.

No low laugh this time. Kris was all focus.

In the old WWII days carriers had plain decks, straight as a Roman highway. When your landing didn't go well you just plowed straight on and crashed into whatever planes were parked up ahead. Until the Brits came up with the idea of knocking the landing strip off at an angle, giving planes in trouble a clear path to escape for a second try. It was the Brits, too, who came up with the term.

Bolter.

*Bolter: n. bohl'ter, from bolt, as in the flight of a crossbow arrow; a bolt of lightning, the bolt of a startled hare or runaway horse; an escaped criminal bolting from prison . . .*

The instant Kristine hit the deck she shoved her throttle forward to "full military"—maximum power without afterburner—in case she needed to bolt a second time. Her jet's tailhook erupting in a brilliant rooster tail of sparks as it screamed across the deck's surface, making its grab for that 3 wire.

"Bolter! Bolter! Bolter!" said the LSO's voice in Kris's ear.

Shit!

*A startled hare, a runaway horse—*

She pulled back on the stick as she shot off the edge of the deck, practically skimming the black water below before pulling up into another climb.

Another bolter.

Big U-turn in the sky and the Hornet came around once more, entering approach for its third try.

In the squad room the popcorn was ignored, bets forgotten, as the space went quiet. Biker was in trouble.

A land-based runway, commercial or military, could
run from 6,000 to 12,000 feet long. The *Lincoln*'s flight
deck was one twentieth of that. The length of a few
football fields. A dot in the ocean.

A pitching, yawing, rolling invisible dot.

Biker closed her eyes.

She'd won her first Harley off a guy on a bet when she
was fifteen, playing a game of high-stakes five-finger fil-
let where the contestants had to stab a jackknife down
rapidly into the spaces between their fingers splayed out
on a tabletop. Kris never missed, not once. Neither did
the other guy. So they upped the stakes and put on blind-
folds. Kris stabbed and stabbed, back and forth across
her spread hand like a sewing-machine shank—hit the
table every time. The other guy made seven nervous
stabs before taking a knife tip square in the middle finger. Just about cut off the damn phalanx. Kris rode off
that night on the guy's Harley. In the squadron, it was
the stuff of legend. It was why they called her "Biker."

Right now felt a lot like that hot summer night outside Nashville. Stabbing her jet down at the deck, blind-
folded. It was the 50,000-pound, $70 million incarnation
of that casual figure of speech: *a stab in the dark*.

A nighttime carrier landing was essentially a controlled crash. There were no other human beings on the
planet insane enough to attempt it but American pilots.
Astronauts who'd piloted their rockets through G-force
multiples and landed the damn space shuttle claimed
that none of that equaled the stress and difficulty of a
night in the barrel.

Another approach . . . *fuck!*

This time she caught the ship in between swells and
the deck held fairly still—but she gave in to a twinge of
panic and twitched back on the stick a fraction of an

inch just before hitting the third wire, and bounced off the carrier's surface yet again.

"Fuck fuck *fuck,*" she muttered, eyes darting from her instrument panel to the dark around her and back. Pushing the panic out of her chest and down into her gut. Forcing herself to keep breathing.

In the air again.

And getting low on fuel.

This was a blue ocean hop, no chance of pulling a "trick or treat," as the pilots called it, and heading off to an alternate landing strip. The nearest beach was hundreds of miles away. And she didn't have the fuel to risk pulling yet another bolter.

Which meant her options were now down to just two.

Grab the wire this time around.

Or eject.

There was no doorway 3.

Option number two would mean flushing $70 million of taxpayers' money down the toilet, which to be honest was not her top concern right now, but also dropping *herself* down into that very same Arabian Ocean toilet, which she cared about very much indeed.

Thoughts of Micaela's last moments flooded her mind and she shoved them out again.

She was *not* going into the water.

She was *not* going into the water.

She was *not* going into the water.

As she came around Kris tried not to imagine treading water alone out there in the ink-black ocean, frantically praying her flotation vest would hold long enough for the SAR team to get there, feeling the salt water tickling at her neck—

She came in at a hard angle, hammering the deck like a battering ram, pushed the throttle to full military even though she had no more bolters left—and felt the sudden jerk as her Hornet's tailhook snagged the last wire. She heard the cable's lunatic shriek as it snaked out into its elongated V, pulling on the massive machinery below in its attempt to stop the nearly supersonic momentum and keep her from shooting off the ship and plunging into the deep.

And then she was still.

Silence.

For a moment she thought it was a trick of perception, a glitch in her wiring. That she must have gone up into the night sky yet again and was now in the process of a slow, terminal dive. After a moment she took a violent in-breath, then slowly exhaled. Then two more quavering breaths. Inhale. Exhale. Inhale. Exhale.

She had grabbed the fourth wire. Her last chance.

She was alive.

In the Kestrels' ready room, a lusty cheer broke out.

"See you boys at midrats," said one pilot as he headed for the ready room door. "Gotta go change mah shorts."

Kris felt her pulse hammering as she taxied her Hornet into place, the goggled and green-jerseyed handlers waving her on. She forced a few long breaths, slowing her heartbeat, and grinned out the cockpit window as a few deck crew added gestures not seen on any other flight deck in US naval history: both fists held out in front, twisting forward and back. Revving on motorcycle handlebars.

*Biker has landed.*

She waited till the plane came to a complete halt, reduced power to idle, let out a breath, then cheerfully flipped her crew the bird. She stood, stepped out onto the wing, hopped down, and made for the catwalk, thanking them all one by one with fist bumps and hugs, her yellow- and green-jerseyed, goggle-faced comrades.

On her way below for her debrief, Kristine stopped.

She needed to take a moment for herself there on the catwalk, alone.

She stood gripping the rail, struggling to get the shakes under control. Looked down at the terrifying expanse of ocean. Gripped the rail harder, willing the tremors in her muscles to slow and still. Feeling the nausea as the rivers of adrenaline drained away.

She closed her eyes, squeezing them tight.

She could still see that black water below.

# 34

Finn had watched the whole thing on CCTV in the ward-room. He stuck around for a while after the tense landing was over, listening to officers' chatter, then came out and up to walk the gallery deck—just in time to see Biker emerge from her ready room, post debrief. He stood aside and nodded, catching a nod and nervous smile from her as she passed.

In the eight days he'd been on board, Biker had lost weight, maybe six or seven pounds. She looked gaunt. And right now she was a nervous wreck. He didn't blame her.

About twenty feet up the passageway he stopped. Sensed that hormonal ozone again. Gathering human thunderheads.

"That was some hot-stuff show up there, Lieutenant." A voice from down the passageway behind him.

Finn turned back just in time to see a tense exchange unfolding between Biker and Movie Star, the CO helo pilot.

"'Scuse me?" said Biker, her voice cracking.

"You know you're supposed to *fly* those things, right? Not play hopscotch with them."

Finn could see from her posture that Biker was caught off guard, grasping for a comeback. Not on her usual game, not at all.

"For a while there," the guy went on, "I thought we were going to have to power up the Knighthawk and go sort through some Hornet wreckage."

It was the kind of trash talk jet pilots took from one another all the time, but this guy wasn't a jet pilot and his barbs weren't banter. They were naked aggression.

And they'd found their target. The encounter lasted no more than ten seconds, but Biker was badly rattled when she walked on. Finn caught a glimpse of the smug rage playing over Movie Star's features.

Finn turned back and saw West Texas, the tall helo pilot, striding toward him. The two locked eyes for an instant and Finn saw her fury as she passed, going after her friend.

" 'Scuse me, *sir*," she spat as she brushed by Movie Star—but it sounded a lot more like *Fuck you, sir*.

Movie Star raised both hands, palms forward, all innocence. *Hey, just kidding around*.

Finn continued on.

He'd seen this dynamic before. A pilot like Biker was there for a reason; she was on a trajectory. The no-future helo pilot wasn't like that. Finn could read the whole story. Movie Star had planned to be a jet pilot, a top-gun guy, swinging dick of the blue skies, flying his machine like a tricked-out hog. It must piss him off mightily that a *girl* got the call sign "Biker." But he hadn't ranked high enough in flight school to get his pick of platform, so he ended up a helo pilot by default. No cool call sign, no yahoo pyrotechnics in the clouds, not for Movie Star. He was still angry about it. And taking it out on Biker.

As he walked Finn noted the usual parade of characters peopling the passageways. Grease-covered mechanics. Riggers and junior officers. A goggled flight deck handler. More pilots breaking up from debrief and heading below to midrats or off to their racks for the night. A few E-1s with their cleaning supplies, heading above or below to wash away evidence of the dying day. The city's night population, going about their business. Nothing to see here, folks, move along.

Finn stopped.

He stepped back into a shallow alcove so he wouldn't block traffic, what there was of it, and stood still for a moment.

Something didn't fit.

In sniper school their training began not with how to shoot but how to *see*. They were taught how to use their peripheral vision, which was anatomically more sensitive to movement and color than the central portion of the retina. They were taught to take in massive amounts of visual information by scanning a scene from right to left, in the opposite direction they'd been taught to use all their lives, because it interrupted the normal leaps of assumption and trained the brain to absorb the raw information and take it at face value.

And they were taught the art of target detection, which hinged on the ability to quickly take in a large field of vision and spot individual elements that were out of place. A straight line or hard geometric shape within a natural landscape. A stray moving branch, an unnatural stillness in the breeze-blown grass. A person doing something they wouldn't normally be doing.

It wasn't just about having keen eyesight. It was about using the information from your eyes to isolate elements that didn't quite fit into the larger picture.

Something he'd seen tonight didn't quite fit. He was sure of it.

But what?

# 35

Kristine had planned to head straight for her quarters, but she was too wound up to lie down, let alone sleep. She paused at the doorway to their berthing area. It was freezing in here, and claustrophobic. She did an about-face just as Monica approached.

"Hey," said Monica.

"Hey, yourself," Kris replied.

"Helluva bronco ride."

Kris gave an unconvincing grin. "Yes, ma'am, that it was."

They both stood silent for a moment.

"You okay?" said Monica.

Kris nodded and heaved a breath. "Asshole." They both knew who she meant.

Monica tilted her head in the direction of their stateroom. "Time to talk?"

Kris sighed. "In a bit. I need to get some air. Actual, real air."

Monica nodded. "Company?"

Kris smiled again, this time a real one. "Nah, I'm good. Thanks, though."

" 'Kay," said Monica. "Later." And she headed on into their stateroom. "Hey?"

Kris turned back.

"Don't be long, okay?" said Monica. "I really do want to talk."

Kris flashed a V with her fingers. "Peace out, baby."

Monica smiled and flashed the peace sign back. "I'll be up."

Kris began snaking her way back out through the dimly lit passageways. Picking through the maze, she made for a small and rarely used sponson, an external access space with its own tiny catwalk, just enough room for one or two people to stand outside and grab some air.

She opened the big hatch and slipped outside. Alone.

She gripped the rail with both hands and closed her eyes, feeling the hot dry breeze caress her face. Gave a few shuddering breaths, then began replaying the recovery sequence in her head. If she didn't do this now it would only replay itself later on when she was lying on her bunk, trying to sleep.

She heard a sound behind her and turned, her eyes snapping open. "Oh—!" Her hand flew to her chest. *A startled hare, a runaway horse.* "Sorry." A nervous laugh escaped her.

Goggles and a green jersey looked back at her.

She relaxed back against the rail. "For a moment I thought—"

His arm shot out, punching his gloved fist hard into her solar plexus.

# 36

A sharp gasp escaped her as she doubled over.

Her assailant followed with a hard right uppercut to the jaw that left her staggering. He caught her before she fell, and for an instant she stood, bent over and dry heaving.

She felt a rag jammed into her mouth, then a sharp prick in her neck as she was lowered to the deck and propped in a sitting position, back against the rail. She struggled to catch her breath, felt her whole body twitch and tremble; when she tried to flex her fingers they responded like semi-hardened clay. Something was happening to her, taking control of her hands, her arms, her legs.

*Drugged*.

Some kind of muscle relaxant. Propofol? No, she wasn't getting drowsy. She just couldn't move. Could barely breathe.

The clay was hardening.

The goggles loomed close, inches from her face.

*"We don't have much time,"* he rasped.

The goggles, helmet, and muffler obscured his face.

She couldn't see who it was. But she knew why he was there.

He was going to rape her.

A convulsion of horror flooded through her. He was going to rip off her flight suit and fuck her, right there on the catwalk. She focused with all her might on her mouth and tongue, summoning the force to spit in his face. She would *not* go down without a fight!

Nothing.

Her attacker reached into one of the green jersey's pockets, extracted a water bottle and unscrewed the cap, which he then carefully placed back in the pocket.

She was confused. If he was going to rape her, he would want to do it fast before anyone stumbled upon them. Why was he stopping?

But he didn't take a drink. Instead, he leaned over her, one hand holding her jaw steady, the other tipping the water bottle to her lips, eking out just a few drops.

She felt the tiny stream snake its way inward past her dead tongue, under her soft palate, into her throat. Her mind went rigid with panic. If it trickled down her trachea, even that tiny amount could drown her. She tried to will herself to cough—nothing. She wanted to scream with fury and frustration. The ghoul wasn't going to rape her. He was going to kill her. And she couldn't fight back.

The bottle left her lips.

Goggles in her face again.

*"If you behave yourself, and everything goes well here, there's a very good chance you'll come through this alive."*

*You're lying!* screamed the voice trapped in her head. *You're lying! You're lying!*

And then it struck her: that low rasp. It was a cheap Clint Eastwood impression. Dirty Harry. Which gave her a flicker of hope. The goggles, the voice. He was taking steps to prevent her from recognizing him. Which would be pointless if he planned to kill her.

Maybe there *was* a good chance she would come through this alive.

The jet pilot training kicked in, her mind a whir of calculations. Speed. Trajectory. How long before she passed out? Before the drug completely paralyzed her lungs? Could she fight through it, come out the other side?

The face was staring at her, peering into her eyes. Like it was watching her thoughts.

It looked like an insect.

Hungry.

A shiver ran through her nerves, though her body was still as stone.

The insect cocked its head. Drinking in her revulsion.

Feasting on her fear.

It reached out to touch her shoulder.

She recoiled in her mind.

*"It's okay,"* Dirty Harry rasped. *"It's okay."*

IT'S OKAY? she wanted to scream. HOW IS IT FUCKING OKAY!

And then—

Oh God. Not again!

He tipped the bottle once more, releasing another trickle of water on its way.

Tickling her windpipe.

All her calculations and false hopes vanished as she felt herself plunge into an abyss of pure terror, the voice trapped in her head thrashing and screaming out of all control—*Stop! Stop! Please no please no please no please no no no no . . .*

The insect giggled.

*"All right,"* it rasped. *"C'mon, up we go."*

He grabbed her with both arms, then pulled her upright and leaned her body against the railing, head flopped to the side like a rag doll. Steadying her against the railing with both knees and the press of his torso, he uncoiled the tie-down chain draped over his shoulders and wrapped it around her several times.

*"Good for you. You've behaved yourself. This has all gone very, very well."*

Slowly, deliberately, he removed the goggles and stared directly at her.

Those eyes were the emptiest thing she'd ever seen.

*You!* the voice in her head screamed. *YOU? Why are you doing this!*

And then he spoke—softly, but in his normal voice:

"And there is no chance, no chance at all, that you will come through this alive."

He peered into her face for another moment, the vacant eyes feeding on her panic—

Then swiveled her body around to face the open ocean and pushed her face forward and down so she was staring into the expanse below.

*Not the ocean! Please God NOT THE OCEAN!*

The last thing she registered before her mind completely snapped was the black face of the Arabian Sea rushing toward her.

# III

# Crossing the Line

# 37

Finn blinked and looked around, trying to remember why he was standing in a passageway somewhere in the middle of the ship.

He'd been up all night combing the decks, anchor room to fantail. Hadn't slept. Had not even stepped foot in his broom closet.

He looked down at himself.

No, that wasn't right. He was wearing a fresh set of cammies. He must have gone back to change. Had he slept?

He rubbed the back of his neck and in the hollows under his ears, trying to shake the sense of dislocation.

Now he remembered.

He was hunting.

When he first arrived on the *Lincoln,* walking his circuits was mostly a matter of reflex. Standard operating procedure. The key to mission success in any new AO, or area of operations, was to master the terrain. Though on the face of it there seemed no strategic point to detailed reconnaissance while aboard an American aircraft carrier, even one as poorly run as the *Lincoln.* No, up till now his explorations had been driven more by habit than by purpose.

Not anymore. Now he had a reason to look.

He was hunting.

He didn't know precisely what he was looking for, but he'd recognize it when he found it. A stray moving branch, an unnatural stillness in the breeze-blown grass. A behavior out of place. A contradiction.

He circled back through the passageway outside the Kestrels' ready room where he'd observed that confrontation the night before between Biker and Movie Star, then on to trace the paths each participant had followed as they entered and exited that nexus point.

He didn't know exactly what he'd find, but he knew what he was hunting. The wriggling creature with the massive head and no arms or legs.

He was hunting death.

He couldn't say how he knew it, but death was still stalking the *Lincoln*.

And death always left traces.

A single tone from the bosun's pipe split the air.

*"All availab—hands to—eck—OD walkdown."*

Finn immediately made for the flight deck, moving purely on instinct. He needed to take a look up there *now*, before this morning's FOD walk had a chance to pollute the scene. He didn't know why, but that didn't matter. His instincts were in charge.

His brain's job right now was just to watch.

# 38

A single tone from the bosun's pipe. *"All availab—hands to—eck—OD walkdown."*

Terrific. After Jimmy Suzuki's departure, the ship's air-conditioning had malfunctioned. Now the 1MC was getting hinky. Only a matter of time before some system broke down completely.

Command Master Chief Robbie Jackson's inquiry into Schofield's suicide had fizzled out. The new chief engineer, Suzuki's replacement, was an idiot. This morning's coffee, inexplicably, was weak as old lady's tea.

Yet none of that was really bothering him.

Jackson had been in a foul mood all morning, but he didn't know why.

"Let's see a little hustle there, shipmates!" At the sound of his voice a small knot of sailors scattered like pigeons at a backfire. "FOD walk waits for no one!" he added as they flew.

He supposed it was Sister Mae.

Jackson stopped at a steep ladder leading to the hangar deck and spirited his considerable bulk up the narrow steel rungs.

Robbie had dreamed about Sister Mae that morning, and it unnerved him. She was humming some primeval tune, punctuated with occasional muttered syllables no one but she could understand, a little cast-iron pot simmering with some evil-smelling brew by her side. His momma's momma was a massive woman, a figurehead of their parish church who led come-to-Jesus Baptist services in the evenings and backroom faith healing sessions in the mornings. Robbie could never tell which she believed in more, the power of Jesus or the sly magic of Louisiana voodoo. Whatever the case, she always seemed to know when there was evil afoot.

Jackson hadn't thought about Sister Mae in ages. Not that he was proud of that. He loved Sister Mae with all his substantial heart, owed his life to her. But what in the name of Damballah was she doing here, disturbing his sleep?

"Morning, Master Chief!"

Jackson nodded his greetings and rolled on.

Born Harlan Robichaux Jackson, Jr., Jackson was "Harlan Junior" till the day of his eleventh birthday, when Harlan Senior got nasty drunk and broke his son's arm. From that day forward he went by plain "Robbie." Six years later, when Robbie was a junior in high school, his daddy came home one afternoon spitting drunk, yelling for his wife, ready to lay into her with curses or fists, or both. But Robbie was there. Sister Mae had taken him aside that morning and told him to skip school that day. "Stay close to your momma," she said. Robbie didn't ask why.

Sister Mae always knew.

When Daddy came stumbling up the dirt-and-gravel drive that day with evil in his eyes, Robbie grabbed a stick of cordwood and told him to scat or he'd brain him. Robbie never forgot the look of fear and fury that flew across the man's face. After Daddy slunk off, Sister

Mae told him he had to *ficher le camp*—scoot, skedaddle, *now*—or he'd be dead by dawn.

And Sister Mae was right. That same night Harlan came looking for the boy. When he found his son gone he raged back to the bar he'd come from. Before the sun rose his switchblade was in another man's liver and Harlan was on his way to Angola, where he was now serving fifteen to life for felony murder. If Robbie had stayed, it would have been *his* liver with the blade stuck into it.

He hadn't been back to the bayou since, not once. Didn't plan to, either. Cesspool of ignorance and superstition.

Arriving up at the flight deck catwalk, Jackson took a big inhale of the salt air.

Normally Jackson did not go above for the morning FOD walk. His regular crew of chiefs managed things up there just fine. This morning, he'd had the urge to come spot this one himself. Maybe he just wanted to breathe the open air for a moment. Get the stench of Sister Mae's foul-smelling voodoo concoctions out of his head.

He stepped out onto the flight deck as lines of crew formed up at the bow.

Maybe *that* was what drew him up here this morning. FOD walk was the very embodiment of military procedure. And military procedure was the bedrock of all things rational.

Procedure was what kept the Terrible Man at bay.

Jackson closed his eyes, took a deep breath, and let the subtropical sun swaddle his face, baking away the dark memories. Exhaled, opened his eyes.

And saw the SEAL, tracking along the blacktop like a bloodhound.

# 39

Finn began scouring the deck, moving as quickly as he could, still looking for anything that didn't fit.

In a moment the crew's vanguard line would catch up and pass him in their aftward sweep. Maybe they'd find whatever it was he was looking for, if it existed at all. Or miss it altogether. Or trample it.

He moved farther astern, looking, moving, looking, moving.

Something.

He bent down to peer close. A small bit of foreign object debris.

Could mean nothing.

He took out his Navy Cash card, then reached into another pocket and fished out a small plastic bag. Using the card, he coaxed the tiny object into the bag.

Straightened and looked across the deck.

The CMC was gazing directly at him.

Finn walked across until he stood face-to-face with the big man, then extended his hand and without a word placed the little bag and its contents in the master chief's open palm.

The master chief looked down and frowned. A thin,

nondescript bit of rigid plastic tube, maybe an inch and a half long. Closed on one end, open on the other.

Cap to a hypodermic needle.

The big man glanced up at Finn, the question on his face mirroring Finn's thoughts exactly. *How the hell did that get up here?*

The 1MC abruptly scratched to life with five urgent tones on the bosun's pipe.

"*Man overboard, man over——hands to mus—all hands to muster.*"

# 40

Monica's first reaction was irritation.

She had just stepped into hangar bay 3 when the passageway speakers erupted in five piercing whistle tones and the voice started blatting.

She didn't buy it. Nineteen times out of twenty, "man overboard" meant that someone had dropped a chem light or a vest off the flight deck, or, even more likely, that someone hadn't shown up to muster because they were still snoring in their rack. Or had snuck off with someone else to attempt a quick copulation in some deserted spot or other. She'd heard of people doing it in supply closets, maintenance spaces, ventilation junctions, even the anchor room, for God's sake. Her mathematical mind couldn't even fathom the odds of getting caught. But people apparently did it all the time.

Whatever. Schofield had been that one case in twenty of an *actual* man overboard, and they were due for at least nineteen more false alarms.

And now the day's whole schedule was going to get upended. Six thousand people on hold while the truant was found, dragged out of the rack, and appropriately humiliated.

Shit fire and save the matches.

*"The following personnel report to deckhouse 3 with their ID cards . . ."*

Leaving her office behind, she began tromping up to her squadron's ready room on the gallery deck for muster. She was halfway there when the droned list of names made her stop in her tracks.

*"OS Courtney Jamieson, Operations. MM Michael Lubschitz, Aircraft Intermediate Maintenance. Lieutenant Kristine Shiflin, Air . . ."*

Oh, no.

Kris had been gone when Monica woke up that morning. She hadn't seen her at breakfast.

By the time she reached her ready room, Monica had started to panic.

*"Time plus three . . ."*

On the next call, the list had shrunk to a single name.

*"Lieutenant Kristine Shiflin, Air."*

"Alert five!" called out Papa Doc from the front.

The words stung her like a scorpion.

There were three levels of alert readiness status. "Alert thirty" meant *stay in the area*, on standby in case a possible mission materialized. "Alert fifteen" meant *mission imminent*: get jocked up and on hand in the ready room, prepared to head up to the flight deck on a moment's notice. "Alert five" meant *you need to be sitting up there in the bird*, auxiliary power unit going, strapped in and ready to rocket.

"Alert five" meant Papa Doc was ordering an SAR team to haul ass up top and board a chopper *now*.

"Alert five" meant they thought Kris was in trouble.

"No way," she murmured, then louder: "No *way*." Someone had screwed up here. She started pushing forward through the rows of chairs. "Did they check the magazines?"

Papa Doc turned toward her and held out a palm. "Hold up, Halsey."

She reached the front of the room and stopped. "Sir, this is crazy, they need to rerun their site checks, there's no way Kris would be—"

"Halsey!"

She stopped short before blundering any deeper into the shit she'd just stepped in. Who did she think she was talking to? *Jesus, Mon, get a grip.*

Papa Doc stared at her, his expression oddly unreadable.

"Halsey," he said, quietly now. "They found a note."

"Bull*shit!*" she blurted. A *note?* No. Not Kris. Yes, she'd been stressed out, and yes she'd skipped a few breakfasts, but if she were feeling that desperate she would have said something—

And all at once the confrontation with Papa Doc from the night before came rushing back. His taunts, Kris's stricken face. He'd pushed her too hard, just like he pushed everyone too hard. God *damn* him. Kris was already fragile. Had his bullying gotten to her *that* bad? Had Kris gone and done something crazy?

All the breath went out of her. She gripped a nearby seat, swaying on her feet.

*Shit. Shit! SHIT!*

One SAR team was already out the door—they'd be readying another ASAP. She needed to be on that second crew.

"*Halsey!*"

Monica snapped to attention. "Sir! I'll go, sir!"

"Stand down, Halsey!"

"*Sir?*"

"You're grounded, Lieutenant."

She stood rooted in place. "*What!* But sir, I have to—we have to—"

Papa Doc leaned in, his face a slab of stone, and said the last thing in the world Monica wanted to hear.

"*Quarters.*"

# 41

For the second time in a week the great ship turned in the ocean, launching its choppers and rescue teams, calculating its search grids, sending out alerts to the other vessels in the strike group. Below, in her silent stateroom, a lone Knighthawk pilot stood helplessly by, confined to quarters.

Monica hauled up onto her rack, forcing herself not to look at the lower bunk, heaved over onto her back, and stared at the overhead inches away, straining to hear the sounds of helicopters lifting off and landing above her head.

In flight school she'd put in hours in a simulator. The exercise that left the deepest impression was a scenario in which she lost her engine and had to make a forced landing. The first time she went through it she hadn't reacted in time. Instead of immediately popping the sprag clutch to disengage the rotor, which would have allowed it to maintain at least vaguely normal RPMs as she descended and given her a fighting chance to land the bird safely, she paused for two seconds to think. Long enough for the stalled engine to cripple the craft.

She would never forget the sense of helplessness as her simulated bird tipped over into that death spiral.

That's how she felt right now.

Her best friend had gone missing—and here she was, restricted to quarters for mouthing off to her commanding officer, pending further disciplinary action while the rest of the squadron flew the mission without her.

Diego. Micaela. And now Kris? She wanted to scream, wail, throw something. Break something. Instead, she lay there turning into hardtack.

All she felt was numb.

She climbed down again and made herself sit on the lower bunk.

Kris had brought her own blanket on deployment, a quilt she'd patched together from remnants of outfits from her teen years. High school skirts, biker jackets, Goth pullovers, the sweater she'd worn (briefly) the night she lost her virginity . . . how the four of them had howled with laughter together the night Kris gave them the tour!

Monica ran her hand over the variegated cloth.

Chapters of a life.

Sectors in a grid.

The search effort would go on for at least a full twenty-four hours and probably longer, assuming Old Eaglebeak didn't pull the plug like he did on the Schofield search. Yet Monica held out little hope. She felt a desperate certainty that in another day or two the quilt under her fingers would be gone, collected and packed away along with every other personal item that belonged to her friend.

She looked around the tiny cabin.

Each of them had her own steel dresser-wardrobe unit as well as a folding desk with additional storage above and below. In a few days a team of two warrant officers would come through and remove everything, carting it off to an office somewhere on the ship to be packed up and flown home to Tennessee. Part of the awful disappearing act that happened when a crew member died.

The CO of Kris's squadron would go to his safe and remove the packet every crew member had prepared ahead of time, containing a form for notifying next of kin, who got the insurance money, prewritten letters to family and loved ones, and an address where personal effects were to be shipped. Normally the skipper would also write a personal letter of condolence to the parents and/or spouse of the deceased. In Kris's case there were no parents, no spouse, no surviving family; the space on the form for "next of kin" would have been left blank.

Monica wondered what they would do with the box.

The numbness was starting to wear off.

In every squadron's ready room, pilots had assigned seats based on rank and seniority, the most senior beginning up front, proceeding from left to right and back through the rows. Each seat had a slip-on head cover with that pilot's name stitched on. In the Kestrels' ready room, the head cover with Kris's name would be slipped off and all those behind it moved forward one seat.

Like a game of musical chairs. Only no music.

Her name tag would be removed from the roster board and flight schedules. In a few hours it would seem as if she were never there. All part of the procedure.

Disappearing Kristine.

A searing ache flared in the pit of Monica's stomach and began to spread up through her chest.

There would be a memorial service, based on whatever religious preference the deceased had indicated on his or her "In the event of my death" packet. And then Lieutenant Kristine Shiflin would cease to exist. After that, if anyone tried to talk about her during work hours they'd be told to knock it off and go cry in their rack after flight ops were over.

She understood the logic, even appreciated it. It wasn't the crisp efficiency of a cold, unfeeling bureaucracy, as they'd explained to her when it was Micaela who was erased. It was a ritual of empathy, designed to serve the morale of the living, so her roommates and teammates wouldn't have to bump into constant reminders of the departed. Also so they could stay focused on the mission.

So, yeah: empathy, and maybe some bloodless efficiency, too.

Monica buried her face in her best friend's quilt and began to sob.


The search effort took two full days. On the morning of the third day, when Monica returned to her stateroom from breakfast, there was a message waiting for her.

Her presence was requested for an interview with the command master chief.

# 42

The first thing Jackson noticed was how exhausted she looked, her red-rimmed eyes set into dark circles on a pale, haggard face.

The second thing he noticed was how pissed off she looked.

Which told him that she hadn't grieved yet, not really. He hoped she would, for her sake, and soon. Before it ate her alive.

"Lieutenant Halsey," he began, then tilted his head toward the man sitting to his right. "Lieutenant Commander Scott Angler, JAG Corps."

There were no particular legal dimensions to the situation, but he trusted Angler's insight and had asked him if he would sit in on the interviews.

The pilot nodded at both men. Her perfect poise concealing her anguish imperfectly.

"Lieutenant Halsey, I like to begin meetings like this on a point of agreement."

"Yes, Command Master Chief Jackson."

"Can we agree that your confrontation with Commander Papadakis two days ago was possibly the most boneheaded move of your career?"

"Yes, Command Master Chief Jackson." Her face rigid.

"Of your very possibly short-lived career?"

"Yes, Command Master Chief Jackson."

"You don't need to address me as 'Command Master Chief Jackson,' Lieutenant. 'Master Chief Jackson' or simply 'Master Chief' will do fine."

"Yes . . . Master Chief."

"Lieutenant, questions of disciplinary action are not my concern here; that's a matter for your chain of command. My concern is the state of morale on this ship."

Jackson hadn't decided up to this moment quite how much to soft-pedal this one. The woman had just lost her roommate and best friend—her second roommate lost in this deployment, *pour l'amour de Dieu*! He'd wanted to spend a minute taking her measure first.

He decided to go blunt.

"It appears your roommate took her own life, Lieutenant, and I need to understand why."

She nodded, still standing at attention.

"Please take a seat, Lieutenant."

She sat down across from him.

"Can you explain exactly what it was that occasioned that outburst in your squadron's ready room? Purely as a question of context."

Monica returned his gaze. "I wouldn't describe it as an outburst, Master Chief."

He nodded. "Fair enough. The exchange, let's say. The one where you used the phrase, 'Bull*shit*!' "

She took her time, assembling her thoughts. Unhurried. Which impressed him.

"I was upset," she began, "when I realized Lieutenant Shiflin was missing. The night before, after flight ops, she'd had an encounter with Commander Papadakis, and I was concerned that this may have upset her unduly."

"An encounter?"

"Yes, Master Chief. She'd had an especially difficult run, involving a string of bolters. He happened to be present when she emerged from her debrief, and he teased her a bit about it."

Jackson let a moment of silence hang before prodding again. "Teased?"

"Yes, Master Chief." Another beat. She didn't want to say more, but he knew she would if he waited.

He waited.

"Taunted her, was how I observed it, Master Chief. She didn't handle it well."

"Huh." Jackson nodded, not a *Yes, I see* nod, more a *So that's what you're going with?* kind of nod. This was a US naval fighter pilot they were talking about here, a Top Gun graduate, and Halsey's position was that Lieutenant Shiflin went and threw herself off the ship to her doom . . . because someone *teased* her?

"As you might be aware," he said, "Commander Papadakis reports that nothing of the kind took place." He saw the startlement register. No, she had *not* been aware of that. "According to him," Jackson looked down at his notes, "he made a comment, something to the effect of 'That was a rough run out there' and that he was glad she didn't go in the drink. And she said nothing in return. All fairly benign." He looked up at her. "That not match your recollection?"

The pilot's cheeks burned. She was pissed off mightily, no concealing that.

"Not in every detail, Master Chief." Jackson then saw her face change, as if she'd just remembered something. She straightened in her chair. "Someone else witnessed the exchange. The SEAL."

Jackson hadn't known this. He covered his surprise by looking down and scribbling on a paper pad. "Noted. And Lieutenant, what led you to make the leap from something as innocuous as a brief, albeit testy encounter in a passageway to a seasoned naval aviator disappearing from our midst?"

She was silent.

"I'm asking because," he added, "in all candor, I really don't see the connection."

"She'd been under a lot of stress the last week or so, Master Chief. More than the usual jet pilot stress, I mean."

"All right," said Jackson. "How so?"

The pilot hesitated.

"I'm all ears," Jackson added.

"Of course," she said. "Here's the thing, Master Chief. I don't think anyone else realized how fragile she was. Everyone in the air wing saw her as a badass fighter pilot. A Tennessee hills spitfire."

Jackson nodded. That squared with everything he'd heard in the past two days as he and Scott interviewed those who knew her.

"But I roomed with her. We talked. The past week, she was more and more anxious. Jumpy. Even a little paranoid."

Jackson's eyebrows shot up in wordless question. *Paranoid how?*

"I caught her glancing back over her shoulder a few times, as if she thought someone was there. One night she asked if I thought we were safe here. On the ship, I mean. Almost like she was being stalked."

"Stalked," he repeated.

"I . . . grew up on a ranch," she said.

"A ranch."

"Yes."

Jackson nodded slowly, as if what she was saying made perfect sense, which they both knew damn well it did not.

"And did Lieutenant Shiflin give you any indication,

any indication at all, as to who in particular might be making her feel . . . *stalked*?"

"She . . . she mentioned that Commander Papadakis had been staring at her." She looked down, breaking eye contact. "At midrats, Master Chief."

There was a brief silence.

Jackson pursed his lips thoughtfully.

"Lieutenant, can you tell us something you actually observed, any specific behavior or exchange, anything at all beyond the brief encounter outside the ready room and the fact that Lieutenant Shiflin mentioned being *stared at*, that would have prompted you to throw yourself on your sword and act out on your own commanding officer, based on what you *thought and felt*?"

"No, Master Chief." She looked up and met his eyes. "I was upset."


After the pilot departed, Jackson sat silent for a moment.

Whatever animosity passed between Lieutenant Halsey and her boss was none of his concern. But losing another crew member? Very much his concern. And there was one thing this green young pilot had said that particularly disturbed him.

He looked over at Angler. "Stalked."

Scott shrugged.

Jackson frowned into his empty coffee mug. "Let's have a talk with the SEAL."

# 43

"Bomb assembly room," announced Tom the ordie.

He ushered Finn through a massive reinforced steel door and into a large, brightly lit space, lined with rows and rows of munitions components stacked deck to overhead, bomb bodies and missile parts everywhere, all pinned tight with wire lines and tie-down chains like those that secured aircraft to the flight deck. The place looked clean as an operating theater.

"This door stays locked when assembly's under way," Tom commented. "At that point the only way in or out is up through the trunk line." He jerked a thumb toward a set of steel rungs disappearing up the wall through a circular opening.

Finn walked over and looked up through the thick glass hatch. From their current location on deck 6 he was looking straight up at deck 2—fifty yards or more through a vertical tunnel barely wide enough for one person.

No thanks.

Places without alternate paths of egress made Finn uneasy. If he'd had his own "Rules to Live By" that would be Rule 1: *always keep an open exit.*

"Your basic five-hunnert-pound bomb," Tom said.

Finn turned and saw a few red-shirted men and women gathered around a large olive-green bomb body, preparing to hoist it up onto what looked like an operating table. High-explosive scrub nurses.

"But that's just the chassis. Depending on what you stick on it you can turn it into a smart bomb, or an undersea mine. You can set it to burrow down and wait, or explode on contact, or in midair, or when it reaches a preprogrammed location. It all depends on which accessories you add on.

"We got about six million pounds of ordnance on board this ship. No real danger when they're all kept separate, but put the right pieces together an' you got serious boom power."

Proud grin on his face. A kid showing off his comic collection.

"Attach some fins, shimmy in a fuse assembly till you hear a nice *click* and she's ready to roll out to one of the bomb elevators and up to the flight deck, where she's stowed in the bomb farm there, right behind the island, till it's time for warheads on foreheads. Then we load 'er on a bird and off she goes."

*Warheads on foreheads?* They were out in the middle of the Arabian Sea. "We planning on loading any birds today?"

"Running a drill," Tom explained. "They'll assemble a full complement, run it all up to the bomb farm, then bring it back down again and restock all the components back in their respective magazines. We're supposed to pick up the pace, get it running a couple times a day, once the, you know . . ." He grew quiet and looked at his shoes. "Now that the SAR guys are wrapping up."

One of the other red shirts nodded to Tom, who turned to Finn and ushered him out the big door, speaking quietly as they went. "Everyone down here's pretty shook up about Lieutenant Shiflin."

"Biker," said Finn.

Tom nodded.

"You guys all knew her?" said Finn. Already knowing the answer. This was the sole reason he'd asked for the tour. He wanted to see where Biker worked.

"Oh yah. She was our assistant O. In here every morning, oh-seven-hundred, like clockwork. Rain or shine, like we say." Tom forced a grin. Ordie humor. As if rainfall or sunlight could penetrate down into these spaces.

Finn understood how this worked. In times of grief, turn up the spigot on irony. It was one way people coped. Hence the term "gallows humor."

Not that it was working right now. Tom's normal good cheer had fizzled like a sparkler dropped in a mud puddle.

"There's a couple dozen smaller magazines all over the ship," said Tom once they were out in the passageway. "I can take you down one of those."

"Down?"

"Trunk line. Only way in or out."

Finn hesitated.

No alternative egress.

"Okay," he said.

# 44

Up in hangar bay 1, Tom led them to a small opening set into the deck. "This one's for the flares the pilots use to decoy heat-seeking missiles." He pried open the little circular hatch, stepped down through the deck, looked up at Finn, and grinned. "Here we go."

Finn waited until Tom's head had disappeared before following him down into the narrow trunk line. The two descended, vertical handhold by handhold, Tom narrating as they went.

"There's thirty-four different magazines on the ship. Everything is stowed separate, according to type. You got your primary magazines, universal magazines, missile magazines, magazines for the little stuff—small arms and ammo, smoke guns, flares, distress signals, things like that . . ."

Despite their physical proximity, the vertical tunnel's acoustics made the ordie's voice oddly distant.

"We're passing deck two now. Most of our magazines are located down here below the waterline so they can flood them in an emergency, like a fire on board . . ."

Speaking of fire, it felt really hot in there to Finn. As if they were climbing down through the Earth's mantle.

Tom didn't seem to notice. "No bomb components in here per se, but there's still a ton of explosive material. If something bad happened here we'd just flood it. Every magazine is equipped with its own sprinkler system. In an emergency you could top this one up with seawater inside ninety seconds."

They got down inside, stepped off the ladder, and looked around. There was barely room for the two of them.

Finn stopped, stood still. Cocked his head for a moment. Looked at Tom. "What's that?"

Tom looked puzzled. "Chief?"

"That sound." It was a faint, high hum. Growing.

Tom frowned. Slowly shook his head. "Not hearing it," he whispered.

Finn cocked his head the other way, then back the first way. Slowly worked his jaw, the way he would if he were popping his ears on a plane on takeoff. The sound began to diminish.

It was in his head. His ears were ringing. That was all.

He looked back at Tom. "So people are pretty upset about Biker."

"Oh, yeah," said Tom. "Everyone liked her. She was a good boss. Intense lady."

"Intense how?"

"Man, *dedicated*. She was down here, in and out of all these spaces, every single day, for hours. More than the O himself. Never missed a day . . ." He went silent again.

Finn could practically hear the sentence finish itself: *until she did*.

"How did she seem that morning?"

Tom rubbed his nose. "Just normal, pretty much. She was kind of distracted that morning. Wound up." His face fell. "Maybe she was depressed or something." Upset with himself for not having noticed.

"Wound up, what, like jacked up on coffee?"

"Oh no, Chief Finn, not a chance. Biker didn't touch the stuff."

"Not a coffee drinker? Not at all?" Interesting. Gauging by the long lines at Jittery Abe's, Finn had thought he must be the only one on the boat who didn't load on the almighty bean.

"Matter of fact, there's quite a few guys work down here who watch their caffeine intake. With her, though, it was like a religion. She said she was born wired, an' if she drank coffee like we did she'd probably blow up the magazine."

Tom's young face lit up as he laughed, but it lasted only a second or two, and in the silence his face fell once more.

"Sucks," said Finn.

"Got that right, Chief. Sucks the big one."

"*Hey, Tom!*"

A voice calling down from above.

"Yo!"

"*Got a message up here for yer guest.*"

Tom nodded to Finn. Time to go. "Yo!" he called up again. "Right up!" He gestured at the vertical ladder. *You first.*

Finn slapped one hand up onto an eye-level rung, then the other onto the next, and pulled to hoist himself up—

And to his astonishment both hands slipped off the rungs, sending him crashing to the deck.

"Whoa!" Tom cried out. He jumped back a step, then quickly bent down to help Finn to his feet. "Man, you okay?"

Finn sat on the deck for a moment. Looked at his hands, working them both, making and unmaking fists.

He couldn't feel his fingers.

Completely numb.

It was as if they weren't there.

"You okay, Chief?" Tom repeated, worried now.

Finn was on his feet, shaking his hands, trying to wring circulation back into them. He turned to Tom. "No problem. Hands fell asleep."

"Okay. Wow." Tom looked uncertain. "You sure? You good to climb?"

"No problem," Finn repeated. He put a Tom-Sawyer-the-ordie grin on his own face to show that everything was right as rain.

Everything was not right as rain.

"Okay," said Tom again, clearly not knowing what to do.

Finn grabbed a handhold to recommence the climb. Ignoring the painful sensation of pins and needles as his fingers started coming back to life, he willed his hands to keep enough of a grip that they would at least partially stabilize his position as he propelled his body upward with his feet. It was like doing rope climbs using only his hands, something he'd done thousands of times—only in this case using only his feet. Basically impossible. Still, he made it up the first six or seven rungs, and by then he'd got enough feeling back into his hands that they could take over their share of the effort.

When Finn finally emerged, like a tunnel rat in a prison escape movie, he found a red-shirted colleague of Tom's standing over him.

"You're Chief Finn?" the guy said.

Finn nodded.

"Master Chief Jackson would like to speak with you."

Finn got to his feet, Tom coming up next to him. "Hey, thanks," he said to Tom.

"No problem," Tom replied. His face was still etched with suppressed alarm. Finn could see it was a struggle not to ask again, *You okay?*

"No problem," Finn echoed back to the boy.

The ordie nodded, looking the opposite of reassured.

# 45

When Finn was ushered into the CMC's inner office he saw the big man at his desk, a JAG officer seated to his right, sporting a golden trident at his left collarbone. Former SEAL. A mustang, probably: former enlisted man who came back through on the officer track. A prosthetic leg, judging by the drape of his trousers. Finn's guess, the same action that took his leg also ended his SEAL career.

"Come in, Chief Finn," said the master chief, but Finn was already in. The CMC rose halfway, probably meaning to gesture toward the empty chair across from him and say *Please, sit* or something of that nature—but Finn was already in the chair. The big man lowered himself back down into his seat.

"Chief Finn, Lieutenant Commander Scott Angler, JAG Corps," said the master chief. "I'm Jackson."

He picked up a sheet of paper from his desk and read from it.

"BUD/S class 251, ranked first in NSW sniper school. SEAL Alpha platoon, seven tours in Iraq, Afghanistan, and I imagine a few more in places we won't mention. DEVGRU Silver Squadron, then Black Squadron. Silver

Star, Combat Action Ribbon." He put the sheet down. "And so forth. A distinguished guest among us."

Finn didn't know what to say to that, so said nothing. His fingers still ached, but it was receding.

"You know what they say 'SEAL' stands for, Chief Finn?"

That sounded like a rhetorical question, so Finn made no reply.

"This would go better if you answered back," the master chief said equably. "You know, back and forth. I ask something, then you offer something in reply. Call and response. Like in church."

Finn gave a single nod, then added, "Okay." Noticing the crayon drawings, school achievement awards, and God's eyes. Taking the measure of the man.

"So, let's go again. You know what they say 'SEAL' stands for?" the master chief repeated.

"It sounded like a rhetorical question."

"See, there you go, Mister Finn," said Jackson. "Back and forth. That's what we call a 'conversation.'"

"Just Finn."

"'Scuse me?"

"Not Mister. Just Finn."

"So, Finn: first name?"

"Only name."

The command master chief stared at Finn for a moment, then half turned to the JAG officer. "Scott, I believe you were a SEAL before JAG Corps. You know what they say 'SEAL' stands for?"

Angler kept his eyes steady on Finn as he replied. "What's that, Master Chief?"

"*Sleep, Eat, And Lift.* Only you don't really seem to be doing any of those things, Chief Finn. If you sleep, no one's quite sure where or when. Since your quarters seem as virginal as the day you arrived. You don't seem to eat much. And when you hit the gym you don't do anything except maybe piss people off."

Jackson waited for a beat.

Finn said, "Okay."

Jackson gave a visible sigh. "Aren't you guys supposed to stay in shape?"

"No real point to weights on a ship."

Jackson regarded him for a moment. "All right, not exactly an answer, but I'm feeling some flow here." He took a sip from his coffee mug, swished the cup around a little, his eyes never leaving Finn. "And why is that?"

"It's not a question of static strength," said Finn. "On a ship you've got continuous fine movements happening around the clock. Even if you're not aware of it, you're making constant microadjustments. Which builds muscular strength automatically."

The JAG officer couldn't hold himself back. "Of what, then?" Like a challenge.

Finn glanced over at him. "Of what?"

"You said it's not a question of static strength. So, what is it a question of?"

"Endurance. Sir."

Finn felt hostility emanating from Angler like summer heat off a city street. Why, anyone's guess.

Jackson glanced down at the file again. "Doesn't say much in here about where you came from. Parents deceased. No childhood history. Like you got sprung full-grown outta the forehead of Zeus. You like a little mystery, Chief Finn?"

Finn gave no reply.

Jackson sighed again. "Yes, that was in fact a rhetorical question." He closed the folder that contained the single sheet of paper and leaned back in his chair. "What are you doing here, Mister Finn?"

"Just—"

"Just Finn, yes, we got that. The mystery I'm interested in at this moment is why you are interrogating my crew. When you're not spending hours at a stretch out on gun turrets staring at the horizon. Looking for answers to life's great questions? Why is there evil in the world? What was God's purpose in creating mosquitoes? Why do officers with perfectly good careers jump off the ships they're serving?"

So many rhetorical questions there.

Jackson picked up his coffee cup, looked inside it, then set it down again. "What are you doing on my boat, Mister I Don't Give a Three-Foot Shit What Your Last Name Is?"

"I can't really say," said Finn.

Jackson nodded. "All right. *Why* can't you really say?"

"Because I don't know."

Jackson glared at him. "I find this hard to believe."

Finn looked back, unblinking. "Me too."

The big man considered that, then nodded once more, slowly. "You're a sniper, right?" He put up a hand. "Rhetorical again." He looked over at Angler. "You know, Commander, most people think snipers are homicidal trigger-pullers. What they don't realize is that a sniper is first and foremost an intelligence asset. They're not paid just to shoot. They're paid to observe." He swiveled his gaze back to Finn. "Am I right?"

"One hundred percent."

"Good," said Jackson. "I like being right." Finn could see him trying to decide whether or not this SEAL was actively trying to piss him off. He didn't seem like he would take the bait if the answer was yes, but Finn thought it irked him not to know. "You've been here for almost two weeks. What have you observed?"

Finn glanced at Angler, then back at Jackson.

"One of your corpsmen is dealing," he said. "Crushed-up pills, probably Adderall, in little home-made envelopes. Your deck-status LSO is banging one of your *Penny Press* photographers. And your XO hates it when the captain calls him 'Artie,' but he'll never say so, because his ambition is bigger than his ego. Rare in an officer."

A cumulus of tension settled over the little space. Finn could feel the JAG officer bristle at that last comment.

Though he was taking care not to show it, Finn could see Jackson was impressed. He hadn't known any of those particulars. He gazed back at Finn. "Anything else?"

"Such as?"

"Such as, anything unusual in Lieutenant Shiflin's general comportment, the day or so before she went missing?"

"Yes."

"Care to illuminate?"

"She'd had a hard time landing that night, on the roof. Outside her squadron's ready room, she ran into a helicopter pilot, don't know his name, short, olive skin, curly hair . . ." Testing the master chief a little, seeing if he could prod him into giving up some information, but Jackson didn't fall for it. Now it was Finn's turn to be impressed. "They had an exchange."

"Any idea what about?"

"He taunted her about the run." Now Finn modulated his voice, giving them a precision playback of Movie Star's delivery. "'*You know you're supposed to fly those things, right? Not play hopscotch with them.*'"

There was a sharp intake of breath from Angler.

Finn's impression was pitch-perfect, as if the helo pilot himself had just stepped into their midst.

"And she said?" queried Jackson.

Finn shook his head. "Just took it. Didn't reply. He said more. '*For a while there, I thought we were going to have to power up the Knighthawk and go sort through some Hornet wreckage.'"*

The silence in Jackson's office stretched out a good ten seconds.

The CMC hadn't yet mentioned the hypo cap Finn had handed him up on the flight deck a few days earlier. He wondered why.

"And that was it?" Jackson finally said.

"That was it."

Jackson paused for a moment, then said, "Thank you, Chief Finn. That'll be all, for now." He began to rise from his chair.

But Finn didn't move. He looked at Jackson and said, "I don't think Schofield jumped."

Jackson stared at him, then slowly sat back down. "Come again?"

"Schofield," repeated Finn. "The ATO officer."

"I know who you're talking about," said Jackson. "You don't think he jumped?" He put up a hand again before Finn could reply. "Rhetorical again." He regarded Finn through half-lidded eyes. "So, what do you think happened?"

Finn looked over at the JAG officer, then back at Jackson. "Don't know. Maybe he was clumsy."

And with that he rose, slipped to the door, and was gone.

# 46

The office was silent for a moment after the SEAL's departure. Finally Angler spoke up. "He's lying, obviously."

Jackson grunted. "About what?"

The JAG officer shook his head slowly. "Don't know. But he won't say why he's here, and that doesn't pass the sniff test."

"Says he doesn't know himself," mused Jackson.

"Right, well *that's* obviously a pile of horseshit."

Jackson frowned at his desktop. The SEAL was a strange one, no doubt about that. Jackson believed him, though, and that bothered him. Pissed him off, in fact. *Because it makes no rational sense.*

He punched a set of four digits on his J-Dial desk phone, then hit the button for speaker. After two rings the phone on the other end picked up. "Lieutenant Desai." A woman's voice, low and musical. Indira Desai, in Jackson's estimation the smartest intel officer on the ship.

"Indy, Master Chief Jackson. I have Scott Angler from JAG here with me. We just spent a few minutes in the company of a SEAL, goes by Finn, no last name. Or maybe that's Finn, no first name. Apparently rerouted here on some sort of 'special assignment.'"

"Yes," the voice said. "Finn. I know about him."

"Good," said Jackson. "I'm wondering if you could dig a little into the man's background. What exactly he's doing here, last known assignments, anything unusual in his CV, and so on."

"On it already, Master Chief."

"Great. Thanks, Indy—"

"No," she broke in, "I mean, I'm *already* on it. I've been looking at him since he came on board." *Bean* looking, she pronounced it, the Bengali accent a distant residue from British rule.

Jackson raised his eyebrows at Angler.

Scott nodded. Indy was good.

"Would you mind stopping over here for a minute, give us a quick sense of what you've got?"

"Copy. Be there in two."

Jackson clicked off the phone and they waited in silence for a moment. Then he turned to Scott. "So this was the first time you two met face-to-face? I thought you'd have some kind of kindred spirit thing going. SEAL to SEAL."

Scott shrugged. "He's lying."

Jackson grunted. "So you said. Corroborated the hell out of Lieutenant Halsey's story, though." He frowned again. "Think we should talk with Commander Papadakis again?"

"For what? On suspicion of being mean?"

There was a soft knock on his door. "Open," called Jackson.

A slight woman with dark eyes stepped inside.

"I was curious," Indy said once she'd pulled a seat up to Jackson's desk. "Once I started digging, I got more curious. It's more opaque than I expected, even for a Six."

"Enlighten us."

"Chief Petty Officer Finn, no last name. Orphan, no family name on record. Only living relative an older brother, no contact info. Enlisted age eighteen in 2001, BUD/S class 251 in '04. Deployed more or less continuously ever since. Officially speaking, Chief Finn has been recalled to Coronado 'on special assignment,' no further details."

"But?" put in Jackson.

"According to a guy on the ground in Bahrain, he's out on medical leave."

That made both men sit back. "Medical?" said Scott. "What's he got, a tummy ache?" SEALs were not known to leave the field for any reason, least of all anything medical, unless they were gravely wounded. As Scott knew better than most. And the SEAL they'd just interviewed certainly didn't seem to be bearing any mortal wounds.

"I can't tell if special assignment is Bravo Sierra and some medical issue the real story, or the other way around," said Indy. Bravo Sierra: BS.

"Either way," said Angler, "why didn't they just stick him on a C-130 and fly him home?"

"No idea. No one knows. Or at least, no one's saying. My guess? They yanked him because he's toxic. And they didn't fly him home because they don't *want* him home just yet. They haven't figured out what to do with him. They're stalling."

"Stalling," Jackson repeated, and then once more: "Stalling." He thought for a moment, then shook his head slowly. "Thanks, Indy. Keep me in the loop if anything else shows up?"

"You bet," she said. "Commander," she nodded at Scott as she rose and left the office.

"Toxic," said Scott. "Well that's . . . disturbing."

Jackson was lost in thought, frowning at his desk.

"Master Chief?" said Scott.

Jackson looked up at Angler. Then opened a side drawer and withdrew a small plastic baggie. Opened it and tipped its contents out onto the desk.

Scott leaned in and took a close look at the item that tumbled out.

"Looks like a hypo cap."

"It is a hypo cap," said Jackson. Using a pencil, he nudged it back into the little bag, resealed it, and handed it to Angler. "Can you find out where it came from?"

"Sure." Scott reached out but hesitated before picking up the thing. "Where'd we get this?"

"FOD walk." Jackson didn't mention he'd been sitting on it for two days. Or who gave it to him.

Scott frowned. "What's this about, Robbie?"

Jackson opened his top drawer, took out two sheets of paper, and slid them over to Angler.

The first was Lieutenant Schofield's brief yet rambling suicide note. *Just another clod, washed away,* and so on. Scott had already seen it. He now picked up the second sheet and read aloud.

I thought I could do this, but I can't. It doesn't matter how fast I go or how hard I fly, it all still comes crashing back down to the same ugly fucking place. I just don't want to be here anymore. Please tell everyone I am so so sorry to cause them pain, but shit happens.

"Shiflin's note?"

Jackson nodded. "See anything odd there?"

Scott squinted, cocked his head. "Odd? Not really. Hell of a thing, though. Tragic." He was silent for a moment. Then looked up at Jackson. "Something I should be looking for?"

"Any similarity between the two?"

Scott read both notes again, then shook his head. "Not really." He looked at Jackson again. "Something in common I'm not seeing?"

"Nothing whatsoever," said Jackson. "Except they're both typed. And unsigned."

Scott put the notes down. "So?"

"So," said Jackson. "Who types and prints out a suicide note?"

Angler looked at the two notes again, then at the hypo cap. Then at Jackson. "What are you thinking?"

Jackson hesitated. He really didn't want to give voice to this thought. *Merde*. He nodded at the little plastic item. "I'm thinking, what if *that* had something to do with Lieutenant Shiflin's unscheduled departure."

Scott's eyes narrowed. "That's a hell of a leap, Master Chief." He looked from the hypodermic cap to Shiflin's note, then at the other note, then jerked his thumb toward the closed door. "Is this because of what *he* said? About Schofield?"

"No." Jackson shook his head slowly. "No, I was already wondering about this."

In truth, the SEAL's unexpected comment about Schofield *was* part of it, but the thought had already crept into Jackson's mind the moment he'd laid eyes on that hypo cap two mornings earlier.

"Honestly? I doubt there's anything to it," he added. "But it needs to be looked into."

"Whatever you think," said Angler. "Seems far-fetched to me." He picked up the little baggie and pocketed it as he stood. "I'll check this out." He stepped to the door.

"And Scottie?" When Scott looked back, Jackson nodded toward his pocket. "Be discreet?"

"No shit." The JAG officer stepped out and closed Jackson's door behind him.

*That's a hell of a leap, Master Chief.* Yes it was.

Made no rational sense.

His thesis advisor had always hated it when he used that phrase. *That's a tautology, Mister Jackson. Rational sense? There is no other kind.*

*Oh, no?* Robbie would think. *You've never lived in the bayou. You've never met Sister Mae.*

He swirled his cup and took a cold, bitter swallow, then set the cup down and rose from his chair. Time to bring this shit sandwich of a problem to the captain. And he already had a pretty good sense how Eagleberg was going to react.

"Ah, crap," he said.

# 47

She didn't hear his approach, didn't even realize he was there until she stirred in her seat and caught a glimpse of that titanium blade leg. For the past hour, Monica had been sitting up near the front of the little chapel, head bowed, lost in a swirl of thoughts and half-formed prayers. Now she looked up and nodded a silent greeting.

Scott slid into the pew next to her and touched her shoulder. When his fingers made contact she jumped as if zapped by a spark of static electricity. "Whoa," he said, his voice gentle. She leaned in against him and softly began to cry. He put his other arm around her and held her like that in silence while she wept.

The SAR effort had shut down hours ago. The pair of warrant officers had already moved through their stateroom, silent as ghosts, to remove her best friend's things. Kris was gone. She knew this, yet it still hadn't felt real—not until she collapsed against Scott and took the space to weep.

*Do you cry when things go wrong on the job?* That dick reporter at Sally Ride's press conference. *Fuck you,* she thought. *Fuck you and the hobbyhorse you rode in on. Goddamn right I do.*

In fact she didn't, not typically. She hadn't cried back when Gram died, and not when they got the news about Dad, either. They'd both been ill for months, everyone saw it coming both times. Their deaths were, in Monica terms, a *known*.

Not this time. Kris's disappearance had come out of left field, *no* one saw it coming. It was a total *X*.

An *X* Monica didn't know to solve for.

"Shit. *Shit*," she muttered, wiping her cheeks with her fingers. She pulled away from him. "Thanks. I'm good now."

"So, I talked with CAG and your flight surgeon." CAG: Commander, Air Group, the top of the air wing food chain. "They've both agreed that the situation calls for erring on the side of leniency. Command is waiving any further action, and you can resume normal duties tomorrow."

Thank God. She felt guilty even thinking about it, but she'd been agonizing over whether her brief insurrection in the ready room might have cost her that HAC.

"Thank you," she said. "That was . . . above and beyond."

This was true. Scott had gone way out on a limb for her, injecting himself into a routine disciplinary action that was clearly outside his province. There was nothing inappropriate about their relationship; friendship was hardly fraternization. Still, his butting in on her behalf could well have raised an eyebrow or two.

"Monica," he said gently. "What the hell were you thinking?"

She felt herself bristle. "Listen, that whole situation got blown way out of—"

"Really. 'Cause the way I heard it you practically told your CO to go fuck himself."

She dug out a Kleenex and blew her nose, then peered at him. "You're angry."

"Damn straight I am. You could have put your whole career in jeopardy."

"You know what, Scott, that is really *not* the salient point here. My best friend's *life* was in jeopardy, and I didn't do a damn thing to help!"

Scott backed away a few inches so he could look her in the face. "*You're* angry."

She put her fingers to her cheeks and felt how hot they were. Took a breath and blew her nose again. "At myself, mostly. I *knew* something was wrong. I kept meaning to sit her down and get her to really talk. That night, when she went off by herself—to 'get some air,' she said . . ." Monica choked up for a moment. Scott waited. "I told her not to be long, that I really wanted to talk to her." She looked at him, tears streaming again. "I said I'd wait up. But I fell asleep!"

He said nothing, just listened.

"Shit, *shit*!" She scrubbed at her face, furiously wiping off the tears. "Every night I lie there listening to that godawful racket up on the flight deck and I can't get to sleep to save my life, and the one night—the *one night* I needed to stay awake—"

"Hey," he said.

"What if I'd followed her out there, forced her to talk to me?"

Scott sat back against the pew next to her and nodded. "I know," he said.

Which was so Scott.

*Don't beat yourself up*, she would have expected anyone else to say. *You can't blame yourself. None of this is your fault.* All those useless clichés. But he didn't say any of those things. *I know.* That was all. And he really did. Strange how it gave her comfort, just hearing that.

"Took a bit of doing, finding you," he said after a moment.

"I couldn't stay in my stateroom. Couldn't go down to the hangar, the place feels like a mausoleum. The whole ship feels like a mausoleum."

"Yes, well," he said. "*That* we can change when we put in at Port Klang."

"Thank God," she breathed. Port Klang, Malaysia. Their first port call in nearly half a year, just a few days away now. The whole ship was looking forward to it. Lord knew they needed it.

Port call was to a carrier crew what spring break was to college freshmen, and it didn't get much more Daytona Beach than Malaysia. On the way out to the Gulf they'd stopped at Hawaii and Luzon, then threaded their way straight through the Malay Peninsula without stopping. It seemed like a decade ago. Now they were all worn and sea-weary, hungry to get out of their steel prison and see land. The prospect of even three days in Malaysia seemed like a ten-week vacation in Heaven.

"Ever been to Malaysia?"

She shook her head. "I've never been anywhere."

"I'll show you the sights. Eat amazing seafood, maybe ride the ferry to Sumatra. Walk on surfaces that don't pitch and yaw. Get sand between our toes."

She nearly smiled.

He stood, looked down at her, and put out a hand. "You gonna be okay?"

She nodded, gave his hand a squeeze, and let go.

After Scott left, the space seemed even more silent than before.

*Ever been to Malaysia? I'll show you around.*

She gave a quiet laugh. From anyone else, that might seem like a classic pickup line. But not with Scott. She thought about how she'd jumped when he touched her. And the hand squeeze when he left. His holding her while she cried. Had they ever actually touched before, physically? No, she was sure they hadn't.

"Oh, Lord," she said aloud to the empty chapel.

# 48

"We could arrange to take on a team from NCIS when we reach Port Klang," said Jackson. "But I'm not sure we want to wait that long. We might want to consider launching our own interim investigation."

Captain Eagleberg nodded thoughtfully, as if giving the information careful consideration. But said nothing.

The three of them—CMC, captain, and Arthur Gaines, the captain's XO—sat together around the parquet mahogany coffee table in the captain's parlor, what Eagleberg referred to as "the Lincoln Room." Jackson had just laid out the bare bones of his concerns: the two suicides, both bodies unfound; the two notes, both typed, both unsigned; the oddly out-of-place hypo cap on the flight deck.

Gaines absorbed it all with mute concern.

Jackson couldn't read the skipper's face at all.

"Of course, I'd suggest we proceed as discreetly as possible," he added. "No point in spooking the crew."

The captain nodded again, paused, then finally spoke. "Thank you, Robbie. I'm glad you brought this to my attention." He tapped one forefinger on his lips a few times. And still said nothing more.

Jackson glanced around the room so as not to seem impatient. Took in the crown moldings and coffered ceiling, the muted slate-green silk-print Colonial diamond-pattern wallpaper, the polished mahogany sideboard with its crystal decanter and matching glasses. The space had received a makeover modeled after the sets on Stephen Spielberg's epic film *Abraham Lincoln*. Spielberg had already spent Hollywood-scale research money making his sets historically accurate. The navy saved taxpayer dollars by simply copying what was in the movie.

*Your box office dollars at work.*

The captain's voice finally broke the silence. "I don't think that will be possible, Robbie. I'm afraid we'll have to forgo port call on this leg. I've already given our new heading to the bridge. We're making straight for Perth."

Jackson slumped back in his chair, stunned speechless. Changing the ship's itinerary without bothering to inform his own CMC, the individual most responsible for ship-wide morale? This was a gross breach in protocol!

On a ship at sea even the slightest disruption in chain of command could pose an existential threat. A carrier's skipper-CMC relationship was central to the ship's smooth functioning. If that trust fell apart it was as catastrophic as a torpedo ripping open a hole in the hull. It would send tremors of concern right up the chain of command. A serious confrontation between the two could wreck both their careers.

The captain turned to his XO. "Artie," he said mildly, "can you give us a moment here?"

Arthur rose from his chair and melted from the parlor.

"Robbie," the captain began, "I'm sensing hesitation. Let's put rank aside for a moment. Please, express yourself freely." He extended an open palm.

*Dieu,* what a patronizing prick he could be.

"I appreciate that, Skipper. Bill. The thing is . . ." Invitation to speak freely notwithstanding, Jackson knew he needed to tread carefully here. "As I'm sure you know, the crew is really looking forward to a break. And honestly, I'm a little puzzled at the change in plans. What's our rush?"

The captain nodded agreeably. "I'll be straight with you, Robbie. I know they'll be disappointed, I understand that. But we just don't have the luxury of time. We need to haul ass down to Perth to replenish and ready ourselves."

Replenish and ready themselves? For *what*? This deployment was basically over.

The captain leaned in and clapped his hands on his knees, a coach wrapping up his halftime talk.

"Listen, Robbie, we cross the line *tomorrow,* right? Equator by oh nine hundred! We'll put the announcement out shortly so everyone can prepare for the festivities. This may be the Age of PC, but they haven't taken that one away from us yet, eh?" He grinned and slapped Jackson on the knee. "A *Line Crossing,* Robbie! Good God, how long has it been since we've done one of those?" He got to his feet, as if the disagreement were now behind them, everything settled and happy. "That'll take people's minds off the skipped port call—and before you know it, we'll all be ashore in Australia."

Jackson stared at Eagleberg. Had the man lost his mind? A sophomoric hazing ritual was going to make up for losing three glorious days on the beach in a tropical paradise? Was he really that out of touch?

No. Eagleberg was insufferable, but no fool. Jackson was being played—and it pissed him off.

"Bill, you really think this can wait till Perth? I realize it's an outside chance that the two disappearances are related, but hypothetically, if these *were* acts of violence, it's not unreasonable to suggest it could happen again."

Eagleberg leaned back against the sideboard and crossed his arms. "Outside chance? Come on, Robbie. Two unrelated notes, a misplaced hypodermic cap, and a hunch?"

So there it was.

Jackson knew very well that this was all, as Scott put it, *a hell of a leap,* and he wasn't keen on the idea of spreading a panic, so he could understand the reluctance to bring an NCIS presence on board. But the captain wasn't talking about being discreet.

He was dismissing the whole damn thing out of hand.

"I see that, Bill," he said carefully, "and to be honest I have the same concerns. There's probably nothing to it. Still . . . I don't know. Do you think we should bring this to Selena?"

Uttering the admiral's name was like pulling the pin on a grenade.

For an instant the captain's face twisted with rage at the veiled threat—and then the features all sucked back into place again. He straightened abruptly, coming up off the sideboard and inadvertently jarring the mahogany piece with a tremor that set the crystal brandy decanter rocking.

Jackson saw the thing teeter and leapt to his feet.

Eagleberg reacted by jerking backward, unaware of the threat to his beloved Baccarat set.

Jackson shot his hand out and managed to arrest the decanter's fall—but one of the crystal glasses tumbled off and hit the faux-hardwood flooring with a musical crash. He looked up, one hand holding the decanter in midair.

Eagleberg's eyes bored into him, lips pressed to a slit that could have cut twine. "Careful, Robbie," he said.

The door flew open and Arthur burst in, alarmed. "Everything all right?" His eyes found the broken glass. "I'll get this." Moments later he was crouching by the sideboard, whisking the debris into a dustpan.

Jackson set the decanter down and took a few steps back. "Sorry about the glass, Skipper."

Eagleberg gave a curt nod. "Could have been worse."

*Yes, it could,* thought Jackson. And that seemed about as clear a signal as he was going to get. The audience was over.

He turned and made for the door, exchanging nods with Gaines as he went. "Arthur," he said quietly, to which the XO murmured, "Robbie," in reply. As he left he heard the skipper's brusque "Thank you, Artie."

The SEAL's observation was dead-on accurate, wasn't it.

Gaines really did hate being called "Artie."

# 49

*"Taps, taps, lights—silence about the decks."*

No problem there. Finn was maintaining silence about the decks just fine, lying right there in his broom closet. Although so far he hadn't actually spent a single night in this little desk drawer of a stateroom.

*You love water, hate ships.*

He flexed the fingers of both hands. They still had that strange foreign-object feeling that had overtaken him that morning in the flare magazine. A vestigial numbness.

He glanced over at the door. Got up off the bunk, slipped over, opened it a crack. Left it that way. Lay back down.

Was he losing his mind? Clearly, he was losing pieces of it. Like the night Schofield went missing. And the night Biker disappeared. Both a blank.

*Scrotal disaster.* As Kennedy would say.

He pressed his fingertips to his thumbs, then did it again.

*Kennedy.*

Glanced back over at the door.

Got up once again and quietly shut it.

Lay back down on his rack.

Thought about that last encounter with Kennedy, the day he left Bahrain.

He'd just emerged from the commander's office and come down to the first floor. The place was bustling with activity. In the hallway he bumped into Kennedy, told him he was shipping out that night. "Literally," he added. "On the *Abraham Lincoln*."

Kennedy nodded and said, "Walk with me?"

They stepped outside and walked together on the paved path out through the yard. Then Kennedy said, "Give me twenty-four." Finn mentioned that his satphone was busted, and he'd put in for a new one. Kennedy nodded again. Then they parted ways, Finn toward his quarters and Kennedy heading off somewhere—

Stop.

Rewind.

Pay attention.

Kennedy nodded and said, "Walk with me?"

What happened next?

They stepped out of the air-conditioned building and Finn was smacked in the face by the sandpaper heat, his eyes half-blinded by dust. Nothing escaped the desert dust there in Bahrain. It found its way everywhere, caking the outsides of windows, creeping up your nostrils, wedging its way into the crack of your ass.

The two men walked the paved path together for a moment in companionable silence—

Correct? Was that brief silence "companionable"? Or "pregnant with something unsaid"? Now that he thought about it, Finn realized he didn't know.

What next?

They stepped off the sidewalk and onto a sand pathway leading *away* from the admin building, because Finn was heading back to the hotel where his platoon was billeted.

Kennedy said, "Give me twenty-four."

Finn mentioned that his satphone was busted and he'd put in for a new one.

Kennedy nodded again.

Like he already knew that.

Then they parted ways, Finn walking on toward town, and Kennedy making a U-turn and heading back to the admin building. Which was where he'd been going in the first place, when the two had crossed paths in the first-floor hallway—

Wait.

Why "nodded *again*"? When did Kennedy nod the first time?

Rewind.

Pay attention.

Inside, when Finn told him he was shipping out, Kennedy registered no surprise at all. Just nodded. Which meant he already knew Finn was leaving. And his reaction was to say, "Walk with me?"

Why?

At the time it had not occurred to Finn to wonder about this. But if Kennedy already knew Finn's situation and had only three words to say about it—*Give me twenty-four*—then why ask Finn to accompany him outside at all?

Why not simply tell him what he had to say right there in the hallway?

Finn stared at his hands, slowly flexing them, methodically working the fingers.

Clench.

Unclench.

Clench.

Unclench.

What was he missing?

# 50

"Morning, all." The three sat in a semicircle facing Jackson, their chairs pulled up to ring his desk like megalithic standing stones hauled into place for some dark ancient rite. Scott Angler, JAG Corps. Indira Desai, from Intelligence. And Lew Stevens, the ship psychologist. No introductions were needed; they all knew one another. None of them yet knew why they were there.

They made small talk for a minute or two, mostly about reactions to the news that Malaysia was canceled and to the Line Crossing ceremony rites that were about to get under way. Consensus around the ship: on a scale of 1 to 10, positive anticipation about the ceremonies was about a 3, negative reactions to the port call cancellation an easy 11.

"All right," said Jackson.

Let the rites begin.

"What I'm about to tell you is confidential. If, after I've explained myself, you decide not to participate, you have my word that there will be no judgment, no further discussion, and we'll pretend the conversation never happened."

The other three sat, waiting to hear more.

"All I ask," he continued, "is that you keep this all to yourselves. Are we clear on this?"

Lew gave a puzzled frown but said, "Fine by me."

Indy nodded cautiously. "All right," she said.

Jackson looked at Angler. "Scottie?"

The JAG officer gave a sharp shrug. "Sure, fine. We listen. Then we decide. So what's it about?"

Jackson looked at them each once more. Then nodded and read them in on the situation. The two suicides, the two notes, the unidentified hypodermic cap.

"We're looking at the possibility that these suicides may, well, may not exactly be suicides." He paused. *Merde alors.* Since when was he squeamish about speaking his mind? "That they may have been homicides."

There was a sharp intake of breath from Indy. Lew's eyebrows shot up in disbelief.

Scott's expression didn't change at all; he already knew this much. "Have we liaised with NCIS?" he asked.

"No," Jackson replied evenly. "At this point, there's no official inquiry. This isn't a working theory, only a hypothetical." He paused again.

"Hang on," said Indy. "You think these two are connected? The same perpetrator?"

"We're looking at that possibility."

"Two connected homicides?" Indy said. "Master Chief, you think we've got a serial killer on board?"

*Serial killer.*

He hadn't yet allowed himself to use that term. Somehow it made the whole proposition seem ludicrously far-fetched.

"No, honestly, I don't think that. I think Lieutenant Schofield had personal problems he couldn't live with anymore. I think Lieutenant Shiflin cracked under the stress of a bad night in the barrel, on top of whatever personal issues *she* was dealing with. And the dropped hypo cap is someone's careless contribution to topside foreign object debris. I'm saying, we're just *looking* at the possibility. I brought you three here to ask if you'd be willing to work with me on an unofficial investigation."

There was a brief silence. Lew glanced at Indy, who looked over at Scott.

"Unofficial?" said Scott softly.

"Yes," said Jackson. Then he added, "When I say, 'We're looking at the possibility,' what I mean is, *I'm* looking."

There was another moment's silence as the implications sunk in. The captain was not on board with this.

Jackson was flying solo.

Lew gave a low whistle. "Well, that's . . . different."

"Sure as sweet fuck-all is, pardon my French," murmured Scott.

Jackson held up one hand. "Before you say anything, let me outline my thoughts. How we do this thing. *If* we do this thing. Indy would work the data side. Sifting through incoming and outgoing emails, web traffic, looking for anything out of the ordinary. Personnel files . . ."

"Cross-checking all ship's schedules in the past ten days," Indy said.

"Exactly," Jackson continued. "See who in theory could have been free to commit both crimes, who would be ruled out based on their documented work schedules, that sort of thing. And any other intel aspect you come up with."

He turned to Stevens. "Lew, I'm hoping you'd be able to pull together whatever evidence and data we have and use it to work up a psychological profile of our perpetrator. If there is, in fact, a perpetrator."

"So," Lew said mildly, "you want me to profile a serial killer who may or may not exist, with no bodies, crime scenes, murder methods, weapons, or hard evidence, for homicides we're not even sure actually happened. Did I miss anything?"

Scott spoke up. "Just the part about no orders or official sanction." He glanced at Jackson. "Or permission."

The master chief gave a rueful nod. "That about sums it up. Which brings me to you, Scottie. I'm hoping you'll conduct whatever interviews and inquiries we might need. Which we'd have to do with tremendous delicacy—"

"Seeing as how this inquiry doesn't actually exist," put in Indy.

Jackson looked over at her. "Correct." Not to put too fine a point on it. "I'd also suggest," looking back at Scott now, "that you serve as the group's tactical coordinator and keep a close watch on everything we do, make sure we don't cross any legal lines in our investigation."

"You mean," said Scott, "other than the fact that the entire effort could be construed as somewhat extralegal?"

They were silent for a moment, all with the same thought.

*If not flat-out mutinous.*

"Right," said Jackson after a moment. "Other than that."

He reached into the bottom side drawer—the one that locked—and pulled out a sheet of paper. Placed it on the desk. "Which is why I've drafted this." He turned it around so they could all read it.

The other three crowded close, reading as he summarized.

"It states that I take full responsibility for what we are about to undertake; that it is exclusively and solely by my initiative; and that you three are acting at my request and direction. If this all blows up in our faces, the hope is, this document will offer the three of you at least some measure of protection."

One by one they finished reading, sat back, and looked at him.

"And, full disclosure," he added, "I can't guarantee even that much. Although I do think it should carry some weight in that contingency. Scottie?"

Scott nodded slowly. Reluctantly. "I'd say the same. *Should*. No guarantee."

"Well." The master chief pulled a pen from the pocket of his blouse and placed it on top of the letter. "This is your opportunity to back out. As I said, no repercussions, no further discussion. No harm, no foul."

One by one, they all signed their names.

Jackson took the executed document, placed it back in the secure drawer, and locked it. Then looked up at his co-conspirators.

"All right, then. Shall we hit the flight deck and spread some good cheer?"

# 51

*Shit fire!* Wasn't this just the very definition of Murphy's Law: her confinement to quarters now over, Monica was finally back at work—only there was no work. Flight ops were canceled for the day, the flight deck cleared and prepped for the Big Event.

Oh boy, a hazing.

She knew she was supposed to be excited. The Crossing of the Line was a hallowed naval tradition, passed down through the seafaring centuries, something she'd treasure for the rest of her life. Blah, blah, blah. She just didn't care. Kris was gone, and she was strung out on grief, confused by this pathetic high-school crush she'd just realized she had, and still burning with shame over her three-day banishment.

Halfway up to the flight deck she did an abrupt about-face and headed against the traffic, back into the ship's interior. The phone down in her maintenance office had outside line access. Not supposed to be for personal use, but hey, this wasn't personal, this was survival. If she didn't talk to someone she was going to burst. Or punch someone.

She keyed in the two digits to get an outside line, followed by the US country code and the Pensacola number she knew by heart.

As she listened to the first ring her eye was drawn to the Harry Reasoner quote over her desk:

This is why a helicopter pilot is so different a being from an airplane pilot, and why in general, airplane pilots are open, clear-eyed, buoyant extroverts . . .

She could certainly use a few words from an "open, clear-eyed, buoyant extrovert" right now.

"Sloane Halsey."

Monica felt the tightness in her chest relax at the sound of her brother's voice. "Hey, Chub."

"Buffy! How're things goin' with Papa Doc?"

"How're things going at home?" she asked, ignoring the bait. "How's Vanessa?"

"Oh, you know. She's Vanessa."

That she was. Their mother had always encouraged her children to call her by her first name. Very progressive. Monica had just felt cheated out of the chance to call someone "Mom." She wished she and her mom could talk right now, woman to woman. Ask her how she coped with it when Gram died, and then when they lost Dad. Fat chance of that.

"How's she doing, though, really?" she pressed.

"I ever find out, you'll be the first to know."

As close to an answer as she would get. All at once a fresh wave of grief swept over her. She realized she couldn't tell Sloane about Kris, or how she was feeling. As much as she loved him, as close as they were, it wasn't the kind of thing the two ever shared.

"Hey," said Sloane. "You'd love it here."

"Flight school?"

"The bomb," he said. "You should think about it. Seriously. Much as I love flying, and you know I do, you can make a *life* here. The kids all look up to you. You're makin' a difference—and you're pullin' scratch up the caboose."

She laughed. "Sounds mahvelous. Puhfectly *mahvelous,* Thurston."

"SensAYshunal, Lovey. On the green at eleven, gee-and-tees at the club with the Hendersons at four, it's just *busy* as *beavers* here."

She laughed again. Amazing how quickly you could fall into the old routines.

"Hey," he said, suddenly serious again. "Speaking of your pal Papa Doc."

"Hey yourself," she said. "And you really shouldn't call him that."

"Yeah yeah, so listen. One of the senior instructors here knew him from his student days. I got an earful last week over coffee. Guy was a real prick."

"I'm shocked, shocked to hear that, Thurston," Monica murmured. "You sure he didn't say 'a real prince'?"

"Ha-ha. So apparently the instructors didn't love him any more than the other cadets did. And he wasn't all that stellar a student, either—but the man had a ferocious work ethic. This guy, the senior instructor, says they kept trying to find reasons to flush him but he kept clawing his way back."

"Why am I not surprised."

"Anyway," Sloane's voice suddenly dropped to nearly a whisper. "This rumor went around, dogged him through his whole last year, nearly got him kicked out. That he went out with a girl, a first-year cadet, and things got . . . preppy."

"Preppy?" Monica sat up.

"You know," said Sloane. "Tried to cash in on his

nonexistent charm?" He paused. "She claimed he date-raped her, Mon."

Monica felt the blood drain from her face.

"When it got out, he said the whole thing was BS, the girl was jealous and made the story up to cause trouble, rank character assassination, blah blah blah."

Oh, Jesus.

"This was years ago. Different times. Nobody believed her. Besides, Papadakis was an obnoxious jerk, but basically a straight-arrow, pole-up-his-ass kind of jerk and way too ambitious to pull a bonehead move like that."

Silence.

"Hey. Hope I didn't ruin your day."

Monica realized she was gripping the phone so hard her knuckles hurt. "No. No, I'm fine. I'm . . . I'm not that surprised. I guess."

"Yeah," said Sloane. Another brief silence, then: "Hey, this has gotta be costing you a fortune. Ha-ha. Anyway, I should go. Listen, you let me know the moment you get your HAC qual, ya hear? We'll pop corks over the phone!"

"I promise. 'Kay. Love ya, Chub."

"Love ya, Buffy."

The phone went dead.

Monica didn't move.

# 52

Ten days into its southeastern transit from the Gulf to Australia, at 0913 hours, the USS *Abraham Lincoln* crossed the zeroth circle of latitude, officially passing from northern to southern hemisphere and triggering the most sacred, time-honored initiation rite in the US Navy, an all-day bacchanal of festivities commemorating its new sailors' first equatorial passage.

The Crossing of the Line.

Stepping through the open hatch out to the catwalk, Lew Stevens heard the chorus of catcalls and laughter from the flight deck, then a burst of applause and more raucous laughter. The island had been draped with a huge canvas poster, courtesy of PAO office printers, depicting King Neptune with his trident and the slogan *Imperium Neptuni Regis,* in front of which King Neptune himself and his first assistant, Davy Jones— Captain Eagleberg in seaweed wig and Disney-pirate regalia, accompanied by Gaines in an equally ridiculous getup—had taken their regal seats.

Lew stepped out onto the deck and saw scores of young sailors, covered with raw egg and shaving cream and hot sauce and other assorted condiments of ritual abuse, laid out on the deck before the King and his Court.

The time of judgment was nearly at hand.

Lew understood the wisdom behind the silliness. In earlier times this was a full-fledged hazing ritual, a way for seasoned sailors to test their green shipmates and make sure they could handle the hardships of a long sea voyage. In these kinder, gentler days actual hazing had been all but abolished and the Crossing of the Line was mostly pure pageantry, a day of letting off steam, acting like idiots, and boosting morale.

He settled into a spot near the edge of the flight deck to watch as a fresh batch of first-timers was forced to lie down across the deck for whatever indignity came next. As one gang of elder handlers dragged a long tunnel into place, another mob of tormentors started rolling out the fire hoses, ready to hose down the newbies when they emerged from their ritual birth canal.

Lew glanced over and noticed the SEAL, Chief Finn, sitting on his haunches a few feet away, taking it all in with something like fascination. Lew leaned over. "Haven't seen this before?"

The SEAL shook his head. "My WestPac, back in the aughts, we never left the northern hemisphere."

Lew nodded at the unfolding scene. "Quite the spectacle."

The SEAL nodded, eyes on the scene some forty feet away.

The elders began swatting the initiates with short lengths of tubing as they moved to the fore of the ragged line and one by one entered the tunnel to push their way through whatever collection of foul-smelling garbage had been piled in there. Lew had seen it before, but he still marveled. That was some weird kind of baptism.

At that moment the group readying the fire hoses started chanting.

The moment of truth.

As part of the Line Crossing tradition, the term used to denote the more experienced sailors was "shellback," while the initiates were called "pollywogs," so up went the chant:

Pol-ly-wog! Pol-ly-wog!
POL-LY-WOG!! POL-LY-WOG!!
POL-LY-WOG!! POL-LY-WOG!!

Lew chuckled, then glanced over again to make another comment to the SEAL—and stopped.

The man was frozen in place, eyes staring, mouth agape, his face gone white.

Lew frowned. He was about to lean closer and say, "Hey, you okay?" but something held him back. The look on the SEAL's face.

It was pure, raw panic.

Baffled, Lew faced forward again to scan the scene before them. A little raucous, but no more so than your average college dorm hijinks. Lew searched for anything bizarre or unusual that Chief Finn might have spotted, anything so far beyond the pale that it might have prompted such an extreme reaction. But there was nothing there to see. Just a bunch of sailors acting like idiots.

"Pol-ly-wog! *Pol-ly-wog! POL-LY-WOG!!*"

He turned back to look at the man again.

The SEAL was gone.

# 53

Finn sat upright on his rack, back pressed to the bulkhead, rocking forward and back, trying to work his jaw. Took a few long, deep, juddering breaths.

What the hell just happened to him up there?

He tried to think it through, to replay the exact sequence, but his focus kept slipping away like feet on a greased log. The way his fingers had gone slipping off the handholds in that magazine.

He tasted blood in his mouth. He was clenching so hard it felt like he was about to break off all his teeth.

Right hand to jaw, left to chest, he focused on his breathing.

Inhale, exhale.

Slow breath in, slow breath out.

He felt his jaws slowly crank apart. He gingerly opened his mouth, wide as he could, and shut it again, then repeated the movement, working out the soreness.

His throat ached as if he had just screamed at top volume for an hour.

He relaxed his neck. Closed his eyes.

And was suddenly, ferociously gripped by a grotesque sensation.

*A billion wriggling tadpoles surged up from his gut into his throat and raced to explode out the top of his head—*

His eyes snapped open as he reeled back. Drenched in sweat.

What the hell?

He slowed his breathing again and tried once more to retrace his steps. He'd been up on the flight deck, watching the Line Crossing ceremony with its shellbacks and polly—

His throat locked up.

Finn lurched to his feet.

Darkness poured into his field of vision, dotted with spots of luminescence that danced before his eyes and blinded him. He fought his way across the tiny compartment, out into the passageway, and over to the cramped little head across the way.

Kicked open the door, dropped to his knees in front of the toilet, and vomited.

And again.

And again.

And again.

# IV

# Monster

# 54

The four sat on two small couches flanking the low coffee table in the forward area of Jackson's inner sanctum, silent under the weight of their shared confidentiality. Jackson nodded at Scott and said, "Let's start with the *what*."

Scott passed out copies of four stapled sheets to add to the sheaf of pages Jackson had already given them. "Here's a minute-to-minute timeline of the victims' last known movements, best as we have at this point. Tomorrow I'll start reviewing CCTV footage from the flight deck . . ."

In times of trial some men sought solace in the arms of a woman, others by crawling into a bottle. Jackson found comfort in procedure.

He had laid this thing out along classical investigative lines, with three prongs of attack. Define the *what*: what happened, where, when, and how. Compilation of all physical evidence and evaluation of its implications. That was Scott. Then, *who*: build a suspect list, which meant data collection, collation and interpretation, schedules and communications, demographics and psychographics of ship's personnel. Indy. And finally *why*:

develop a profile of their hypothetical killer to focus their suspect pool so they could identify the *who* who did the *what*. That was Lew's domain.

A solid plan. A crack investigative team.

Or a gang of mutineers, depending on how you looked at it.

"Both notes are on plain copier paper," Scott was saying, "and could have been printed on any one of the dozens of printers around the ship, by just about anyone. Including Schofield and Shiflin, for that matter.

"Those with access to the staterooms where the notes were found would've included admin, cleaning crew, anyone in supply. Plus the victims themselves, of course, and their roommates. Schofield and Shiflin would've kept their stateroom keycards on their persons, but since neither body was recovered there's no way of knowing whether the keycards were still on them when they died. In other words, the perpetrator—if there was a perpetrator—could easily have taken their keycards and accessed the staterooms himself."

In other words, thought Jackson, the "suicide" notes were a dead end.

"Speaking to the *how*," Scott continued. "Me, I'd want this to be quick and quiet, and I'd want to avoid leaving any blood trail. That's a challenge. Schofield was a big guy. Shiflin was small but tough. Neither one would've been a pushover."

"Which could explain the hypodermic cap," interjected Indy.

Scott nodded. "If you had the element of surprise you could dope your target right off, or kill him or her outright. Preemptive strike. Easier said than done, though. And you'd need something fast-acting, like fentanyl or propofol. We should run a list of available fast-acting sedatives, check it against inventory at sick bay."

"I'll take that one," said Jackson. He'd ask the general medical officer, whom he knew and trusted. "Anything on the hypo cap itself?"

Scott shook his head. "One hundred percent generic. Could've been used with anything. And we don't have the lab tools to sniff for spectroscopic residue."

Another dead end.

"All right," said Jackson. "On to the *who*." He looked across the coffee table at Indy.

"I've been sifting all incoming and outgoing email." (*Bean* sifting.) "For Kristine Shiflin that is an empty set. She kept to herself, as far as email goes. Sam Schofield wrote quite a lot. He stayed in touch with a few friends, a sister, and two nieces. Tonight I'll expand the search.

"I've also been collating schedules for those known to be on duty at the time, so we can rule them out and narrow the suspect pool."

Here Indy consulted her notes.

"On both nights, flight ops were already over by the time the subjects disappeared, so the entire air wing was mostly off-shift. The bridge is fully staffed at night. So are combat systems, CVIC, and comms. Engineering and maintenance run a good-sized overnight crew. The galley is staffed and running. Most of the rest are pretty much on skeleton. This is a preliminary number, but so far I have a total of four thousand, three hundred seventy."

"That's everyone you've ruled out?" said Jackson.

Indy looked up. "No," she said. "That's everyone we've still ruled in."

The group fell silent for a moment.

Four thousand, three hundred seventy.

Dead end number three.

"I know," she added quietly. "It's a lot of *who*."

"Right," said Jackson. "So we keep refining the funnel. Which brings us to the *why*. Lew?"

Lew Stevens nodded and glanced around the coffee

table. "At this point I've got three avenues of inquiry. Victims, methodology, timing." He held up an index finger. *One*. "The victims."

Even from his position sitting on the little couch across from Jackson, Lew somehow conveyed the impression of a professor pacing before a lecture hall jammed with grad students.

"Both officers, obviously. Both well liked and respected by their peers, which might suggest jealousy from another officer, someone who sees himself on the other side of the scale. Someone disliked, in other words, or not respected. Or it could suggest resentment, for example, from an enlisted person who feels unfairly treated by the upper class. These are broad categories, of course, but it's a start."

He held up his index and middle fingers. *Two*.

"Methodology. The subject took elaborate care to cover his tracks in establishing the suicide cover story. There's nothing especially revealing about that—except the notes themselves, which exhibit a considerable level of intelligence and artifice."

He picked up the top sheet of the little stack in front of him. All four had identical paper stacks, including copies of the suicide notes, notes from Jackson's interviews, the personnel files of both missing officers, and the brief timelines Scott had just handed out. Stevens read from one of the unstapled sheets.

Another day, another dolor. Oh God, I'm so very weary of all of this. Weary to the bone.

He placed the paper back down on the table and picked up a second sheet.

Please tell everyone I am so so sorry to cause them more pain, but shit happens.

"The two notes are strikingly different," Lew continued. "There's no hint of being from the same hand, and they both do a credible job of evoking the personality of the intended author."

"And slipping in and out of both staterooms undetected to plant the notes," said Indy. "That would take a significant level of skill."

"And nerve," added Lew. "All of which suggests not only skills and smarts but also a marked degree of premeditation." He hesitated, then said, "That is, preparation."

Jackson look at him sharply. "Meaning?"

"The execution seems too smooth for ad hoc improvisation. I'm guessing this is not our guy's first rodeo."

There was another brief silence.

"Oh, my," said Indy softly.

Jackson looked at Lew again. "Shiflin's roommate said she'd been unduly stressed, possibly experiencing some harassment. 'Stalking' was the word she used. Did Shiflin come to you at any point for counseling?"

"I wish," said Lew. "But officers avoid coming to medical unless they've got an actively rupturing appendix, and least of all for counseling. It's that zero-defect mentality—as if admitting to any kind of stress would be tantamount to saying they'd got a crack in their fuselage. They'd rather tough it out."

Jackson nodded. This was just as true of chiefs as it was of officers.

"You mentioned timing," said Indy.

"Yes," said Lew. He held up more fingers. *Three.* "Why now? We've been at sea for nearly eight months. What would have triggered these two events to happen now, and in such rapid succession?"

"Couldn't it just be a cumulative thing?" said Indy. "A burning resentment builds and builds, until it reaches the boiling point?"

"Sure. Could be." Lew shrugged. "I've got no conclusions there, it's just one more factor to keep in mind."

Jackson looked around the table. "Questions? All right." He got to his feet, the others following suit. "Let's keep at it. Tomorrow evening, same time." He glanced at Scott, who was frowning. "Scott?" The JAG officer, he noted, had not spoken a word since concluding his own report.

Scott hesitated, then looked at Jackson and said, "Robbie, you sure we're not on a wild-goose chase here?"

Jackson sighed.

Of course he wasn't sure. Not even close. And by running this unauthorized little operation he was risking four good careers. If he was wrong, and they acted, there could be courts-martial in it for all of them.

And if he was right, and they didn't?

Chances were, more people would die.

"Scottie, if it turns out there's nothing there and we're all chasing our tails? I'll be the happiest damn squid in the whole damn bucket."

Indy chuckled softly. "Now, that is something I would pay money to see."

The three men turned to look at her.

She gave another quiet laugh. "Master Chief Jackson—smiling."

## 55

Color drained from the sky, painting the ocean in a palette of pewter and ash.

Finn had found a tiny electronics access sponson, barely big enough for one person to squeeze in. From its tiny catwalk he had climbed out onto a small projection from the ship's hull where he now sat, perched some ten feet above the water's surface, straddling the jut with his legs and gazing out at the darkening ocean. Holding a white plastic bucket with one hand, he reached in with the other and withdrew a small slimy object.

A chicken heart.

He tossed it out into the sea churn.

A huge shape leapt out of the water. There was a harsh *clump* of jaws closing and the thing crashed back into the water.

A swirl of bubbles curled around it and vanished.

Finn had been observing the tiger shark for hours, watching it trail alongside the *Lincoln*, trying to parse just why it was there. Yes, tiger sharks liked to hunt alone, at night, and they favored warm waters. But this far from the shallows? Out in the middle of the ocean? It shouldn't have been there. Yet there it was.

"You're out of your depth," said Finn.

*Says the SEAL who spent an hour this morning hunched over a steel toilet.*

Now the roiling sea surface, with its flicks and curls, reminded Finn of the icing on a big fat chocolate cake.

*A fat slice of chocolate cake on a plate, left on a card table in a dimly lit kitchen. A faint beam of late afternoon sunlight carving through the room, trapping a silent swarm of dust motes—*

Finn shuddered, then blinked, twice.

Early memory? Stray fragment in the gaping bomb crater that was his childhood?

A gust of night breeze stippled the water's surface, the waxing moon a million tiny echoes like an insect's mosaic eye.

Scientists talked about "water memory," the ability of water molecules to retain the impression of dissolved substances even after exhaustive dilution should have erased all traces. The idea defied all current physical and chemical understanding, but homeopathy worked anyway. And poets were thousands of years ahead of the scientists. They'd been talking about the ocean's memory for eons.

*Where is your tribal memory? Sirs, in that gray vault, the sea . . .*

*When water turns ice does it remember one time it was water? . . .*

*Sea-nymphs hourly ring his knell . . .*

Finn leaned back against the ship's steel skin and closed his eyes. Slowly, gingerly, he walked through that morning's sequence of events.

Climbing up onto the deck to watch the Line Crossing. Sitting by the rail, watching. Brief exchange with one or two people. Observing sailors as they went through their sophomoric rituals—and then, *boom!* He was in his broom closet, sitting on his rack and holding his paralyzed jaw.

Two scenes, side by side in his mind, seamless. Here—there. Nothing in between.

Like a skip in an old vinyl LP.

He took another slow breath. Reached into the bucket. This time his fingers found some chicken feet. He tossed them.

The monster leapt, gulped, crashed back into the water.

He brought his thoughts back again to the flight deck that morning. The sailors, the rituals. *Pol-ly-wog. POL-LY—*

He quickly shut that thought down. Looked out at the ocean, breathing in, breathing out, watching the chocolate cake curls.

Without permission, the thought crept back in again. *Pollywog.* What the hell did *that* mean?

But he knew, didn't he.

It meant death.

He had no idea why. But that's what it meant.

Death.

The creature with a massive head and no arms or legs.

Finn reached back in the bucket and his fingers closed on what felt like a slippery, serrated bamboo flute. Chicken neck. He picked it up. This time, instead of tossing it he leaned as far forward as he could and reached out over the water, holding the chicken neck out with his fingertips.

Tiger sharks could grow to twelve, fourteen feet and longer. A thousand pounds plus. He knew this one could take his arm off if it wanted to. And that fucker could jump, he'd just seen that.

Suicidal.

Insane.

He gripped with his thighs and leaned out a few inches farther.

Felt a tug, and his hand was empty.

*Splash—CLUMP—crash*.

Finn slowly withdrew his hand and straightened, his back pressing against the ship's hull again.

He had not even flinched.

He could lower himself down into the water, right here and now, come face-to-face with that tiger shark, armed with nothing but his four-inch ring knife—and he would not be afraid. The shark might kill him. Or not. Either way, he still would not be afraid.

So why was he paralyzed by some childish chant about a tadpole?

Fingers back in the bucket. Nothing left but a slick of guts. He tossed the mostly empty bucket out in front of him. The big tiger shark reared up one last time, then the chocolate icing melted in around it, and it was gone. Like a bad dream.

Like a memory.

# 56

"Is there someplace we could talk?"

She'd been avoiding him for the past day and a half, trying to sort out her feelings. She couldn't afford a romantic entanglement right now, let alone an illicit one. Her HAC had to be front and center, every waking moment. *Eyes on the prize.*

Fine. She knew all that. But right now, this morning, she needed to talk to someone about what Sloane had told her, and who else was there but Scott?

"Sure," said the JAG officer. He picked up his breakfast tray and walked with her to an empty table at the back of the wardroom.

"I talked with my brother last night. In Pensacola . . ." She stopped.

"And how is he?"

She watched Scott take a bite of eggs. The thought of eating nearly made her gag. "He's great."

"Family doing okay? Your mom?"

"Yeah."

She'd lain awake most of the night, waiting for morning so she could come find him and talk. Now that she was here she couldn't get out the words.

She put her hands in her lap and took a breath. "Scott . . . I think I know why Kris was acting weird. I think she'd been assaulted." She didn't dare say by whom.

Scott stopped chewing and stared at her. After a moment he resumed chewing. Then swallowed, speared another bite, and paused. "I'm trying not to say the cliché thing here."

"Monica, you have to stop torturing yourself?" she said.

He smiled. "Monica? You have to stop torturing yourself."

She pinched off a bit of toast, balled it up, and threw it at him. "Predictable, Commander."

He continued eating. "True, though." After a moment he set his fork down and wiped his lips with his napkin. "I want to tell you something." He tapped a knuckle to his titanium leg. "You already know how I got this. You want to hear *why* I got it?"

"I know," she said softly.

She knew the whole story: how his leg was shredded by 7.62 rounds in the same ambush that killed two of his friends; how the docs said they could save the leg but he'd never regain anything like full function; how he'd made the brave decision to go ahead and take the leg off just below the knee, then pushed himself back into fighting shape with his new titanium leg and worked his way back up the officer track.

"So you'd have a shot at getting back into the field. So your friends wouldn't have died for nothing."

He was silent for a moment. "Yep," he said. "That's the story. Wanna hear the truth?" He paused again. "Once the morphine wore off and I saw where I was, lying on a hospital bed in Frankfurt, I started to cry. And I couldn't stop. Every time I looked at that chewed-up scrap of leg, all I could see was those two brothers I left behind, and I couldn't live with the reminder. I begged them to take it off." He looked up at her. "That's it. I didn't *need* to lose the leg. I got rid of it out of pure guilt."

Monica's heart churned with conflicting reactions. She was moved that he would share such an intensely personal confession with her. There was something broken in Scott, something deep inside. She'd sensed it from the day they met. Maybe that was part of what drew her to him.

At the same time, she felt placated—and it pissed her off. He was telling her she needed to stop feeling guilty and "move on."

Move on? Monica? Whose mantra was *Never back down*?

"I get what you're saying," she said gently, "and don't think I don't appreciate what you just told me. But this is different. The firefight that took your friends was completely beyond your control."

Scott sighed.

"No, listen," she said. "I knew Kris was in trouble. I *knew* something was wrong. I should have forced her to talk to me. I can't be positive that would have changed anything, but I sure as hell can't be positive it wouldn't."

Scott pushed his plate to the side and set his elbows on the table. "Hey. This was not your fault." She started to argue but he cut her off. "No, seriously, I mean, factually *not* your fault."

She looked at him sharply. "What do you mean?"

"You just have to trust me on this. You need to let this go."

Her face hardened. "Let this *go*?"

Scott sighed again. "Shit. Okay, listen." His voice dropped to a whisper. "The thing with Kris? It may not have been suicide."

"Like what, maybe she tripped and fell? Jesus, Scott!" Monica grabbed her tray and got to her feet.

"No, wait. Wait." He put out a hand to stop her. "Christ." He looked around, muttered "Shit" once more, then leaned in close. "Listen, this stays between us. I mean, no-shit classified, heads-will-roll-level stays between us. Okay?"

Monica sat back down. "What are you talking about?"

"Okay?"

She nodded. "Okay. No-shit classified."

He leaned closer and whispered. "There's some thinking in play that it may have been a homicide."

Monica's face went blank. In an instant she was back in her stateroom lying on her rack, staring at the overhead in the semidarkness, Kris's voice floating up from the lower bunk.

*Do you feel . . . safe here?*

"Who thinks that?" She spat the words without looking at him. "Based on what?"

Scott leaned back and ran both hands over his face.

Monica glanced around the wardroom—and happened to catch a glimpse of her CO striding in with a tray and taking a seat up front near the door. He hadn't noticed them. She quickly averted her eyes, staring at the wall, the floor, anywhere but in his direction.

Her mind spinning.

Papa Doc?

*Papa Doc?*

Oh, Jesus.

"It's a working hypothesis, all right?" Scott still talking. "That's all I can say. Which I never said, okay?"

Monica didn't hear him. She was back in that passageway outside Kris's ready room, watching the two of them face off. *You know you're supposed to* fly *those things, right? Not play hopscotch with them.*

And what had Monica herself said about that confrontation? That he pushed her too hard. Just like he pushed everyone too hard.

He pushed her.

*He pushed her.*

"Monica?"

She saw exactly how the scene would have gone down. Kris goes out to the catwalk to be alone. Papa Doc follows her out. They exchange words. She tells him she's going to report him for assaulting her. He knows the inquiry will dig up the old Academy rumor. The past will come spilling out. His career is over . . . he'll do prison time. He loses his cool. One aggressive shove—

"Monica?"

"Mmm?"

Scott was watching her, wary. "What are you thinking?"

She finally looked up and met his eyes.

"Nothing," she said. "Nothing at all."

## 57

They were too far away to hear a word, but Finn didn't need audio. He saw her face go rigid. The JAG officer—the captain's own Supercop—had just dropped something major on her. Something highly confidential, judging from his *don't repeat this* posture. And judging from her reaction, something heavy.

He also caught the black look she darted over at Movie Star when he walked in. But she'd controlled herself. Covered her reaction. She might be in love with Supercop, but she didn't exactly trust him. And she was quietly seething with rage at Movie Star. Finn could feel the heat from over here.

If looks could kill.

Finn quietly deposited his breakfast tray and slipped to the exit. As he stepped out of the wardroom a voice called from down the passageway.

"Chief Finn!" He looked around. Stickman, the SAR swimmer. "Hey, Chief, I got your stuff."

The electronic components he'd asked for.

"Outstanding," said Finn.

"If you can swing by avionics in an hour or so, I'll have it bagged up for you."

Finn gave a nod. "Be there in an hour."

Up a few ladders to the gallery deck, through a passageway, and over to his broom closet. Closed the door. Lay on his rack, hands folded behind his head.

Thought his situation through again.

He'd spent the night thinking about it.

Somewhere out there was an incident file on Mukalla. He was in that file. He needed to see it. Needed to know what they were saying about him.

But even if he did work out a way to get through to SOCOM, or WARCOM, or Naval Intelligence, or whomever, they wouldn't talk to him. "Smitty" had made that clear. He was radioactive. A leper.

He needed to find someone else to do it for him.

Master Chief Jackson?

If there was anyone outside the captain's immediate sphere who could get his hands on that incident file, it would most likely be the CMC. And a telling detail about Jackson: in their interview, he had never asked Finn anything about that hypo cap he'd handed him. Never even mentioned it.

Which was interesting.

Maybe he, like West Texas the helo pilot, didn't entirely trust Supercop. Which, if so, made Finn *more* inclined to trust Jackson, not less. Finn wouldn't have trusted Supercop, either. Too much hostility.

And here was the clincher: Finn had something Jackson needed. Jackson had said so himself.

*A sniper is first and foremost an intelligence asset.*

Good. Jackson it was.

He would set it in motion the next morning at chow.

Meanwhile, he had a second problem to solve. Which called for help on yet another front.

He needed an expert opinion.

# 58

"How can I help?" Lew Stevens pulled up an empty chair to face his own.

Finn closed the door to the psychologist's office and took the offered seat.

"I have this friend," he said.

Stevens sat back. "Tell me about your friend's issue."

Finn told him. A ringing in the ears, numbness of fingers. Disproportionate response to a trivial event. An unexplained gap in memory.

"My friend is wondering if there could be some organic issue," he said. "And how one would tell."

"Organic, like a brain tumor?"

"Or MS. ALS. Parkinson's. Whatever."

"Has your friend had other unexplained memory lapses?"

Finn hesitated. "Once or twice. At least. Probably more like five, six times. Nothing dramatic, just brief time spans with no recall."

"Like the tape was erased," suggested Stevens.

"More like a lightbulb that's not fully screwed in. So it occasionally flickers or blinks out for no evident reason. Like an incipient short in the wiring."

"Good description. Your friend is observant." Stevens thought for a moment. "You asked about organic causation. That's possible. MS, ALS, they're basically shorts in the wiring. But it could just as easily be psychological."

Finn frowned. "The numb fingers?"

"Psychologically based physical symptoms can follow symbolic rather than anatomical pathways. Someone who can't bear to see something that evokes a particular trauma, say, may go 'blind.' And it's real, they truly cannot see. Yet if you ask them to walk over to a window and put a chair in the way, they'll walk around the chair."

Finn thought about that, then nodded. "Okay."

"Let's try something. Mind if I run a quick mental status exam, ask a few standard questions?"

"My friend isn't here."

"You can answer for him."

Finn considered that, then nodded again. "Go."

"Does your friend feel like the room is spinning, or that *he* is spinning?"

"No."

"Any double vision?"

"No."

"Atypical clumsiness, reeling, falling over, like that?"

Finn thought about falling from the ladder in the flare magazine. But that wasn't lack of coordination. His fingers just stopped working.

"No."

"Can your friend tell me what day, month, and year it is?"

He did.

"Count backward from one hundred, counting by sevens?"

Finn did so, stepping back through 93, 86, 59, 52, and 45 before the psychologist stopped him.

"Okay," said Stevens. "Question: If I said, 'A rolling stone gathers no moss,' and asked for an interpretation, what would your friend say?"

"He'd probably say it means people who are always on the move never form healthy attachments."

Stevens nodded.

"Proving?"

"Not proof. It's a pretty imprecise test. But someone with an organic brain dysfunction might tend to interpret the proverb in a more concrete way. People who move around a lot don't collect a lot of stuff, maybe. Like college students. Whereas someone with a serious psychiatric disorder, like schizophrenia or psychosis, might interpret it more literally: the stone's moving too fast for moss to attach to it."

Finn thought about that, then nodded once more. "Which leaves us where?"

"We can't rule out an organic causation without real testing. Nor the possibility that your friend has a genuine thought disorder, such as schizophrenia."

"Or psychosis."

"Or psychosis. But if I had to take a running jump at it, I'd say you're looking at an episodic anxiety associated with some sort of lacunar amnesia."

"Lacunar."

"Memory lapse over a discrete interval. A gap. Psychologists call them 'lacunae.'"

"Which would be caused by?"

"The mind knows how to wall off a traumatic event, encapsulating it to protect the rest of the system. Much like the body cordons off an abscess."

"It dissociates," said Finn.

"It dissociates," Stevens agreed. "When something gets close to or touches upon the traumatic event, like some sensory or emotional trigger, the subject might respond with heightened anxiety and a whole range of symptoms without knowing why. It might seem wholly irrational."

Finn frowned.

"I'm sure your friend's considered the obvious," said Stevens.

"PTS." *Shell shock,* they used to call it before the age of acronyms. Finn slowly shook his head. "Don't think so."

"That is the logical first place to look. Assuming your friend is, like you, a SEAL who's probably seen a good deal of war, this wouldn't be a surprising consequence."

Finn put his head down for a moment, thinking. Then looked up.

"I've been in the field for close to two decades," he said. "More or less continuously. I've seen a lot of terrible things. Some too terrible to put into words."

"Happens in war," said Stevens.

They were silent for a moment.

They had both seen terrible things.

"But I can pull up every single one, with total clarity," Finn added softly. "In detail. I couldn't honestly describe any as walled off, or buried, or repressed. Some were so horrific, no sane person would want to hear about them, or even know about them. But I can think back over every one, replay each one in my mind. Doesn't even raise my heartbeat."

Stevens nodded. "Well," he said. "Maybe those are just the ones you remember."

# 59

*Just the ones you remember.*

Finn sat at the foot of his rack and spread out the items Stickman had procured for him. Two little component frames, designed to hold a pair of AAA batteries. A jeweler's tool kit, including a few tiny screwdrivers, a miniature pair of pliers, wire cutters, and tweezers. A small soldering iron. A jeweler's magnifying headset. To which he now added a pocket digital recorder he'd brought on board with him and a roll of duct tape from the ship's store.

He slipped on the magnifying headset and picked up the first component, a miniature amplifier. Removed each of the tiny screws that held the case together and pulled it gently apart. Removed the circuit board and placed the empty casing pieces to the side.

*An incipient short in the wiring.*

Next he unsoldered the wires leading to the amplifier's two tiny microphones, extended them several inches and resoldered them, then located the power wires and extended those and connected the free ends to one of the AAA battery frames.

He set the device down, picked up a second component—a mini-transmitter—and repeated the procedure, removing the board from its case and extending its power wires, then attaching those, too, to the AAA battery holder, using heat-shrink tubing wherever he made connections to prevent shorts.

He plugged the two components together, then set that whole assembly to the side. Now he turned his attention to the next bit of electronics, a miniature receiver, and began disassembling that one.

Once the miniature receiver's innards were exposed, he picked up his little digital recorder and began peeling the electronic meat out of its shell.

*Has your friend had other memory lapses?*

It had started two weeks earlier, with that botched raid in Mukalla. They breached the compound, found themselves staring at nothing but smoke—and his next clear memory was of waking up the following morning at daybreak, lying on the ground on his Gore-Tex blanket back at their base camp.

Finn's memory was among his most precious assets, possibly the most powerful weapon in his sniper's tool kit. Far more than being able to aim and shoot a rifle, it was his abnormal talent for observation, storage, and retrieval that caused SOCOM to pour a small fortune into training, equipping, and deploying him.

The other guys in Spec Ops training had to work like fiends to develop their powers of observation and recall. Building memory muscle was a critical part of sniper training, and he'd watched his teammates struggle. Not him. For Finn, it was just there. Among the teams he was known for it. Legendary, even.

A memory prodigy with holes in his memory.

*Fucked-up mass of contradictions.*

He set the finished assembly down on his bunk, went over to his locker, and retrieved a thick, leather-bound volume he'd persuaded Olivia, the writer at the PAO office, to "loan" him from their reference library.

Did he miss something critical that night in Mukalla? *See* something critical? Some pivotal footage buried in that hours-long trench between crashing into the empty building and lurching awake the next morning?

He opened the big book, picked up his steel ring knife, and began slicing into the pages.

# 60

Lew Stevens swiveled slowly in his desk chair, gazing at the anthropological artifacts that graced the bulkheads of his office as he mused about his odd visitor.

Situated by itself down a short passageway around the corner from the main medical suite, Lew's office had been dubbed "the museum wing" by some medical wit for the series of tribal masks on display there: a Maori *haka* mask, an ancient Etruscan death mask, a Japanese *ko-omote* Noh drama mask, a Hopi ceremonial *katsina* mask, and a number of others.

This was Lew's fascination. Happily for him, it was also his job: decoding masks. Not, as most laymen might assume, to dig behind the mask in hopes of finding the "real person," but to decipher the mask itself, why it was there, its purpose to the wearer. What Lew understood was that masks were for most people not a way to conceal but a way to express. The "real person" didn't hide behind the mask so much as he or she sought to make sense of their world and their place in it *through* the mask.

And this SEAL wore one seriously intriguing mask.

Like Indy, Lew had been curious about the SEAL

from the day he boarded the *Lincoln*. He, too, had been poking around, looking into his military record, which was unusual to say the least. But that strange encounter on the flight deck? The man's bizarre reaction to the Line Crossing ritual?

Just what the heck was that all about? And was it connected to the memory gaps?

He pulled out a small notebook and looked up the number of a colleague, a Navy psychologist in Coronado. He entered the number, heard two rings, then a familiar voice.

"Dan Van Ness. Hold for the beep, then state your case."

Lew held for the beep.

"Dan, hi, it's Lew Stevens. Listen, I'm calling from the USS *Abraham Lincoln*. Looking for some background on an active-duty SEAL, goes by the singular name of Finn, last posted to Black Squadron Echo Platoon in the Gulf. Looking for any unusual issues, early history, treatments, et cetera. Appreciate it, Dan. You can reach me here on the *Lincoln*."

He hung up the phone and leaned back in his chair. Swiveled around, looking again at his collection of masks.

Lew Stevens had seen a lot of deeply troubled souls in his twenty-odd years as a psychologist. One thing he'd observed consistently was that everyone, no matter how conflicted or scarred, was the hero of their own story. And everyone had a story. One's story was one's mask, as expressed over the dimension of time. Or to put it the other way round, the mask was simply the story encapsulated. To unwrap the mask was to unravel the story.

Most stories, in Lew's experience, were fairly transparent. A rare few were so opaque they were almost impossible to read. He suspected Finn's story was such a case.

Still, he knew early trauma when he saw it.

## 61

**Midrats.** *Act normal.*

Monica moved down the food line, placing a few items on her tray. Taking her time, she wove through the tables and found an empty spot next to a quiet, studious-looking pilot.

Alan Rickards. Flew one of the air wing's gigantic E-2 Hawkeyes. The E-2 was a long-distance radar detection craft, not a fighter, and the Hawkeye pilots were less showy than their fighter jet cousins. Monica knew Rickards by reputation; a serious but easygoing guy. Well liked by his peers.

She took the seat next to him, pulled her fat NATOPS manual from under her arm, and plopped it down next to her tray. Took a bite of her late-night snack.

Rickards nodded at the manual. "Need directions to study hall?"

She grinned. "I know, it's a little hard-core." She took another bite and turned a page.

"Cramming in every minute you can spare. Remember it well," he said.

They went on like that for a few minutes, back and forth. She admitted that she was nervous about getting through the next few weeks leading to her checkride. That her CO was one seriously tough boss. She mentioned his name.

Rickards laughed. "I'm not surprised."

"No?" she said.

"Papadakis and I were in the same class at the Academy."

"Really," she said—although that was precisely the reason she'd tracked him down. "I had no idea. So you know him."

"Oh yeah," said Rickards.

"Sometimes it feels like he's, I don't know, tougher on those of us who are women."

Rickards smiled. "To be honest, that doesn't surprise me, either. Nikos was never a guy you'd accuse of being *woke*. Not that we had that term in those days." Warming to the topic. "Contrary to popular belief, though, we weren't all Neanderthals. I mean, everyone knows the stories, Tailhook and all that. People assume it was systemic."

He took a bite and frowned as he chewed.

"I'm here to tell you, it was not systemic. There were some jerks. Quite a few jerks, actually." He swallowed. "But when that kind of ugly stuff went down, you know what, we hated it as much as anyone. Hey, I've got sisters. I've got a mom." He shook his head. "That was some ugly stuff."

They ate in silence for a moment.

*So far, so good.*

"Was there," she began, then she paused and started over. "When you were there, was there anything, I don't know, weird, or off, in terms of how he treated women?"

Rickards's demeanor changed instantly. "Off, how?" Cautious.

"I don't know," she said, "just, any scuttlebutt about

stuff he did, anything specific you heard about? Off the record?"

His eyes narrowed. "Such as?"

It felt like the room temperature had just cooled ten degrees.

"I just, nothing specific, I guess I just wondered, if there were any rumors, or talk, about how he got along with his female classmates, or—"

Rickards cut her off. "I'm sure you'll be judged on merit, Lieutenant. You've got nothing to worry about."

"Of course," she said quickly. "I'm sure you're right." She felt her face go red. Thank God for the low lights at midrats. "I've heard my NATOPS officer is a super-nice guy. What was it like for you, your first checkride?"

She managed to steer the conversation back to aviation and current events aboard the *Lincoln*. After a minute or two she even tried to nudge them back toward the Academy days again, but it went nowhere. Rickards had closed up shop, pulled down the steel shutters for the night.

After another few minutes the Hawkeye pilot stood, bade her a cordial good night, and left.

Monica felt almost nauseous, in part from the adrenaline aftermath and in part out of sheer relief that the conversation was over. Mostly, though, from that sickeningly familiar sense of boys closing ranks.

Guys protecting guys.

Rickards seemed like a decent enough person.

She didn't believe him for a second.

# 62

When he didn't see CMC Jackson at Chief's Mess the next morning, Finn headed above to check in general mess. Sure enough, there he was, sitting alone: reading, eating, greeting passersby.

"This seat taken?" said Finn. Without waiting for a reply, he sat down in the next seat over and went to work on his breakfast. Oats, sardines from a can. Spring water.

They ate in silence for a minute.

Finn spoke first. "Come here often?"

Jackson grunted. Finn guessed that was as close as he got to a laugh.

"Food's better down in CPO mess," Finn commented.

Jackson nodded. "This is true," he said. He took another bite of whatever it was they were calling "breakfast hash."

Finn gestured vaguely at the space with his spoon. "I'm guessing you eat here now and then just to keep your thumb on the pulse." It was highly unusual for chiefs to eat with the enlisted ranks, practically taboo. The fact that Jackson did it anyway impressed him.

"No better place," agreed Jackson. He glanced over

at Finn's tray. Withheld comment. Not a sardine fan, Finn's guess.

"Pulse seems like it's running a little ragged today," said Finn. "Not so popular, the whole skipping-Malaysia thing."

"True again," said Jackson. "Say, you're good at this."

"This?"

"Small talk."

Finn took a bite, chewed, swallowed. "You too," he said.

The two ate in silence.

Finally Jackson spoke up again. "Tell me something? Why just the one name."

Mid-bite, Finn took a moment. "Never knew my parents' last name."

Jackson nodded. "Foster names?"

"A bunch. None stuck." He lifted his shoulders in a shrug. "So Finn it was."

"And they let you get away with that?"

"When I enlisted they said I had to list a last name. So I put 'X.'"

Jackson looked at him. "You're shitting me. That's it? Finn X?"

"That's it."

Jackson shook his head. "Finn X."

Finn heard someone walking toward him from behind. Heavy treads. A single quiet cough: *ark!*

Tucker walked by with his tray, glowering at Finn as he passed. Finn figured he didn't dare bark more overtly with the CMC sitting there.

"Friend of yours?" said Jackson, without looking up.

"Sparring partner," said Finn.

Jackson grunted. Another few seconds passed in silence. Then Finn said, "So how goes the investigation?"

"'Scuse me?" Now Jackson looked up.

Finn shook some pepper onto a sardine and popped it in his mouth.

The CMC sighed. "If I were investigating anyone, I'd probably start with you, Finn X. They say you're all over the ship, asking questions everywhere. A regular Joe Friday."

Finn nodded. "I think your captain thinks I've been put here to spy on him."

Jackson looked surprised, then thoughtful. "Maybe he's right."

Finn gave a soft chuckle and glanced sideways at the other man. After a moment he said, "You don't smile much, do you."

Jackson took another bite. "So you're, what, like a wandering samurai? Down these mean streets, and so on? Looking for justice, Finn X?"

"Justice isn't really my thing."

"Well now that prompts the question, doesn't it. What exactly *is* your thing?"

Finn took a long drink of water. Set the glass down. Then said, "Commodities."

"Commodities."

Finn went back to his oats and fish.

"Like orange juice?" prompted Jackson. "Coffee, pork bellies?"

"Something like that."

*Commodities.*

He could see Jackson wondering what on God's green earth *that* was supposed to mean but not about to give Finn the satisfaction of asking. Instead, he put his knife down and pointed at Finn with his fork. "It occurs to me that you were one of the last people to see Lieutenant Shiflin alive. *The* last person to see Schofield alive, far as we know. You wouldn't happen to be the angel of death, would you, Mister Finn?"

"Just—"

"Just Finn, I know." Jackson sat, waiting the other man out.

Finn took another bite. "I see a lot. It's—"

"It's what snipers do?"

Finn saluted him with his fork, scooped up the last sardine. Stood up with his empty tray, said, "Good talk," and walked off.

He'd sunk the hook. That should be enough.

On to the next op.

# 63

If you observed this passageway often enough, as Finn had, you began to learn its rhythms. Right now mess was over, morning shifts were fully staffed, people had settled into their routines. Traffic on the gallery level was light. It was never fully deserted, but every so often there would come a lull long enough that you could stand in one spot and experience five or six seconds of solitude.

Finn had timed it in his mind. Five or six seconds was all he needed.

He strolled down the passageway, past the captain's suite. A few doors down he reversed course. By the time he passed back that way again he was alone.

He set his mental timer to zero and clicked into action—

—reached over and punched in the sequence of digits he'd watched a steward enter on the security keypad

—quickly glanced up and down the passageway

—cracked open the door

—slipped inside

—pulled the door shut behind him

—and stopped his mental timer—

Five and a half seconds.

He snaked across the small anteroom, oozed through that door and into the captain's parlor. Took a slow breath, listening to the silence. Looked around, taking it all in.

He saw why they called it the "Lincoln Room." The place was decked out like a museum exhibit of nineteenth-century life. Dark hardwood furnishings, period wallpaper, the whole nine yards.

Finn slipped the go bag off his shoulder and set it on the parquet mahogany coffee table. Approached a big bookshelf set against one bulkhead and surveyed its contents. Crouched down to examine the big leather-bound volumes on the bottom shelf.

Carl Sandburg's six-volume biography *Abraham Lincoln: The Prairie Years and the War Years*. Evans and Grossnick's *United States Naval Aviation, 1910–2010*, the definitive two-volume work on the subject. John Darrell Sherwood's *War in the Shallows: U.S. Navy Coastal and Riverine Warfare in Vietnam, 1965–1968*. Off to the right a few lesser paperbacks, popular leadership stuff.

Curious, he pulled out one of the cheaper books. *Patton on Leadership: Strategic Lessons for Corporate Warfare*. Dozens of pages were marked with meticulous underlinings and marginal notes. The paperback fell open to a page with this gem highlighted:

You are not beaten until you admit it. Hence don't.

Captain Eaglebeak's bedtime stories.

He slid the book back into place, stood, crossed over to the mahogany sideboard. A crystal brandy set. Looked expensive. He removed the stopper and sniffed. Cognac. Nightcap of champions.

A faint glint from floor level caught his eye. He replaced the crystal stopper in the decanter and bent down to take a closer look. Tucked down against one of the sideboard legs was a tiny shard of glass. He fished it out with the corner of his Navy Cash card, stood up, and examined it. Looked over at the crystal brandy glasses again. Three of them. Finn was pretty sure glasses like these would come in sets of two, or four. Not three.

Which meant one broke.

He thought back to a scene he'd observed a few days earlier, Jackson emerging from the Lincoln Room looking steamed. Must have been quite the argument.

Finn walked slowly along that bulkhead, examining the various wall hangings. The nineteenth-century navigational maps. The Andrew Jackson portrait. A framed deployment patch with three lines of lettering:

WestPac 2003

CVN-72 CVW-14

GET OVER IT!

He'd heard the background.

In the late fall of 2002 Eagleberg was serving as ship's XO right there on the *Lincoln*, supporting the one-year-old effort in Afghanistan. They steamed down to Australia on their way home—exactly as they were doing right now—and pulled into Perth for a well-earned port call, at which point they got new orders: they weren't going home after all. They were turning the boat around. It was time to go back and kick Saddam's ass.

The crew was upset. They'd been at sea long enough. Their strike group commander got on the 1MC and addressed the grumbling head-on. "We don't need to be back home holding our loved ones," he barked over the ship-wide PA system. "We need to be right here holding the line. So *get over it*!"

The *Lincoln*'s official motto was "Shall Not Perish," from the Gettysburg Address; it was painted onto the side of the ship in ten-foot letters. Ever since that announcement, though, this had become their other motto, the unofficial one.

"Get Over It!"

Hence the patch.

This mattered to the captain, mattered enough that he'd had it framed and placed here. Finn bent close, looked at the frame tops of the hangings on either side, then back at the framed patch again. The dust on this one had been disturbed.

The piece had been recently handled.

The captain wanted to relive the glory days of Operation Iraqi Freedom.

And down in the bomb assembly room, Tom Sawyer and his pals were running drills. *We're supposed to pick up the pace,* Tom had said. *Warheads on foreheads.*

Those steel-gray eyes, that eagle's claw of a nose.

The captain had a hard-on for some action.

His deployment was going to shit. His leadership style, if you could call it that, had made the crew brittle. Vulnerable. Now people were dying.

He was losing control of his ship and he knew it. Solution? Reassert control. Go to war.

*You are not beaten until you admit it. Hence don't.*

Whatever mess was happening on the captain's watch right now, taking part in a major military action would overshadow it. History—and his superiors—would overlook this tour's first eight disastrous months and he would be the navy's equivalent of a made man.

Finn thought about the delay in getting out of the Gulf, the talking heads on CNN. Was the Iran threat real? Didn't matter—the captain wanted it to be real. He was hoping to be called up, have his ship pressed back into service. That's what the change of course was about.

That's what the argument was about.

The captain wanted to haul ass to Australia, replenish, then turn around and steam back to the Gulf to go kick Khameini's ass. And bury his shitty record in a fireball of glory.

The CMC had probably wanted to bring someone in to investigate the "suicides." NCIS. FBI maybe. The captain said no. He wanted his crew to *get over it*.

The master chief wanted to protect his people.

The captain wanted to protect his record.

Which made him dangerous.

Small men in high places.

Finn began moving through the space again, examining every shelf and drawer, nook and notch. When he was finished he slipped back out and into the passageway, go bag back on his shoulder, leaving everything exactly as he'd found it.

Or *almost* exactly.

# 64

Monica was in the open space of hangar bay 3 going over a helo when she heard Scott's voice, a single clipped syllable. *"Hey."* She pulled her head out of the engine. One look confirmed what she'd heard in his voice: he was furious.

"Somewhere we can talk?" He practically spat the words.

She nodded in the direction of the stern, then walked aft through the hangar bay and into the empty jet engine shop. She pulled up a stool, turned to face him, and sat. "Hey?"

Scott took his time pulling over a stool and sitting before he looked at her. "So," he said after a brittle pause. "I just came from a brief chat with your flight surgeon. Who just came from having a brief chat with Alan Rickards."

Monica closed her eyes. Shit.

"Monica. Just what the *fuck* were you thinking?"

"Hang on a sec—"

"Are you actively *trying* to torpedo your fucking career? Can you even imagine what kind of hell your life would be if Alan had gone straight to Papadakis instead of your flight doc? Who by the way deserves a fucking Albert Schweitzer humanitarian award for keeping this between us and not taking it to CAG!"

Monica felt her face flush—shame? fury? maybe both? "Listen, I'm sorry this blew back on you—"

"You're *sorry*? Christ, Monica, this was way, *way* over the top—"

Monica raised her voice to speak over his. "*I'm sorry this blew back on you* and I'm grateful for their discretion—" Scott wasn't listening to a word, just shaking his head "—but all I was doing was asking—"

"Monica, you've got to stop this—"

"*All I was doing was asking about a rumor I'd heard!*"

They both stopped and glared at each other.

"A credible rumor," she added.

Scott closed his eyes and kept them closed as he spoke, low and measured. "Listen. I know how much this whole thing hurts. She was your friend. I get it. But you've got to leave it alone. Besides," he lowered his voice even more, "Papadakis is not a credible suspect."

"Well who is?"

"Jesus, Monica, I can't tell you that, and you shouldn't be asking!" He paused. "No one is. There are no suspects, not at this point. It's just a theory, and a damn shaky one. The more we look for hard evidence, the more there's none there."

"No you don't, goddammit." Now it was Monica's turn to shake her head. "You don't drop this ten-megaton bomb on me and then come back twenty-four hours later and try to take it back!"

"I'm not—" He stopped, took a breath, and lowered his voice again. "I'm not trying to take anything back. I'm just—Christ, I shouldn't have said anything." He sat back on his stool. "I couldn't stand to see you sitting around blaming yourself. But I'm not kidding, the whole idea is no more than a sketchy hypothesis based on evidence that's about as strong as a piece of wet Kleenex. *There's nothing there.*"

"No." She shook her head again. "I don't care what evidence you have or don't have. I've been thinking about this for the past twenty-four hours, and it's the only thing that makes sense. Swallowing a handful of pills, that I can see her doing. Putting the barrel of a sidearm in her mouth and pulling the trigger—"

"Jesus, Monica—"

"No, *listen to me,* dammit! I can see those or a dozen other scenarios. But jumping overboard? Intentionally committing herself to the water? *Kris?*" She started poking him in the chest to punctuate the words. "No. No way. She would have been too terrified."

"Didn't seem to me like she was afraid of anything."

"*You didn't know her!*"

Scott put up both hands. "Hey."

"Sorry." She realized how loud she'd gotten and lowered her voice to a hush. "I'm sorry. But you didn't *know* her, Scott." Her eyes welled up.

Scott put his hands on her shoulders. "Hey," he said softly. "Listen. We'll figure out what happened to Kris. Trust me. But the most important thing right now is securing your HAC. Right? And not doing anything that jeopardizes that. Okay?"

Scott leaned in closer, gripping her arms.

And kissed her.

Monica was so caught off guard she didn't react, or even know how to react.

The kiss went on, and it went deeper, his tongue exploring the inside of her mouth, the warmth of his lips intoxicating, the smell of his skin filling her nostrils. His hands were behind her now, pressing into her back, his arms encircling her, and she felt herself dissolve into the inexpressible comfort of being held. A part of her longed to let go altogether and be wholly consumed. She couldn't breathe. She didn't *want* to breathe.

She placed both hands on his chest and gave a push.

Scott backed away, putting his palms up in that *Hey I surrender* gesture again. "Sorry. I'm sorry. I shouldn't have done that."

It was the apology that did it.

And that gesture—all innocence and plausible deniability.

He was *sorry*? What, he momentarily lost control? No—anyone else, maybe, but not Scott. She knew him well enough to know that "Oops, I didn't mean to" was not a gear in his drive shaft.

It was the first thing he'd ever said to her that rang false, and it hit her like a slap in the face. He was placating her again. Trying to get her to back down.

Not a gear in *her* drive shaft.

All at once that messy tangle of feelings fell away, all sorted and clear now.

She was not about to flirt with disaster by slipping into some kind of onboard romance. She couldn't afford the distraction. She liked Scott, liked him a lot. But she needed to stay focused and on task.

Someone had killed her friend, goddammit. And if Scott wouldn't help her nail the bastard, she'd find someone who would.

"Scott," she said, her voice husky with emotion. "You're a wonderful man, and a good friend. But . . . back off."

## 65

Lew Stevens was late to work that morning, and because of it he nearly missed what would prove to be a highly consequential phone call.

Normally Lew was in at 0700 sharp, a half hour before the medical offices opened. This morning, though, he'd spent some time meeting off-site with a junior pilot who was having anxiety issues and wanted to avoid a recorded visit to medical.

This was a delicate matter. Visits to the staff psychologist were supposed to be a disclosure item for the squadron's flight surgeon, but any psychological issue could be viewed as cause to temporarily suspend one's UP status for flight. A career killer. Lew understood this, which was why he didn't mind spending a quiet hour with someone out of the office—and off the books—when such situations arose.

He was still thinking about the young man's disquiet when he heard his phone ringing through his office door. He hurriedly keyed in the four-digit code, let himself in, set his tall Americano down, and picked up the phone on the fourth ring. "Stevens."

"Lew? Van Ness here," said the voice.

"Dan! Thanks for getting back to me." He did the quick calculation: 0830 there meant it would be 5:30 p.m. on the West Coast. He was surprised Van Ness was still in his office.

"Well, you almost missed me. Heading out in a few minutes. For good, in fact."

"You're kidding."

"Hey. Put in my twenty, figured I'd get out and go into private practice while I still have a few marbles rolling around. So, not to be rude, but may I cut to the chase? Got your man's enlistment records in front of me."

"Fantastic," said Lew.

"Don't get too excited," the voice replied. "I'll give you what I have, but there's not a lot and what there is isn't great. No family background. Finn X, listed as an orphan on his sign-up papers, no extant contact info for foster homes. Kid had been on his own for a few years, in and out of trouble on the Southern California docks. Worked as crew on a few dive boats, in between stints on the streets."

"Tough life for a teenager."

"Tough." Van Ness snorted. "That's one way to put it. Street life in those neighborhoods? In those days? Jesus Van Christ. Picking your way through a 3D chessboard of drug kingpins, Chinese mafia, and bent cops. Most of the kids he hung with would've ended up in jail, chronic rehab, or the morgue."

"But not him."

"Not him. He managed to stay straight and vertical." He paused.

"But?" said Lew.

He heard the other man sigh. "There's something fractured about the guy, Lew. Jesus, I'd love to run an fMRI on that brain."

"Fractured, how?"

"He'll go into these lulls where he seems zoned out, almost comatose, like there's nothing going on inside. Only the feeling you get is it's really the opposite, right? Like *everything's* going on in there. Tick, tick, tick. Part of what made him such a phenomenal operator."

Lew thought for a moment. "Weren't you on the board that made recommendations on DEVGRU candidates during that time?"

"Sure was."

"So you recommended him?"

"Sure didn't. I recommended in the strongest terms that he be flushed. I don't know what unit he ended up in, where he is or what he's doing now, but I can tell you this: it ain't good. The guy is damaged, Lew."

Lew nodded to himself. "Any ideas on what's behind that?" he asked.

"Unfortunately, that's all I got. You might want to talk to Harry Holbrook, the shrink up at Great Lakes who would've been on staff when he went through basic."

He gave Lew the man's name and number.

After hanging up with Van Ness, Lew tried the Illinois number, asked for Harry Holbrook, and learned that the man was off on a late-summer fishing trip. Lew left a brief message and his callback number, and hung up.

Lew Stevens spent a good deal of his time inside other people's heads, which could be a strange place to explore, even terrifying at times. But Lew enjoyed the adventure of charting the shadowy territories, puzzling out explanations for the inexplicable. Identifying the monsters that lurked under people's beds.

And right now what interested him most was whatever monster lurked behind the puzzle of Finn.

*The guy is damaged, Lew.*

Just *how* damaged?

# 66

He'd been out on the big portside Gatling gun mount for about an hour, watching the ocean and sketching, when West Texas pushed her way out through the door behind him and plunked herself down on the narrow catwalk a few feet away.

"Just so you know," she said, "far as I can see all SEALs are arrogant, self-absorbed pricks. Worse than male fighter pilots."

They both sat silent for a minute. No sounds but the wind and the faint scratch of his charcoal pencil on the paper.

"Glad we got that out of the way," said Finn.

She seemed to hesitate a moment, weighing her next move. Finally she said, "I need your help."

"I doubt that," said Finn. "You didn't need any help with that big guy in the gym."

"Tucker? He's not that big."

Finn couldn't help smiling. He watched the ocean and sketched. Whatever it was she came to say, she would say it eventually.

"On the ranch, when I was little, there was this particular horse. A little blue roan. Amelia. For most of my childhood she was my closest companion on the planet."

On her twelfth birthday, she told him, they were out riding when a rattlesnake spooked them both. Amelia reared up and came back down hard. Too hard. It broke her leg and she had to be put down. Monica's daddy was up in Amarillo for the day, so her big brother, Sloane, did it. Monica was heartbroken—and spitting mad. She took a machete and went after the snake on foot.

"At twelve you knew how to hunt with a machete?" said Finn.

"I'm a fast learner."

She tracked down the snake, whacked off its head, then hacked its body into pieces. Her mother was horrified. Her daddy didn't say a word when he got home, but a week later she overheard him telling his friends about it. "And *that's* how we do it in West Texas," he said, and they all laughed with him.

Finn went on sketching, eyes never leaving the horizon.

"There's a rattlesnake on board this ship," said Monica. "I want it." She glanced at him. Then she said, low and fierce: "He killed my friend."

Finn looked over at her for a moment, then went back to sketching. "Sounds like a job for NCIS."

"Nobody's calling in NCIS, far as I can see."

"Talk to your chain of command."

"Not really an option."

"So why come to me?"

"You're a SEAL."

He slowly shook his head. "Not my fight."

This was true, technically speaking. Although not really. It had become his fight the day Schofield went missing. But he didn't see how getting her involved would help the situation.

She sat silent for a moment, watching him. "You have any brothers or sisters?"

Finn's hand paused for a long beat, then continued. "One brother. Ray."

"Is Ray a SEAL, too?"

Finn shook his head. "He left that to me. Moved on to bigger and better things."

"Parents?"

He shook his head again. "Dead."

"Sorry to hear that."

Finn glanced at her, then back at the ocean. "They died when I was a kid. I hardly remember them."

"Grandparents?"

"Negative."

"So it's just you and Ray."

"Just Ray and me."

She sat silent for another moment. Then turned to face him again. "I never had a sister. Brothers, but no sister. My friend Kris, who disappeared last week? *She* was my sister." She kept looking at him. When he didn't reply she spoke again in that same low fierce tone: "If someone killed Ray, what would *you* do?"

Finn stopped. He set his pad and charcoal pencil down on the catwalk grating and turned to look her full in the face, eyeball to eyeball.

Five seconds ticked by.

He turned back to the horizon. "Not my fight."

She was silent, but he could feel her simmering fury. Finally she got up and walked back into the interior of the ship without another word. As she pulled the big hatch behind her Finn added one more comment.

"It wasn't your CO."

She froze for a moment. "How—?" Finn could practically hear the unvoiced question. How did he know she suspected her CO? But she stopped herself at the one word. After a moment, she shut the hatch.

Finn picked up the pad and looked at what he'd drawn.

Night scene, heat lightning. Shattered door.

He stared at it for a moment.

*Lacunae.*

He tore off the sheet, crumpled it into a ball, tossed it overboard into the sea, and began again.

# 67

Jackson's dinner, brought up to his office that evening, sat untouched on his coffee table, the master chief buried in his fourth reread of their interview notes.

A little Adderall dealing, the occasional fistfight, people caught with their hands in each other's pants; that stuff happened all the time. There was as much petty theft on board a naval warship as in any small city. Welcome to the human comedy. But homicide? Jesus. How were they supposed to deal with that?

He rifled back through the pages, then tossed them on the coffee table and sank back. What they needed was hard, tangible evidence. Something that would take them logically from point A to point B to point C. Which was exactly what they did *not* have. No suspects, no witnesses, no weapons, no bodies. They were grasping at smoke.

He glanced over at the God's eyes gracing the office bulkheads.

Divine surveillance.

"If this were a city murder," he said aloud, "it'd all be so damn easy."

Five'd get you ten the guy got robbed for money.

CCTV footage'd show it all from ten different angles. Twenty-four hours max, and *boom!* you've got your man.

But this wasn't some American city. Shiflin and Schofield weren't robbed, and the only CCTV they had was up on the flight deck. Which had revealed nothing.

He looked again at the God's eyes.

"What I'd give," he said, "to have a pair of especially observant eyes on board. Someone, say, who was trained to notice things."

He sighed.

*Commodities.*

Lew Stevens said he'd talked with a psychologist in Coronado who knew the SEAL from BUD/S days. Screened him, recommended he be flushed. *Damaged goods,* the guy said.

Then again, how many top-tier SEALs had Jackson ever met who *weren't* damaged goods?

# 68

The call for lights-out came at 2200, but there was still plenty going on around the ship. People peeling potatoes and soaking beans in the galley. Lots of mopping and cleaning everywhere. Up in the big hangars mechanics were taking planes apart and putting them back together. *The ship that never sleeps*, as Manny always said.

And down here on deck 3, Luca Santiago was in the laundry, folding clothes.

The other sailors hated working here. Working laundry was worse than peeling potatoes, they said, worse than swabbing decks.

Not as far as Luca was concerned.

He did his best not to let anyone know it, so they wouldn't make fun of him. Secretly, though, Luca liked the laundry. He liked looking at all the clothes and thinking about who they might belong to.

Who went with this pair of socks?

Who put on this shirt?

As he folded each item he would picture the person who wore it, sometimes even give them names and personalities, make up stories about them and where they came from.

And Luca loved, absolutely loved, the smell of clean, pressed laundry.

He picked up the stack of clean undershirts he was working on, pressed them to his face, and breathed in. *Cielo!* It made him think of summer in El Paso, of being in the woods all by himself, the clean pine-needle floor, no one there to pick on him or give him grief, just Luca, walking and smelling the grasses and the leaves and the moss.

Being alone—that was another reason he liked it there in the laundry. There were other guys who worked there, of course, but they mostly left him to himself.

Which meant he could talk to his friends.

There was Manny, who was like an older brother to Luca.

Little Boss, who was not too smart but very funny, and had a good heart.

And there was Lulu, who liked Luca and was the prettiest girl he had ever seen.

*Los amigos especiales.* His special friends.

He knew they weren't real. Luca wasn't stupid. But he'd never had any other friends. Ever since he was *un niño pequeño* he always had his special friends around. When they were there, he never felt lonely. Of course he knew they only lived in his head, but that was fine with Luca. That way he didn't have to share them with anyone else.

His Special Friend was different, though.

His Special Friend really *was* real.

Luca placed the last folded undershirt on top of the stack, then looked around to see that no one was watching. He reached into his back pocket, pulled out the note, and unfolded it carefully.

He read it again, whispering the words out loud.

Luca—I've got another secret assignment for you! Come to Sponson F, off the hangar deck, on the port side. I'll be waiting for you tonight at 2400.

Luca looked around once more, then carefully re-folded the note and placed it back in his pocket.

And smiled a secret smile.

## 69

Luca stepped through the hatch and out onto the tiny steel grate catwalk. His face lit up in a big smile when he saw his Special Friend.

His Special Friend put his finger to his lips. "Shhh," he said. "Close the hatch and come stand over here."

Luca closed the hatch, took a few steps, and stood over by the railing.

"Now, we're going to do something that will seem a little odd for a moment. But just go with it, okay?"

Luca gave a sharp nod. Of course.

"Close your eyes. Just for a moment."

Luca closed his eyes.

He felt his Special Friend put something around his mouth, some kind of strap, and fasten it behind his head. Then he instructed Luca to put his hands behind him, and he fastened them together with another strap around his wrists.

Luca started to say, "What's *that* for?" but of course it came out "Mwhh *mwhh* mwhh?" because of the strap tied over his mouth.

He began to feel a little anxious.

What kind of game was this, exactly?

"It's okay," his Special Friend assured him. "Can you breathe okay through your nose?"

Luca nodded.

"Good," said his Special Friend. "That's good."

Luca felt a sharp sting in the neck, and then his Special Friend had him sit down on the catwalk and lean his back against the railing.

"Now open your eyes."

Luca opened his eyes, though it took some effort. He was feeling strange all over.

He tried to talk again, momentarily forgetting that he had that strap across his mouth—but strap or no strap, he couldn't make any sound at all. Nothing. Not even a *Mwhh* mwhh *mwhh*.

It was then that Luca Santiago understood.

This was not a game.

He was going to die.

*Manny! What's going on? Why is this happening!* he tried to scream—but there was only silence and the sounds of the water below and the strap around his mouth being unfastened.

Now the strap loosened and came off, but he still couldn't talk. He couldn't do anything. He could feel everything, just like normal, but he couldn't move. He couldn't even blink.

A sharp smell came to him. It was pee. His own pee. Oh, God—he had just peed right in his clean clothes, and there was nothing he could do about it. He was going to die right there in his own pee, and he would never smell clean pressed laundry, ever again.

A great sadness welled up inside him.

His Special Friend crouched down in front of him and looked into his eyes.

"Luca, Luca," the man said softly. "We need to turn that frown upside down!" He picked up Luca's right hand, holding it up between them by the thumb. "Let's play another game."

With his other hand he brought out a pair of metal snips.

"This little piggy went to market," he said in a soft singsong.

He placed the snips' two little arms on either side of Luca's little finger, right where it connected to his hand.

Luca knew what was going to happen next, yet somehow he did not feel afraid. There wasn't room to feel any fear. The great sadness crowded out everything else. No more dancing, no more song. No more life.

It was more than he could bear.

There was a soft crunching sound.

An explosion of pain crashed through him, blotting out all his thoughts. He was dimly aware of the man holding up Luca's little finger and tossing it overboard. "Didn't really need that one," the man murmured, and he smiled at Luca, an empty smile that made Luca's flesh crawl.

"And this little piggy stayed home." He held up the snips again.

There was blood on them now.

*Crunch.*

Another explosion of pain, way worse than before, like his whole arm was on fire, all the way up to his neck. Not being able to scream made the pain even worse.

The man tossed his ring finger overboard, too. Then something in the water must have caught his attention, because he looked down over the rail and said, "Well, hello." He turned to Luca. "Looks like you have a *new* special friend!"

Luca didn't want a new special friend. All he wanted was to be back in the laundry room again—or alone in the woods at home in El Paso, where he could lie down on the moss by himself and weep openly.

The snips. His middle finger.

"This little piggy had roast beef."

*Crunch!*

KAAAAAH! In his mind Luca screamed at the top of his lungs. In his body, he just sat there on the catwalk, sadder than the saddest song he ever heard.

"And this little piggy . . ."

*Crunch!*

"That's your pointer finger, Luca." The man was crouching in front of him again now, holding the severed finger up to Luca's face so he could see it. "And you know what? This one I actually need!"

He dropped Luca's index finger into a little plastic sandwich bag and put it in his pocket. Then he set down the snips and turned back to Luca.

"And this big little piggy?"

He grabbed Luca with both hands, under the arms, got him upright and turned around, leaning him over the rail so his eyes looked down.

That was when Luca saw it, too.

And now he *was* afraid—so terrified that all thoughts of El Paso and the laundry room and sadness and pain vanished with a *POP!* and in his mind he shrieked and shrieked and shrieked—

Down there, down in the water, was an enormous fish, the biggest fish Luca had ever seen. With teeth.

And stripes, like a tiger.

"And this little piggy—" the man grunted with effort as he lifted Luca up and over the railing "—goes Wee! Wee! *Weeeeeee!* . . ."

Luca was in the water.

Luca was in the teeth.

*I'll miss you,* whispered Lulu.

## 70

"Morning," said the big man as he set his tray down and slid into the seat next to Finn's. Eggs, sausage, biscuits, gravy. "Thought I might find you here."

Finn nodded. "Only place you can get a decent poached egg." Two poached eggs, one sliced mango. Although he wasn't there for the food.

He was there for Jackson.

The master chief put back a fist-sized bite of sausage. "Yesterday," he said after a moment, "you asked, how goes the investigation. I'm curious what exactly you meant by that."

Man didn't beat around the bush.

"Someone's got to chase down the clues," said Finn. "But quietly, so you don't spook the crew. Which means a small task force. Probably just you, Supercop, and one or two others."

"Supercop?"

Finn took a spoon and tapped it twice against his leg. *Tink, tink.*

Jackson let out a long sigh. "I don't like you, Mister Finn."

There was nothing to say to that.

"I don't like you, and I sure as hell don't trust you. So just so you understand, I'm throwing up in my mouth a little when I say this. I want your help."

Finn said nothing. Everyone wanted his help. Popular guy.

"Specifically, as an intelligence asset."

Finn pointed his fork at himself. "Not exactly a homicide detective."

"Neither am I. But that's what you do, right? Observe?"

Finn cut off a slice of mango and ate it before replying. "Captain know you're recruiting the spy?" He sensed the master chief stiffen. Finn put down his utensils and looked at the other man. "You're doing this on your *own*?"

Jackson kept eating.

Finn picked up his fork and knife again and went back to his breakfast. After a moment he said, "Whoa."

They both cleared territory on their plates, the lull in conversation filled by the ambient sounds of clanking cutlery and three dozen chief petty officers talking.

"I can help," said Finn.

Without looking at him, Jackson said, "Why do I feel like I'm about to hear the drop of another shoe?"

Finn said, "There's a file I need to see." He took another bite and waited.

Jackson took a long pull on his coffee, set it down, and grunted. Still staring straight ahead, he said, "Commodities."

"Commodities," said Finn. "Call and response. Like in church."

Jackson sighed. He pushed his plate away, leaned back in his seat, and said, "I'm all ears."

Finn pushed his plate back, too. "July twenty-nine. There was an incident in Yemen, little farm settlement on the outskirts of Mukalla. Somewhere at SOCOM there's an incident file."

"And you're in the file."

Finn took a slow sip of water. "And I'm in the file."

Jackson finally looked at him. "Are you in the file as a white hat, or black hat? Or some shade of gray?"

"I guess we'll know when we see the file."

"Ah," said Jackson. "And you're telling me this why?"

"I've been locked out."

Jackson grunted.

"You've got some sharp intel people on board," said Finn. "Probably one right in your little task force."

Jackson grunted again. He seemed to Finn to be going through an internal debate, one he was in no rush to resolve. Finally the CMC said, "Official information notwithstanding, word on the street has it you're out on some sort of medical leave. Any idea why that is?"

Finn blinked once as he reorganized his data. *Medical leave.* Stan L. was right on the money. Not just a leper. An invisible leper. Not just exiled. *Erased.*

Jackson squinted at him, as if to see him better. Then he leaned back in his seat. "Sonofabitch," he murmured. "You didn't know that, did you."

Finn didn't reply.

"But you're not surprised."

Finn took a slow drink of water from his glass. "I'm never—"

The bosun's whistle erupted from the 1MC.

"*All personnel report——ster stations. All pers—— muster stations.*"

Finn and Jackson looked at each other.

A second announcement came over the speaker. "*Master Chief Jacks——port to medical.*"

Jackson frowned and got to his feet.

So did Finn. "Time to observe," he said.

# 71

It was a finger. A fat, bloody index finger, sitting on a bed of gauze in a small stainless-steel container. Severed at the first joint, turned slightly bluish-gray and already puckering.

"This was discovered on the flight deck thirty minutes ago, during this morning's FOD walk," said the ship's general medical officer. "By a seaman who was unfortunate enough to pick it up before realizing what it was. Now under sedation in sick bay."

Jackson leaned over to inspect the severed end. "Could this have been from a hatch cover?" It wasn't all that rare to see a careless hand or foot caught in a slammed hatch cover and lose a digit.

Finn shook his head. "Don't think so. You'd see a combination crush injury and laceration injury." He looked up at the GMO for confirmation.

"Correct," she said. "The bone would be at least partially fragmented, with a rougher pattern of skin tearing. If I had to guess, I'd say this was hacked off with cable cutters or a pair of aviation snips."

Jackson grimaced. "Any idea who this belongs to?"

"We're trying to identify its owner now, based on ethnicity and relative bone size, matching against records of people we've seen. Not much to go on."

A corpsman knocked lightly on the door and poked his head in. "Master Chief Jackson? XO calling on this line." He nodded at the phone on the GMO's desk.

Jackson picked up, and Finn heard him updating Gaines in murmurs.

Finn could hear the urgent buzz out in the medical suite. People were freaking out. On their way from Chief's Mess, he and Jackson had passed dozens of sailors rushing to their muster stations, scrambling to get past one another in the passageways and on the ladders. It didn't take someone with Finn's skill to read the panic on their faces.

The grisly news was flying fast.

Finn saw Jackson's face cloud over. "Say *what*?" the master chief growled.

Finn took two quiet steps toward him, close enough to hear Gaines's voice.

"We've got a man missing a finger here, Arthur," continued Jackson. "No, scratch that, we've got a finger missing the whole *putain* man! Are we getting out an SAR or not?"

"*That's a negative, Robbie,*" said the voice on the phone.

Jackson was silent for a moment. "Once more?"

A slight pause, followed by a sigh the XO probably didn't mean to be heard. "*The skipper feels a man overboard alert may be an overreaction. Could put undue stress on ship's company.*"

"Is he serious?"

"*I would say that's an affirmative.*"

Jackson clicked off the phone and put one hand to his forehead, eyes closed. After a moment he opened his eyes again and looked at the GMO. "Will you let me know the instant you make an ID?"

"Of course."

He stepped out of the office, Finn following.

"Master chief," said the GMO. "Before you go, can I ask you something?"

Jackson turned back and looked at her.

"What the hell is happening here?"

## 72

Selena Kirkland's face was all smooth planes and sharp angles, like fragments of a fine china set refashioned into an instrument of war. She reminded Jackson of Pallas Athena, the Greek goddess of wisdom and democracy. Also of warfare. And everyone on the Attic plain knew, gods and mortals alike: you did not fuck with Athena.

There were seven of them seated around the polished wood conference table in the admiral's war room: the admiral herself, with her chief of staff, a dour-faced rail of a guy; the CAG, or commander of the air wing; Eagleberg, Arthur Gaines, Jackson, and Scott Angler.

Nobody had spoken for a full minute.

"So," said the admiral. "Where are we?"

If Captain Eagleberg was the mayor of this mobile city, Admiral Kirkland was the governor, chief executive of all ten vessels that made up Strike Group Eight. It was the biggest job on the ocean. She rarely got involved with the business of running the *Lincoln* itself.

But then, it wasn't often a human finger turned up on the flight deck.

"They X-rayed the finger," Gaines reported, "and

confirmed that the cut was most likely made by a pair of aviation snips."

It had taken less than an hour to make the ID; it was Seaman Santiago's right index finger. They couldn't get DNA confirmation without sending it ashore, but the medical department had been able to make a 95-percent-likely match. And Santiago was missing.

A hasty review of CCTV footage had not revealed any trace of his presence on the flight deck. The finger appeared to have been tossed onto the deck, apparently from the adjacent catwalk.

The admiral's lugubrious chief of staff spoke up. "So, unless Seaman Santiago snipped off his own index finger, lobbed it up onto the flight deck, and then pitched himself overboard, we have to consider the possibility of foul play."

All eyes turned to Admiral Kirkland, who now looked at the captain.

"Bill," she said, "do we need to call in the cavalry here?"

Jackson watched the captain struggle. Multiple suicides, losing an entire helo crew, and now the possibility of a homicide investigation right there on his boat? It was enough to make even the hardest skeptic wonder about that shark curse.

Sailors were a superstitious lot—even those who sat at DC desks and gave sound bites on CNN. Eagleberg would never admit it, but he believed in bad luck and cursed voyages, and so did at least some of his superiors. He couldn't afford to let anyone think he was losing control of his ship. The last thing in the world he'd want was some independent authority poking around his ship. His career was on the line.

The captain cleared his throat. "No, ma'am. I don't believe we're at that point."

The admiral nodded, letting her gaze drift around

the table, as if silently feeling for any rift in consensus. Then frowned. "The two officers," she said. Looking back at Eagleberg.

"Officers, ma'am?"

"The jet pilot. And Schofield, the ATO man. Any possible connection there?"

Jackson felt his heart rate accelerate. There it was, right out on the table—and from the admiral's lips, no less. Would Eagleberg acknowledge the possible links he had refused to hear from Jackson?

The captain cleared his throat once more. "No, Admiral," he lied. "There's no evidence of that."

Kirkland looked at him. Again, the thoughtful nod. "Very well," she said. "Keep me posted."

As they walked out into the passageway, Eagleberg leaned in close to Jackson and spoke in a harsh whisper.

"Investigate, Mister Jackson."

Robbie nodded and started to turn away, but the captain grabbed his arm and glared at him. Then mouthed one more word:

*Quietly.*

# V

# The Other Shoe

# 73

**Dusk. A cold Australian drizzle.**

Two days after the discovery of the severed index finger, the USS *Abraham Lincoln* dropped anchor at the mouth of Fremantle Harbour, the busiest seaport in Western Australia, and a total of zero people disembarked.

Port call had been canceled—again.

The official explanation was that a particularly virulent strain of flu was sweeping the city of Fremantle and the captain could not afford the risk to his crew's health and safety. The "Eaglebeak flu," some called it when their superior officers weren't listening.

Few believed the official explanation.

The more obvious truth was that they didn't want to let anyone off the ship and risk the possibility of escape. Not with Santiago's killer still on board.

Either way, quarantine or stakeout, there the ship sat, moored some twelve hundred meters from the dock. As far as its population was concerned, it might as well have been twelve hundred miles. For the next two days the *Lincoln*'s convoy of helos buzzed back and forth, replenishing its supplies, and the ship's six thousand inhabitants walked through their chores and routines, subdued and claustrophobic, within shooting distance of the shore but unable to *go* ashore.

The ship had become a floating prison.

## 74

"We don't have much time." Scott glanced at his watch and looked up at Jackson.

In the forty-eight hours since they docked, this was their first chance to meet all four together, and it would have to be brief. Scott and Jackson were both due at the Lincoln Room in twenty minutes with the captain and Gordon MacDonald, the captain's chief of security, who had apparently developed a few theories on the case.

Now that Captain Eagleberg had sanctioned Jackson's investigation, he'd put Mac in charge of conducting interviews with anyone connected to Santiago; Scott was liaising among Mac, Jackson, and the captain.

Any suggestion that the other two disappearances could be connected was still to be kept strictly under wraps, with those discussions confined exclusively to Jackson's office and the Lincoln Room.

"There's something here I'm still not seeing." This was Indy. "If our killer is so smart, how can he be so dumb?"

"How so?" said Lew.

"That finger," said Indy. "Dropping a hypodermic

cap is one thing, but a finger? Either that was an accident, which is careless beyond belief, or he left it there on purpose—which is even more careless, because now the whole suicide story is out the window."

Jackson had been wondering about that, too.

"And it gets worse," said Indy. "For the killer, I mean. If Santiago's disappearance were chalked up as one more suicide, there'd have been no lockdown. The killer could have debarked at Perth along with everyone else and slipped away into the crowd. But . . ."

"But Santiago's finger closed the door on all of that," said Scott.

Indy shrugged. "As I said. How could someone so smart be so dumb?" She looked back at Jackson, who was flipping through his notes on the Santiago case and frowning.

"The finger was a trophy," said Scott. "So he could reexperience the thrill of the kill. Serial killers are famous for it. For all we know he took fingers from Schofield and Shiflin, too."

"And he just happened to drop this one?" said Indy.

"Heat of the moment," said Scott. "Rushing to slip away unseen. By the time you realize you dropped it, it's too late to go back."

"Maybe," said Indy. "Or maybe it wasn't entirely accidental *or* entirely on purpose, but a little of both. Perhaps he *wants* to get caught."

Jackson looked up from the page he was studying and spread it out on the table so all could see. It was a diagram of the flight deck indicating where the severed finger was discovered. "Anyone notice the location?"

The others looked at him.

"Where they found the finger. Just aft of elevator 4, that little spot where there's just enough room to park a single plane. Know what they call that spot?"

Every carrier's flight deck was divvied up into staging areas with idiosyncratic nicknames, such as the Point, Corral, Hummer Hole, Junkyard, Sixpack, Crotch, and—

"Christ," said Scott. "Finger."

Indy gave a quiet gasp.

Jackson looked sideways at Lew, who had listened to this exchange without saying a word. "Lew?"

Lew slowly shook his head. "No," he said. "I don't think he wants to get caught . . . but I don't think he's being careless, either."

"Explain," said Jackson.

"The hypo cap, the bogus suicide notes, now the finger, even the forced cancellation of port call—my guess would be that it's all deliberate, calculated, right down to the timing of it. He's raising the stakes."

"To what end?" asked Indy.

Lew looked at Indy. "That," he said, "is the sixty-four-thousand-dollar question."

"Robbie?" said Scott, getting to his feet and glancing at his watch.

"I know." Jackson nodded but didn't move. Still frowning at his notes, from which he'd pulled a summary of all three timelines: Schofield, Shiflin, Santiago. "Just one more thing." He sighed.

It occurred to him that he'd been doing that a lot lately. Sighing. Sister Mae used to say chronic sighing was a sign you had a lost soul clinging to your lungs. Now, there was a disturbing thought.

"Speaking of timing. Sam Schofield went missing the night of August second. Lieutenant Shiflin, on the eighth. Santiago—"

"The fourteenth," said Indy. "Oh, my."

There was a brief silence.

"Could be pure coincidence," said Scott.

"Or not," said Jackson. "In which case, another six days past the fourteenth would be—"

"The twentieth," said Indy.

*Tomorrow.*

Jackson got to his feet and nodded at Scott.

"Like you said. We don't have much time."

# 75

"So far we've got three hypotheticals." Gordon MacDonald, the captain's chief of security, was beanpole thin and sat straight as a crease; when he spoke, the only thing that moved was his trim red mustache.

"Scenario One: these were hate crimes. You can see the pattern. Schofield: gay man. Shiflin: strong woman in what some, regrettably, still regard as a 'man's job.' And finally, Santiago: Hispanic. Three demographic groups the killer despised."

"So our guy is a misogynistic bigot?" said Scott.

"Correct. Male, almost certainly white. Likely an enlisted man, ship's crew. At least that's hypothetical number one."

Jackson frowned, a disturbing thought occurring to him. He pushed it aside for later contemplation.

Mac plowed on. "Scenario two: the assaults were driven more by a sort of class resentment, someone with a grudge against officers in general. Again: enlisted man, possibly flight crew, though I'd lean toward ship's crew, someone who spends his days cooped up below. Possibly Schofield and Shiflin both insulted him, intentionally or not. Or maybe he just took their very existence as an insult."

Now Arthur spoke up. "Santiago?" Not an officer, obviously.

"Witnessed something. Stumbled onto the killer's identity somehow."

"And the finger?"

"A warning to anyone else who might finger the killer. Classic witness intimidation. Like cutting out a rat's tongue before whacking him."

Jackson noticed Scott suppressing an eye roll at that last remark, and he had to agree. Mac may have watched a few too many gangster movies.

"And theory number three?" prompted Scott.

"The least helpful possibility, but it needs to be considered: that these were purely crimes of opportunity. Our three victims, in other words, all happened to be out on the exterior, isolated, and at night."

"Chosen at random."

"Correct. Wrong place, wrong time."

"So why attack them at all?" asked Captain Eagleberg, irritably. "What's the supposed motive here? Killing for killing's sake?"

Mac looked at the captain. "Your guess is as good as mine, sir."

Jackson noticed that Mac had consistently used the past tense. They *were* hate crimes. The assaults *were* driven. He was not describing a clear and present danger. There was no sense of urgency here. None at all.

Despite his vow to sit back and observe, Jackson needed to speak up.

"Skipper," he said. "I wonder if we should look at stepping up security on the ship. Specifically, at all perimeter points."

"Why?" snapped the captain.

Jackson chose his words carefully. "To forestall the possibility of any further incidents."

"I hardly think that's necessary. If these *were* assaults, which I'm still not at all convinced is the case, then our putative killer has bollixed it up with that bloody finger business. I don't expect we should see any further episodes."

The captain looked around as if gathering a consensus, then nodded and got to his feet.

"Good," he said. "In any case, no point unnecessarily spooking the crew."

*You mean any more than they're already spooked?* thought Jackson.

# 76

*"What do you think of Mac's analysis, Artie?"*

*"Hard to say, sir. All three seemed plausible enough."*

An audible snort, no doubt from Eagleberg.

*"Occam's razor, Artie, Occam's razor. When did all this business start? I'll tell you when: with Schofield, just two days after we took a certain guest into our midst. Which prompts a question, doesn't it? If these really were homicides at the hand of one man . . ."*

Finn sat on the deck of his broom closet, his back to the bulkhead so he faced the door, motionless, earbuds in, listening to his recording of the previous evening's conversation in the bugged Lincoln Room. His sliced-up Sandburg *Lincoln* volume with its embedded bug was performing flawlessly.

And here came the punch line.

*". . . wouldn't the most likely suspect be our good friend Chief Finn?"*

He pressed PAUSE.

He'd known it was coming, even before Schofield disappeared. He'd known it from his first morning on this ship, from the moment he gazed up at the Vulture's Nest and saw those steel-gray eyes fixed on him, radiating mistrust.

Sooner or later the man behind that eagle's gaze would be coming for him.

He looked at the little electronic assembly in his lap, thinking.

After a moment he pressed START again.

*"I can't trust Jackson, Artie. So here's what I want you to do. Talk to Scott Angler. Quietly. Explain our concerns. Have him look into the SEAL himself. His movements since arriving on the ship. Any possible connections with the three disappearances. Clear?"*

*"Aye, sir."*

*"And have him keep a close eye on the man at all times."*

*"Sir, that may be problematic. Logistically, I mean. He may need to recruit some manpower."*

*"Whatever. A few people he trusts. But as few as possible. And—"*

*"On the QT, sir."*

*"Exactly. Thank you, Artie. And make sure he understands that he reports directly to me, through you. No need to involve anyone else in this."*

Finn pressed STOP.

So. The captain was recruiting Supercop as his own secret police—without telling his CMC. Divide and control. Finn wondered which paperback had offered that particular leadership tip.

And he could hear the stress in Arthur's voice. The XO knew how far out on a limb the captain was going. This was a wary career sailor who would cover his own six. He'd follow his CO's orders but keep his eyes wide open. At some point the sewage was going to hit the propeller, and Commander Arthur Gaines would make sure he wasn't standing next to whoever's head it landed on.

Finn listened again to the conversation with Gordon MacDonald, then switched off the recorder.

Three working theories. Hate crimes; class resentment; crimes of opportunity. As Gaines said, all three seemed reasonable, on the face of it. But Finn thought there was something deeper going on. A more careful calibration at work.

All three scenarios were based on thinking two-dimensionally, drawing logical inferences from the facts in evidence. Viewing the disappearances as a straightforward, tactical sequence.

Not the killer.

The killer was operating on a strategic level.

Yes, he'd selected as his victims a strong woman, a gay man, and a Hispanic sailor. A misogynistic bigot? Maybe. But Finn didn't think it was a simple sequence of events. There were layers to what the killer was doing.

Biker, Schofield, Santiago.

Pilot, officer, swab.

One snatched from the air wing; one from ship's company officer corps; one from the lowly enlisted.

The meta-message? *Eenie meenie miney mo*. This wolf could snatch his sheep from any corral he chose. He could come and take anyone—which meant, in terms of psychological warfare, he'd already taken everyone.

And now Finn thought he knew why poor Luca had been directed to take his charcoal pencils.

He thought he knew why, and he didn't like it.

Time to get into the fight.

He stood, stowed and secured his eavesdropping equipment in his locker along with his steel ring knife. He wouldn't be needing either for the next few days.

# 77

Down on deck 4 Finn showed up at the gym he hadn't visited since his second morning aboard. There was West Texas, grim-faced, punishing herself on the lat press. And yes, there was Tucker, seated at the weight bench, flanked by his two rat-faced buddies.

Tucker watched Finn's approach, his eyes narrowing. He set his weights down with an ostentatious *hfff* and wiped his hands off on his pants and stood. "Well, look who's here. The pacifist SEAL." He barked a few times. Ratface 1 and Ratface 2 *hyuk-hyuk-hyuk*ed.

"The thing I said about fighting, not seeing the point?" said Finn. "I changed my mind."

His right arm shot out like an adder's strike.

Tucker rocked back on his legs, grabbing at his throat and gagging for air.

Finn had a philosophy about fighting. He preferred not to; mostly it was a waste of time and energy. But when a fight became necessary, the only way to do it was to win, and quickly.

In Finn's book there were three types of fight.

The fight to kill. That was the simplest and easiest. The fight to avoid being killed or prevent someone else from being killed. That one you accomplished by putting the other combatant out of commission, not necessarily permanently, just for the purposes of the moment. Still, the general rule in a type 2 fight was to inflict, if not lethal damage, then at least damage sufficient to ensure that the immediate danger was extinguished. Nobody was more dangerous than a committed and only partially disabled combatant.

And then there was the third type: the fight to make a point.

Which was what Finn was looking at right now.

"Hey!" A full two seconds had elapsed from the instant of impact, but Ratface 1 was just now reacting, a look of outrage and fury so exaggerated it was almost comical. Apparently he was winding up to execute some sort of counter. Not so Ratface 2, who was still frozen in place, stunned disbelief on his face.

Typically the goal in a type 3 fight was to cause more psychological than physical pain. In a word, to humiliate. Since there was seldom any real danger involved, there was rarely need for serious physical damage.

Regardless of the specific goal, though—to kill, to avoid being killed, or to humiliate—it was *always* best accomplished immediately. Less wasted energy, more certainty, and you retained the advantage of surprise. The fights in movies, stretched out for suspense and entertainment purposes, were pure horseshit. In a real fight the outcome was usually determined within the first ten seconds of action.

Ten at most.

This one took about half that.

Tucker had reeled back two steps, retching and coughing but not fully out of the game, which impressed Finn. There was something to be said for the inertia of sheer bulk.

Finn half turned toward Ratface 1 and punched the

point of his left elbow into Ratty's left temple, then launched off his left foot and delivered a left-hand palm strike to Tucker's nose.

The nose is one of the more sensitive human extremities, even in a less than super-sensitive guy like this one, and smashing its delicate cartilage up against the nose bone is quite painful, as Tucker would have been able to attest if his brain were not currently distracted by firing on all sorts of normally unused cylinders. The nose also houses a dense matrix of tiny blood vessels, a number of them right then in the process of rupturing. All in all, a nose strike like the one Finn had just executed could be relied upon to make the eyes tear up to the point of shutting down vision.

Finn turned his face sharply a few degrees in the direction of Ratface 2, who responded by promptly sitting down on the deck.

Ratface 1 had slumped back against the nearest machine, a leg press.

Tucker was on his knees, a supplicant weeping before the unfamiliar god of defeat.

Finn turned to the stunned scattering of gym patrons watching this all go down and lifted both hands in the air, open palms forward, in the universal sign language for *It's all good, fighting's over*. Nobody moved.

West Texas watched him curiously.

Tucker let out a low moan.

Finn sat down against a bulkhead and waited.

# 78

It took a full two minutes for security to show up. Long enough for a crew of sailors to lift and haul the big guy out of the gym and off to medical, his entourage in tow. The others in the gym didn't move a muscle, just gawked at Finn.

After a half minute of silent stares he spoke up quietly. "He'll be fine," he said.

No one said a word. They didn't believe him, but it was true. Finn's fighting style was a cross between water and lightning: fluid, electric, lethal. Though not literally, in this case. Delivered with full force, that throat strike would break the windpipe and sever the vessels, causing the opposing combatant to bleed out in minutes. Or choke on his own blood. Whichever came first. Finn had pulled it. No major damage, and certainly nothing permanent. Although Tucker wouldn't be able to talk in anything over a whisper for the next few days.

What a loss to the world.

When the security team arrived Finn was still sitting in the same spot. The two MAs stood him up, read him his rights as they cuffed him—moving warily, as if he were made of high explosive that might detonate at any moment—and marched him out of the gym.

Two minutes later they ushered him through a massive, capsule-shaped door, then a second, steel-grated door, down a narrow ladder and through yet another door to the subfloor suite that constituted "Precinct 72," the ship's brig, and into the custody of the two masters-at-arms currently on duty.

"You're kidding," said one in a high gravelly voice.

Frank and his silent partner, Dewitt.

Lo and behold.

After dismissing the two escorts, Frank proceeded to pat down the prisoner, starting with his torso, then carefully along one arm, then the other, then starting on the legs.

"So, Chief Finn," he said.

"Frank," said Finn.

"Have to say, I am surprised. How the hell did you get yourself in here?"

"Getting in is easy," said Finn. "Getting out, that takes practice."

Frank chuckled as he patted down Finn's left leg toward the foot.

Just then the bolts on the brig's door shot back and in walked Cheryl Hawkins, the security officer who ran Precinct 72, triple-sized morning mocha in hand.

Hawkins was a skinny, wiry thing, tough as sheet metal rivets, with a hacksaw voice that could cut through anything. She also had the foulest mouth on the ship. "The Sheriff," they called her.

The Sheriff ordered the same damn coffee drink every single day: a triple mocha, at 0630 on the dot. According to Finn's internal timepiece it was now 0635. A five-minute amble from Jittery Abe's to Precinct 72.

Creatures of habit.

"Well, fuck me sideways, mean and hard." The Sheriff stood just inside the door and stared at him for a long moment, then walked over behind her desk and took her seat. Noted Finn's gaze and turned in her chair, looking up behind her.

There, mounted on the bulkhead behind her desk, was a photo of a much younger Cheryl Hawkins, standing proudly on the deck of a fishing boat, holding a speargun at port arms; a second photo of her posing with an enormous yellowtail; and in between the two framed shots, a short American-style mahogany speargun, mounted along with a single steel-tipped bolt.

Finn had heard her bragging about this speargun in the coffee line, about how she'd won her "little beauty" in a shooting contest during a training workup. Seemed the Sheriff cut her teeth on the California docks, too.

The Sheriff swiveled back to look at Finn.

"See something you like, Chief Jizz?" she said.

Finn gave no reply.

She leaned forward on her desk and spoke in a soft rasp.

"Listen to my words, Mister Titanium Ballsack. I see you up to anything suspicious, I see you even *thinking* anything suspicious, so help me God I will pull my little beauty down and send that steel shaft straight up your butthole and out between your googly eyes."

Finn nodded. He tried to picture her swimming in the deep, hunting yellowtail and abalone, cursing at the sharks. He could see it.

Frank put one hand on Finn's forearm and ushered him out of the office, past genpop (currently empty), and back to one of the solitary cells, where he would be their guest for the next three days.

Finn sat down on the steel bunk's thin padding, then lay back and stretched out his frame, hands folded behind his head while his grated door clanged shut and locked.

"Don't envy you, Chief," said Frank through the door's steel-mesh grating. "Three days in a cell, no exercise, nothing but bread and water."

That was not a figure of speech. Actual bread-and-water punishment, referred to officially as "diminished rations," was not supposed to exist anymore, having been recently retired from the books; the new mandate was for all prisoners to be fed a normal three squares. The Sheriff, though, she was old school. Chain of command looked the other way. Bread and water it was.

"It's not perfect," Finn agreed. "But it has its advantages."

"Such as?"

"If anyone else gets killed out there while I'm in here, you'll know it wasn't me who did it."

Frank started to chuckle, then abruptly stopped. "You serious?"

"I'm always serious."

Frank chuckled again as he walked away, leaving their prisoner in the semi-gloom. Finn stared at his cell's ceiling and thought about his last conversation with Jackson.

*Commodities.*

He knew the CMC's team had no leads, nothing at all, and that Jackson was counting on Finn to give him something.

All Finn had to work with was the files in his head.

He thought about Stevens, the psychologist, and what he'd said about Finn's memories. *Maybe those are just the ones you remember.*

What was he not remembering?

Finn closed his eyes, took a series of long, slow breaths, and began to think back.

From outside there came a long loud booming sound, a single five-second blast on the ship's horn, audible for miles around: the signal for getting under way. They were pulling out, bound for their Pacific crossing, their killer still on board.

# 79

Jackson was about to go take some chow when a light knock came on his office door. "Open," he called out.

Indy poked her head in. "I have something to report," she said, in a tone that said, *Fasten your seatbelt*.

Jackson ushered her into his inner office, where they both took their seats on his little facing couches. "Let's have it," he said.

"I've been sifting through all the email and web traffic in the days around the disappearances. Since you asked me to look into Chief Finn's background, I decided to take a closer look at his Internet usage. His second day on board he did several web searches, all based on the word 'Mukalla'—that's a city on the coast of Yemen . . ."

Jackson recognized it: the location Finn mentioned, where the "incident" occurred.

"The other search terms included 'terror attack,' 'massacre,' and the date July twenty-ninth."

"I don't remember any news about a recent massacre in Yemen."

"There wasn't any. So I dug a little."

It had taken a bit of digital forensics to tunnel down

to it, and all she could unearth were references in an obscure Naval Special Warfare report, withheld from the public and classified as "investigation pending," plus a few unsubstantiated rumors.

"There was an AQAP cell operating in the area, carrying out local assassinations and grand theft—mostly drug money."

Jackson nodded. AQAP: al-Qaeda in the Arabian Peninsula.

"According to the report, nearly four weeks ago, on July twenty-seven, the group tortured and killed an American journalist. Two days later a SEAL team stormed their safe house, but they managed to evade capture. That same night, they slaughtered a nearby settlement of farmers who had given up their location. You didn't read about this because the whole thing was buried, kept completely out of the press."

Jackson gave a low whistle. "An American journalist. Wonder how they kept *that* quiet." He frowned. "And why?"

"Why indeed," said Indy. "Which is where the rumors come into it—and where it gets weird. As I said, that is the *official* report. But there's also a story, entirely unsubstantiated, that it was not the terrorists who killed the locals, but a few rogue SEALs from that same team who went off the reservation and committed the atrocities."

Indy paused. The office was so quiet Jackson could hear his own heartbeat.

"There have been no charges brought," she went on. "No formal investigation. Right now there is nothing but a vague cloud of suspicion."

"This SEAL platoon," said Jackson. "Would that happen to have been Chief Finn's unit?"

"It was."

Another silence.

"So I'm guessing you're going to tell me what Chief Finn's role may have been in all this, if anything?"

Indy looked up from her notes. "Nobody is drawing that connection, at least not that I've been able to find."

Jackson sighed. "You used the word 'atrocities.'"

"Yes. There is one more ugly detail. Whoever it was that killed these families, the rumor is that they took trophies. Ears. Scalps."

Jackson closed his eyes. "Let me guess," he said quietly. "And fingers."

"And fingers," said Indy.

*Mère Marie.*

# 80

*July 29. Near midnight and still infernally hot. The air shimmers with unspent static charge. It's been two days since the journalist's murder. Finn and his squad approach the cell's safe house silently, invisibly. Their breacher plants his charge. Finn gives the signal. The charge goes off with a roar and they sweep through the place. There is no one there . . .*

And then?

A gap.

Finn opened his eyes.

He was on the floor of his cell, back against the bulkhead, where he'd been sitting all day with the light switched off, looking for lost memories in the dark. He took a slow breath, shut his eyes again, and once more slipped back into July 29 . . .

*A flicker of heat lightning rips open the sky, a flash bulb instant.*

*He is somewhere else now, standing by himself in front of a small dwelling of plaster rubble and sun-baked mud bricks, facing a wooden door. He waits a moment for the flash's night blindness to fade.*

*It feels all wrong. He shouldn't be alone. This is what*

*a squad is for. Like the civilian police: always call for backup. But he hasn't. He doesn't.*

*His eyes regain their sensitivity, and now the darkened scene in front of him starts to resolve.*

*Now he sees the door clearly.*

*Shattered to pieces.*

*Someone has smashed it in.*

And then? Only disconnected fragments.

*A flickering lightbulb, skips in an old vinyl LP.*

*He pushes aside the shattered wooden fragments and steps through the mud-brick doorway—*

Skip.

*Now he's walking through the house, entering a room—*

Skip.

*Now he's inside the room, sitting on the earthen floor, legs splayed, his back to the wall. A few feet away, a shape on the floor, too dark to make out. A sleeping child? boy? girl?—another lightning flash illuminates the room—the child's eyes stare sightless, blood oozing from both ears, blood pooling black on the floor in the strange light—*

Finn's eyes snapped open, his heart racing in the dark.

The massacre.

He was there.

# 81

Indy sat silent.

"All right," said Jackson. "Information has come to me," he paused again, then continued, "that there's an incident file on this whole thing buried somewhere at SOCOM. I want that file."

"That will not be easy."

"I wouldn't think so," said Jackson. "Meanwhile please don't share any of this with anyone."

"Of course," said Indy. "Shall I update Commander Angler?"

Jackson hesitated.

He hadn't yet told the others about his meeting with Finn, and now he realized why. Because they would think he was crazy for even entertaining the idea. More specifically, because Scott would think that. Scott had been so quick to judge the SEAL, right from the start, and that concerned Jackson. He worried that the JAG officer might respond to this news with a knee-jerk conclusion that Chief Finn must be their killer.

Which Jackson was not yet prepared to believe.

Besides, Jackson had his own suspicions, and they pointed in a different direction. A disturbing thought had nagged at him ever since hearing Mac's first scenario. The one with the "misogynistic bigot."

"No," he said. "I'll talk with Scott."

Indy nodded and got to her feet. Turned to go.

"Indy? One more thing?"

She turned back.

"Can you also get me whatever you can pull up on Commander Papadakis?"

She raised her eyebrows. "Ah." She paused. "So, going with hypothetical number one?"

"Just following the leads."

"Wow," said Indy. "Okay." She thought for a moment. "They're not adding on extra security yet, are they?"

"They are not," Jackson agreed. "The captain doesn't believe there'll be 'any further episodes.'"

"What do you think?"

What he thought was that this was day six, and his crew was in danger.

He rubbed his hand over the close-shaven dome of his head and got to his feet as well. "I think it's gonna be a long night."


All that night Jackson patrolled. Walking, watching, listening.

As he walked he thought about Sister Mae and her shell figurines and voodoo accessories, her foul teas and tinctures, her stories of the Chupacabra, the Grunch, and the Rougarou, and how he would run into his momma's room in the middle of the night, having worked himself into a terror.

He thought about Nikos Papadakis and that confrontation Lieutenant Halsey had described, how rattled she said Lieutenant Shiflin was. *Like she was being stalked.*

He thought about Chief Finn. *Damaged goods.*

Mostly he walked, watched, and listened.

At 0600, reveille sounded. Jackson stood stock-still for another minute, craning his ears, dreading the sound of five long whistle blasts on the bosun's pipe.

Finally he let his breath out, not realizing he'd been holding it.

# 82

When Finn came to, he heard the Sheriff stir. He knew it was the Sheriff because every time she sorted a new piece of paperwork she spat out a single compound-word obscenity. "Fuckweasels." "Pencildick." And so forth. Kennedy would get a kick out of her.

He wasn't sure exactly when he'd dropped off, or whether the dreams he'd had were really dreams or fragments of actual memories.

*Heat lightning. Shattered door. Black pooling blood.*

It must have been reveille that woke him. He was not aware of having heard the call, but his internal clock told him it was a few minutes after 0600.

Sure enough, another minute later the Sheriff got up from her chair and headed out. Finn knew precisely where she was going, and why. She'd be at the front of the line when Jittery Abe's opened at 0630.

Trained rats.

He closed his eyes again and thought back to that pointless raid on that empty compound. That much was memory, he was sure, and not dream. They burst in. No one there. And after that?

He touched his fingertips to his temples.

Radio silence.

When the rumor reached them the next morning Finn went out and shook the bushes, talked quietly with every local contact he had, and he had plenty. But his HUMINT network had gone dark. No one was saying a word. Why?

Exactly who were they afraid of?

At 0635 the Sheriff returned, prompt as an alarm clock.

A few minutes later, Finn's thoughts were interrupted by the Sheriff's rusty hacksaw. "You got a visitor, buttwipe."

Finn opened his eyes but didn't sit up.

Through the door he heard a deep rich voice. "Can you give us a few minutes alone?"

He heard the Sheriff hesitate, a faint throaty grumble like an ancient car engine about to quit. "Five minutes," she growled. No obscenities, incredibly, but she didn't sound happy. "We'll be right outside."

Finn heard the scrape and shuffle of the Sheriff moving out with her two MAs in tow. He heard the brig's outer door clank shut, followed by the *thunk* of the closing lock. The scrape of a chair being pulled up to his cell.

Finn sat up in the semidarkness. Didn't turn on his cell light.

"Anything I can get you?" said Jackson. "Loaf of pound cake with a nail file inside? Poster of Rita Hayworth?"

Jackson sounded fatigued. Finn's guess, he'd been up all night. "What brings you to the dungeon, Master Chief?"

"And here I was going to ask you the same thing."

Finn waited.

"All right, then," Jackson said amiably. "I'll go first. I thought I'd drop by and see how that recon's going."

"It's going."

"Uh-huh," said Jackson. Finn saw him glance around at the brig's sparse interior. "I can see that. Got things nicely under control."

"How's the incident file search going?" said Finn.

Jackson grunted.

Finn waited. Jackson seemed to be weighing what to say next.

"I've got questions for you, Finn X."

"Okay."

Another pause.

Finn could guess what some of those questions were. *What are you doing getting yourself arrested? Why are they really sending you home? Why are you on this ship at all? What's your endgame? Why are people dying on my boat, and what do you have to do with it?*

"Are you a bad guy, Chief Finn?" said Jackson.

Finn smiled in the dark. "Tell me something," he said. "Anyone else disappear last night?"

Jackson grunted again. He leaned close to the steel grate and spoke quietly. "Now, why would you be asking a question like that?"

"Because I can count to six."

Jackson straightened back up and rubbed his eyes.

In the silence Finn parsed the progression of thoughts Jackson would likely be having right now. He'd figure Finn had to know he was under suspicion. Today was August 21, which meant another six days had passed without incident. Which could be confirmation of his guilt: if he was in fact the perpetrator, then it stood to reason there'd be no further homicides as long as he was locked up.

On the other hand.

If Finn was *not* the perpetrator and the actual guilty party was setting him up for it, then there still wouldn't be any further homicides as long as he was locked up—

because if there were, that would take him off the board as a viable suspect. Which could mean Finn had gotten himself thrown in there intentionally to prevent any more murders from happening.

Either way, as long as he was in the brig the people on the ship were safe.

But were they safe because Finn was outmaneuvering the killer—or because he *was* the killer?

"The lady or the tiger," said Finn.

Jackson gave another grunt.

In any case, the ship's population wouldn't be safe for long. The captain had no cause to keep the prisoner locked up for more than three calendar days, which meant Chief Finn would be out on the streets again, so to speak, by the end of the following day.

"About that finger," said Finn.

"Oh yeah," said Jackson. "About that finger."

"Not a hate crime. Not a reprisal."

"How in God's—?"

Finn could hear the unspoken thought. *How in God's name could you possibly know about Mac's theories?*

After a long beat, the CMC quietly said, "No? What was it, then, Finn X?"

"A start signal."

More silence. Jackson thinking hard.

"CMC?"

"Still here."

Finn whispered, "Watch out for Supercop."

There was the sudden *thunk* of heavy door bolts being thrown back.

"Time," crowed the Sheriff.

# 83

For the rest of that morning and on into the afternoon Jackson continued roaming the passageways and cat-walks, nodding and exchanging words with passing crew members as he reviewed his conversations of that morning and the past few days.

*Watch out for Supercop.* Meaning what, exactly?

*They took trophies.* Jesus.

And, *start signal*? Jackson wasn't familiar with the term but its meaning seemed clear enough. Something like a shot from a starter pistol at the track. Was that a warning? or a threat?

The fact that day six had come and gone gave Jackson little comfort. With Santiago, the killer had already changed his pattern substantially. Who was to say he wouldn't also change his schedule?

That afternoon he returned to his stateroom to grab a few hours' sleep so he could walk the passageways again—and especially the exteriors—come the night hours.

He dreamed about his daddy, coming for him that sultry Louisiana night with his switchblade in his pocket and murder in his heart.

At dusk Jackson arose and resumed his circuits, patrolling like a beat cop. Fantail, gun mounts, sponsons, aircraft elevators, anchor room . . . everywhere that involved direct access to the outside. What was he watching for? Would he know it when he saw it? Pick up the scent of Terrible as it drifted past? He had no answers. All he could do was walk, watch, and listen.

He rolled on through the night.

The moon was one day from full.

August moon, tail end of the Australian winter. In these parts of the world the locals called it "Snow Moon," "Storm Moon." "Hunger Moon." "Wolf Moon."

All that night, nothing happened.

Finn sat in solitary.

Some six thousand souls snored in their racks or went about their night jobs as above their heads jets shot off into the sky and crashed down to the deck again. The ship hurtled on, shoving aside 5,000 tons of seawater per second as it ate up the miles.

The Wolf Moon watched.


Jackson was out on the flight deck catwalk the next morning when dawn broke, cold and drizzly. He doubted their evildoer would attempt the doing of any further evil during the daylight hours, but he could not be certain of that, so on he walked, through that morning and into the afternoon—when he got word that security would in fact be increasing that night.

The captain had finally agreed to beefing up their detail, with the proviso that it be done as quietly and discreetly as possible.

Jackson had no problem with that. No problem at all. Maybe he'd even get in a few hours of sleep himself tonight.

At 2200 hours, as darkness settled in over the flight deck and catwalks, the extra security detail began moving into place.

At 2300 hours, the incessant rain gave way to a dense, cold fog. The Wolf Moon took its place above the ocean's horizon, pale and blood-hungry.

At midnight, Finn was released from custody.

# 84

When he emerged from the brig Finn noticed three things straight off.

First, as he headed back to his quarters to change and retrieve his knife he became aware of darted looks in his direction. He thought back to his first day on board, how when he walked the narrow passageways people would stand aside out of respect. Now they shrank from him as he passed.

People had to be making the same connection as Eagleberg had, and drawing the same conclusions. After all, the "suicides" started happening right after Finn came on board. And he'd gone off like a Claymore mine on those dudes in the gym. What was to say he wouldn't go off on others?

What was to say he hadn't gone off on Santiago?

The second thing he noticed was that they'd put increased security in place throughout the periphery of the ship, every spot with direct access to the open air.

Third, he'd picked up a tail.

A warrant officer, hefty guy. Finn had seen the face, didn't know the name. When he came back out after changing and began his stalk, the WO had been replaced by another. No doubt there was a third in the wings. Tag-teaming it. An eyes-on scout rotation from Supercop.

This did not surprise him, but it did complicate things. Finn was on the hunt again. And putting surveillance on him was like belling a cat. Proceed with these well-meaning goons hovering in his wake, and it would almost certainly spook his quarry. He could easily shake them—but if he did, they would just redouble their efforts, which would make the bell jingle even louder.

He chose the middle path: keep his watchers on as long a leash as possible without seeming like he was doing so. Not ideal. But what was?

At 0100 he was making a pass on the mess deck when he saw Jackson coming his way. The two men stopped for a moment and eyed each other.

"Extra detail out tonight," said Finn.

Jackson looked back at him with no expression. "Can't have too much security, Chief Finn."

"Exit points."

"Seemed like the smart play."

Finn saw the logic of it. Rule 1: *always keep an open exit.* Or, if you're a serial killer: *always do your killing as close as possible to where you can dump the body.*

Thinking tactically. Not strategically.

"If it were me," he said, "I'd do the opposite now. Go deep."

"Deep?"

"Freezers. Machine rooms. Nukes. Deep."

Jackson gave him a long look, as if trying to penetrate that blank face and see inside his head. Was Finn there to give assistance to Jackson's vigil? Or was he the reason for the vigil? The CMC gave one slow, uncertain nod and rolled on.

Finn stood in place for a moment. Freezers. Machine rooms. Nukes. Fifty acres of interior. A good deal more territory than the periphery. Exponentially more. Impossible for twenty men to cover adequately, let alone one man.

Jackson was placing his bets on the tactical logic. Stick to the periphery.

Finn headed below.

# 85

Lieutenant James Bennett was up on the flight deck, unloading his turboprop Greyhound. At least that was his excuse. Really he just wanted to be up there in the quiet of the night, in the open air. Sammy used to spend time up there after everyone else was gone, just watching the stars, thinking. No stars out tonight, though. Nothing but fog, stilled planes, and loneliness.

Ever since Sammy went missing, Bennett had been little more than a hollowed-out shell. The news that his friend had taken his own life shattered his world. Sammy had always been the stable one of their relationship. James was prone to drama; he was the first to admit it. Sammy was a rock.

But . . . murder? And a *serial* murderer? That had freaked him right out. Try as he might (and he had! oh, he had!) he could not shake the sense that he was next on the psychopath's list.

Bennett glanced around. He was completely alone. Flight ops had been canceled and only a handful of aircrew and pilots were up top. Somehow the rest had already gone in ahead of him.

The fog caught the full moon's illumination and scattered it over the flight deck, diffusing the light in such a way that despite the brightness, visibility was little more than a few meters.

He checked the chocks on his Greyhound one more time, then began crossing the deck to the catwalk.

The fog seemed to muffle the sounds of his footsteps.

After he'd gone about ten yards he stopped, craning to listen into the murk.

Heard nothing but his own ragged breathing.

He walked another eight or ten yards, then stopped again. Now there was no mistaking it.

Footsteps.

Not his.

A bubble of panic rose up and burst open, and he broke into a run, bolting the last ten meters to the edge and scrambling down the short ladder to the catwalk, his unseen pursuer's footsteps practically in his ears.

Miscounting the steps, he lost his footing and toppled headlong.

Slammed against the catwalk railing.

Felt his collarbone snap.

He let out a scream—in pain but even more in terror—and felt two strong hands snatch hold of him and set him upright. He shut his eyes to avoid looking at his captor.

"Bennett!"

He opened his eyes.

Master Chief Jackson stared at him like he'd lost his mind.

Olivia sat at her editorial desk deep inside the inner office at Public Affairs. Working late; last-minute edits on the next edition of the *Penny Press*. Thinking about their SEAL guest, how she'd known the moment they'd met that here was a man with a colorful past, a man with a story to tell.

Someone she would just about kill to have the chance to interview.

She hadn't seen him in over a week, not since she loaned him that big Lincoln volume. And look at what had happened since then! A third missing crew member; that bloody finger; good grief! She was itching to get their mysterious guest on record and hear his take.

When she heard he'd been arrested for brawling she nearly jumped out of her skin. Now she *had* to get a sit-down with him. Talk about color!

Huh. The sound of someone in the outer office. Footsteps, stopping now; then starting again, coming her way.

She felt a quick spark of panic and squelched it just as quickly. *Don't be ridiculous, Liv.* Whoever it was, if they needed her they'd find her back here. If they didn't, they wouldn't.

She returned to her edits, her thoughts wandering back to her piece on the SEAL. She'd heard he was being released that night. *Tomorrow,* she thought. *Tomorrow I'm gonna hunt him down.*

She heard the door behind her open and the spark in her stomach puffed into a small blue flame of alarm.

Who besides herself would be coming in here in the middle of the night?

She pivoted in her chair and stifled a scream.

The overhead light snapped on.

It was Drew, one of their staff photographers.

"Jesus!" he said. "You scared the shit out of me!"

She forced a laugh and turned back to her desk. "Don't be a dork, Andrew," she said over her shoulder, thinking, *You scared the shit out of me, too.*

———

Willy Chavez hated it when Ángel smoked on the job. Even in a place as funky as the recycling compartment it was totally against the rules, and if someone walked in on them Willy knew it would be his ass hung out to dry, too. And now Ángel was telling him about some porn DVD Willy just had to see to believe. Ángel had sneaked a whole collection on board, man! This one *chica,* you will not believe what she does!

Willy was doing his best to pretend he was interested. Truth was he could care less about Ángel's stupid DVDs.

Ángel paused to take a drag and Willy tried to think of a way to change the subject. But Ángel did it for him. "Hey, man," he said, serious now. "How's it going with Marisa?"

Willy was surprised Ángel remembered her name. They'd been together almost two years now, Marisa and him, since high school. He had been with other girls before, but she was different, special. And then, just before they embarked on the *Lincoln,* she had stunned him with her news. "Stunned" didn't cover it. Blew his freakin' mind.

"She must be gettin' pretty big now, uh?"

"Like, seven, almost eight months big."

"Whoa, man," said the smoker. "Li'l Willy, gonna be a daddy."

"Yeah," said Willy. "I can't believe it." But he did. He was gonna be a daddy. A good one, too, way better than his own pop ever was, straight up.

Ángel took another drag. "Whole new kind of life, bro. Seriously, man. Congratulations."

"Thanks, Ángel," said Willy. "I just hope we get back in time, you know?"

Ángel stared at him. "Whoa, man. You gonna, like, be there? For the birth an' shit? Watch the little guy make his big entrance?" He hooted and grinned.

Willy was about to reply when he heard the latch to the compartment door behind him *snick* open.

Ángel stumbled to his feet and hastily stamped out the smoking butt.

At that moment, his biggest concern in the world was that he not get caught yet again, smoking on the job.

The man who came through the door stood still, looking at the two of them.

Why was he wearing goggles?

# 86

*Jackson was lying on his back in the dark when the switch-blade came at him. He felt his daddy's hot breath on his face as the blade slid into him and buried itself deep in his liver, the hot blood rushing out of him—*

The phone in his stateroom rang, jerking him awake.

He grabbed at the receiver in the dark.

*"It was recycling."*

Click.

The SEAL, calling from God only knew what phone. "Sweet Jesus," muttered Jackson as he fumbled the thing back onto its base. "What are we, partners now?" He glanced at the luminescent dial on his watch: 0530. Barely an hour of sleep, if you could call it that.

He sat up and started pulling on his trousers.

The phone rang again. He snatched at it. "Jackson."

"Robbie? Arthur. Better meet us down at recycling. Right away."

Recycling. *Dieu.*

Jackson ran his hand over the dome of his head. *Start signal,* the SEAL said. He'd looked it up. "A communications term; a signal that prepares a receiver to begin receiving data."

Had they just begun receiving data?

He hoisted himself to his feet and headed below and aft to the recycling compartment, arriving to find Arthur, Captain Eagleberg, Scott, and one terrified-looking E-2.

Arthur nodded to the E-2, then at Jackson. "Tell him."

The boy was so frightened he could barely stutter out the words.

"Me and Dougie, we got morning shift. Willy—Willy and Ángel, they, they got graveyard."

"William Chavez and Ángel Cristobal," inserted Arthur. Nodding again to the E-2. "Go on."

"When we got here—me and Dougie, I mean—when—when we got here . . ." At this point the E-2 seemed to run out of sentence. He opened and closed his mouth a few times, looking from Jackson to Arthur and back again.

"When you got here this morning?" Arthur prompted gently.

"They wasn't here. I mean, it was *empty*."

A warrant officer stepped into the compartment and murmured in Arthur's ear. Arthur nodded and turned to the E-2. "You can go with this gentleman," he said quietly. The warrant officer and the E-2 withdrew, leaving the four men alone. Arthur repeated the warrant officer's update for the group: a cursory search had not turned up the two boys. Awaiting further orders.

Eagleberg turned to Scott. "That'll be all for now, Commander." Then, to Arthur: "Will you wait outside for me, Artie?"

As Scott and Arthur both left the compartment, Jackson thought about the E-2's stammered pronouncement. *Willy and Ángel, they, they got graveyard.* That certainly summed it up, didn't it. Summed it up like poetry.

Alone now, the captain scowled at Jackson. "Selena is on board the *Stockdale* till day after tomorrow. She doesn't know about this."

Jackson opened his mouth to ask a question, then thought better of it. Was Eagleberg saying what Jackson thought he was saying?

The captain leaned in close. "*Robbie*," he hissed. "*Fix this.*"

# 87

Scott had waited for him around a corner. As Jackson approached he growled, "We need to talk."

Reveille was still a few minutes off; there was hardly anyone in the passageways. The two men easily found a nearby alcove where they could grab a minute in private.

"Robbie," said Scott. "Are we overlooking the obvious?"

Jackson feigned innocence. "Such as?"

"Who showed up just before this all started? And just happened to be on hand to witness both Schofield's and Shiflin's last documented moments?"

"I don't know, Scottie. That's a little—"

"He's released from the brig, and *blam*!" Scott snapped his fingers. "Two more gone. I'm sorry, Robbie, but what else do we need, a Venn diagram?"

"Correlation doesn't equal causation, Scottie. Didn't they teach that in OCS?"

"What did Lew's man say? *'The guy is damaged.'*"

Jackson held up both hands. "Hang on—no, hear me out. Has it occurred to you that those same circumstances you just mentioned, the timing, all of it, could constitute the elements of a perfect frame-up?"

"Oh, come on!"

Jackson pressed on. "That the killer could be using all that to set the guy up and take the heat off himself?"

"That's a reach, Robbie. I mean, that is one serious reach." He shook his head. "I don't get this. Where the hell are you coming from here?"

Jackson felt a pit in his stomach. How could he even have this conversation when he hadn't yet shared that Mukalla bombshell? Or at least told Scott about his private conversations with Finn?

"I talked with him. Chief Finn."

Scott's eyes narrowed. "About?"

"About using him as an asset. An intelligence asset."

Scott took a step backward, glaring at Jackson.

"Well, sonofabitch," he said. He looked away, shook his head. Looked back at Jackson. "I don't know how else to put this, Robbie—are you out of your fuckin' Creole mind?"

Jackson sighed. "I don't know, Scottie. I honestly don't."

"When we started this thing I thought you were jumping at shadows—"

"Hell of a leap, you said."

"Yeah, hell of a leap, but I was wrong, and you were right, the shit truly had hit the fan and you were the first one to see it. I give you that. But now you've got a prime suspect staring you in the face, and you refuse to look at it?"

"Scottie—"

"I can't do this anymore. I'll keep working with Mac and have one of his guys liaise with you and the others."

"Scott—"

"I'm sorry, Robbie. I'm *out*."

He turned and walked away.

# 88

"And then there were three," said Indy.

Jackson had told them that Scott would be focusing on his work with Mac and their interviews. He had not mentioned their disagreement, but neither Indy nor Lew were naïve.

Also not mentioned—by any of them—was the pressure they all felt bearing down on them. The captain was frantic to have their culprit caught before the admiral returned in two days. With Scott and Jackson running what were now essentially two parallel investigations, the task felt even more daunting. And with the killer's pattern and apparent timetable both up in the air, there was absolutely no way of guessing where or when he would strike again.

"Speaking of three," said Jackson. "Factoring Chavez and Cristobal into the picture, which of Mac's theories seems likeliest at this point, if any?"

Lew thought for a moment. "That may not be the right question," he said. "The three scenarios are not necessarily mutually exclusive. And my guess is, no one of them goes quite far enough on its own."

"Explain," said Jackson.

"It's possible that he could be acting out of inflamed bigotry, for example, or resentment, but at the same time be motivated by a broader purpose."

"Such as?"

Lew was pensive for a moment. "Well," he said, "look at the result."

"Okay. Which is what?"

"Look around," said Lew. "Look at the crew. They're terrified. This thing has been building for weeks in a carefully laid out sequence. And now you have some six thousand people locked up on this boat together, terrified of one another and their own shadows."

"Point being?" said Jackson.

Lew once again thought for a moment before replying.

"In my career I've heard thousands of people spill their worst fears. Ninety-nine percent of those fears are basically insubstantial: echoes of traumas long past, baseless anxieties about imagined future calamities. Maybe one fear in a hundred concerns something *real*, something bad that could genuinely be about to happen. The hungry lion circling you in the jungle; the wildfire surrounding your house.

"That's what we've got here. This place *is* on fire—on fire with fear. And not the hypothetical kind, not the typical anxieties of modern living. We've got six thousand people all terrified of the monster under the bed—*but the monster is really there.*

"My guess is, *that's* the result our killer is after. Not the thrill of the kill: the thrill of the emotion his kill elicits. Yes, he's started taking trophies, but in this case the trophies aren't for himself, they're for us. For everyone on board. I don't think he gets off on the killing per se. He gets off on the building terror."

Lew pursed his lips and frowned. "In fact . . ." he

added. "You know, that helo crash, back in the Gulf, that cast quite a long shadow. What if our killer took advantage of what was already a haunted mood and used it as . . . well, as his stage setting."

He turned to Indy. "And that's why he didn't care about not slipping away into the crowd at Perth. He didn't *want* to slip away. He wasn't finished."

There was a long silence.

Indy cleared her throat before she spoke again. "So does any of this narrow the profile down?"

Lew sighed. "Just the opposite, I'm afraid."

"Because . . ."

"We're likely talking here about APD, antisocial personality disorder. In this case, your classic psychopathy. A genuine sociopath would have zero affect, basically a flat screen with nothing projected on it—yet that wouldn't necessarily be something you'd see. Sociopaths are often extremely bright, keenly observant. Our subject could be quite skillful at aping affect."

"Aping affect," said Jackson.

"Projecting normal responses, such as empathy or bonhomie, to blend in. Simulating emotions as the situation calls for it."

"Pretending to be normal," said Indy.

"Exactly."

"Which means it could be more or less anyone on the ship."

Lew spread his hands apologetically. "Wish I had more."

There was another long silence.

Jackson was thinking about the rumor.

According to nautical lore, crossing the line was supposed to neutralize any shipboard curses. Not this one, apparently. And now, according to crew scuttlebutt, their ghost-shark curse had a cause: it was because they'd left the Gulf without finishing the search for Schofield.

Sailors' curses: the seagoing version of conspiracy theories.

*Madone.*

"When I was little," he said, "they told us stories about a swamp creature. A kind of demon, I guess you'd say. The Rougarou."

He spoke softly, gazing at his bulkhead display of drawings and God's eyes.

"Stood seven, eight feet tall, all covered in wet matted hair, big canine incisors. Glowing red eyes. Least that was his natural form—but the Rougarou, he was a shape-shifter. Could transform himself into any animal he chose. A bear. Wolf. Snake. Anything.

"In the bayou the Rougarou was more than a bedtime story, more than just one more boogieman cooked up to scare the young pups into behaving. Grown-ups believed in him, too, plenty of them. Still do today. Some say after Katrina the Rougarou stepped out of the bayou waters and roamed the streets of Nawlins, riding the diseased floodwaters, feeding on the misery, spreading chaos and evil far and wide. Some say the beast can travel anywhere, unseen, long as there's water to carry it."

After an awkward silence Indy said, "What exactly are you saying, Master Chief?"

He looked at her, then at Lew, then let out a heavy sigh.

*Damn you, Sister Mae,* he thought. *Stay out of my head!*

"I'm saying, I grew up with that crap, and those stories scared the living bejeezus out of me. But I was an ignorant little kid." He looked at Lew again. "What you're describing makes sense. Maybe our guy is a sort of shape-shifter. But he's no Rougarou. He's just a man—flesh, blood, and bones."

He took a big breath and forced his shoulders to relax.

"Just a man. And we're gonna find him."

# 89

Lew Stevens had just stepped out of his office that evening to grab some late supper when he saw Chief Finn sitting on a bench outside, waiting.

"Chief Finn."

"Lieutenant Stevens."

Stevens regarded Finn for a moment, then cocked his head. "Forget something?"

Finn stood.

Stevens opened his door again and beckoned Finn to follow.

"I just have one question," said Finn once they were inside the little space, sitting in two chairs side by side.

"Please," said Lew.

"How do you remember something you can't remember?"

"Now, that is an excellent question." Stevens thought for a moment. "A traumatic memory is like a cornered bear. You don't want to go charging in after it. But you might be able to coax it out."

"How would you do that?"

"Don't try to recall what you don't remember. Just let yourself recall what you do remember."

"Such as what?"

"Such as whatever you can. What's the earliest memory you can pull up? Where did you grow up?"

"I'm not sure that's especially relevant here."

"Humor me," said Stevens. "Think about your boyhood, your neighborhood. Anything you remember."

Finn closed his eyes.

He remembered running through the trees . . .

*The sun-dappled forest floor, a canopy of broadleaf maples, the sweet-tangy scent of the grand firs . . . tracking through the woods together, Ray showing him how to follow the deer tracks, elk tracks, black bear tracks . . .*

*Ray making grilled cheese sandwiches for the two of them when their parents were away, showing him how to make a Duncan Hines Devil's Food chocolate cake out of the red box . . .*

*Ray taking him down by the millstream, showing him the place where you could lie down by the bend in the stream and watch the minnows and goldfish, with their rainbow colors and bugeyes, the water-skeeters and mayflies and dragonflies, the frogs and salamanders . . .*

*the frogs and—*

His eyes jerked open. The biting odor of ammonia carbonate—smelling salts—in his nose. Eyes tearing.

He was on the office floor curled on his side, no sense at all of how he got there, Stevens kneeling over him and holding a damp washcloth against his forehead.

His jaw ached.

He touched it, massaged it. Tasted blood. He looked up at the other man. "How long?"

"Maybe twenty minutes."

Stevens helped him to a sitting position, back against the bulkhead. Then sat down next to him while he took a series of long slow breaths.

Finally Finn looked over at him.

"Looks like you poked the bear," said Stevens.

# 90

After Finn left his office Lew thought about what Master Chief Jackson had said that morning. *Just a man. And we're gonna find him.*

Maybe so, thought Lew as he woke up his computer. But his own quarry—the childhood version of Finn X—was proving difficult to track down. He had not heard back from Harry Holbrook, the old psychiatrist at Great Lakes, who apparently was still on his fishing trip. And even Indy had not yet been able to unearth anything further about the man's pre-military background.

Lew figured it was time to go on a fishing trip of his own.

Unlike the rank and file of the *Lincoln*'s population, key personnel in medical had access to the ship's dedicated high-speed Internet service, which enabled them to conduct efficient online research on medical, pharmaceutical, and other topics.

Lew began looking.

No last name. No arrests, no police record. No known hospital stays or prior medical records. Schooling unknown.

Lew thought back over what Van Ness had said.

Drug kingpins. Chinese mafia.

He began combing the San Diego newspaper archives for pieces on the street trade, starting a few years before Finn enlisted. For the next hour, he kept reading, finding nothing.

Then, a story. A sixteen-year-old, arrested in connection with a DEA raid on a known Triad connection. In a sidebar titled "Teens on the Docks" the writer mentioned a few of the kid's associates, including another sixteen-year-old who went by "F/X."

The Hollywood term for "special effects." Classic SoCal nickname.

He looked back at Jackson's notes from his original interviews. His observation about how the SEAL had replayed that altercation he'd witnessed outside Shiflin's ready room with such startling precision. An uncanny skill of mimicry. *Special effects.* It fit him.

F/X.

Finn X.

For the next two hours he searched every archive, every database, every story on the drug wars or life on the docks or troubled teens that he could find for references to a kid going by the tag F/X.

Not counting the Triad-related drug bust story, he found exactly three.

First up was a story about the shady goings-on alleged to be taking place on several Santa Catalina Island boat tours. According to that piece his quarry had done an eight-month stint at age fifteen on a dive boat called "the *Frieda*." No details.

The second was another drug-related story that mentioned that same teenage associate. This one provided no new information, but it did at least offer independent confirmation that this kid had existed.

The third was a puff piece about a summer swim contest for youngsters. One of the day's races was won by a thirteen-year-old identified in the story as "going by the name F/X."

This story had photos.

Lew manipulated the browser, enlarging the window in an effort to see the boy more clearly. The crude, pixilated quality of the scanned newsprint didn't help.

He sat back in his chair and squinted at the image.

Chief Finn at thirteen?

Possibly.

He copied the photo and pasted it into a separate file, then sat back to think.

As far as he could tell the trail went cold at that point. He'd found no trace of the boy before that swim race at thirteen. Not in Southern California anyway. It was as if he'd dropped out of the sky at the age of thirteen.

He sat back again and thought about the SEAL's odd reaction to the Line Crossing ritual up on the flight deck.

"Where did you come from, F/X?" he murmured. "And what happened to you?"

# 91

Command made an effort to keep the lid clamped down tight, but the story was as uncontainable as an oil spill. Within hours everyone on board knew the basics. No trace of Chavez and Cristobal had been found in the recycling chamber. A half-smoked cigarette; that was it. There was no way the two could have gone over the side; too much extra security that night. For three straight days a crew conducted a lengthy search of the entire boat.

The boys did not turn up.

When the admiral returned and learned what had happened, she immediately got on the horn with the mainland and arranged for them to take on a joint NCIS-FBI task force when they reached Hawaii. The threat of which greatly increased the pressure on Eagleberg—and therefore on Jackson and the others—to wrap up this investigation before then. The captain grew increasingly paranoid.

Finn followed it all through his bugged Lincoln Room conversations.

The week dragged past like Marley's chain.

Flight operations were resumed, along with their attendant daily FOD walkdowns, the unspoken message from command being, *See? Everything's back to normal!*

No one was fooled.

"Nothing like a crisis to bring people together," so went the popular wisdom—but this particular crisis seemed to work in exactly the opposite way. Every petty conflict was magnified, every rift driven deeper. Fear, withdrawal, and distrust—*they* became the new normal.

The rain that had dogged them since arriving at Fremantle finally stopped. At first the weather turned sunny and balmy with a warm dry breeze, then the breeze stopped and it grew blisteringly hot.

The AC system failed, was fixed, failed again.

Humidity hung in the air like wet woolen blankets, itchy and pestilential.

An outbreak of food-borne bacterial illness swept the ship, sending sailors by the hundreds through sick bay and back to their racks. Work hours were stretched, nerves frayed. Scuffles and fights broke out, with several violent assaults. All at once the brig's genpop was busy.

Back in Fremantle Harbour the ship had reminded Finn of a floating prison. Now it felt more like a floating death row, everyone on board wondering when and where the killer would strike next.

But he was already striking, throughout the ship.

As Finn knew all too well, a sniper could function as a precision instrument of psychological warfare, crippling an entire battalion by sowing confusion and chaos among its ranks. That's what their killer was doing. The dead and missing were his victims—but not his targets.

No, his real targets were the thousands of crew who were still alive.

By now everyone on board had twigged to the rhythm of the first three murders. Assuming the killer's six-day plan was back on track, after being interrupted by Finn's incarceration, the twenty-eighth should be the big day.

Finn could feel the crescendo of anxiety.

The twenty-eighth arrived.

Six thousand people held their breath.

Nothing happened.

Nobody went missing.

Yet no one felt relieved.

In fact, the anxiety deepened.

Another day went by.

And another.

Everyone waiting for the other shoe to drop.

# 92

**Monica was going crazy.**

The chief of security and his team were still interviewing people, but they hadn't called in either her or Papa Doc. Whatever theory they were pursuing, apparently they were interested mainly in talking to enlisted crew.

To her the truth was so obvious it practically screamed itself.

When Kris called Papa Doc "a classic male chauvinist, fucking racist, and unreconstructed homophobe," she'd hit it right smack on the nose. It was no secret, either, everyone in the air wing knew it. And wasn't that a precise description of the kind of person who would seek out these particular victims? Talk about finding for X! Add on a history of assault (even if unproven), plus that hostile encounter between the two of them the night Kris disappeared, and wouldn't you have enough to warrant an arrest?

She thought about asking Scott, but they hadn't spoken since she told him to "back off," and she was sure he'd want nothing to do with *this* conversation.

She itched to tell someone about Papa Doc's alleged date rape, to give up Alan Rickards's name. Rickards knew something, she'd seen it in his eyes. The man was a loose thread; one good yank and the whole sweater would come unraveled.

But did she dare? She had no way of knowing whether whoever she told would keep her confidence. Whistle-blowers were supposed to be protected—but this was the military: short of high treason, there was no sin greater than ratting out a superior officer. She would be gambling her career.

Besides, even if nobody revealed what she said, if they hauled Rickards in for questioning immediately after talking to her, wouldn't it be obvious that it was Monica who'd steered them his way?

And anyway, who would she tell? The chief of security was too close to Scott—and as much as she wished she could, she couldn't trust him. Could she trust Master Chief Jackson? She didn't know. He was already skeptical about her testimony from their brief interview.

Monica lay on her bunk, running her fingers over the patches and seams of Kris's quilt, which she had quietly pilfered and slipped into her own locker just minutes before the warrant officers arrived for their wordless sweep.

*August 31.* It was just a number, she told herself, the end of one calendar month and start of another. Still, somewhere in the course of that month, Kris had been stolen away, and now the month itself, the last month in which the two of them had been here in this stateroom together, talking and laughing, was zipping itself shut. Like a body bag.

*"Shit fire and save the matches,"* she muttered.

She threw aside the quilt and hopped down.

Two minutes later she was knocking on the door to an office she'd never visited before. "Come in," said a voice from inside. "It's open." She turned the handle and stepped inside.

"Can I help you?" said Commander Gaines.

# 93

On September first, halfway into its northeast passage to Hawaii, the USS *Abraham Lincoln* crossed both the Equator and the International Date Line at the same time, a juncture that the captain, determined to pull ship-wide morale out of its funk, had seized upon to commemorate with a Beer Day and a talent show.

The concept of Beer Day was simple: everyone on board who was not on essential work detail got one beer to drink—quite a luxury, given that alcohol was otherwise forbidden on board and they hadn't had a single port call in over half a year. There would be those who opted to sell their beer to some other swab, which meant there'd be some lucky sailors drinking multiples. Things would get a little rowdy. Add a talent show into the mix and the hilarity would only escalate. Count on it.

The crew loved it.

Monica could give a shit.

She'd told Gaines everything—about Kris's state of mind those last few days, the missed breakfasts, the weight loss, the drawn look, the paranoia. Her concerns that Kris might have been assaulted. That altercation between Kris and Papa Doc. The Academy rumor. Rickards. She should have felt unburdened—but now, waiting to find out what she'd stirred up, was somehow worse.

And that remark the SEAL made, last time they talked. It was driving her nuts.

She'd spent the past hour trying to hunt him down. He wasn't in his quarters or any of the mess facilities. Not in the library, not the gyms. Not out on the gun mounts or fantail. Time to check up on the flight deck, where the day's festivities were already under way. Oh boy.

Traversing the portside main artery on the gallery deck, she passed two sailors who already reeked of beer. Monica shuddered inwardly. The smell, the swagger, the up-to-no-good sparks in the eyes, it all reminded her of her Academy days . . . which made her think of Papa Doc back in the day, Papa Doc as an upperclassman, Papa Doc plying some semi-willing cadet with drinks and more. Movie-star good looks, frat-boy intentions.

The moment she pushed open the hatch to the catwalk she heard the ruckus from above: hooting, clapping, laughter, a screech of distortion from a jury-rigged PA system. She climbed the familiar five steel steps to the deck's surface where all the action was happening.

The first person she bumped into—literally—was Rickards, mid-joke with a few pilot pals. When he turned to see who it was the easy grin vanished.

"You," he said.

So much for confidentiality. "Alan! Hi," she began. "Listen, I hope you—"

"*Fuck you,* Halsey."

She stopped as if she'd been slapped.

He took a step forward and leaned in close, deliberately invading her space, his face inches from hers, and spat the words.

"*Fuck. You. Halsey.*"

Without waiting for a response he turned back to his friends and laughed at whatever joke they'd just told. She no longer existed.

Monica walked a few steps, shaken. She knew what it was to be cursed at, yelled at, verbally attacked; she'd been through that a hundred times, a thousand times. Par for the course. It was the deliberate leaning in that had got to her. The unalloyed venom. She felt like she'd been physically assaulted.

How had she not seen this before? Rickards and Papadakis. Classmates. Buddies. Of course.

She wanted to go take a shower.

She took a breath and looked around—and there he was. The SEAL, sitting off by himself. People avoiding him like the crazy neighbor's pit bull, which she could well understand; she'd heard the rumors. She'd seen the guy in action herself, down in the gym.

The SEAL seemed focused on whatever was going on up onstage. She turned and looked. The flight deck was now home to a crowd of maybe a thousand, most of them nursing plastic cups of beer, heckling and laughing at whatever lame skit was happening. She couldn't see any reason why he'd be watching so intently.

She turned back, walked over to the SEAL, plunked herself down next to him.

"You remember what you said about my CO?"

He turned his head to look at her but said nothing.

"You said, 'It wasn't your CO.' How did you know that's what I was thinking?"

The SEAL turned back to watch the stage. After a moment, he said, "I see where you'd get that. Decent theory."

"But wrong?"

"Yup."

All at once she felt irritated. Why couldn't the guy have a normal conversation? And why was he so convinced of Papa Doc's innocence? He'd witnessed that confrontation in the passageway himself. How could he say there wasn't something suspicious about that?

"Whoever's doing all this," the SEAL replied as if she'd voiced her thoughts aloud, "is putting on a hell of a show. Not this." He gestured toward the stage. "I mean the killings. That takes imagination."

"Oh? And why is that not my CO?"

"This is not a guy with a rich interior life."

Monica thought that was the lamest reasoning she'd ever heard. *My client couldn't have done it, Your Honor. He doesn't have a rich interior life.*

Had the SEAL ever even spoken with Papa Doc?

She was about to ask him about that when someone screamed.

# 94

Finn had just watched as the master of ceremonies gestured with his cane to a rolled-up canvas affixed high up at the back of the makeshift stage.

Some in the crowd who guessed what was coming were already starting to laugh. Even though the gigantic poster's exact content was a closely guarded secret, they knew what it would display: something truly, insanely ridiculous. A photoshopped image of the captain in drag, maybe, riding on top of Master Chief Jackson, rendered as a tank in a tutu. Or who knew what. Whatever the crew who put this on thought they could get away with.

With a soft *thoop!* the poster unfurled.

The laughter stopped. A thousand sailors froze in place as if God Almighty himself had just hit PAUSE.

Then someone near the stage let loose with a bile-curdling scream.

Others joined in, a wave of screams ripping through the crowd like a fire in a dying forest.

"Shit! Oh, *shit!* Ohhh, *SHIT!*" one guy moaned. "*Ohhh FUCK!*"

Another voice: "What—Oh, Jesus, oh, Jesus, Willy! WILLY! Oh, Jesus! Fuck me, man, FUCK me!"

"Holy mother of God," murmured someone near Finn. The person next to him vomited, right there on the deck.

It was not an image of the captain, or of Jackson, or of any other subject of lighthearted ridicule.

It was a diptych of two high-definition photos, side by side, each depicting a nearly identical scene: a squarish opening in a wall of charred steel, blazing fire inside, like a pizza oven. What looked like two logs jutting in through the narrow door.

Not logs.

Legs.

An iron shovel pushing in the prone figure of Seaman Willy Chavez in one shot, Seaman Ángel Cristobal in the other, the skin on their faces starting to bubble and smoke, wild eyes staring at the camera as they were fed feetfirst into the ship's jet fuel–powered, two-thousand-degree incinerator.

Finn heard a voice bellowing, *Cut it down! Cut it down!*—the chief of security, fighting his way up onto the stage, shoving people aside as he went—but nobody was listening.

*"QUIET!"* That was the air boss, whose voice carried like a thunderclap even without his PA system. The screaming and crying stopped as if someone had yanked the power cord. *"CUT IT DOWN! NOW!!"*

Three guys scrambled up onto the stage and managed to wrench the canvas free from its moorings.

The two incinerating boys crumpled and folded to the deck.

The talent show was over.

# VI

# Rubik's Cube

# 95

The weather that day looked foul from the start.

Like everyone else on board, Monica spent the morning trying to put the horror of the day before out of her mind.

Was it ridiculous to expect they'd all go about normal business in the face of what had just happened? Of course, but that was the navy for you. *Semper fortis, semper Gumby.* Always strong, always flexible. *Hooyah.*

And today was the big day, make or break.

Her HAC checkride.

Which, thanks to Alan Rickards, she was pretty sure she'd already flunked.

When she reached the flight deck the sky had turned an ugly, splotchy gray with green striations. As she climbed into the Knighthawk with her crew she tried to read the NATOPS officer's face. "Okay," was all he said, once they were all strapped in and he'd gotten tower clearance.

Monica lifted them off the flight deck, then banked them to port as they climbed into the gray sky and out over the open sea. For the next two hours the officer pushed her through her paces, checking every move she made, every response to every simulated emergency, Monica reacting, adjusting, adapting, drenched in sweat.

And then it was over.

She lowered the Knighthawk to brush the flight deck, kicked the engines back to idle, and sat dreading her instructor's feedback.

"Okay," he said without looking at her. "This is my stop." He abruptly hopped out of the chopper and someone else climbed in his place.

"Lieutenant," said Papa Doc with a curt nod, as he buckled himself into the co-pilot seat. "Let's go."

Monica sat frozen. What was happening here?

Papa Doc strapped on his helmet and spoke into his comms. "Gents," addressing Stickman and Chief Harris in back, "we're taking her up again for a brief spin around the block."

Monica heard Harris and Stickman behind her, buckling back in. She still hadn't moved.

"Let's go," Papa Doc repeated without looking at her. "Already cleared with the tower."

What the *hell*? What was this, some sort of checkride postscript? An extra punishment round?

"Lieutenant?" he said.

She pushed the Knighthawk's rotor blades back up to full power, got the plane captain's signal for takeoff, and once again lifted the bird off the deck and banked away to the left.

As they angled up and away from the ship she shot a glance at her CO—and was thrown by what she saw. He looked terrible: haggard face, sunken eyes, his normally olive skin now a faint gray-green.

Like a man who'd seen his own ghost.

Once airborne he reached over and switched the in-

ternal comms to front-seats-only, an option that allowed
pilot and co-pilot to speak privately, without being
heard by the crew in back. Monica steeled herself for
whatever tongue-lashing her superior officer was about
to unleash.

Yet for a full minute he said nothing at all, just stared
out the windshield as Monica, for lack of any other in-
struction, settled into the standard D-loop. When he did
finally speak it was in a low monotone.

"The rumor you've heard is accurate."

Did he just say . . . *accurate*?

"It was my senior year," he continued in the same
monotone. "She was a frosh. Wide-eyed at being asked
out by an upperclassman. At the time I thought—" His
voice faltered, then caught and continued. "At that time,
in that circumstance, I thought she was saying 'yes.' Or
that's what I told myself. It was not—" again that brief
stumble and recovery "—it was not my proudest moment."

Good Christ. That's what they were doing here? He
wanted to make a *confession*? Monica felt her pulse
pounding in her throat.

"It happened a second time. Different girl . . ."

Monica's breath stopped. Sloane had talked about
*one* assault. There were *more*?

"The second girl—woman—tried to speak up about
it. But I'd covered my tracks and again, I was an upperclassman. And of course, a man. Nobody believed her."

He paused for a sickening eternity, like the nausea of
free fall, then droned on, staring out the Knighthawk's
windshield as he spoke.

"Third girl—woman . . ."

Jesus. Monica thought she might throw up.

"That one tried to kill herself. Ended up dropping
out. After that I stopped. No more. That was it. It all
happened years ago."

Stickman and Harris had to be wondering what the hell was going on up there in front, but she didn't dare make a sound, didn't dare even look Papa Doc's way. She just kept flying the D, wishing she weren't there, wishing she weren't hearing any of what she was hearing.

Papa Doc took a shaky breath. "I just wanted you to know, you were right." He looked away, out the far side of the helo. "Of course I'll deny this conversation ever took place. Though I expect it'll all come out now anyway." He nodded toward the *Lincoln* below. "You can take 'er in."

As she began her reapproach, Monica debated furiously whether to ask the question. Better not to say a word. But she had to. It wasn't enough to know. She had to hear him *say* it.

"And Kristine?"

She waited for a reply, then realized he hadn't heard her.

"And Kristine?" she repeated.

He turned back and looked at her vaguely. "What?"

"Kristine," Monica said again, quietly. "What about Kristine?"

He seemed genuinely puzzled. "Shiflin?"

She stared at him.

"You think . . . God, no. What are you saying?" He frowned at her—and then his face congealed into an expression of horror. "You think *I* had—?" He slumped back in his seat and stared forward at the darkening sky. "You think *I* had something to do with . . ."

He was silent for a moment. "God, no," he repeated. "When she disappeared, I was heartsick."

*Heartsick?* Her CO, Papa Doc, the arrogant self-confessed rapist prick . . . was *heartsick*?

She wanted to believe he was lying. She wanted to believe that with all her heart. She wanted to scream at him, go at him with her nails, rip his lying face off.

She began their descent.

As they neared the deck she saw a small knot of men gathered by their landing spot just forward of elevator 4.

Papa Doc's face curled into a frown.

"Christ," he said. "Is *that* what they're saying I . . . ?"

Now they were close enough to see the men clearly. There was Mac, the chief of security, and two masters-at-arms.

One held a pair of cuffs.

"Christ," he repeated softly. "They'll crucify me."

# 96

The library was empty today. Finn sat at the first PC station and fired it up. Since his coded warning from "Stan L" and "Smitty" he'd returned once a week. So far there'd been no more messages. He didn't expect any.

He tuned out the CNN talking heads and went directly to Gmail, starting with the two anonymous accounts he hadn't yet deleted. Nothing. Next he opened one of his regular Gmail accounts and checked that one. Nothing. Opened the other account.

Something.

Not a reply from Kennedy nor from any of his teammates. Not another coded note from "Stan L."

It was an email from squidink28@gmail.com, time-stamped less than half an hour ago.

The *Lincoln* was passing through the Baker Island time zone; it would be five hours later for Carol. Which meant she would have sent this in the evening, when she would be at home, probably triple-locked into her darkened houseboat, watching television.

No subject line.

Finn clicked on the entry to open the body of the email.

Carol's messages were always brief to the point of telegraphic, rarely more than one line. Still, this one was short even by Carol's standards.

It consisted of a single word.

Run

Finn stared at the screen. What could have given Carol the sense that he was in danger? She wouldn't have had any contact from "Stan L." They didn't know each other.

Run

Run from what? And how would Carol know it was headed his way?

The television droned on. Something caught his eye on the TV screen. His brain had caught it through his peripheral vision, something meaningful but which he hadn't yet consciously registered.

He consciously registered it now.

The news crawl along the bottom of the screen.

He stopped breathing.

. . . HUNDREDS MORE TURN OUT FOR BOSTON MEMORIAL SERVICE,
LT MICHAEL JOSEPH KENNEDY TO BE POSTHUMOUSLY AWARDED
MEDAL OF HONOR NEXT WEEK AT . . .

Finn sat stone still.
Kennedy—*dead*?

# 97

He fumbled out one hand to pull the PC's keyboard toward him. Forced himself to focus on it. Called up Google.

Key by key, he punched in a search string. Then sat staring at the screen as he waited for the snail-slow browser to serve up its results.

He scanned the first few stories. They all said the same thing. Lieutenant Michael Joseph Kennedy had been killed on an unnamed mission, location classified, on August first of this year. In excess of one thousand people showed up for the memorial services . . .

Finn's brain was on fire, sparks flaring in all directions but one thought outshouting all the others.

*August first.*

His first day on the *Lincoln*.

Was it possible that they'd flown out of Bahrain early that same morning, just hours after Finn's departure, and deployed to some Middle Eastern hot spot where they'd immediately come under fire and Kennedy had taken a hit?

Sure, it was possible—in a world where pigshit could fly.

"Unnamed mission"? "Location classified"? Bald-faced lies, fabricated for public consumption.

So what really happened?

They last saw each other on July 31, the day that started with a busted satphone and ended with an escort off the island and on to the *Lincoln*.

*Give me twenty-four.*

Why had he steered Finn outside that day to finish their conversation?

To avoid the possibility of eavesdropping, electronic or otherwise. Because Kennedy knew they were being surveilled.

By whom?

By whoever executed those Yemeni families. And then silenced Kennedy. Because he knew. And they would have suspected Finn knew, too.

Hence the busted satphone.

If Finn hadn't been whisked away onto an aircraft carrier, would he have been the second casualty of that "unnamed mission"? Had Kennedy himself somehow engineered Finn's hasty exit, for Finn's own protection?

Now Finn understood.

Saw the whole thing.

They were set up that night. The people who did this planted that false intel. The people who did this wanted Finn and Kennedy out of the way so they could take out that settlement. No doubt because someone who lived there could finger them for the murder of the American journalist. Who no doubt had stumbled onto the rest of their dirty little criminal enterprise.

No wonder Finn's team couldn't find the terrorist cell they'd been hunting. The ones doing the stealing, the ones terrorizing locals and assassinating civic leaders.

There was no terrorist cell.

Never had been.

It was men from that third squad, the one hanging

back to cover their flanks. Only they didn't "hang back"—they took off to go carry out their own bloody mission five klicks to the east.

They murdered the journalist.

They murdered the Yemeni families.

They murdered Kennedy.

His team.

His own guys.

*It's the assholes who keep their contradictions hidden you have to worry about.*

*RUN.*

And they would be waiting for Finn, too, when he set foot off the boat.

Yes, there would be a welcoming committee of navy cops, or FBI, or DOD, there to escort him to HQ for a classified debrief. To get him in a room and ask him just what the hell happened out there. But there would be someone else there waiting, too.

A second welcoming committee.

With cuffs.

Maybe someone inserted in HQ with a needle on his person. Or someone at the dock, tucked behind a tenement window or on an office building rooftop, some retired Teams guy who wasn't exactly retired. Someone as skilled as Finn.

*Special assignment.*

Finn would never make it to that briefing alive.

He looked up again at the TV screen. The news crawl had moved on to other headlines.

Carol would have seen the same item. She would have known immediately that it was a whitewash. That Finn was in danger.

Suddenly the images flooded his head again—

*the shattered door—*

*the child's sightless eyes, black pooling blood—*

*the flies—*

A wave of nausea slammed into him like a car crash. He bolted upright so abruptly he flipped over the PC keyboard.

He lurched to the door, stumbled out into the passageway. Made his way to a ladder at the far end, hauled himself up, paused at the top and gripped the rail, waiting for the nausea to subside.

It didn't.

He pushed through the exterior hatch and emerged out onto the starboard-side catwalk, where he steadied himself and took several long breaths of the thickening ocean air.

The images faded.

He mounted the five steps to the flight deck and stood, leaning on the railing. Took a few more steadying breaths. His vision finally came into focus.

There was some sort of commotion happening on the deck, over on the port side. A Knighthawk had just landed, the crew standing half in and half out of the bird, staring.

Two masters-at-arms had Movie Star in cuffs.

# 98

Finn watched as the pair of MAs ushered the helo squadron CO aft onto elevator platform 4 to take him below. He glanced over at West Texas, sitting frozen in the pilot's seat. She looked like someone who'd just struck and killed the family dog with her car.

"Hey!" A scuffle.

Movie Star had just shoved one of the MAs off his feet. Now he swung his cuffed fists at the other, whacking him in the head, and took off at a run. Where did he think he could run to? Maybe he wasn't thinking at all. Maybe he was acting out of pure panic.

Or maybe he'd do anything—literally *anything*—to avoid prison.

Hands still shackled, Movie Star made a dash for the far side of the elevator.

And leapt off.

The helo crew scrambled back into the bird, their plane captain frantically clapping his outspread arms over his head, giving them the "cleared for liftoff" signal.

But Finn saw all this only after he was already in motion.

He took off like a rifle shot—

Ran full tilt across the flight deck—

Accelerated when he reached the edge—

And flew off the ship.

The sea state was now belching up ten- and twelve-foot waves, the water a deep burgundy.

Falling feetfirst, eyes on the horizon for clean entry, Finn pierced the surface like a lance and plunged twenty feet under before the water resistance slowed his momentum. He pinched his nose and blew out to equalize the pressure in his ears—at this depth he was at nearly double normal atmospheric pressure—then executed an instant flip and ripped back toward the surface, searching as he swam, scanning for Movie Star.

There!

Finn had experience swimming in cuffs; not elegant, but doable. And Movie Star knew what he was doing.

First thing you did in this situation was put distance between yourself and the ship to avoid getting sucked into its churn. Every experienced sailor knew this. Finn willed his thoughts to reach the man. *Swim away from the ship!*

Movie Star swam toward the ship.

Toward—and aft.

Cresting the surface, Finn was vaguely aware of the Knighthawk above and behind him, Stickman leaning out the side door and shouting directions back into the cockpit, helping West Texas navigate the helo to a spot where it could safely hover and drop him.

*Don't do it, Stickman. You'll only die here, too.*

Finn homed in on Movie Star's trajectory like a heat-seeking missile, closing the gap, churning gallons of the Pacific with the most powerful strokes he could muster—but Movie Star was still a few dozen meters ahead and closing fast with the ship's stern.

Heading for the propellers.

Behind him Finn heard Harris shout "Go!" and Stickman make the dive.

Movie Star was a determined man. He made it to his destination just a dozen strokes ahead of Finn.

Into the propellers.

One moment he was there and the next he was gone, sucked under and into the blender-blade chop of those massive brass screws.

Commander Nikos Demetrius Papadakis was now a cloud of blood, tissue, and bone fragments.

As Finn would be, too, within seconds.

Being this close to the ship's wake was like jumping into a black hole's event horizon. Finn knew this from countless exercises off the San Diego pier. There was a point where you still had enough energy to break free. And a point where you'd be swallowed. He executed an impossible turn and began swimming away from the ship—but he'd gotten too close. Even as he powered forward, away from the ship, he was being sucked backward by the churn.

Event horizon.

Stickman was now six meters away and getting closer. Bad move. Damn him. If he tried to grab Finn's flight suit they would just get sucked in together.

Stickman grabbed Finn's flight suit.

For what felt like a span of minutes they seemed to hang motionless, suspended in space between the pull of the ship and the force of their own efforts in the opposite direction.

In this tug-of-war there was no way the ship could lose.

Yet, foot by watery foot, swimming in tandem now, Finn and Stickman pulled steadily away from the carrier's hull until they finally reached the lip of the furiously bobbing rescue basket. Grabbed at it over and over, snagged it on the fourth try.

Pulled themselves over and in.

Collapsed.

Let the hoist do its work.

As they reached the hovering chopper, Finn looked over and gasped, "Thanks—Stickman—owe you—one."

The kid's face flushed with pride—but only for a moment, before being overtaken by the horror of what he'd just witnessed.

West Texas navigated her Knighthawk back over to their landing spot.

When they touched down, a second pair of masters-at-arms stood waiting for them.

With cuffs.

# 99

"By your rash actions, you put *lives* in jeopardy! By what Christforsaken delusion did you imagine you had the right to take matters into your own hands and risk the safety and welfare of *my crew*?"

The captain sat at the fore of the bridge, gripping the arms of his big pedestal chair, the one with COMMANDING OFFICER stenciled on the back in gold letters.

"Your guys wouldn't have made it in time," said Finn, standing in cuffs between the two MAs. "Sir," he added.

"And you felt it was your divine prerogative to insert yourself into the situation?"

"I'm a rescue swimmer. It's what we do. We rescue."

Captain Eagleberg's face turned a shade whiter while his ears turned a simmering red.

"Well, *I'm* the commanding officer on this ship, mister, and that's what *we* do. We *command*."

Finn shrugged.

The captain shook his head in disbelief. He turned to his XO. "Artie, our guest seems awfully casual about the situation he's put us in, doesn't he? Perhaps he thinks running this ship is like cooking a small fish."

He swiveled back to face Finn. "That right, Chief

Finn? You think running this ship is like cooking a small fish?"

Finn gave no reply. He was looking at the captain's nose.

It looked like a lily's pistil, swaggering and self-important.

The captain leaned in and dropped his voice to a tone of soft menace. "You have anything to say in your defense, *Mister* Finn? Because right now would most assuredly be the time."

Finn nodded. "I do, sir."

The captain sat back in his big chair and spread out his hands. "Well, I can't wait to hear it."

Finn waited a beat before speaking. He glanced at Arthur Gaines, then around the compartment at the rest of the staff, then back to the captain.

"Sir," he said, "you are an asshole."

Every face froze.

"Possibly the biggest asshole I have ever met," Finn continued, "and I have met my share of assholes. Worse than that, you're an asshole with power, and that's dangerous. The slipshod way you run this place, you've put *six thousand* lives in jeopardy. You're a stain on the US Navy. Sir."

For a long moment the captain sat stone still, a tremor of rage playing over his features. Then he rose from the chair and closed the distance between them in three long strides, got right in Finn's face, staring down at him nose to nose.

Pistil to nose.

*"I could have you court-martialed! I could bury you under a rock you'll never crawl out from under!"*

"I don't know." Finn frowned as if thinking it over, then shook his head. "I don't think so."

A guttural sound rose up from the captain's throat and erupted into a roar of fury, and as it did his arm whipped around and delivered an open-hand round-house slap to Finn's face.

Without taking his eyes from Finn he addressed his chief of security. "Mac, please have Mister Finn escorted below to the brig to be remanded into solitary, where he will be held until we make port in Hawaii . . ." As the two MAs took Finn by the arms the captain continued, shouting his last few words after them as they hustled him off the bridge. ". . . *pursuant to a general court-martial WITH THE MAXIMUM PENALTY!!*"

He wiped the spittle from his mouth with the back of his hand and turned to face a half circle of stunned faces.

*"What are you looking at?"* he snapped.

Once inside the brig Finn was thoroughly frisked—once again, by Frank, exactly the same way as before: torso, then each arm, then each leg.

Trained rats.

"Back for a return engagement, Chief Finn," said Frank. "Couldn't stay away?"

"Encore performance."

Frank laughed quietly as he finished at Finn's left foot, carefully checking the ankle. "Hey, Dewitt said to ask, you master the getting-out part yet?"

Finn called out to the main section of the brig, where Dewitt was seated. *"I'll let you know, Dewitt."*

Frank chuckled again, then stood and faced his prisoner. Shook his head and sighed. "Okay, then, you know the drill." He walked over to the cell door and held it open. "Your suite awaits."

Finn stepped into the cell, turned to face Frank, and sat down on the steel bunk.

Frank hung his head inside the door for a moment before closing it. "You know they caught the guy who did all the killings, right?" He shook his head. "A pilot. You believe that?" His voice dropped a notch. "Guy took a footer, they said, ate the prop."

Finn looked at him and nodded. "That's what I heard."

"So what are you in for this time?"

"GCM. Maximum penalty."

Frank's jaw dropped. He spoke in a hoarse whisper. "Are you shitting me?"

Finn lay back on the thin mat, fingers laced behind his head.

"I shit you not," he said.

Maximum penalty for a general court-martial, if the captain could make it stick, was death.

# 100

Midnight.

Flight ops had been called off for the night; they were skirting some sort of tropical storm system and the sea state was getting too rough.

Monica sat in the pilot's seat of her Knighthawk, staring out through the helicopter windshield at the darkened space of hangar bay 3, tears of fury and frustration running down her face.

*Do you cry when things don't go well?*

"You better fucking believe it," she said. A mechanic in the helo next to hers glanced over at her, startled, then looked away again when he realized she was talking to herself.

Everyone on board had breathed a huge sigh of collective relief. Murders solved, killer found, case closed—and that terrible curse was finally behind them. In just two days they'd be docking at Hawaii—port call at last!

And then, that time-honored Navy tradition the whole crew had been looking forward to for weeks: Tiger Cruise! The final leg of the deployment, where crew members would be joined in Hawaii by friends and family, who would be allowed to come on board and finish out the ship's last few days as they steamed homeward. Finally.

There was good news for Monica, too: late that afternoon, after all the drama was over, she got word that she'd aced her checkride. Her HAC was in the bag.

She should have felt triumphant. She didn't.

She felt drained and defeated.

Papa Doc had been telling the truth. She was sure of it. He was a petty, angry man with a nasty history, and he'd chosen suicide rather than face his crimes. But he hadn't killed Kristine.

"Shit!" she muttered.

She didn't want to accept the idea that her best friend really had taken her own life. It made no sense. But maybe the truth didn't always make sense.

Maybe sometimes there was no X to find.

If Monica had forced the issue, sat Kris down, looked her in the eye, and got her to open up about what was *really* going on for her, might things have turned out different?

She'd never know.

In any case, Papa Doc didn't kill her. And now Papa Doc was dead himself.

Thanks to her.

*Never back down.*

And she hadn't.

No, she sure hadn't.

Scott warned her. Rickards pushed back. The SEAL flat-out told her that her CO had not done what she was convinced he had. Even Master Chief Jackson, when he questioned her, put it right out on the table. *Can you tell us something you actually observed, any specific behavior or exchange, anything at all?* No, she couldn't—but she still wouldn't back down, and she had pushed her way into the investigation and handed them a convenient suspect for their bullshit theory. Not that she could really blame the investigators.

There was only one person to blame here.

Her own damn self.

# 101

Midnight.

The mood at midrats was celebratory. Practically giddy. Tiger Cruise!—the navy's version of *We're goin' ta Disney World!*—and then home again, home again, jiggity fucking jig.

He'd watched his compadres yak and stuff their faces and tell one another sophomoric jokes for as long as he could stand it. And now here he was, back in his cramped, gray office space where he had spent the past two weeks with Mac and his people, grilling half the boat, and to what purpose?

He balled up a meaningless meeting memo from his desktop and tossed it across the little office space toward the five-inch hoop he'd taped to the back of his door. The shot missed.

To most people who knew him, the USS *Abraham Lincoln*'s JAG officer was a hero. A kind, patient person, solid officer, compassionate leader.

The truth?

Scott Angler was all those things, yes.

But he was also an angry, bitter man.

In the gun battle that took his leg and his friends' lives, Scott had also lost a core part of himself, the part that answered to the hero's call. He'd thought becoming a JAG officer would help him get that back, but it hadn't. And he missed it sorely, every bit as much as his leg. More.

He didn't like SEALs. He saw them as gunslingers, swinging dicks, egomaniacs who believed the rules applied to everyone but them. Yes, he was a SEAL himself, or used to be, but that only meant he knew what he was talking about. Scott Angler didn't like SEALs. And he especially didn't like this one.

*No last name. Give me a fucking break.*

He was also irritated as fuck at Harlan "Robbie" Jackson. A damn good CMC, he'd give him that, and that mattered to Scott—but that didn't mean he had to agree with the man.

Captain Eagleberg? Scott wouldn't cross the street to piss on that one to put out the proverbial fire. A grade A dick and one of the shittiest leaders Scott had ever come across—but he was a smart man with some serious family pedigree and he was, for better or worse, the commanding officer of this vessel. It had never sat well with Scott, the way Jackson had gone behind the captain's back to initiate his own investigative team. And then to top it off, refusing to consider the SEAL's obvious guilt?

Unbefuckinglievable.

Except that he'd been right. It wasn't the SEAL, after all.

And Monica had been right, too, right about her CO all along. And Scott had refused to listen to her, refused to take her instincts seriously.

And because of it, three more murders had happened before they finally caught the guy.

Some hero.

He balled up another memo, this one from Mac's summary conclusions, and one-handed it at the hoop on the door. Another miss.

"Fuck me," he said.

# 102

**Midnight.**

"Here's to fair winds and a following sea," Jackson said aloud to the empty office, and he hoisted a mug of hot coffee from midrats.

Earlier that evening he had officially disbanded the team, quietly thanking Lew and Indy for their service and their trust in him and repeating his promise of confidentiality concerning their clandestine formation. Now he was taking a quiet moment to, what? To mark the passage of an era, he supposed.

Savoring the victory. If you could call it that.

He sat brooding into his mug.

Trying to shake the thought twisting in his gut.

What if Papadakis wasn't the guy?

What if he was set up? What if the killer went out of his way from the start to target victims in a pattern that would point toward a bigot, to throw any investigations off the scent? In a couple days they would be in Hawaii, and the mainland a few days after that. The boat would empty out. The killer could walk away free.

And that finger. If Papadakis was playing out some kind of vigilante fantasy, Keeping the Navy Pure for

Straight White Males, okay—but why leave a finger? Why *take* a finger? And if it *was* Papadakis, how did that fit with Lew's whole piece about the killer wanting to create a reign of terror?

It made no rational sense.

He took a hot sip, made a face, set the mug down. Weak as piss tonight.

Jackson had talked to Scott that afternoon, tried to anyway. It was a brief, strained encounter. He didn't ask, but Jackson had wondered if Scott still liked Chief Finn for the murders.

But *that* made no sense—not after today. Let's just say Finn *was* the perpetrator of these crimes and had set up Papadakis to take the fall. Then why in God's name would he try to save the guy's life?

Okay . . . but did he really?

The man was a SEAL, and not only a SEAL but a top operator. And before that he was an SAR swimmer. You didn't get any more capable. He could imagine exactly what Scott would say: *If he wanted the guy's life saved, it would've been saved.*

An excellent point.

And Jackson had to admit, the circumstantial evidence against the SEAL was impressive. The killings started right when he came aboard. Then stopped while he was in the brig, and started again the night he got out.

And it couldn't be easy to track and kill someone, then dispose of the body, all completely without detection in such tight quarters as an aircraft carrier. Let alone do it four times. (Or five, depending on whether you were going by incident count or body count.) All that had to take some skill.

No, not *some* skill. An extremely high level of skill.

All of which pointed guess where.

And speaking of pointing, there was that damn finger, too. A trophy. Just like in Mukalla. Which Scott didn't even know about.

His thoughts were interrupted by the sound of his phone. He stared at it. The last time he'd gotten a call at such an unexpected hour it had been the morning they found the two incinerator kids missing. He didn't much care for the reminder.

It was Indy, calling from her office up in CVIC.

"You're still up?" said Jackson.

"I can't sleep."

"No. Neither can I."

"Well," she said. "Even if you could, you won't after you read this."

"This?"

"That incident file you asked about? I have it." She paused. "It's ugly."

# 103

Finn did not feel things the way other people did. But that didn't mean he didn't feel them. In fact, it was precisely because he didn't feel things "normally" that when he did, he felt them far more acutely than most. Or maybe it was the other way around. Maybe it was the very fact that he felt those things to such an unbearable depth that had led him to forge different, more indirect emotional pathways.

He had never stopped to think about it, didn't think about it now. All he knew, lying on his back in his darkened cell, was that there was a two-thousand-pound weight crushing down on his chest.

Kennedy?

Gone?

Kennedy had been more than his OIC, more than a teammate. A brother.

And Finn knew what a brother was.

One January night in the middle of Hell Week, Finn's BUD/S class had spent hours on and around the rocks of the San Diego coast, navigating out and back again in Zodiacs, rigid-hulled inflatable boats that could carry a dozen men each. They were soaked to the bone, covered in sand, bare degrees from hypothermia. Bleeding in a dozen places. Every move felt like being rubbed all over with coarse-grade sandpaper. The task was to ignore all that and focus on the rolling sets of incoming waves to avoid having their rafts—and themselves—sliced to ribbons on the rocks.

That's what this felt like right now. Bleeding in a dozen places.

Groaning with the effort, he pushed away thoughts of Kennedy, fighting the sense that he was betraying his brother by doing so, and tried to focus. He heard his own breathing, coarse and heavy, forced himself to take a long, even inhale, then let it out. Slow. Controlled.

Focus.

Think it through.

Naming Movie Star as their perp might have satisfied the chief of security, and it might satisfy the captain, but it wouldn't wash with the CMC. He was too sharp, too conscientious. Same for Supercop. They would keep at it, both of them, more so than ever, now that everyone else considered the problem solved. They wouldn't stop till they had their man.

Which meant at least one of them would be coming after him. Because Finn himself was the most obvious suspect. There were a dozen airtight circumstantial reasons that said he was the one who did these things.

Which forced the sobering question:

*Was he?*

He had no solid memories of his whereabouts those hours during which both Schofield and Shiflin went missing. Or Santiago. Or the two E-2s in recycling.

So, yes, technically speaking, it was possible.

The one they were looking for, the killer—*it could be him*.

The notion made no sense to Finn. No sense at all.

Why would he kill Schofield? Or Biker? Or any of them? Yes, Finn knew what it was to kill another human being. Had done so himself, more than once. But not like this. No, he didn't for a moment think he would have done these killings.

The problem was, he couldn't remember.

He needed to.

Mukalla he would deal with later. First things first. He needed to clear himself *on* the boat before he faced what was waiting for him *off* the boat.

Which meant he needed to ID their killer.

Assuming it wasn't himself.

Focus.

Remember.

According to Stevens, he *did* remember, it was just that those particular memories were locked away in a cave and there was a bear in there. He needed to get past the bear. Stevens said you didn't just charge in, but that's exactly what Finn had done in his office. He made a run at the bear, and it whacked him.

He needed to go back into that cave again, but as quiet as a shadow. To tread carefully, one memory fragment at a time.

Not poke the bear.

Stalk it.

In the dark, Finn sat up, swiveled, and placed his bare feet square on the cold deck.

Slowly, he breathed in through his nostrils.

Let the breath hold itself for four, five, six, seven seconds.

Slowly let it out, through his mouth.

And in, through his nostrils.

And let it pause.

And out, through his lips.

And in.

*Where did you grow up?*

# 104

**Midnight.**

Lew Stevens sat hunched over his desk, consulting the little notebook he'd been using to keep his Finn research notes. He'd hit a brick wall at age thirteen, when Finn first showed up in Southern California. When he'd seemed to appear out of nowhere.

He knew, or could at least surmise based on the evidence thus far, that a thirteen-year-old boy named Finn Something had first appeared in Southern California without any evident family or family history, most likely from somewhere nearby. He decided to broaden his search radius to include western Arizona and western Nevada. He considered the northern tip of Mexico, from Tijuana to Ensenada, but he thought it more likely that they were dealing with an American boy from a contiguous American state.

And with some sort of traumatic past.

Car accident? Too enormous a data sector to search, and anyway, he had a hunch that what he was looking for involved trauma from some sort of violent crime. Home invasion. Shooting. Domestic violence.

He began combing through news archives for stories

of violent crime whose victims or witnesses included boys age ten to thirteen.

After a fruitless half hour, he widened his search area to all of Arizona and all of Nevada. Nothing. He pushed the boundaries out to include western Oregon. Still nothing. Then all of Oregon.

And, bang. He found something.

# 105

0045 hours.

*Where did you grow up?* That was the question Stevens had asked, so that's where Finn started.

He was surprised how difficult it was. He tried to stay on one memory, to bring it more sharply into focus and see how far he could play it, but it would shift and crackle and blur and another completely unrelated memory would cut in. Like radio signals gone awry in an ocean of static.

*Running through the trees, the sun-dappled forest floor . . . Boyd, scrabbling to reorient himself, getting sucked into the maw of the destroyer's ballast pump . . . following deer tracks with Ray . . . sitting against the interior wall of the brick-and-plaster dwelling, heat lightning searing his field of vision . . . black blood pooling, flies buzzing—*

His eyes jerked open as a wave of nausea slammed into him, knocking him breathless. The darkness of his cell felt terrifying.

Breathe in, let it hold, four, five, six, seven, breathe out.

Breathe in . . .

During the pool competency phase in BUD/S, instructors would devise the most fiendish torments possible—tie your air hose in knots, rip your respirator out of your mouth, shackle your wrists to your feet, anything to push you to the point where you *had* to come up and gasp for air. But if you did, you flunked, and Finn had seen a dozen guys pass out underwater and pop unconscious to the surface like dead goldfish. Not Finn. He would just sink to the bottom and sit, waiting out the instructor.

He needed to do that now, to sink to the bottom of this dark pool. And wait.

He closed his eyes and sank.

*Sun-dappled forest floor . . . following deer tracks with Ray . . . Ray making grilled cheese sandwiches . . . the place by the millstream where you could lie down and watch the minnows and goldfish and frogs and the—*

His eyes jerked open as he gasped for air, the wave of nausea slamming into him again, nearly forcing him back onto the rack's thin mattress.

He fought it, rocking forward and back, slowing, stilling himself. Gripped the edge of the bunk with both hands. Drew a shuddering breath in, then heaved it out with a *whoosh*. Then another. And another, slower, more measured.

And again, slipping down into the deep.

Remembering.

*The cabin in the woods, canopy of broadleaf maples, scent of grand firs . . .*

It was almost an hour before he found it.

He was deep in early memories (*fat slice of chocolate cake on a plate, a dimly lit kitchen*) when his eyes jerked

open again—for the tenth time? eleventh? twentieth?—
and he burst back up to the surface.

His hands had gone numb, his cell filled with a buzzing sound.

He shook his head.

It was that ringing in his ears, the same one he'd ex-
perienced a few weeks earlier with Tom the Ordie.
They'd been down in that flare magazine, talking about
Biker the jet pilot and how she never drank coffee—

And that was when he heard it.

Somewhere in the depths of Finn's brain there came a
soft *click*—a neurochemical spark flying between tem-
poral lobe and prefrontal cortex as one among thousands of innocuous memory fragments suddenly burst
open, a single rocket against the night sky.

Coffee.

Finn sat straight.

Closed his eyes again.

Sorted through the stills and clips.

Saw images of sailors getting coffee at Jittery Abe's—
dozens, hundreds, thousands of sailors, a forest of
lattes, a landscape of grande double-shots.

And one coffee order that didn't fit.

"Americano, tall," he heard her say.

A short, black-haired jet pilot.

Biker.

Who never drank coffee.

He opened his eyes and called out to his jailer.

"Hey, Frank," he said. "I need to get a message out."

# 106

0145 hours.

"Well, look at you," said Jackson. "Mouthed off to the teacher, got yourself sent to the principal's office again. Some kids never learn."

"I have something," said the voice behind the steel mesh–covered door.

"It's late, Chief Finn." Jackson looked at his watch. "No, as a matter of fact it's early. Too early for BS."

"A lead."

Jackson shook his head. "Time for a lead's behind us. Suspect charged, sentenced, executed by propeller. Or hadn't you heard."

The SEAL didn't reply. He had to know that Jackson suspected him. What game he was playing at now, Jackson couldn't begin to guess at.

He sighed. "What's the lead."

"The jet pilot who disappeared. Biker."

Jackson stiffened. Hearing the woman's name spoken by the man who very possibly killed her . . . it gave him the creeps. "Lieutenant Shiflin," he said.

"She got coffee. Three times. August first, August fourth. August eighth."

August eighth. The day she disappeared.

"Uh-huh."

"She didn't drink coffee."

Jackson rubbed his big hand over his head. *Madone*. "She bought a cup of coffee for a co-worker. Heck of a breakthrough, Columbo."

"Not a co-worker."

Jackson got to his feet.

"Have your intel person look at her schedule on those days," said the voice behind the grate.

Jackson shook his head. "She's already done that."

"Not with the squadron. With her day job."

"This is what I'm saying. She's gone over all those schedules, from a week before each disappearance to a week after. Gone over them with an electron microscope. There's nothing there."

"Have her look closer."

"If you say so." Jackson stepped away from the solitary cell and toward the outer door. "Good talk."

*"Jackson."*

Jackson stopped. Had the man ever called him by his name before?

"Have her look closer."

# 107

0200 hours.

Lew had been at it now for nearly two hours.

He'd found a short piece in an eastern Oregon newspaper on a shooting incident in a rural unincorporated community along the Snake River, by the Oregon-Idaho border. Hunting accident? Robbery? The piece didn't say, only that two young boys were found at the scene, ages eight and eleven; that the younger boy had been transported to an area hospital; and that the parents were still being located.

It didn't give either of the boys' names, nor did it mention the fate of the older boy.

Eight years old. Lew noted the date of the article and did the simple math. It fit. The younger boy could be Finn.

Continuing his search, he'd found a second story from the following day, and then another—and then, silence. He scoured larger newspapers in the bigger cities to the west, looked up local network affiliate newscasts. Nothing.

Whatever happened, it had generated buzz for something like twenty-four hours and then the lid had clamped down. Curious.

He browsed some more, leaving behind the incident and following minor tributaries and feeder streams. About a month later he stumbled upon a "Letters to the Editor" entry that asked the question, whatever happened to the search for the boys' parents? He found no trace of an answer.

He went back to the original article and reread it. In the latter part of the piece, they ran a brief quote from the detective on the scene. Dalton Mosley.

He looked at the name. Talk about a long shot: this was nearly thirty years ago. Was there any chance the man was still on the force?

He looked up the number of the local police department there and placed the call. Not quite eight o'clock in the morning, their time, and he figured he'd still get the night desk. He was not expecting a geyser of information.

"Crane Neck Police Department, Jerry Anderson speaking."

"Good morning, Officer Anderson. The name is Lewis Stevens, I'm a lieutenant with the navy, staff psychologist for the USS *Abraham Lincoln*. On board right now, somewhere in the Pacific."

"Uh-huh."

"I'm wondering if by any chance there's still a Dalton Mosley on active duty with your department?"

"Mosley?"

"Yes. I'm looking for some background information on a case he worked on, that'd be nearly thirty years ago now. Eight-year-old boy, some kind of accident. First name Finn, don't have a last name."

"Mosley?"

Ah. Definitely not a geyser.

"Yes," Lew repeated. "Detective Dalton Mosley. He would have been active there in the early nineties."

"Early nineties?"

"Yes."

"Hang on." After an interminable wait, the voice came back on. "Retired."

"Yes, I was kind of expecting that. Would it be possible to get in touch with him?"

"With Mosley?"

*So this is how major crimes are solved,* thought Lew.

"Yes, please. If that's possible. It's important," he added. "Could be a matter of life and death."

"Hang on." Good Lord. Another wait, as long as the morning line at Jittery Abe's.

The voice finally returned. "Moved to Montana."

"Ah," said Lew. "Do we have any idea where in Montana? A phone number, maybe?" He expected another "Hang on" followed by a wait long enough to usher in the Rapture, but was surprised to get an immediate response.

"Bozeman, somewhere. Don't have a number."

"All right," Lew said, feeling a combination of defeat and triumph. "Well, thank you very much."

The man had already hung up.

Bozeman, period. No address, no phone number. Not much of a thread. But at least he knew where to start.

Lew thought about the legend of Theseus threading his way through the labyrinth. Except that Theseus had followed the thread to find his way out *after* he'd slain the beast. Lew was finding his way in.

Into the heart of the labyrinth.

He wondered what sort of Minotaur he might find when he got there.

# 108

Captain Eagleberg had been asleep no more than forty-five minutes when he was awakened by a phone call from the bridge letting him know he was needed up top, right away. At the bridge he found an aerographer's mate from the weather shop waiting for him, who informed him that there was a major tropical storm system ahead; that it had abruptly changed direction and was now on course to slam Hawaii over the next ten hours; and that they were saying it might make landfall as a Cat 5, their worst on record.

The captain closed his eyes.

"Balls," he said.

He opened his eyes again and saw his XO had joined them just in time to get the gist of things.

"We're going to have to skirt the whole damn island chain," the captain said.

Gaines nodded. "We are."

"Balls," the captain muttered once more.

"Sir," said Gaines, "shall I get started moving all the aircraft below and getting everything secured?"

Eagleberg nodded.

"We should probably notify the family members in Hawaii," added Gaines.

Eagleberg closed his eyes again. Dear Christ. No port call. No Tiger Cruise. A thousand eager friends and family anticipating the experience of a lifetime, a week on a real aircraft carrier! Not going to happen.

What a Christ Almighty cock-and-balls disaster.

*Christ to hell. Shit, piss, and corruption.*

Why was this happening to him? Eagleberg was starting to wonder if there wasn't some truth to that goddamn rumor about that goddamn ghost shark. Schofield, damn him. Damn all of them. He was *not* going to let this take down his career.

"We should also notify the crew," Gaines was saying.

Eagleberg opened his eyes, took a breath. "Later," he said. "Not now."

"Aye, Skipper. Make the announcement at chow?"

The captain leaned against the back of his big leather COMMANDING OFFICER chair and rubbed his forehead. "No. Maybe. We'll see."

# 109

0533 hours.

She couldn't sleep. Lord knew she was beyond tired. In the last twenty hours she'd burned through enough adrenaline to call in a week of sleep. Yet sleep would not come.

Monica could feel the distant swell and heave of the ocean. Somewhere out there, a storm was brewing.

She left her stateroom and crept below to the hangar deck. Sat at her desk, looking at her silver Rubik's cube and its scrambled array of black dots.

The onyx eyes looked back.

"Shit," she said.

She'd gone at these last few weeks all wrong. Monica worked out the solutions to impossible puzzles. She always knew to start with known quantities and find for X. Yet when her best friend went missing she'd done the opposite. She'd seized on a conclusion about the nature of X—Papa Doc's guilt—and tried to work the equation backward from there. She'd let herself be completely swayed by her feelings.

She'd been wrong about Papa Doc.

What else had she been wrong about?

She reached down and hauled out the big notebook.

She'd spent weeks trying to understand how Diego could have so badly lost control. But what if it *wasn't* "pilot error"? What if the investigating board had seized on a faulty conclusion?

She leafed through the book's pages, past the voice transmission transcripts, flipping forward to the final maintenance report, the one she'd conducted herself just hours before flight 204 lifted off. She remembered that inspection, every detail of it. That helo was in perfect condition when she sent it above on elevator 4.

Fuel? Tested right there on the flight deck, moments before liftoff, as always. Right?

"Let's go to the videotape," she murmured.

She woke up her computer with a keystroke and clicked through folders to bring up the CCTV footage of the helo's departure, which she'd obtained back when the investigation was still under way. Fast-forwarded to the point where one purple-shirted fuel handler stood just yards away from the Knighthawk, testing the fuel from the hose.

Looking up at the cockpit: thumbs-up.

Diego in the pilot's seat, signaling back. Thumbs-up.

Monica hit PAUSE and sat back in her chair.

No problem with the bird.

No problem with the fuel.

So what were they missing?

She set the footage back to the beginning and let it run. The grape rushing in with his big fuel hose, twisting the nozzle onto the pressure seal to gas up the Knighthawk; the brown-shirted PC stepping forward to initiate his takeoff routine; two green-jerseyed handlers running forward to pull the forward-wheel chocks as a few others swarmed over the bird in last-minute checks—

She lunged forward in her chair and clicked PAUSE again.

Who was that?

To Monica, these men were like her Rubik's cube algorithms: she had each one memorized, knew them so well she could pick out any one of them from a lineup, goggles and all.

Except *that* one.

She rewound fifteen seconds and played that last bit of video again.

Hit PAUSE.

There. That handler. Thin, lithe, tightly controlled movements. She'd never seen him before. Except . . . hadn't she? At least once. But not on the flight deck. Where?

Something pulled her glance down to the cube in her left hand.

Fifty-four onyx eyes looked back at her. Nine groups of six, neatly arranged in three rows of three.

Her hand had run the algorithm by itself.

All at once her blood ran cold.

She remembered where she'd seen him.

# 110

0533 hours.

Finn was in trouble.

At first he'd tried to ease his way back into those random patches of childhood memory. Slow. Cautious. Carlos Hathcock, the legendary Vietnam-era Marine sniper, once took three full days to slither a thousand yards through heavily defended territory before sending a bullet ripping through a general's heart. Finn didn't have three days, but he did his best to slip into the bear's cave as undetected as Hathcock.

Didn't work.

Every time he got close the bear lashed out—and he would find himself sitting up, gasping for air, gripped with nausea.

Now it was worse. The dizziness was back. In the dirty red haze of the safety lights the walls of his cell seemed to be slanting inward, crashing into one another at impossible angles. It hurt to keep his eyes open, hurt worse to close them.

The buzzing in his head came and went, a distant police siren having a psychotic episode.

He sat up and leaned against the wall, panting with effort. Consulted the clock in his head. After 0530.

Which left him barely half an hour.

Focus.

The danger was coming at him from three directions. Danger at the beach, when they landed. That could wait. Danger here on the ship. Imminent. Danger from inside his head—worsening by the hour. But he wasn't making any progress on that last, so that would have to wait, too.

Leave the old memories for now. Deal with the imminent danger.

Which meant a different kind of reconnaissance. He needed more than an unaccounted-for cup of coffee.

He needed to ID the guy.

Assuming it wasn't himself.

Finn lay back on his prison cell rack, hands clasped behind his head, and closed his eyes. The nausea swept over him like a poisonous wind, rushing up from his legs to his head. He let it run. Breathe in, let it hold, four, five, six, seven, let it empty out, then roll in again . . . a slow surf of breath, a tidal heartbeat.

He'd already run through footage in his head of the days Schofield and Biker went missing. Ditto Luca Santiago. Ditto the night the two boys from recycling were killed, the night he and the CMC ran into each other patrolling, the night of the full moon. Nothing but gaping holes.

He started unpacking the files of memories of that Beer Day talent show scene, the day of the killer's big reveal.

Breathe in, four, five, six, seven . . .

*Sitting by the portside edge of the flight deck, watching the crowd. West Texas, the helo pilot, walks over and sits down. Starts talking to him, asking something about her CO. Finn watches the stage. Master of cere-*

*monies pointing to the rolled-up canvas. A few laughs in the crowd, people guessing at the joke to come. The canvas unfurling. The first scream.*

At the time Finn was dimly aware of the poster depicting the two kids being burned alive, but unlike most of the crowd he was not shocked by it. Not even surprised. In fact he hadn't paid much attention to the poster itself. He was focused on everyone's response. He began replaying those observations now, subject by subject—the screaming, crying, shouting, vomiting. He didn't care about any of that. It wasn't the reactions that interested him.

It was the reactions to the reactions.

Finn flipped rapidly through the mental files, pausing only to examine images of the scattered few who responded proactively—those who, rather than recoiling or freaking out, acted instantly to protect or support the person next to them. The sheepdogs of the group. These were not conscious, thought-out responses. There wasn't time for that. They were reflexive. Instinctive. And all virtually identical.

Except one.

He rewound the footage in his head, watched it again.

Something was different here. What, exactly? Different how?

He rewound and scanned it again.

And a third time—

There.

One man, an officer, putting out a hand to support the screaming woman standing next to him. Much like a few others.

Except that this one started putting out his hand a split second *before* the poster unfurled.

He knew what was about to happen.

He knew before it happened.

He was the guy.

# 111

0533 hours.

"Dalton Mosley here."

A small sigh escaped Lew's lips. It had taken him more than two hours, but he'd finally tracked the man down to a remote municipality north of Bozeman, Montana. And more's the wonder, had found a working number and got the man himself on the line.

"Detective Mosley! You're a tough man to find."

There was a wheezy laugh on the other end. "That's more'r less the idea, son. And you are?"

"Lieutenant Lewis Stevens, sir, with the US Navy. At sea, as a matter of fact, right at the moment somewhere in the Pacific."

"That right?" The wheezy laugh again, like a rusted-out gate. "What's the US Navy want with an old former back-country bull?"

Lew explained briefly what he was looking for, and the old cop told him the whole story, or at least the part of it that he knew.

Two boys were involved; parents evidently not at home when the incident occurred. Older boy's name was Ray, Mosley remembered; wasn't sure about the younger boy. Frank? Phillip? Something like that. Older boy was in the parents' gun closet, showing his kid brother one of their handguns, when it accidentally went off.

"Damn fool kid shot himself straight up through the head. Body fell across the closet door, blocking egress. Result being, the younger boy sat there on the floor, trapped and in shock, for more'n twenty-four hours till neighbors found him and called the cops."

The line went silent for a moment.

"And that was you?" prompted Lew.

He heard the man draw a breath and let it go. "Oh, yeah. That was me. For about twelve hours, till the Feds showed up and shut that whole shit show down."

"Feds?"

"Parents were known anarchists, wanted in three states for gun-running, arson, armed robbery, had themselves a whole rap sheet of subversive and violent activities. Never did see what any of that had to do with our situation. We had one dead kid, 'nother one just about comatose. Didn't matter—we were roped off and out of the picture."

Ah. That explained why Lew hadn't been able to find any further reports after that first day; the media were shut out, too.

"I followed the case, best I could. Parents never showed, no doubt spooked off by the alphabet boys. Surviving kid became a ward of the state. Hospitalized for weeks, had to be sedated when he came around, which didn't surprise me one bit. I wouldn't lay odds that poor kid'd *ever* come out of his briar patch."

"You saw him?"

"That I did. Oh, yeah. Heard the first call come in, got there just a few minutes behind the uniforms. There when the EMTs carried him out of that hell hole. Spent ten, maybe fifteen minutes in that closet myself. Felt like a God damn lifetime. Blood all over the floor, flies all over the blood, stink of cordite still hanging in the air after God knew how many hours. Older boy's body'd started to go, too, you know? Like a God damn torture chamber, son, some serious Stephen King shit. Tell you something, Lieutenant. I was not a young man, been on the force more'n two decades at that point, seen more death and ugliness than most. But that closet, that morning? Gave me the God damn willies."

Lew had said as little as possible, not wanting to interrupt the man's flow, but there was one detail he was curious about. "So, what happened to the parents?"

"The parents? Ha. Nothing. Not a God damn thing."

"I mean, how did they die?"

The voice laughed, that rusty wheeze again. "Who says they died? Feds tracked those pieces of shit for years, never did pin 'em down. All I know, they're still out there somewhere. Probably hiding out from the law and plotting against their government."

Lew heard the man breathing heavily as he paused. His mouth must have been right against the phone. Finally he spoke up again.

"Always wondered what happened to that poor kid."

"He joined the navy," said Lew.

"That right? Sonofabitch. Good for him."

Lew thanked the cop and hung up, then sat back in his chair and looked up at the masks on his wall.

*Gave me the God damn willies.*

Lew Stevens was not a man who cursed with great frequency, but there were times when nothing less would do.

"Ho-lee shit," he said.

# 112

Monica sat staring at the freeze-frame image on her computer monitor.

She had to tell someone.

She put her hand on her phone, then stopped.

Would he listen?

She had to *make* him listen.

She looked up his stateroom number, punched in the four digits. No answer. *Shit*. She'd have to leave a message on his office line. Looked up that number.

The phone picked up on the first ring. "Scott Angler."

It took her a moment to realize it wasn't a recorded voicemail prompt. "Scott? You're there?"

"Long night," said Scott. "What's up?"

"Listen, it's about Kris—" She heard his hiss of exasperation. "Please—don't hang up. This is important!"

She heard him pause. "What," he said, not disguising the impatience.

"The night she went missing, after we talked in the passageway, she went out to be by herself for a bit. Right?"

"Okay."

"That night, there was a guy in the passageway, in goggles and a green jersey, a guy I didn't recognize."

"Uh-huh."

"Scott—I don't think he was a genuine handler."

She heard him sigh. "Monica. You can't expect to recognize every single—"

"I *know* them, Scott! I'm telling you, this guy was not a handler, he was just wearing the outfit! Scott—I think he may have been following Kris."

There was a silence, so long she thought she'd lost her connection. Finally Scott said, "Papadakis ran, Monica. Guilty men run."

Monica said nothing, just waited.

After another silence he said, "You're sure about this?"

Monica swallowed, her throat dry as leather. "I am."

"And you don't know who it was?"

"No. But definitely not Commander Papadakis."

"Okay."

"*Okay?* That's *it*?"

"I'll look into this, I promise. I mean it. All right?"

"All right." She felt hollow, the rough emptiness that followed an adrenaline rush. "Scott—"

"Hmm?"

"I'm sorry. For what I said."

"Tell me over breakfast in Hawaii."

He disconnected.

*Tell me over breakfast in Hawaii.* That would be nice. Monica almost smiled, but her face was too tired to make the shape.

She sat still for a moment, looking at the freeze-frame on her screen.

It occurred to her that she hadn't told Scott just how she stumbled upon the unidentified handler in the first place. In fact, she'd been so focused on her revelation that this man was in that passageway the night Kris disappeared, she hadn't stopped to ask herself the obvious question—

What was he doing there on the flight deck, just moments before Black Falcon 204's final flight?

"Oh, God," she murmured. A fresh stream of adrenaline surged through her body.

She reset the footage and went through it once more, this time frame by frame, following the movements of the unidentified handler. She saw him emerge from the right side of the frame and approach the bird. Duck under the main deck, by the fuel lines.

Wait.

She isolated a single frame. Something in his hand, something he was holding to the fuel line. A wrench? Screwdriver?

A pen?

Not a pen.

A hypodermic.

"Oh!" Monica gasped and jerked back, sending her chair rolling back a few feet. She stared at the screen in horror.

Not pilot error.

*Sabotage.*

She snatched at the phone and dialed Scott again. No answer. She hung up and immediately dialed back. It rang four times, then went to voicemail.

# 113

Finn squeezed his eyes shut in the darkness, gazing inside his mind at the Beer Day scene, trying to zoom in on the man's face. Impossible. At the time, he'd been positioned way back and to the left and had only a momentary glimpse of him from behind.

Still, he thought he recognized him.

From where? When? He couldn't quite pull it up.

He slowed his breathing down.

Slowly at first, then picking up speed, he began flipping through thousands of mental files, one by one: his walks through the ship, forward and aft, starboard to port, deck by deck, starting back at his first full day on the *Lincoln*. Jittery Abe's. *Yo, Billy, you in?* FOD walkdown. Library. Midrats. Scanning, scanning, watching the faces, the shoulders, the gaits. Searching for the guy.

Day 2. The lower decks, The Jungle, Tucker, Jittery Abe's again, Tom the ordie, Frank and Dewitt. CIWS mount. Library again. Flight deck. Searching, sorting, cataloging. Midrats at general mess. Mukalla memories. A hot prickling up the back of his neck. This was the night Schofield went missing. The people he saw passing in the passageways. Unrated E-1s and E-2s, swabbing and polishing. Air traffic and intel crew heading to their berthing compartments after a long day. Flight deck crew and mechanics heading above to the flight deck or below to the hangar deck to service their aircraft. There went Schofield himself, heading in the direction of the fantail. A pair of yellow shirts, laughing quietly over some private joke. Another handler in his green jersey and goggles. Dozens of faceless individuals all going their separate ways yet all—

Wait.

He hit the PAUSE button in his head and scrubbed backward, frame by frame, then hit STOP.

*Another handler in his green jersey and goggles.*

Why was an aircraft handler wearing deck goggles when he was below, on the gallery deck, well after flight ops were done for the night?

And with that it all snapped into place.

He remembered where and when.

He knew the face behind the goggles.

"Hey, Frank!" he called. "Need to get another message out."

He needed to warn Jackson. The lead Finn gave him might have put him and his intel person in jeopardy.

"Sorry, Chief, no can do," Frank called back. "No more messages. Sheriff's orders." He sounded fried. Half the security staff was still out sick. He and Dewitt had been on duty now for more than twelve hours.

Finn lay back on the hard bunk, felt the heave and pitch of the boat.

He had to get to Jackson.

He consulted the clock in his head: 0556.

Four minutes to go.

# 114

0556 hours.

It took Scott no more than a minute to locate the place, a cramped little compartment tucked in a portside corner just below the flight deck. Not much bigger than a broom closet.

The door had no lock.

The search took only minutes. There was a small secure locker; he broke into it and found what looked like an improvised bugging/recording setup. He listened to a minute of what was stored on the thing, just long enough to identify it as taped conversations from the captain's parlor.

Set the device down on the bunk.

Continued looking around.

Pulled out the locker under the rack, rifled through it. Lifted out a folded deck crew jersey. Green.

Underneath that, a pair of goggles.

"Fuck, I knew it. I *knew* it! Mother*fucker*."

So it wasn't Papadakis. It was never Papadakis. It was always the SEAL.

The motherfucking SEAL.

He quickly wrapped the goggles and bugging contraption inside the jersey, jammed the whole mess under his arm, stepped out into the passageway.

And stopped.

Stepped back inside, shut the door again, and stood, thinking through his next move. He was taking this straight to the captain. Of course he was.

"Fuck," he said again. *"Fuck."*

He was torn.

Duty told him to bring this evidence to the captain so they could bury that prick for good. But as pissed off as he was at Jackson, he couldn't deny the fact that he felt some tug of loyalty there.

Jackson had fucked up royally, but as much as it was that stubborn old Creole motherfucker's own fault, he deserved this shot at redemption. He should be the one who got the credit for reopening an investigation and burying that psychotic, fucked-up piece of US Naval Special Warfare dogshit.

*"Fuck!"* he whispered.

He opened the door once more and headed out, making his way below toward the CMC's office to put the incriminating evidence in the man's hands so he could bring it up to the captain himself.

# 115

Jackson stared at the thing sitting on his desk, wondering exactly what he was waiting for. Or avoiding.

That damn incident file had sat there unopened for a few hours now, ever since Indy gave it to him, while Jackson attempted to catch some sleep jammed into one of his little couches, his feet jutting out over one end like a victim on Procrustes' bed.

Finally he'd gone over to his desk and read the whole bloody, horrifying thing, all five single-spaced pages of it.

How Indy managed to get hold of it he'd never know, didn't want to know. Wished he'd never read it. But he had, and he couldn't unread it now.

What to do with it: that was the question.

*Madone.*

He looked up at the God's eyes on the bulkhead. Jackson thought about the slender little fingers that made them, about his two daughters bent over their craft tables at school, frowning in concentration. His daughters, now grown women with lives of their own. Lives that existed only because they had survived childhood—because they had not been cut short, had not known the horrible intimacy of deadly violence.

There were eight kids in that little farm settlement in Mukalla, eight kids killed along with the rest. Slaughtered. Dismembered. Defiled.

Just five pages, but dear God. The whole massacre was there in all its ugly detail, and while the file didn't name Chief Finn, they did place a "rogue SEAL" at the center of the whole bloody mess.

Their own Lieutenant Calley.

Why Finn wasn't arrested right there in Yemen, or later in Bahrain, was beyond Jackson. Probably Indy was right: they wanted to keep him under wraps, keep the entire damn thing from going public. Some mediocre mind had decided the navy couldn't afford the exposure. So they dropped him on a boat in the middle of the Pacific while they worked out some antiseptic way of making the thing go away.

Maybe SOCOM got it wrong. Maybe Finn wasn't involved.

And maybe the moon was made of green cheese.

No, SOCOM was right, and Scott was right. Chief Finn had committed unspeakable crimes in Mukalla, and when he came aboard Jackson's ship he kept on committing them. Chief Finn was the psychotic Lew had described to them, the twisted bastard cooking up his theater of horror. Hadn't Finn told him as much? *A start signal.*

He was guilty as sin.

Everything rational told Jackson that.

He pushed back his chair and stood.

He should be turning the file over to Eagleberg. Should, but wouldn't. He'd lost all trust in the captain's capacity to act rationally.

But he could take it to the admiral.

He picked up the file and headed for the door.

# 116

*Tap-tap, tap-tap.* There was a gentle knock at Lew's door, which he'd left open a crack. "Open," he said. He swiveled in his chair and saw Indy's face poking in.

"Hi," she said. "Got a moment?"

He smiled and put his monitor to sleep. "Of course. What brings you out at this hour?"

She stood just inside the door, holding a sheet of paper. "I saw your light was on. I know you're in early sometimes." She sounded apologetic, almost embarrassed.

Lew nodded. "So. What's on your mind?"

"I . . . I need to talk to you about something. It's about Lieutenant Shiflin."

"Indy," said Lew patiently. "I hate to say this, but you know as well as I, we're officially off the case. No more moonlight sleuthing for us nerds."

Indy gave a soft laugh. "I know. It's just, there's something that's just a little puzzling."

Lew nodded. "This whole thing has been unsettling, to say the least. I suspect there are a thousand questions we'll never know the answers to."

"I know. You're right. But . . ."

Despite his best effort to gently close the topic it was clear that Indy was going to persist, so he relented. "All right," he said. "Come on in. Let's see what you've got." He gestured to the other seat and pulled it closer to his so they could sit at his desk side by side.

Indy sat, still holding the sheet of paper.

"Early this morning," she began, "Master Chief Jackson asked me to take one more look at Lieutenant Shiflin's schedule the week before she disappeared. So I did."

"And?" said Lew.

"I went back over transcripts of all the interviews and noticed something. Lieutenant Halsey and her roommate both mentioned Shiflin skipping breakfast a few times. I checked once more. Shiflin wasn't at work on those days, or in the squadron ready room. Or in her stateroom. So where was she?"

Lew thought for a moment, then shook his head and shrugged. "I'd imagine she could have been almost anywhere. Off by herself? Time to think?"

"Maybe," said Indy. "But this is where it gets curious . . ."

# 117

0600 hours.

When Jackson reached the door to the admiral's suite he met Arthur on his way out.

Both men nodded their greetings.

Not a word passed, but Jackson knew why Arthur was there. He was putting his concerns on record. Putting some daylight between himself and the captain. Covering his rear. Arthur was no fool. He could sense as well as Jackson that something on the USS *Abraham Lincoln* was not going to end well.

*"Reveille, rev—nds heave out and—"*

The speaker barked its fractured wake-up call, then fell silent.

Jackson shook his head and sighed. The red lights should be switching over to normal daytime lighting right now, but of course, they weren't. Delayed again. Engineering going to crap.

He turned and looked down the short passageway through the open porthole at the end, out at the sea. He couldn't quite make out the horizon. Dawn had long since broken but it was still dark out there, the roiling cloud cover pressing down like a thousand gnarled black hands, angry ocean rising to meet it.

Getting darker by the moment. Summed up their whole situation.

Summed it up like poetry.

He turned back and stepped through the door, where he was met by an aide. The admiral was tied up for a bit. Could he wait a few minutes?

The aide retreated back inside the admiral's war room.

Jackson took a seat and waited.

# 118

0600 hours.

*"Reveille, rev—nds heave out and—"*

Scott waited for the 1MC speaker to go silent, then reached out and gave the door three quick raps. No answer. Tried the handle. Locked.

Not in his stateroom, and not here. Must be out on his rounds already, doing his den mother/beat cop thing.

Should he let himself in? He had the pass code to Jackson's office; everyone on the team had it.

Or should he come back later?

No, this couldn't wait.

He should take it to the captain.

"Fuck!" he said quietly.

He let out a breath and nodded to himself. He'd take it to the captain.

*Fuck!*

He took another breath. Then punched in the sequence of digits on the door's keypad and stepped inside the darkened compartment.

No one there.

He went into the inner office and sat down to wait for the master chief to show.

After a moment, he picked up Jackson's phone.

# 119

0600 hours.

*"Reveille, rev—nds heave out and—"*

Lew looked at Indy and smiled. "I suppose it's official now: we're all awake."

She gave a soft laugh. "Yes."

"Anyway," he said, and he nodded at the sheet of paper in her hand.

"Right," she said. She laid it down on Lew's desk so he could take a look. On it she'd hand-scribbled a quick chart of dates and times. "I remembered a co-worker mentioning that a few days earlier Shiflin had skipped breakfast for a doctor's appointment, but there was no record of her seeing anyone at medical. Which was no surprise. Pilots hate having medical visits on their record. Makes them seem mortal."

"Tell me about it," Lew agreed.

"So I thought—"

She was interrupted by Lew's desk phone ringing. They both glanced at it. "Sorry," said Lew. He touched a switch that shut off the ringer, letting the call go to voicemail. He looked up at Indy again. "You were saying."

"So," Indy said, "I thought perhaps she had arranged to see her doctor privately, off the record. Meeting in a private office, say, over coffee. Which would explain the missed breakfasts."

"Huh." Lew nodded, intrigued. "Go on."

"But I double-checked on the actual whereabouts of medical personnel on those mornings Lieutenant Shiflin skipped breakfast. I've accounted for everyone in the medical department. Everyone but you."

Lew frowned. "That *is* strange."

"Lew, this could be important. I know those sessions would be privileged, but she might have said something significant, perhaps without your realizing it at the time. And besides, I don't think that privilege would apply anymore. So I'm just wondering, if Lieutenant Shiflin was seeing you for counseling, off the record, before office hours . . . why didn't you say something?"

"Well," he began, then stopped. Smiled at her.

Then drove his right fist hard into her solar plexus.

# 120

0600 hours.

"*Reveille, rev—nds heave out and—*"

Finn sat up, planted his feet on the deck, and stood.
It was time.

# VII

# The Storm

# 121

He grabbed her by the hair with his left hand, forcing her head back, and with his right delivered a vicious jab to the throat, crushing her larynx.

He saw her eyes fly open as she fought to take a breath. Nothing but a muffled, strangled choking. No more oxygen would be going down that pretty throat. He released her hair and watched as she collapsed forward like a rag doll—

*Ow!*

SHIT!!

Lewis stared at her in disbelief. That witch! He didn't know how, but she'd managed to lash out with one hand and rake her fingernails across his face.

His face!

Sonofa*bitch,* that hurt!

For an instant they glared at each other—she, still struggling to breathe, hands flailing; he, momentarily stunned that she'd had the audacity to fight back—

Then he moved.

In one quick motion he snatched at her head with both hands, right hand grabbing the back of the head by the hair, left hand on the chin, and gave it a hard yank.

Then he gave it a second violent twist and felt Indy pop open like a jar of vacuum-sealed pickles. With a loud *crack!* her neck snapped, fracturing two cervical vertebrae and severing her spinal cord.

He placed her back in the chair, vaguely upright, head lolling.

He touched one finger to his cheek, still in disbelief. The witch drew blood. *His* blood. She scratched a gouge across *his face!* He wanted to kill her all over again. He heard panting and a low growl, realized it was coming from himself.

*Control, Lewis.*

Assess, formulate, execute.

He looked at Indy.

He sat back in his chair for a moment, too, making his posture just like hers, even lolling his neck a little, waiting for his own breathing to slow. It took no more than eight or nine seconds.

He picked up the phone, punched in a number.

*"Brig. Hawkins,"* hacked the voice on the other end.

He sat up straight and put a friendly-but-concerned look on his face as he spoke into the phone. *Voice pattern conveys physiognomy.*

"Lew Stevens here. Hey, I need to have a word with the prisoner. Yes. It's sensitive, I'll need a few minutes alone. That's fine. All right, I'll be right over."

He set the phone down, stood, took his jacket down off a hook and put it on, rehearsing as he did.

*"As I was speaking with the prisoner he produced a weapon—no idea how he got it—then he overpowered me and shot the security team. Forced me at gunpoint back to my office, where we were surprised by Lieutenant Desai. The SEAL snapped her neck—and I, I grabbed at his gun and it just, it just went off . . ."*

Lewis unlocked the bottom side drawer of his desk, pulled it open, and slid out three items, carefully laying each on his desk: hypodermic needle, pistol, set of zip ties.

Could he make that story work? He smiled as he rose from his chair.

Of course he could.

# 122

The Sheriff hung up, spat "Butthole!" at the now silent phone.

"Shrink's coming over to talk to shithead for five," she announced.

*Endgame,* thought Finn.

The Sheriff glanced up at the wall clock, pushed back her chair, and got to her feet—0605 on the button. Gotta get in line early if you want to be first at Jittery Abe's.

"Keep 'im honest, boys," she rasped as she walked to the door. "Five minutes, no more." She opened the door and headed out for her triple mocha.

Frank followed her to the door and shut it behind her, locking them in.

Finn slowed his breathing.

Like the tides.

Pulling in. Rolling out.

Frank turned, ambled back in the direction of his seat. As he passed Finn's cell, the prisoner's dinner tray from the night before slipped out of the feeding slot in the door and clattered to the deck.

Pulling in. Rolling out.

"Oh, fer cryin' out . . ." muttered Frank. He bent down to retrieve the tray.

An arm snaked out and wrapped around his neck.

Before he could react Frank was pinned to the door, the tip of Finn's ring knife kissing the flesh of his left temple.

"*Dewitt.*"

Frank's partner was already scrambling to his feet and reaching for his sidearm—but something in Finn's voice froze him in place, hand still on the butt of the holstered weapon.

"Wh-what?" he stammered.

"*This is the getting-out part.*"

Without warning, the red safety lights switched off and the full white lights flashed on.

Then there was a loud *POP,* and everything went to black.

# 123

He was just leaving his office when the lights blew.

The blackness lasted no more than a moment, at which point the emergency lights kicked in, their glow about as strong as a few candles. In the ghostly light Indy's sagging figure looked like a poorly made wax mannequin.

Standing at the door, fingers on the handle, Lewis remembered the call that came in while he and Indy were talking. The caller left a voicemail. He made a mental note to retrieve it as soon as possible, as soon as he'd gotten this other business out of the way.

*No, now.*

Something deep in his reptile brain sparked and sizzled. *Lisssten now.*

He'd learned to heed his reptile brain.

He went back to his desk and played the message.

*"Lew, Scott Angler. I'm in Jackson's office waiting for him to show. Listen, I just spoke with Lieutenant Halsey, the helo pilot who roomed with Shiflin. She's got a hell of a story. I think she can ID our killer—and it's definitely not Papadakis."*

He sank back into his chair and spun it slowly back and forth for a moment.

In the pale glow of the emergency lights the little compartment looked like a cave, the masks on his wall like cave paintings, records of ancestral exploits.

*I think she can ID our killer.*

Well, that changed things a bit, didn't it.

He thought quickly, processing the implications as his chair swung to and fro.

Now he needed to go find Halsey and silence her. Right away, before she shared her insights further. If she really could finger him, that was. Which he doubted. But he didn't have the luxury of hoping otherwise.

Finn X could wait; he wasn't going anywhere.

Finding Halsey was now priority one.

But exactly where would she be right now? Wardroom? Ready room? Maintenance office? He didn't have time to check all possible spots. He needed to know *now*. And there was someone who could tell him— someone sitting in Master Chief Jackson's office, just a one-minute walk down the passageway.

Lewis Stevens unlocked his bottom drawer again and took out three more items.

Another hypo. A scalpel.

And a charcoal pencil, sharpened to a fine point.

*Talk to me, Scottie. I'm a doctor. You can tell me anything.*

# 124

In the dark Frank started to make micromovements, a tensing of muscles. Finn spoke in a voice so soft the man could barely hear him even from the distance of a few inches.

"I like you, Frank. But I'll kill you without a thought."

Frank stopped struggling.

The emergency lights popped on, releasing their pale glow into the compartment and diluting the blackness to a dark murk.

"Listen close," Finn said, loud enough for them both to hear. "Here's how it works."

He walked them through it.

Dewitt unlocked Finn's cell door via the electronic locking system at the Sheriff's desk, then came over and slowly knelt down, hands clasped behind his head. Finn released Frank and in the same instant had his knife point pressed to Dewitt's temple, freeing Frank to perform the next task, which was to set two chairs facing the back bulkhead, six feet apart. Finn then cuffed them both to the chairs and gagged them with strips of material he hacked from their own shirtsleeves.

"I know what you're thinking, Frank," he said.

"*How?*" He leaned closer as he tied Frank's gag. "Next time, frisk both legs at the same time."

He could see the thoughts racing through the man's head, trying to work out how Finn had slipped that goddamn knife from spot to spot while Frank was frisking him.

The e-lights blinked out—and now the red safety lights came back on again.

Finn shook his head. A $5 billion warship, coming apart like a piece of cheap prefab furniture, all because of the arrogance and incompetence of one man.

He tightened Dewitt's gag, then leaned down by Frank's ear again.

"Hey, Frank, that thing I said before? How I liked you, but I'd kill you without a thought?"

Frank nodded, eyes wide. Finn gave his shoulder a pat. "I was kidding."

As Finn headed to the door Frank struggled to speak, eyes bulging with the effort. "Uh-ah ih *AH*!"

*About which part?*

But the prisoner was already gone.

# 125

Finn shut the brig door behind him and stood for a moment, leaning back against the passageway bulkhead. The effort it had taken to push away his grief over Kennedy, to dive deep into that cave of memories, to poke at the bear again and again, it was all catching up to him now. The assault on his senses, not from the outside but from the inside, had left him drained.

Breathe in, two, three, four. Breathe out.

Conscious of his back against the steel.

Conscious of the soles of his feet pressing against the deck, his toes gripping.

Conscious of his hand's grip on the little mahogany speargun.

He looked down at the speargun—Reason One for getting himself arrested in the first place. He knew he might need a primary.

He could have taken one of the guard's sidearms, but those were so rarely used that he didn't trust they'd be in good working condition. Besides, only a lunatic would start a gun battle inside a steel maze.

He stepped away from the door, slipped around a

corner into a narrow recess cobwebbed with cables and pipes and ductwork.

Breathe in, two, three, four, breathe out.

The Sheriff would be back inside ten minutes, max. Psycho Doc was on his way down, too, and if he got there first, Finn would take him. But if the Sheriff got there first, Finn needed to be in the wind. He had an extremely narrow window in which to escape undetected. He needed to use those few minutes to maximum advantage. He needed—

Finn slid to the deck and passed out.

## 126

Captain Eagleberg was losing it.

Now the lights were back on, but flickering. Then there was a *POP!* followed by a split second of darkness. Then those blasted, useless e-lights again.

"Mother of God!" he barked into the phone. "Whatever it is, just find it and fix it! Put your best man on it!"

Arthur Gaines knew that wasn't going to happen—their best man was miles away on the *Stockdale,* banished there by the captain himself—but he wasn't about to share that thought. Arthur's mind was on Chief Finn.

Something bothered him.

"Cap," he said once Eagleberg was off his phone. "Anything strike you odd about that encounter with Chief Finn last night? Anything strange?"

"Everything about that knuckle-dragger is strange," the captain snapped. "Man's a walking freak show."

"No, I mean, the way he went off on you. It wasn't just disrespectful. It was over the top. Almost as if he *wanted* to be tossed in the hole."

They looked at each other.

"Call," barked the captain.

Arthur dialed the four-digit number for the brig and

put the handset to his ear. After a moment he hung up without a word and looked at the captain. "No answer."

He punched in another number.

"Mac. Arthur. We're not raising anyone in the brig. Have your nearest MA get over there on the double and report back. I'll hold." He looked at Eagleberg. "Man's on his way down to the brig now."

Thirty seconds went by, Arthur listening, head down. Then he gave a grim nod. "Copy. Hold a sec." He looked up at Eagleberg. "Security overpowered. Finn's gone."

"*FUCK!*" said Eagleberg.

Everyone on the bridge froze. None had ever heard the captain utter any oath stronger than "Balls."

"Tell him to have every goddamn MA fan out across the ship," he snapped at Arthur. "Launch a full security sweep. Find this lunatic!"

Arthur spoke quietly into the phone. "You heard?"

"*Bring him in at all costs, Mac,*" the captain shouted. He snatched the handset from his XO and barked directly into it. "The man is extremely dangerous. I am authorizing the use of deadly force. *I repeat: deadly force.*" And handed the phone back to Arthur.

A kill-or-capture command.

Emphasis on the kill.

## 127

**Scott Angler was pissed off.**

He was pissed off at their fucking thin-skinned captain for reassigning Jimmy Suzuki and leaving the whole engineering department a rudderless mess. If the fucking lights hadn't gone on the fritz again, if full lighting had come on when it was supposed to and they weren't still drenched in that dim fucking red light like a block of Copenhagen whorehouses, he might have noticed something was off.

He was pissed off at Arthur Gaines for not standing up to his boss and straightening some of this shit out.

He was pissed off at Selena Kirkland for letting that dick run this ship his way and not jumping all over his Yankee blueblood ass.

He was pissed off at Jackson for . . . fuck, he couldn't focus well enough through the haze of shock and pain to work out exactly what the fuck he was pissed off at Jackson for but let's just say for being fucking Jackson.

Mostly he was pissed off at himself.

He was pissed off that he'd let himself be blinded by his own certainty that Finn was the psycho they needed to worry about, that he'd been so goddamn cocksure of himself that he let his attitude override his instincts.

He was pissed off that when Lew got to Jackson's office and he showed him the jersey and goggles and explained what Monica had told him, and Lew said, "What else did she say?" he didn't pick up the edge in his voice.

He was pissed off that he'd let Lew get behind him, whack him on the back of the skull with a pistol butt, and shove a needle into his neck.

He was pissed off that he and Lieutenant Halsey were not going to do breakfast in Hawaii together.

And it was his own goddamn fault.

And now here he was, trussed like a boar, his skin hanging in strips off his face, about to die—and for no good fucking reason.

He hadn't been afraid to die in the bush or on the battlefield. He'd gone into the shit willingly. Fuck it, he'd gone in *eagerly*. The thought that there might be an IED out there with his name on it, or a 7.62 round, a mortar shell, hell, a rusty bayonet carving up his guts, he truly and heartily did not give a three-*inch* shit. Dying out there in the thick of things, giving his life to help make his country a better place or at least maintain its status as toughest and meanest motherfucker on the block, that would be an honor.

But being wasted here? Now? By this piece of dirt?

It was an embarrassment.

Gave new meaning to the word "waste."

So Stevens, that twisted little fuck, thought the threat of extreme pain would terrify him into talking, telling him where she was. And, when that didn't work, that actually *inflicting* some of that agony on his person would inspire an even greater terror, a terror impossible to deny.

His mistake.

It didn't terrify Scott.

It just pissed him off more.

"Okay—okay," he groaned.

His capacity to speak was nearly gone, frozen out of him by whatever drug Stevens had shoved into him. Succinylcholine, probably, a partial dose, not enough to paralyze him, just enough to turn him into oil sludge. He was losing strength and mobility—but not feeling. No, he felt every bit of it. When Stevens made those little horizontal incisions in his forehead, then grabbed the little skin-tabs and pulled, peeling his face like strips of flypaper, old Scottie felt it, all right.

He felt it plenty.

Maybe Lew was right.

Maybe it *would* make him talk.

"No more . . ." he whispered. "No—more. She's . . ."

Just to breathe was an effort.

His tormentor paused, hands in his lap, then cocked his head and leaned in closer to hear. An undisguised look of triumph on his face. *I win,* that look said. *I knew you'd talk.*

Scott marshaled every atom of will he could to speak one last time. It felt like pulling up a tree stump with his bare hands. He took a breath, then another, then croaked out the words.

"She's—crawling—up your ass crack—you pathetic dipshit."

He tried to laugh, but all he could pull off was a faint wheeze.

It would have to do.

# 128

Finn had been out for no more than a minute when he was stirred to consciousness by the first MA barreling down the ladder. He darted away from the brig's door and into a recess just behind the ladder as the man came huffing through to check on the prisoner's status and inquire as to why the hell no one was answering the phone.

By the time the Sheriff came stomping down Finn had pulled himself up to hug the ladder's underside, hanging by his fingers and toes in the surreal crimson shadows, hugging his body to the structure like a Ninja sloth, the Sheriff's speargun with its single bolt strapped to his body.

Clutching on to the ladder's steps from underneath, he fought to beat back the waves of nausea and dizziness. The shards of memories were crashing through him now, disjointed and in no logical sequence, and he couldn't stop them—

*The sound of the destroyer's ballast pump,* whoojah, whoojah, whoojah—

*His back against the brick-and-plaster wall, the child's sightless eyes—*

*A fat slice of chocolate cake on a plate on the kitchen table—*

He had just managed to find his footing in the present moment—and then the churn of images snatched at him and pulled him back in, a psychic undertow sucking him down, then spitting him out again to totter briefly on the sand and rocks, only to suck him back under seconds later.

Finn was drowning.

*"Goddammit—find that sneaky little cocksucker!"* The Sheriff's voice came blasting out from the brig's interior. "Pappyfucking piece of shit took my little beauty!"

Breathe in, let it hold, five, six, seven, let it out . . .

It had been over fifteen minutes since Psycho Doc had called down saying he was coming to visit the prisoner. He hadn't showed.

He wasn't coming.

Which meant he had shifted his game plan.

Finn had to get to Jackson. Had to warn him.

If it wasn't already too late.

He felt the treads shake as the Sheriff and her MAs went storming back up the ladder. He waited ten seconds, then began to move, silently slipping out sidewise, around and up onto the ladder, then through the grated door and out into the labyrinth.

# 129

Sitting outside Admiral Kirkland's war room, Jackson reminded himself why he was about to turn over the incident file and let command know just how bad this bad actor was. That every rational consideration told him to turn over the file. That Procedure itself told him to turn over the file.

The problem was, he didn't believe it.

SOCOM be damned, he just didn't buy it.

He had no idea why the guy had put himself back in the brig, or whether Eagleberg really could make his threats stick, but if Jackson handed this file over to the admiral Finn would never see the sun again.

And he didn't believe Finn had done it.

Any of it.

He stood, quietly walked out, and made his way back down through the maze to his own neighborhood. When he reached his office he put his hand on the door handle—and stopped.

Jackson took his hand away and stood still. Smacked his lips, then did it again. Made a face. He sniffed the air.

Impossible.

He sniffed the air again.

He shook his head.

*Pull it together, Robbie.*

He grabbed the handle again and opened the door. Stepped into his outer office and flipped the switch for the overheads. The compartment's red safety lights came on. Still no daytime lights.

He crossed the small space to the inner door, to enter his own office—

And stopped. Sniffed the air one more time. Made a face.

"*Foutaise,*" he whispered. *Bullcrap.* There was a distinct scent in here. Unmistakable.

Impossible, but unmistakable.

One of Sister Mae's foul-smelling concoctions. He could smell it. He could taste it on his tongue.

He would stake his life on it.

All at once the full daytimes snapped on, the white lights momentarily blinding him. There was a *POP!* and the light began flickering off and on, like a bad connection about to blow.

He thought he heard a faint grunt. Coming from where, out in the passageway?

Now the white lights crapped out altogether and the e-lights popped on yet again, the faint illumination so weak it gave the compartment and everything in it a spectral cast.

He opened the door and stepped inside.

In the pale gloom he could just make out the form of Scott Angler, slouched on one of his couches.

"Scottie?" he began. He took a step toward the figure. "What're you—"

He froze.

Scott wasn't moving.

Some kind of mask hung from his face in strips, like strands of papier-mâché.

Something protruding from his left eye socket.

A *pencil*?

# 130

Jackson stood blinking in the near-darkness, trying to make sense of the visual information, when a voice thundered at him, punching him like a haymaker in the gut—

*DROP!* it bellowed.

Sister Mae's voice.

Right in his ear.

Jackson dropped.

Without thinking, just crashed to the deck.

As he went down he felt a sharp sting in his upper back, something stabbing into the meat of his trapezium.

He spun and lashed out with one foot, connecting with his attacker's legs. The man fell to the floor but twisted away like a swamp eel, Jackson's roundhouse hitting nothing but air.

He felt something slash through his jacket across his back.

He struck out with a backhand but hit—nothing—and, then . . . he . . .

felt himself going into

slow motion

as if he
were drunk
and thought
*Craaappppp* . . .

That hypo cap.

The sting in his shoulder—a hypodermic. Slowing him down.

The red safety lights snapped on.

Lying on his back now, Jackson got a glimpse of his assailant.

In the unreal crimson glow, the face looked like a Halloween mask.

Jackson thought his brain would go *POP!* like the lights.

*Lew?*

The mask leered, the figure lunged forward.

Jackson felt the scalpel being thrust into him, just under the rib cage.

# 131

"God*dammi*t," said Eagleberg. "The SEAL. The goddamn SEAL. I *knew* that man was trouble."

Arthur wasn't listening; he was calculating. They had approximately seventy masters-at-arms on board the *Lincoln*. With more than thirty out sick that still left nearly forty, all small-arms qualified, most of them carrying. Which sounded like a big number—but there were more than four thousand different compartments and spaces on the ship. That was a lot of space to cover. And the SEAL was smart. When it came to evading capture, probably the best there was.

"Artie. Have all mess facilities shut down, PDQ. And put me on the PA. I need to make an announcement."

"Sir?"

The entire time they'd been at sea the captain had addressed the ship on their PA system exactly once, and from Arthur's perspective it had been a mild disaster. Ye gods, he hoped the man didn't cock this up.

"The 1MC," Eagleberg repeated. "*Now.*"

Arthur switched on the hand mike to the 1MC system and handed it over.

Eagleberg put his mouth up against the mike and began to speak.

*"THIS IS YOUR CAPTAIN SPEAKING. THIS IS NOT A DRILL . . ."*

*Don't say anything about the escaped prisoner,* thought Arthur. *Not to the general population. Don't create a panic.*

*"THERE IS AN ESCAPED PRISONER ON BOARD,"* the captain continued. *"HE MAY BE ARMED AND DANGEROUS . . ."*

Arthur closed his eyes.

*"ALL MESS HALLS ARE TEMPORARILY CLOSED. ALL NONESSENTIAL PERSONNEL ARE CONFINED TO QUARTERS UNTIL I GIVE THE ALL CLEAR. REPEAT: ALL NONESSENTIAL PERSONNEL ARE CONFINED TO QUARTERS UNTIL I GIVE THE ALL CLEAR."*

Eagleberg handed the mike to Arthur. "Artie," he growled, "stay on top of this mess. I'm trusting you."

He turned abruptly, leaving his XO in charge of the bridge as the ship skirted the edge of the gathering storm, and went to fetch his sidearm and go below himself.

# 132

Jackson had read that yogi masters could slow their own heartbeats. If he were a yogi master, maybe he'd take longer to bleed out and someone would find him before it was too late.

Jackson was many things. Yogi master was not one of them.

He tried to look around the dark office, but couldn't move his neck. Lying on his back, head cranked at an angle, all he could see in the gloom of the red safety lights was the series of God's eyes hanging in a row like lights on a Christmas tree.

Jackson wondered if God Himself was looking at him through those eyes. And if He was, what was He seeing?

A foolish man.

Foolish, dying man.

So wrapped up in logic and sequence and procedure he hadn't seen what was right in front of his face.

He thought about Lew Stevens, sitting right there in that very office just over a week earlier, giving them all his little discourse on their mystery killer's possible motivation.

*I don't think he gets off on the killing per se. It's the thrill of the emotion his kill elicits. He gets off on the building terror.*

Nice profiling work, Doctor Stevens.

Uncanny.

Almost as if you *knew* the guy.

What was it Lew said about sociopaths?

*Extremely bright, keenly observant. Our subject could be quite skillful at aping affect.*

Nailed that one, too.

Skillful at aping affect.

A practiced shape-shifter. A Rougarou.

*The beast could travel anywhere, unseen, long as there's water to carry him.*

*He could change into any animal he chose.*

*A bear, wolf, snake.*

A naval officer.

A minute ticked by. Then another.

Jackson's pulse began to fade.

Black clouds surrounding his field of vision now.

As he lay still, feeling his life flicker like a candle in the wind, one last thought occurred to him.

One way or the other, it looked like his daddy's blade had finally found its way into Robbie's liver after all.

As Harlan Jackson Robichaux, Jr., slipped down into the black water he heard a voice drifting over him from miles above.

*Listen*, it said. *Don't talk.*

# 133

On the bridge the phone rang, and Arthur Gaines picked up.

"Gaines," he said.

*"Listen. Don't talk,"* said the voice on the other end.

Arthur froze.

In that instant, Arthur knew his life was about to change forever. Whatever he did in the next few minutes—in the next few *seconds*—would determine whether that change would prove propitious, or catastrophic.

His commanding officer, the commanding officer of this entire warship, had just gone full Ahab on him, charging below with a sidearm to hunt the SEAL.

And the SEAL he was hunting was now on the horn with Arthur.

"Chief—"

*"Don't talk."*

He hesitated.

*"I need you to get a team of two hospital corpsmen over to Jackson's office, stat."*

Arthur turned his back to the others on the bridge

and spoke as softly as he could. "Is that where you're calling from?"

*"And have security break into Stevens's office."*

"You should stay—wait, what?"

*"Your psychologist. His office. Break in. Full caution. And Jackson's office—two corpsmen. Now. He's in danger."*

"Where—are—you?"

The voice paused, then said, *"Arthur. Please."*

Gaines was silent for a few seconds.

Propitious? Or catastrophic?

"Hang on—stay on the line. *Tommy!*" he called out to the nearest officer. "Ring medical. And Mac." Then he spoke quietly into the phone again. "Chief?"

The line was dead.

# 134

"Sir!"

The voice came from right behind him. Another master-at-arms.

"You need to be in quarters, sir!"

The moment he'd heard the captain's announcement, Lewis had leapt over Jackson's body, hit the door, and sprinted in the direction of the brig, calculating furiously as he went. The SEAL was out and on the move. Which meant what? He couldn't exactly go break out a prisoner who was already broken out!

*Don't panic, Lewis.*

Assess.

Formulate.

Execute.

As he fast-walked down a level and aft to the sector where the brig was located, he ran through his new story, probing for holes.

*The SEAL set up Papadakis, but when Jackson's investigative team got too close he broke out and tried to kill them all. Why he also killed Halsey, we may never know. Maybe Angler had told her some-*

*thing, the two were close. The only reason I sur-*
*vived was I managed to grab at his gun while he was*
*attacking Lieutenant Desai—we struggled, it went*
*off.*

Rickety, but doable. He could sell it. As long as he could locate the SEAL before Mac's MAs did and force him back up to his own office.

Tall order.

But Lewis had superpowers.

Obviously, he was no match for the SEAL physically. The man could snap him in half like a matchstick. But if he could maneuver him into the right situation, he knew exactly how to subdue him, make him malleable as putty. Given the chance to talk to him, Lewis could snap *him* in half—

These were the thoughts swirling through his mind when the voice from behind surprised him.

"Sir! You need to be in quarters, sir!"

Lewis was about to turn when he remembered: that gouge the witch left in his face! Impossible to hide, but difficult to explain away—how could he bear scratches from a struggle he hadn't had yet?

*Assess.*

*Formulate.*

In a flash of inspiration a new tactical element dropped into his mind, the winning silver dollar in a slot machine.

*Cha-ching!*

He whipped around and faced the MA, a look of startled terror on his face.

"Oh, thank God!" he said, clutching his hand to his cheek.

"Sir, you all right?"

Lewis tottered for a moment and leaned against a bulkhead for support, catching for a solid breath.

"The SEAL," he gasped. "Saw him—attacked me—just . . ."

"Easy, sir." The guard helped Lewis to a sitting position. "How long ago did this happen?"

"Just—a minute—maybe two. Oh, God . . ." He put his head between his knees.

"Did you see which way he was headed?"

Lewis gestured vaguely down the passageway. "Ladder—heading below—the nukes, I think—something about—blowing up the ship." He looked up at the young guard, his face suddenly full of alarm. "Can he *do* that?"

"Jesus," the young man muttered. "You sit tight, sir, all right?" He grabbed his radio, pushed a button. "Callan here, just fore of the brig, got a wit here says subject headed for reactor compartments. May have sabotage in mind."

Callan's radio squawked back.

In moments the ship's entire security force had been rerouted below to make a meter-by-meter search of decks 5 and 6.

Leaving Lewis free to work the upper decks.

The perfect diversion.

Recalibrate.

Halsey first. Easier to find—and she might even lead him to the SEAL. There was some kind of connection there. He'd observed them talking.

*Think.*

She wouldn't be in her squadron's ready room—with the ship's flight ops shut down, the captain's order would have evacked her to quarters as "nonessential personnel." But she wouldn't be in her stateroom; she was too stubborn and too personally involved to retreat to quarters, orders or no orders. She'd be someplace where she could stay mobile, waiting to hear from either Scott or Jackson.

She'd be in her office.

Lewis waited a few seconds until his little passageway was empty. Then he stood. With a quiet chuckle, he headed above to the hangar deck.

People were so easy to read.

# 135

Monica was on her way below, searching for Scott, when she rounded a corner and stopped short. Down at the other end of the passageway, Lew Stevens, the ship psychologist, was wigging out, babbling to a master-at-arms about being attacked by the SEAL. Something about . . . *blowing up the ship?*

That was crazy.

But that announcement, just a few minutes earlier. Escaped prisoner, armed and dangerous? That had to be the SEAL. She'd watched them arrest him barely ten hours earlier.

Oh.

*Oh!*

The SEAL. Jesus. *He'd* been in the passageway that night, too, outside Kris's ready room, watching. She remembered thinking how creepy it was, the way he was skulking the passageways. Could *he* have . . . ?

And then she remembered what she'd told Jackson about Kris's state of mind. "Almost like she was being stalked."

*Stalked.*

She turned and ran.

Back through the passageway, back above toward the hangar deck, slipping once on a ladder and nearly falling. Get to her phone. Find Scott, find the chief of security, find *someone*.

She reached her office, yanked open the door, and stepped inside. Closed the door, put her back to it—and stifled a scream.

In the shadows, a figure sat splayed out on the floor, his back to the bulkhead.

"I need your help," said the SEAL.

# 136

"Christ!" she cried out.

The SEAL looked terrible. Crumpled on the deck, like a heap of old clothes.

He shifted slightly—and she saw the speargun.

*Armed and dangerous.*

Monica raced through a mental inventory of her office, searching for anything she might use as a weapon. Should she risk turning and grabbing at the door to make a run for it?

"Did you kill Kristine?" She blurted out the question without even knowing she was going to do it.

The SEAL gazed up at her.

Didn't move.

Didn't reply.

She took two steps forward. "Goddamn you—*DID YOU KILL MY BEST FRIEND?*"

*BAM-BAM-BAM-BAM-BAM!*

A loud fist pounding on her door.

"*Lieutenant!*"

She froze.

"*Lieutenant! Are you all right in there?*" A second voice. A pair of masters-at-arms.

"I'm—I'm here," she called out, still staring in horror at Finn.

The man she'd seen in the video footage, with the goggles. Thin, lithe, tightly controlled movements.

Chief Finn was thin and lithe.

*"Stay there, Lieutenant,"* called the first voice. *"Do not come out. Chief Finn, the SEAL—he's on the loose somewhere. Armed and dangerous."*

Monica felt herself swaying on her feet.

She took a breath.

Shouted, "He's right—"

She stopped.

The man in the goggles . . .

*"Lieutenant?"*

"He's right below us," she shouted back over her shoulder, "deck 3, maybe deck 4 by now. Heading for the nukes, I think."

She heard the two break into a run, the sound receding into silence.

She was alone with the SEAL.

## 137

He hadn't moved. Just sat watching her.

For a moment, neither one spoke.

Then she said, "The guy who killed Kristine posed as a handler."

The SEAL nodded weakly. "Goggles."

"Yeah," said Monica. "Goggles. Green jersey." She took a shaky breath. "Same guy who took out that Knighthawk that crashed in the Gulf. He sabotaged their craft, just before it lifted off. Injected some type of contaminant into the fuel hose."

It would have taken a few hours to work its way through their fuel supply. When the engine stalled out the fuel gauges would've read normal, which would have created a few moments of confusion for Diego and Micaela. Maybe they worked it out in those last seconds. Maybe they had time to wonder who did it, and why, as they cracked the surface of their watery grave.

Not pilot error.

Not Diego's fault, and not Monica's fault, either. It wouldn't have mattered if Chuck goddamn Yaeger had been in that pilot seat. The helo was doomed before it lifted off the deck.

She picked up an object from her desk and held it out toward the SEAL.

Fifty-four onyx eyes stared at him.

"Took me a moment to work it out." She placed the cube back on the desktop and stared at it. "That crash happened weeks before you showed up," she added. Now she looked over at him. "Which means it wasn't you. None of it was you."

The SEAL exhaled and sank back against the bulkhead, eyes closed. "Yeah," he said.

Was that a look of . . . *relief*?

# 138

So it was true.

Whatever neural footage Finn had lost into the maw of those gaping holes, he'd probably never know. But it didn't matter. He hadn't killed Schofield. Hadn't killed Biker. Hadn't killed any of them. It wasn't him.

*None of it was you.*

Although . . . what about Mukalla?

But he'd have to worry about that later. He had a predator to stalk. A smart one.

Where would he be right now?

He looked up at Monica, sharply. "Have you told anyone?"

"So far? Only Scott Angler."

Finn paused, sifting through the implications. Supercop knew. But did the killer know that Supercop knew?

"They think you've gone below to sabotage the reactors," she added.

He looked up again. "Why would they think that?"

"Lew Stevens told them. The ship psychologist. I just heard him a few minutes ago, down on deck three, saying he was attacked—by you." When Finn didn't say anything to that, she pressed. "Did you attack Lew Stevens?"

Finn slowly pulled himself up onto his feet. "Lew Stevens is your rattlesnake."

"*Stevens?* Are you fucking *kidding* me?"

"You just saw him?"

She looked thunderstruck. "Briefly. Just a glimpse. Are you *sure* . . . Lieutenant *Stev*—"

"Did he see you?"

"I—I don't know. I don't think so. Why?"

Finn pushed between her and her desk on his way out. "Lock this door after I leave."

"It doesn't lock."

He stopped, looked around the office. "You have a weapon in here?"

"No. Why?"

He handed her the speargun.

"He'll be coming for you next."

## 139

Finn stood just outside the little maintenance office, lean-ing against the doorframe and taking stock.

Stevens would have a sidearm. Finn didn't believe he'd use it in here—too much noise and risk of ricochet—but he couldn't be sure of that. And he'd just left his primary with West Texas.

He needed a weapon.

Finn pressed both palms to his head. Here came that faint high hum again, the sound he'd started hearing the day he toured the bomb assembly room and magazine.

The magazine.

Where they stored flares.

It would take no more than sixty seconds to scoot down the ladder, find and secure a small flare, get back up and out. With any luck he'd be armed, hidden, and waiting by the time Psycho Doc arrived.

Pushing off from the wall, he threaded his way through the maze of chocked and chained aircraft and forward through the hangar deck until he found the hatch to the little magazine. Punched in the code he'd memorized the day of his tour. Opened the hatch silently and slipped down inside, leaving the hatch open for quick exfil.

*Rule 1: always keep an open exit.*

Lowered himself in.

Hand over hand, feet finding each rung.

As he descended the dizziness worsened.

The nausea rose up.

That distant demented police siren returned, circling closer and closer.

Rung by rung.

Lower.

Lower.

Finally one foot touched the deck.

He removed his hands from the ladder and flexed his fingers gingerly. His hands ached. He took a breath, then began looking around to locate the right-sized flare—when he heard the *snick* of a valve relay being thrown, followed by the gurgle of rapidly flowing water. He felt water around his feet.

The magazine was filling.

A man's voice filtered down from above, quietly echoing.

*"Hello, F/X."*

# 140

Emergency sprinkler system.

Psycho Doc was flooding the magazine.

To drown him? Flush him out?

Either way, he was dead.

*"A little unsteady on your feet there. Have you been drinking, F/X?"*

The faint echo gave the voice a ghostly quality, as if it were coming from inside his head.

Fighting back the nausea, Finn pulled a small flare from its containment. Couldn't fire it from here, too far to the opening. He'd only blast the inside of the magazine.

*"Ha-ha, kidding. I know you're not a drinker. No, you're a claustrophobe, aren't you, F/X?"*

He strapped the flare to his side and began to climb.

Focus on the breath. In through nostrils, four, five . . .

*"My gosh, the willpower it must have taken, plowing through all those training scenarios, keeping your little secret. But you still can't stand enclosed spaces, can you? That's why you're always out on the sponsons and catwalks and not in your little bedchamber."*

Finn was nearly halfway up now. A little farther and

he'd take the shot. At worst it would distract the target, buy him time to scuttle up the ladder and out.

"*I put something in your little bedchamber today, F/X. A green jersey and goggles. They'd look good on you. Make you look a little like, I don't know . . . a pollywog?*"

Breathe out through pursed lips, pause, in through nostrils—

The voice started softly chanting.

"*Pol-ly-wog . . . Pol-ly-wog . . . Pol-ly-wog . . .*"

Finn froze.

Felt the color drain from his face, his jaw clench.

He scrabbled at the flare and pulled it free—

The voice picked up in pace and volume.

"*Pol-ly-wog! Pol-ly-wog! Pol-ly-WOG! Pol-ly-WOG!*"

His hands went numb and he felt himself starting to slip—the flare fell from his fingers, clattering down the ladder.

"*Pol-ly-WOG! Pol-ly-WOG!!*"

Finn jammed his arms and now useless hands through the rungs to hold him in place, his body dangling from the ladder like a broken shutter. His throat locked.

"*Pol-ly-WOG! Pol-ly-WOG!*"

He felt water licking at the soles of his feet, tickling his ankles.

"*I know what happened in the gun closet that day, F/X, the day that made you what you are.*

"*Ray never shot himself, did he. When that handgun went off, it wasn't in his hand, the way everyone assumed.*

"*It was in yours.*"

A billion wriggling tadpoles came swarming up through the water, up through his gut, into his throat, all of them shrieking in unison with that leering voice . . .

*Pol-ly-wog! Pol-ly-wog!*

*"You shot him."*

*POL-LY-WOG!! POL-LY-WOG!!*

*"You killed your brother, F/X."*

*POL-LY-WOG!!! POL-LY-WOG!!!*

*"You killed Ray."*

## 141

Ray was a god. He knew everything. When the boy grew up he wanted to be a big brother like Ray.

It was a sunny day but there were thunder rumbles, and he thought that was weird but Ray said, that's Oregon for ya, and the boy felt like a smarter person knowing this wise thing. That was Oregon for ya!

They spent the morning out in the woods tracking deer and elk and hanging out by the millpond, and when they got back Ray showed him how to make grilled cheese sandwiches. Their parents were gone for the day—again—or maybe a couple days, the boy didn't know and didn't really care, the longer the better as far as he was concerned, things were better anyway when it was just him and Ray.

Just Ray and him.

When they were down by the millpond Ray showed him that place where the stream twisted around a bend and you could lie on your stomach and watch the water, the minnows and goldfish, the water-skeeters and may-flies.

And tadpoles. Billions of them, wriggling and swarming in the water.

Those're also called *pollywogs,* Ray told him as they sat in the kitchen and ate their grilled cheese. In ancient Egypt hieroglyphics, they used one tadpole to stand for the number *a hundred thousand,* Ray said. In some parts of the world, people ate them for food.

The boy thought they looked scary.

All big heads and no arms or legs.

They gave him the creeps.

Ray took a fat slice of Duncan Hines Devil's Food chocolate cake out of the fridge for his little brother and set it on the card table in the kitchen to let it warm a little. He said it would taste even better when it wasn't totally cold.

While they waited for the cake to warm, Ray said, hey, you wanna see something really cool?

The closet was locked, but Ray knew where the key was.

They had guns in there. A bunch of them. Ray took one out and held it in his hand. This is the coolest one, he said, it's an H&K, they're the best there is. Ray held it out to Finn. Check it out! The boy wasn't so sure he wanted to touch it. It looked cool, all right, but it also looked big and cold. It's not loaded, goofball, Ray said, just feel the weight of it in your hand.

He took it, felt the weight of it in his hand. It *was* really cool.

His brother beamed at him.

His big brother.

His world.

*BOOM!*

The boy wasn't aware of squeezing anything or pulling anything. He wasn't even sure exactly which little piece of metal was the trigger.

It was like it just exploded in his hand.

They were watching TV one day, him and Ray, and they saw a big hotel in Portland that was condemned and they were televising the demolition, the TV guy explaining how they wired the whole thing with explosives, and all they had to do was press a little button and *BOOM,* a whole bunch of explosions would go off at the same time and the building would just collapse—and then right as they were watching it *happened,* just the way the man said, this big humungous hotel just melted down into itself, collapsing like a puppet when you cut all its strings.

That's what Ray did now.

Ray just stared at him, and then collapsed like a puppet, his knees slammed into the floor, and then his body crashed down too—

a big *THUD!*—

then a second, smaller *thud*—

and then a million billion *trillion* pollywogs came surging up into the boy's throat and burst out through the top of his head—

## 142

**Finn screamed.**

The cry of something primordial, a banshee wail, the howl of a dozen dying wolves, a thousand tortured souls, a train whistle shrieking into the mouth of Hell—

And took a breath—

And he screamed again—

A roar of pain and grief and anguish—

for Schofield,

for Biker,

for Luca—

for Kennedy—

for Ray—

for that terrified boy sitting frozen in his blood-soaked closet forever—

the scream ripped through the hangar deck and startled the man standing at the top of the tunnel, causing him to rear back—

Finn surged up the ladder like a geyser—

His arm shot out and over the lip of the magazine and plunged the steel ring knife into Lew Stevens's right foot.

# 143

Bellowing in pain and fury, Lewis tugged the knife out and hurled it away. He staggered, caught his balance, and lifted the sidearm to shoot—

But Finn was gone.

*Shit.*

Where?

Somewhere out there in the darkened hangar, among all those sleeping aircraft.

Lewis lowered his head and half closed his eyes, straining to hear something, anything, even the slightest movement. Nothing. There was no one in the hangar but himself and his prey—and neither was making a sound.

If "prey" was still the right word.

*Shit!*

Ten seconds ago Lew was standing on the outside of the rat cage looking in.

Was he now the rat?

Recalibrate.

He was at a disadvantage. Finn could be anywhere, could jump him from any direction.

He took off at a sprint, making for open ground, knowing Finn would pursue, giving Lewis a clean shot.

Timing, that's all. Just a matter of timing.

Lewis ran.

# 144

Finn shook all over, his body trembling with the after-shocks of an epic earthquake. He'd poked the bear, all right, and it hadn't just whacked him back, it had lashed out at him with both paws and ripped the flesh off of him, left him naked and bleeding.

But he was still there.

*Still here, Ray.*

*I'm sorry, Ray.*

*I'm so sorry.*

He had to move.

Breathe.

Still wracked with tremors he couldn't control, he started across the hangar deck, slipping from craft to craft, reaching out with his ears and instincts far ahead of his feet, moving silently, monitoring in all directions.

The ship was rocking hard now, the storm in full swing. He didn't care. Didn't affect him. The police siren was silent now, the dizziness gone.

He was on the stalk.

Fighting to tamp down the full-body shakes, he worked his way aft through hangar bay 2, past the maintenance office and on through hangar bay 3, through the jet engine shops and finally out onto the fantail—

Where Psycho Doc stood off to the port side, back to the rail, struggling to keep his footing on the storm-rocked deck. Leveling his unsteady handgun at Finn.

Every security detail had gone below to join the others in their wild-goose chase. The fantail was empty.

There was no one there but the two of them.

Finn stood in the doorway facing Psycho Doc from about four meters' distance. Empty-handed.

The wind howled. The sea pitched up fifty-foot waves, some washing up over the rail and sluicing over the deck.

Psycho Doc was having trouble holding his aim. Still, from that distance his chances of a center-mass hit with his first shot were decent. Maybe better than decent.

On the other hand, the first shot could just as easily be a miss—and shot meant recoil, which meant a few precious seconds to retake aim, which upped the odds of Finn successfully rushing him between shot 1 and shot 2.

Finn had played those odds before, and won. But that was no guarantee.

Time slowed to a halt, each man taking the other's measure.

Both weighing the options, calculating the odds.

Would Psycho Doc shoot Psycho SEAL—or would Psycho SEAL explode into a sudden feint-and-lunge and try to get the jump on Psycho Doc?

Finn would never learn the answer.

Because right at that moment a third possibility presented itself.

# 145

Finn felt it more than heard it—a whisper of hot air darting past, barely an inch from his side, as the missile found its target.

*Thwonggggg.*

The crossbow bolt buried itself in Stevens's solar plexus and pinned him against the rail.

Monica let the crossbow fall clattering to the deck and stepped uncertainly out onto the fantail, both arms out for balance, her face gone white.

Shaky but still standing.

Sitting on the deck some five meters off, legs asprawl, Monica's lethal shaft protruding from his solar plexus, Lew Stevens heaved a strained grunt.

Finn and Monica both stared at him.

His face twisted into something not recognizable as Lew Stevens. A grin so lewd it didn't look human. He twitched once, then again, then went still, his face still twisted in that fey leer.

Like a mask.

Which was when they both heard the distinctive *shuck-shuck* of a sidearm chambering a round.

# 146

He saw them both freeze in place the instant he racked the slide on his Beretta 9mm. "Hold it right there!" he shouted over the wail of the wind.

Captain Eagleberg was aghast at what he'd just witnessed. The SEAL he'd expected—but holy Mary mother of God, the young helo pilot . . . was his *accomplice*?

He stepped out from the doorway at the far side of the fantail, a good six meters from where the two assassins stood. Close enough to shoot.

And Eagleberg was trained.

He stood, legs well apart and knees slightly bent to brace himself from the pitch and roll of the deck underfoot, and held his pistol out with both hands, aimed in their direction. "I'm placing you both under arrest, Article 31, UCMJ," he shouted, "for the murders of Lewis Stevens, Sam Schofield, Kristine Shiflin, Luca Santiago, Ángel Cristobal, and William Chavez."

The pilot stared at him, openmouthed.

The SEAL didn't seem surprised, just frowned, as if he were concentrating, aiming a weapon. Though he clearly had no weapon to aim.

He had nothing.

He was empty-handed.

They both were.

"Or," said Eagleberg. "Or I could save the navy the time and expense, and put you both down right now. Bring the killers to justice. Not the NCIS, not the FBI, not Angler, not Jackson. Old Eaglebeak."

He lifted the pistol to chest height, aiming at a point between the two of them.

"Self-defense," he said. He sneered. "You think anyone will doubt it?"

# 147

Finn was too far away to get to him before the gun went off, and from the look of his stance the captain was a far better-trained shot than Stevens. Finn had given his primary to Monica and left his secondary sticking in Stevens's foot.

No primary. No secondary.

*This,* he thought.

*This* was why you *always* deployed a tertiary.

A backup to your backup.

And then the helo pilot did something neither Finn nor the captain expected. She slowly began to turn around. Hands out to her sides. Putting her back to the captain.

Finn understood what she was doing an instant before Eagleberg did. If she turned all the way around she would force his hand.

Tough to claim self-defense when you shot the other person in the back.

"Stop it!" His voice cracking, gun hand trembling. "Don't move!"

She froze again, then resumed her painfully slow turn, shouting over the wind as she did. "It wasn't Chief

Finn, sir!" she shouted. "It was Stevens. Stevens killed them all."

"I'm warning you, Lieutenant—stop moving, that's an order!"

She kept turning. If he really meant to go through with it, this was his last chance.

"*Stop,* goddammit!" he screamed. "I *will* shoot you!"

Finn believed him.

Endgame.

He moved like a flash of lightning—a slingshot twist of his body and flick of his left hand.

The captain cried out in pain and surprise.

He dropped the sidearm, both hands flying to his face, and fell to his knees with blood pouring through his hands. He stared up in horror at Finn. Then looked down.

On the deck in front of him sat a bloodied, silver-plated Rubik's cube.

"Shuck! *Shuck!*" he screamed.

He looked up at Finn in disbelief.

"You jush broke my shucking *nozhe*!"

Captain William James Eagleberg sat kneeling on the deck of the USS *Abraham Lincoln* and began to cry.

# Epilogue

# 148

*A week later*
*Ten miles off the coast of San Diego*

"The USS *Abraham Lincoln* is proud to welcome their new commanding officer . . ."

An audience of some three hundred sat in folding chairs on the flight deck, there to witness the change-of-command ceremony.

"I had the privilege of working with this distinguished gentleman several years ago . . ." The speaker, some visiting rear admiral, droned on under the hot September sun. Off to his far left, facing the audience, sat Captain Eagleberg, decked out in his finest dress whites, his nose so heavily bandaged it looked like the Mummy had just stepped off the silver screen and lay down on his face.

The captain would be shipping out the next day to the central Indian Ocean, where he would assume command of the Chagos Archipelago's Diego Garcia naval base. "A capstone to his distinguished career," the speaker had called it.

Diego Garcia was one of the worst assignments in

the navy—a little piss pot in the middle of nowhere. The navy's way of shuffling him out to pasture without the embarrassment of a court-martial.

Everyone present knew it.

Watching from his seat in back, crutches tucked under his chair, Command Master Chief Robbie Jackson checked his timepiece.

In his own gratefully brief speech, Old Eaglebeak dutifully extolled the virtues of his successor, Commander Arthur Atticus Gaines. Now *Captain* Arthur Atticus Gaines.

*Good for you, Arthur. And may no one ever call you "Artie" again.*

Jackson had heard the rumor that they were planning an award ceremony for him, too, but he hadn't paid much attention. It hadn't been announced yet; maybe it never would. They probably couldn't figure out what medal you give to someone for surviving a homicidal attack from one of your ship's own crew.

The scalpel had not gone into his liver after all, but it had lacerated his spleen and caused massive internal bleeding. Would have killed him, too, if the medical team Gaines dispatched had not arrived so quickly. And Gaines and his corpsmen were not the only ones Robbie had to thank. The sharp sting he'd felt in his trapezium was a hypodermic filled with succinylcholine—a lethal dose, even for someone as big as Jackson.

Except that Lew had been prevented from pushing the plunger all the way in when Jackson went suddenly crashing to the deck. He'd gotten enough sux in him to slow him down and create a near-paralytic state. But not quite kill him.

Sister Mae had saved his life.

Once he got stateside, Robbie had some time off coming.

He'd use it to pay a good long visit to the bayou.

Scattered applause. Finally the ceremony was winding to a close.

Jackson got up and crutched his way across the flight deck to head below to his office.

He'd been up there since an hour before the ceremony, watching as they loaded a series of three black rubber body bags onto Lieutenant Bennett's big Greyhound for transport: Commander Scott Angler, JAG. Lieutenant Indira Desai, Intelligence. Lieutenant Lewis Stevens, Medical.

He'd thought about all the bodies they weren't able to recover. Kristine Shiflin. Sam Schofield. Luca Santiago. Willy and Ángel, the two boys from recycling. Commander Papadakis. The crew of four from the ill-fated Knighthawk. Casualties of war—not with a named enemy but with whatever dark imperative it was that animated people like Lew Stevens.

*We steam around the world,* Jackson mused, *offering protection from our enemies.* But the greatest mortal threat Jackson had ever encountered came from one of their own.

And that, he thought, was the most dangerous thing about the Terrible Man.

How often he looked just like the good guy.

Jackson checked his timepiece again, then stepped cautiously down onto the catwalk and headed below.

## 149

When he reached his office there was a message from the ATO shack.

"Delegation's on their way below in ten minutes," it said.

Finn's welcoming committee, making the hop out from the beach to provide their guest an escort back to WARCOM headquarters at Coronado for a debrief.

Jackson had sent a petty officer up to see if the SEAL would stop in at his office before heading ashore. The delegation would be escorting him from here.

He went back into his inner sanctum to wait.

Earlier that day he'd met with Admiral Kirkland, who'd thanked him on behalf of the US Navy for his heroic if unorthodox efforts to maintain order on the ship and secure the crew's safety, and apologized for the treatment he'd received at Eagleberg's hands. She also let him know she had personally cleared him of any wrongdoing or impropriety in connection with his un-sanctioned investigation, as well as having all the captain's charges against Chief Finn dropped—gross insubordination, disorderly conduct, and on down the list.

As they stood to conclude their meeting, she'd asked, did he know anything about some sort of top-secret incident file concerning Chief Finn in Yemen? Apparently a few handwritten notes alluding to it had been found among Lieutenant Desai's personal effects.

Jackson thought for a moment, then shook his head. Sorry, he lied. First he'd heard of it.

Now he looked over at the God's eyes on his bulkhead. "So sue me," he said.

The God's eyes said nothing back.

Jackson took that to mean God had no problem looking the other way.

"Ah, Master Chief Jackson?"

The petty officer was peering in his half-open door. He was alone.

Jackson nodded at the guy to come on in.

The young man took two steps inside the office and stood there, his arms loaded with a stack of large sheets of paper.

"Go ahead," Jackson prompted.

"Ah," the kid stammered. "We, ah, went to get Chief Finn." He stopped.

"And?" said Jackson.

"We, ah, we found these."

The petty officer spread the sheaves of sketch paper out on Jackson's desk. In Finn's tiny compartment they'd found what looked like a complete set of sketched blueprints of the ship, all drawn by hand.

Jackson leafed through them, one by one, shaking his head in amazement. Every deck, nearly every compartment, all rendered in meticulous detail like an architect's drawing. He got about halfway through the stack and stopped.

Stared.

Turned the next sheet over. Then the next.

Mixed in among the architectural-style renderings

were a few sketched portraits of the *Lincoln*'s crew members.

Kristine Shiflin, alone in the cockpit of her F/A-18, laughing.

Sam Schofield, at his desk in the ATO shack, in conversation with his assistant, Campion.

The captain, peering imperiously down at the flight deck from Vulture's Row.

Jackson himself, standing in deckhouse 3 in the midst of a muster, his eyes fixed straight ahead as if staring directly at the viewer.

Jackson felt the gooseflesh rise on his arms.

It was uncanny how lifelike they were, how the personalities leapt from the page. These were not simply photographic, they were somehow even more real than photographs—as if the artist had captured the very essence of each subject. Like psychological CAT scans.

"*Mère de Dieu,*" he murmured. Looked up at the petty officer. "And the man himself?"

"Ah, we haven't quite located him yet, Master Chief."

There was a brief silence, heavy as granite.

"You haven't quite located him?" repeated Jackson.

The young man looked like he wanted to crawl onto Jackson's desk and hide inside the stack of drawings. "He doesn't seem to be, ah . . . anywhere, Master Chief."

Jackson lurched to his feet and bellowed at the man: "*You search every compartment, every locker, every trunk line, every toilet, shine a flashlight up every sailor's butt if you have to, but find that goddamn sonofabitch!*"

The petty officer blanched. He'd never heard Master Chief Jackson raise his voice before, let alone use that kind of language. No one had. "We already h-h-have, Master Chief. He's just, he's just not there!"

"*WELL, SEARCH IT ALL AGAIN!!*"

"Aye, Master Chief! On the double!"

The petty officer turned and fled.

The big man lowered himself gingerly back into his leather chair, swiveled around to his desk, and took a sip from his coffee mug. Set the cup down. Made a face.

*Dieu*, that was some bitter brew.

Perfect, to his way of thinking.

He pulled open the bottom drawer of his desk, the one that locked, and pulled out a thin sheaf of stapled papers. Five sheets, single-spaced.

He dropped it in a burn bag and sealed it. Thought about the SEAL, who at that moment was probably miles from there, slipping in among the rocks and onto shore somewhere on the Southern California coast. Imagined that within another hour or two, half of San Diego's military security forces would be looking for him.

They'd have their work cut out for them.

A smile stole over Jackson's broad features.

And then he laughed and he laughed and he laughed.

# 150

*Two days later*
*Lummi Island, Washington*

She checked all the locks. Lowered all the lights. Brewed herself a cup of oat straw tea, added half a teaspoon of local wildflower honey, took it to her couch. Remote in hand, flicked on the news. Felt with both hands on the couch's surface beside her in the dark, triple-checking.

Phone and tactical flash on one side, HK P2000 9mm on the other. She liked the P2000. It had no safety, which suited her just fine.

Flipped through the news channels, taking time to assess each story's basic information. Switched to the Internet, did a series of searches, found nothing worth tracking further. Back to the news to pick up on any back-page items. Then called up the show she was currently watching, a documentary on aquatic predators of the Antarctic. Whale, squid, albatross, and so forth. She was rooting for the krill.

Her phone lit up.

Message.

She muted the set and looked at the phone's flat surface.

"I'm here," it said.

# Note from the Authors

Prior to becoming a SEAL, Brandon did two six-month WestPac (Western Pacific) tours as a search-and-rescue swimmer, one on the USS *Kitty Hawk* and one on the USS *Abraham Lincoln*—much like Finn in the book. The idea for this novel was inspired by an actual serial-molester event that occurred during his tour aboard the *Lincoln* in the mid-1990s, when the US Navy had just integrated women on board. The identity of that serial molester was never discovered.

A ship's crew is ill-equipped to deal with a complex crime, not to mention the external political forces that would come into play. At the time, Brandon thought, *What if these were* murders?

It took twenty-five years and a writing partnership with John to bring that idea to the page.

While the characters of *Steel Fear* are fictional, the USS *Abraham Lincoln* is as real as blood and bones, as Finn would say, and we've sought to depict the ship as accurately as possible. For example, the décor of the captain's "Lincoln Room" really was remodeled based on the set of Spielberg's 2012 movie. (And yes, that little spot just behind elevator 4 is in fact called "The Finger.") That said, there are certain features, locations, and other details of the ship's layout that we have intentionally changed, simplified, or obscured for security reasons.

Running a military vessel like the *Lincoln* takes a vast crew of talented and dedicated people whose tireless efforts often go unseen and unsung.

Turns out, the same is true of making a novel.

The authors send their abiding thanks:

To Alyssa Reuben at the Paradigm Agency for brilliantly shepherding our maiden voyage as novelists every step of the way (and for her Ninja-level editing skills).

To Anne Speyer, Jennifer Hershey, Kim Hovey, and Kara Welsh at Bantam Books for being our enthusiastic partners-in-crime; we could not have conceived of a more ideal publishing partnership.

To Carlos Beltrán for his stunning cover design, and Virginia Norey for the perfection of her book design.

To Hilary Zaitz Michael and Jack Beloff at William Morris Endeavor, Ben Smith and Adam Docksey at Captivate Entertainment, writer Aaron Rabin, and Alex Sepiol and Jake Castiglioni at Peacock for their dedication to bringing *Steel Fear* to the screen.

To Captain Putnam H. Browne, commanding officer; Command Master Chief James W. Stedding; Captain G. Merrill Rice, senior medical officer; Rear Admiral John F. G. Wade, commander, Carrier Strike Group 12; Lieutenant Charlie Koller, Lieutenant Christian Litwiller, MC3 Amber Smalley, and MCC Mark Logico, all from the USS *Abraham Lincoln;* and at Naval Air Force Atlantic in Norfolk, to Commander Dave Hecht, Deputy PAO Officer Mike Maus, MC2 Kaylyn Jackson-Smith, MCCS Dustin Withrow, MC Alan Lewis, and Ensign Clara Navarro for their generous assistance in John's visit aboard the *Lincoln*.

To David Krueger, M.D., George Pratt, Ph.D., and

J. T. Swick II, M.D. for lending their psychiatric, psychological, and medical expertise.

To Nick Coffman, George Hand, and Sean Spoonts for sharing their technical and military expertise.

To Geoff Dyer, author of *Another Great Day at Sea;* Cary Lohrenz, author of *Leadership Without Fear,* and Icon Productions, producer of the documentary *Carrier,* for their outstandingly informative descriptions of life on an aircraft carrier.

To Harry Bingham and Hal Croasmun for their expert guidance in how to put one word in front of another and have it all go somewhere (these two guys are SEAL-level in the writing sphere!); and to Eve Seymour (aka G. S. Locke) for her life-savingly expert critique of our first draft.

To Michael Ledwidge for his generous early endorsement.

To Deb and Charlie Austin, Dan Clements, James Justice, Ana Gabriel Mann, and Abbie McClung, for soaking up every word of early drafts and offering their own words of critique and encouragement.

And finally to you, the reader following these words right now, for coming with us on this journey. Don't unpack your bags just yet; if you're willing, we have more travels still ahead of us.

Read on for a sneak peek at
the next explosive thriller by Webb & Mann:

# COLD FEAR

Coming soon from Bantam Books

# Prologue

*A deserted city street. The distant ruckus of drunken revelers, laughter, Christmas carol fragments. Under the faint glow of street lights a flurry of snowflakes drifts to the frigid cobblestone surface, then swirls aside as a girl sprints past.*

*Bare feet. No coat. Mid-twenties.*

*She darts through an intersection. Then another. Street names she can't pronounce. On a wild guess she takes a left at the next corner and runs another block before stopping, bent over, hands on knees, breathing like a trapped animal.*

*There's nothing but the silence of the snow and her own rapid panting. She looks around, frantic.*

*Has she gone too far?*

*Takes off running again. Squinting at the street signs, pleading for them to make sense. Fighting back the urge to stop and scan the darkness behind her.*

*The sound of her feet slapping the slick street surface drums against her ears . . . images explode through her mind—*

*the mines . . . the Englishman . . . the lake house—*

*She pushes them away. Her feet are bleeding, but she has to keep going. She has to—*

*Wait.*

*Was that a glimpse of someone passing on the far side of the street?*

*She slows long enough to peer back through the murk. No one there.*

*the drugs are still too strong.*

*She can't tell what is hallucination and what is real.*

*Keep going.*

*her feet slapping the cobblestones . . . the mines . . . the Englishman . . .*

*She won't make it. It was a crazy idea. Should have known it was pointless to try. She reaches the next corner—*

*And there it is. Spread out before her like a banquet.*

*She stops again, hands on knees, gasping, the Arctic air searing her lungs. Squints into the dark and feels a rush of bitter relief. Not a hallucination. Really there.*

*A patch of open water.*

*The driver told her about this the day she arrived. In December the pond is covered in ice, he said, ice so thick they hold hockey matches on it. Except right here, at this spot. The city keeps this northeast corner heated year-round. "For the ducks!" he chortled.*

*And sure enough, through the gloom she can see their little bodies, tucked into themselves for warmth, still and silent. Living, breathing ducks, asleep on the water.*

*How do they survive the winters here?*

*How does anyone survive the winters here?*

*She whips her head around, suddenly alert, eyes and ears straining in the dark. There's no one behind her. The only sounds she hears are her own hard breath and the faint splish-splash as she steps into the shallow.*

*From her pocket she pulls a stick of lipstick, blood red.*

*Stares at it, her heart thudding.*

*She isn't supposed to know.*

*Isn't supposed to know about any of it.*

*But she does.*

*Hands trembling from the cold, she twists the lipstick open, pulls up her shirt with one hand and with the other scrawls a single word upside down across her abdomen.*

*Then lets the lipstick fall from her fingers.*

*She strips out of her clothes, tossing each item behind her. Stark naked, she takes a few more steps into the water. Another flurry of snowflakes falls around her, the air a blast freezer on her skin. Teeth chattering, she kneels. Places her palms down against the shallow pond floor. Slides down onto her stomach and pushes herself away from the edge with her feet, propelling with her arms, each stroke drawing her further toward the pond's center. After a moment her outstretched fingers find the lip of the ice sheet.*

*She slips underneath the ice, then twists around so that her back is to the pond floor, her face to the ice above. Stretches out her arms as wide as she can.*

*And pushes farther in.*

# Sunday
## 1

*Temperatures in the low twenties (F°),
snow flurries; bitter winds.*

Gunnar slipped out of his family's townhouse and closed the front door, soft as a spy. He wasn't supposed to be out here on his own, but his parents wouldn't notice. And anyway, he'd be back inside in just a few minutes. Quick as a flash.

It was past ten in the morning but still dark out. The sun wouldn't come up for another hour. He looked around at their street. It had snowed in the night! Only a little dusting, but snow was snow. It looked just like the powdered sugar on the Christmas cookies his Danish au pair had made the day before, on Christmas Eve.

Gunnar descended the steps and trudged around the corner, scooted across the street and out onto the ice. He knew it was safe. In fact, he'd be out there later that day with his parents to watch the college kids play hockey. Right now, though, there was no one on the pond, no cars on the streets. Christmas Day. Everyone was at home eating oatmeal and staying warm, or still in bed ("sleeping it off") like his parents.

He ventured farther out onto the ice, halfway to the middle of the pond, then laid down on his back, gazing up at the gray clouds against the violet morning sky, imagining bears and dragons and brave men with swords chasing them. He made snow angels. Laughed at the fresh tickle of snowflakes on his face.

After a few minutes of this glorious fun, Gunnar rolled himself over to get up on his feet. Gotta be home before they noticed him gone. He slipped on the ice and fell flat on his frontside. *Good one, klaufi! That takes talent!* That's what his big brother would say if he'd seen that clumsy move.

Taking it slow and careful now, Gunnar got back up onto his hands and knees—and stopped.

This couldn't be real. Could it?

He was looking down at the ice, and someone underneath was looking back up at him.

He stared into the ice.

Into her eyes.

*The Little Mermaid* was Gunnar's favorite story. His au pair had read him all the Hans Christian Andersen stories, and that was the one he fell in love with. He'd seen the Disney movie, too, but that was different. It felt fake. He liked having the story read to him better. Closing his eyes and hearing the words, in her voice, it all came alive. He never admitted this to his big brother, or to anyone, not even his au pair, but in his heart of hearts Gunnar believed that mermaids were real.

And there was one staring up at him right now from under the ice!

His palms were starting to hurt from the cold, but he couldn't move a muscle. It was like he was as frozen as the ice.

He *wanted* this to be real.

He wanted so badly for this to be proof that he was right all along, that his brother and his parents and teachers were all wrong, that there really *were* mermaids, and that Gunnar—not his brother, not his parents, but Gunnar himself—had found one!

But there was this cold feeling in his tummy, a bad feeling, really bad, bubbling up like Geysir.

He was terrified.

Gunnar knew this was not a mermaid.

He knew this, because the lady in the duck pond wasn't moving.

Not at all.

Then Gunnar heard a horrible sound, like the shriek of a hockey referee's whistle, but he didn't stop to wonder what it was or where it was coming from, didn't even think to realize it was coming from himself.

Didn't think at all.

He was too busy running.

# 2

Krista Kristjánsdóttir stood over the vague form in the ice and cursed a blue streak.

She pulled her phone from her vest and tapped the screen to life. "Surface too opaque to see limbs and torso clearly." She held the phone close and spoke low and quiet, enunciating each word. "Only the face visible."

She paused, aware of how inadequate the word sounded. *Visible*. How about *indelible*. *Haunting*.

The police had arrived within minutes of the boy's first screams, but not before some citizen showed up with his phone and snapped photos, then trotted off to sell them to the city's daily newspaper. Terrific. By the time the cops had the scene locked down, the dead girl's face was staring out through iPad screens in households across the country, under the headline "LITLA HAFMEYJAN Á ÍS!"

*The little mermaid on ice!*

Krista's partner Einar plodded over, texting as he walked, and relayed a brief from one of the officers on the scene.

No ID in the woman's clothing. A lipstick that might be hers, might give up prints, might not. No other clues to her identity. A team of divers was slipping in under the ice sheet right now to see if it was possible to pull her free without damaging the body. Otherwise they'd need to cut her out.

They waited in silence, puffing clouds of icy breath.

Moments later the lead diver emerged, looked over at Krista, and shook his head. They'd have to cut out a section of the ice, secure it with a tarp, and transport her to pathology that way. "Like a fly in amber," murmured Einar, his nimble fat thumbs tap-dancing over his phone again.

Krista glanced at the crowd along the duck pond's edge that was pushing up against the barriers the police hastily put in place, craning to catch a glimpse.

And cursed again.

Media.

She looked at Einar and nodded in the direction of the throng of reporters. He stopped texting and grinned. *No problem*, he mouthed. He turned and trundled over toward the pack to give a statement that would say nothing at all, but say it in the most polite and interesting terms.

Krista hated this part, talking to the press. Always made her feel like a politician. Einar had no problem with it. Which Krista had never understood. It seemed to her that cops and reporters should be natural enemies. Or at least opposites. A detective's toughest job was getting people to talk. The hardest thing about reporters was getting them to stop talking.

She watched as an officer brought over a blue vinyl tarp and set it down next to her. Another officer with a portable saw kneeled at the foot of the young woman's frozen crypt and lowered the spinning blade to the ice.

Like a bone saw at an autopsy, its metal edge let out a scream that sliced through the brittle morning air.

Krista winced.

# 3

At the back of the crowd, a squarish face with oversize eyes watched from under a hooded parka as the little knot of police officers instinctively took a step backward from the scream of the saw. Their elongated shadows stretching out over the duck pond's frozen surface reminded the hooded man of the strange statues of Easter Island. Silent sentinels, watching over their people, keeping them from harm.

Too late for the woman they were cutting out of the ice.

He looked around at the city's storybook architecture, everything illuminated by the liquid amber light. Eleven fifteen, and the sun was just now coming up, struggling to breach the horizon by a few degrees before falling again and plunging the city back into darkness barely four hours later.

Iceland, the "land of fire and ice," at the darkest time of year.

He'd been here before. Visited briefly, years earlier, just before they withdrew all American forces from the nearby air base. A lifetime ago. Before he made chief.

Back then he was plain Finn, a freshly minted Navy

SEAL sniper on his way to help train a Coalition team in Norway. It was summer then, balmy, sunny. Iceland's famous temperate summers. Herds of tourists—Americans, Canadians, Brits, Malaysians, French, Germans—there to experience the daylight that stretched clear around the clock, to see the glaciers and geysers, the lava fields and lunar landscapes, the milky Blue Lagoon, the ooh and the ahh.

Not now. Now the tourists were mostly gone. This was the island community in deep winter, when the sun showed its sallow face for no more than a few hours a day. The bitter Arctic climate that forged this people's national character for a thousand years. No midnight sun, no balmy lava-field tours, no ooh, no ahh. This was not the Iceland of the travel brochures and vacation websites. This was the Iceland outsiders seldom saw. Right now, the land of fire and ice was mostly ice and darkness.

And death.

The night before, after being dropped off a few blocks from his destination, Finn had walked the streets of the city. It was an eerie mix of old and new, a mash-up of Heidelberg or Prague or some other quaint European burg, with a futuristic scene out of *Final Fantasy*. Rows of wood-and-corrugated-iron houses brightly painted in pastels and primary colors, a medieval village on an LSD trip. Even as he walked the paved streets of the city, images of the gouts of steam he'd seen geysering up out of the treeless landscape on his ride from the airport were a constant reminder that this was a land formed on the face of a volcanic crack in the Earth.

When he'd gotten safely into his bolt-hole and turned on the tap, the water that poured out was near the boiling point and gave off the unmistakable smell of sulfur.

All the amenities of hell.

On the ride into the city his driver had asked what he was doing here in Reykjavík. "Research," Finn told him. "Crime writer." As good a lie as any.

The driver snorted. "Then you will have a boring time here, my friend. We've got no crime in Iceland worth writing about. We have husbands who beat up their wives and idiots who drink too much and beat up their friends. And this, my friend, is all she wrote."

Finn looked back at the pond, the milling crowd pointing at the saw-cut hole in the ice, conversing in whispers as one would in church.

*All she wrote.*

He slipped away and melted into the city, winding through the back streets of Parliament Hill until he arrived at an old townhouse on a quiet block. He mounted the steps and produced a makeshift housekey, which he slid into the lock along with a slim torsion tool.

Finn felt the lock put up mild resistance for a moment, then gently give way. He turned the knob and the door clicked open a crack—

"Halló!"

He glanced over at the townhouse next door. An old woman's face poked out at him, its features twisted into a suspicious scowl.

Finn nodded. "Halló." The torsion tool salted away in a pocket.

Her face darkened. "Ert þú vinur Ragnars?"

*You a friend of Ragnar's?*

Finn nodded again. "Já."

The crone took a step out onto her stoop and eyed him up and down a few times, her scowl deepening.

"*He said nothing about any friend,*" she grunted in Icelandic.

Finn shrugged. "Ragnar," he said, rolling both *r*'s hard, like machine-gun fire. He sighed and shook his head as if to say, *What a dick, am I right?*

The scowl relaxed by half a degree. The woman looked out across the street, gazing in the direction Finn had just come from.

"*Terrible, what happened,*" she murmured, still in her native tongue. The Icelandic words reminded Finn of someone gargling.

"Já," he murmured.

Her scowl went harsh again, her voice low and guttural, like a dark priest casting a curse. "*Some drunk partier got a little too friendly. Like poor Birna in 2017.*"

"Já," Finn agreed.

"*Too many foreigners,*" she added, spitting the words: "Pólverjar. Finnar. Rússar."

*Poles. Finns. Russians.*

Finn looked back toward the pond, too.

"Fuckers," he said.

She looked at him in surprise and barked a laugh. "Já," she said. "Fokking fokk." She turned her gaze out toward the pond again.

"Greyið," she said softly. To Finn it sounded almost like the word "crying," and the look in her eyes conveyed much the same thing.

*Poor thing. What a terrible shame. Crying.*

"Greyið," Finn echoed.

The old woman raised one finger in a wave.

Finn waved a finger back.

They both retreated into their respective houses.

Finn closed the door behind him and strode silently through a narrow hallway, coming out into a small dining room. The place was spotless, meticulous, tiny. Polished hardwood floors, disappearing black acoustic-tile ceilings, soft recessed lighting. Old made modern, like an Upper West Side apartment. Walls hung in good art—except for one which lay bare, cleared of its artwork, the framed pieces neatly stacked against a far wall.

Prep, for the task ahead.

Finn slung his backpack off his shoulder, dropped it on the dining room table, which was empty save for three large sketch pads and a dozen charcoal pencils, purchased on an earlier swing through the neighborhood. He began unloading the results of his resupply run.

Two gaudy, traditional Icelandic wool sweaters, the kind only tourists wore. Two ratty pullovers. A second, scruffier parka and an oversize pair of cargo pants. Expensive suit jacket, dress shirt, and tie. Half a dozen cheap, preloaded flip phones. Two disposable cameras, ball of twine, small screwdriver, wire stripper, a foot of insulated wire, a few small screws. He didn't expect to need the hardware, but better to have it on hand.

As he unpacked his gear he thought about what the old woman said.

Or at least, what he guessed she said.

Finn neither spoke nor understood a word of Icelandic. Other than "Já."

He knew the accent usually fell on the first syllable, knew how to put that assault-rifle roll in his *r*'s with the tip of his tongue, knew that if he aped a Norwegian accent he wouldn't be far off. Although he didn't know any Norwegian, either.

Not that it mattered much.

Even in English, most people were a mystery to him.

Still, he was pretty sure he understood the old woman's final comment. More or less.

"Greyið," he murmured in her voice.

He took a breath, held it to the count of five, then let it out again.

This wasn't why Finn was here.

He had a quarry to hunt, and scarce time to do it before the noose tightened.

No distractions.

Not his problem.

He opened one of the sketch pads, selected a charcoal pencil, and began sketching a layout of what he'd seen of the city so far.

# 4

Ten blocks to the east, Krista and Einar sat in their cramped office at the Reykjavík metro police station. The ice-encased, vinyl-wrapped body was making its short trip to the university pathology lab. The pathologist had been called at home and was on his way in, grumbling, to perform an immediate autopsy. Christmas or no Christmas, they needed to get in front of this.

Krista was especially keen on seeing the results of the tox screen. Drugs. Had to be. What else could explain a girl stripping naked in the middle of the night, in late December, and sliding herself under the ice? "Like a letter through a mail slot," she murmured.

"A dead letter," her partner added with a fat grin.

In her mind, Krista sighed. That vintage Einar humor, driving her nuts for the past twenty-six years.

An officer poked his head in the door and handed her the surveillance photos she'd asked for. Good. Take her mind off the scene she'd just left.

"I'll leave you to it, then," said Einar, as he hauled himself out of his chair and lumbered off to hunt down a pastry and hot coffee.

Einar thought she was wasting her time. He was probably right.

Krista stared at the first grainy enlargement, a screen capture from CCTV footage taken at the airport the day before. The facial recog software at customs had flagged half a dozen travelers, Brits and Kiwis and one American, but it was just an A.I. hiccup, and after a cursory passport check by an actual human they'd let each one pass. Now, at Krista's request, they were running another check on the ID the American had used to enter the country. It would come back clear, she'd bet money on it. But something about him still felt off.

It was the name on the passport.

Marlin Pike.

That seemed an obvious fake to her, but then what did she really know about American names? They all seemed fake to her, strange combinations with no logic or consistency to them. Marlin Pike. Two fish? She sighed. Real as any, she supposed.

Krista had no love for Americans. Some half a million of them flooded her country each year—half a million too many, in her view. "Their dollars help pay your salary," as Einar had pointed out a thousand times, to which she would reply: "I'd take a pay cut."

But why did this particular American bug her so? She couldn't say. Some foreigner with an odd name enters their city and trips a cyberwire, and on the same night an unidentified girl winds up dead in the heart of downtown . . . No, there was no logical connection. Nothing there but a random confluence of unrelated events. The very definition of coincidence.

Or maybe she just had too much time on her hands.

And like any one of ten million other cops on the planet, Krista did not like coincidences.

She tapped the screen on her phone and began voice-to-texting another memo.

"Marlin Pike . . ." She stopped.

Marlin Pike what? Looked odd? Bothered her?

"Fuck."

She set the thing down.

Krista hated her phone as much as Einar lived on his. It was only the relentless mocking from everyone else in the department that had made her finally give up her little notepad and pencil stub and follow the high-tech herd.

She studied the photo again.

Oversize eyes, set wide on a squarish face. Expressionless.

God, she missed that pencil stub. Made it so much easier not to smoke.

She switched to the second photo, shot at a distance from behind. A little blurred, but she could make out the figure. Short. Lithe. Thin wiry limbs, knobby joints.

Now she studied the two photos side by side, the face and the frame. Awkward looking, like a cartoon. Almost geeky. But there was something wary there. An alertness in the eyes. A strange grace in the posture.

Who was this guy?

An officer burst into the room. "The mermaid!" he stammered.

Krista silently cursed and threw the man a weary look. Did her own officers have to refer to the deceased as a "mermaid"?

"What about her? Isn't the pathologist there yet?"

"Já, he's there. He just—he just went in to autopsy the girl."

"And?"

"She's gone!"

"Of course she's gone. She was dead when the boy found her. Probably been under the ice for hours."

"No, I mean." He took a shaky breath. "Her body. It's *gone*."

# About the Authors

BRANDON WEBB and JOHN DAVID MANN have been writing together for a decade, starting with their 2012 *New York Times* bestselling memoir *The Red Circle*. Their debut novel, *Steel Fear,* is their seventh book together and the first thriller of many to come.

SteelFear.com

After leaving home at sixteen, BRANDON WEBB joined the US Navy to become a Navy SEAL. His first assignment was as a helicopter search-and-rescue (SAR) swimmer and Aviation Warfare Systems Operator with HS-6. In 1997 his SEAL training package was approved; he joined over two hundred students in BUD/S class 215 and went on to complete the training as one of twenty-three originals.

He served with SEAL Team 3, Naval Special Warfare Group One Training Detachment (sniper cell), and the Naval Special Warfare Center (sniper course) as the Naval Special Warfare West Coast sniper course manager. Over his navy career he completed four deployments to the Middle East and one to Afghanistan, and redeployed to Iraq in 2006–2007 as a contractor in support of the US Intelligence community. His proudest accomplishment in the military was working as the SEAL sniper course manager, a schoolhouse that has produced some of the best snipers in military history.

An accomplished and proven leader, Brandon was meritoriously promoted to Petty Officer First Class, ranked first in the command, while assigned to Training Detachment sniper cell. Shortly thereafter he was promoted again, to the rank of Chief Petty Officer (E-7). He has received numerous distinguished service awards, including Top Frog at Team 3 (best combat diver), the Presidential Unit Citation (awarded by President George W. Bush), and the Navy and Marine Corps Commendation Medal with "V" device for valor in combat. Webb ended his Navy career early to spend more time with his children and focus on business.

As an entrepreneur and creator Webb founded two brands, SOFREP.com and CrateClub.com, and bootstrapped them to an eight-figure revenue before successfully exiting the Crate Club in 2020. He continues to run SOFREP Media, his military-themed digital media company, and as its CEO has created several hit online TV shows, books, and podcasts, including the series *Inside the Team Room* and the award-winning documentary *Big Mountain Heroes*.

Webb is a multiple *New York Times* bestselling author of nonfiction and is now focused on his new thriller series with his creative writing partner, John David Mann. The first in the series, *Steel Fear,* is a high-seas thriller that follows the US Navy's first serial killer.

Brandon pursued his undergrad studies at Embry Riddle Aeronautical University and Harvard Business

School's two-year OPM program. He is a member of the Young Presidents' Organization and has served as an appointed member on the veterans advisory committee to the US Small Business Administration.

He enjoys spending time with his tight circle of amazing family and friends. When he's not traveling the world, being in the wild outdoors, or flying his planes upside-down or on floats, you can find him at home in San Juan, Puerto Rico.

brandontylerwebb.com
Facebook: /brandonwebbseal
Twitter: @brandontwebb
Instagram: /brandontwebb

JOHN DAVID MANN has been creating careers since he was a teenager. At age seventeen, he and a few friends started their own high school in New Jersey, called "Changes, Inc." Before turning to business and writing, he forged a successful career as a concert cellist and prize-winning composer. At fifteen he was recipient of the 1969 BMI Awards to Student Composers and several New Jersey state grants for composition; his musical compositions were performed throughout the US and his musical score for Aeschylus' *Prometheus Bound* (written at age thirteen) was performed at the amphitheater in Epidaurus, Greece, where the play was originally premiered.

John's diverse career has made him a thought leader in several different industries. In 1986 he founded *Solstice,* a journal on health and environmental issues; his series on the climate crisis (yes, he was writing about this back in the eighties) was selected for national reprint in *Utne Reader.* In 1992 John helped write and produce the underground bestseller *The*

*Greatest Networker in the World,* by John Milton Fogg, which became the defining book in its field. During the 1990s, John built a multimillion-dollar sales/distribution organization of over a hundred thousand people. He was co-founder and senior editor of the legendary *Upline* journal and editor in chief of *Networking Times.*

John is the co-author of more than thirty books, including four *New York Times* bestsellers and five national bestsellers. His books are published in thirty-eight languages, have sold over three million copies, and have earned the Axiom Business Book Award (Gold Medal), the Nautilus Award, Bookpal's "Outstanding Works of Literature (OWL)" award, and Taiwan's Golden Book Award for Innovation. His bestselling classic *The Go-Giver* (with Bob Burg) received the Living Now Book Awards "Evergreen Medal" for its "contributions to positive global change." His books have been cited on *Inc.*'s "Most Motivational Books Ever Written," HubSpot's "20 Most Highly Rated Sales Books of All Time," *Entrepreneur*'s "10 Books Every Leader Should Read," *Forbes*'s "8 Books Every Young Leader Should Read," CNBC's "10 Books That Boost Money IQ," NPR's "Great Reads," and *New York Post*'s "Best Books of the Week." His 2012 *Take the Lead* (with Betsy Myers) was named Best Leadership Book of the Year by Tom Peters and *The Washington Post.*

Over his decade of writing with Brandon, John has logged hundreds of hours of interviews with US military service members, along with their spouses, parents, children, and friends, to gain an intimate understanding of the military life and Special Operations community. In preparation for writing *Steel Fear* he spent time on the aircraft carrier USS *Abraham Lincoln,* where the novel is set.

John is married to Ana Gabriel Mann and considers himself the luckiest mann in the world.

johndavidmann.com
Facebook: /johndavidmann
Twitter: @johndavidmann
Instagram: /johndavidmann